RUNNING ON

Instinct

N. M. LUIKEN

A TOM DOHERTY ASSOCIATES BOOK
NEW YORK

RUNNING ON

Instinct

RUNNING ON INSTINCT

This book is printed on acid-free paper.

Design by Jane Adele Regina

A Forge Book
Published by Tom Doherty Associates, LLC
175 Fifth Avenue
New York, NY 10010

www.tor.com

Forge® is a registered trademark of Tom Doherty Associates, LLC.

Library of Congress Cataloging-in-Publication Data

Luiken, N. M.
     Running on instinct / N. M. Luiken. — 1st ed.
          p. cm.
     "A Tom Doherty Associates book."
     ISBN 0-312-87344-1 (acid-free paper)
     1. Violence—Fiction.   2. Nursery rhymes—Fiction.   I. Title.

     PR9199.3.L83 R86 2001
     813'.6—dc21

                                                    2001023205

First Edition: July 2001

Printed in the United States of America

0   9   8   7   6   5   4   3   2   1

For Dad, who has never owned a John Deere tractor

Thanks go to Stephen Humphrey, for making a phone call, and to Marg DeMarco for sharing her medical expertise. Thanks also to Karen Bacsanyi of the Purdy/Kresge Library for last-minute details. All mistakes are mine.

part one

Instinct

• 1 •

When Jeff Lacrosse saw the Bronco in the ditch, he almost didn't stop.

Five, even two years ago, there would have been no question about it. He wouldn't have stopped. Eyes trained since childhood not to see would have slid past, and Jeff would have kept on driving, whistling cheerfully, just as he had been moments before.

He liked driving, and he liked to whistle as he drove, even though his wife, Penny, insisted he couldn't carry a tune in a washtub.

Thinking about Penny made him smile. She was eight months pregnant and round as a melon. He loved her and his three-year-old son, Bobby, to distraction.

Sometimes his own happiness scared Jeff. His life was going too well. He had a well-paying job with the phone company, a house in the country, a family. For a Mètis kid from the slums his success was almost frightening. He kept thinking, *It can't last*, and the specter of his mother's voice would rise up to haunt him. *You're worthless. You'll never amount to anything.*

For the first six months he'd dated Penny, he'd lived in fear that she would somehow find out about his background. Find out he wasn't good enough for her. His young offender's record had long since been expunged, and his chances of running into his old gang were low to nonexistent, but Jeff still worried.

He had so much more to lose now. So much that could be taken away from him.

First your house, then your wife, then your son, then your life . . .

Although his mother was still alive as far as he knew, her parting words to him whispered through his mind like a death curse.

Impatiently, Jeff pushed the memory aside and concentrated on driving. In his opinion, Alberta had the best roads in the world. The two-lane secondary highway unfolded like a ribbon in front of him, smooth and flat, made for driving.

The station wagon was a ten-year-old Reliant K, a far cry from the hot rods he'd once stolen for joyrides, but it was his, every cent of it paid off.

No one could take it away from him.

As a child Jeff had had too many things taken away from him. Too many evictions and middle-of-the-night skipping-the-rent moves in which a cherished toy was left behind. Too many treasures which had been "borrowed" and then broken by his half brother, Todd.

Todd had always said he was sorry, but his eyes had watched Jeff for signs of distress, ready to make fun of him if he cried. Their mother had favored Todd, her blond, light-skinned son, over Jeff's Indian looks, and she'd always taken his side, laughing along with him.

As a result Jeff had gotten very adept at fixing broken toys, from model airplanes to clocks. He had a talent for tinkering with things, and his worktable at home was always overflowing with toasters in need of repair and gadgets he was working on.

He called them gadgets. Penny called them inventions and teased him about "saving the world" with one. He was never quite certain she wasn't a little serious.

Jeff was toying with the idea for a mini–grappling hook to add to the Batman-style utility belt he'd made Bobby for Christmas — maybe if he used the reel from a fishing rod — when the station wagon bumped across a set of railroad tracks.

Up ahead he saw a brand-new Ford Bronco canted sideways in the ditch.

His eyes started to slide past. The Bronco was somebody else's problem, and nothing to do with Jeff. He'd learned long ago that poking your nose into other people's business was a good way to get it sliced off.

The blue Bronco was unfamiliar, but he recognized the older

man standing next to it as his neighbor, Will Halvorsen. Without making a conscious decision to do so, Jeff pulled over onto the shoulder.

Being neighborly was a foreign concept to Jeff—the dish-throwing, screaming couple in the next apartment during his childhood had hardly counted as neighbors—but he liked the idea. Last December, when he and Penny first moved out here, Will had used his tractor to pull the station wagon out of a snowdrift. Will's wife, Janet, had helped Penny plant her garden and stuffed Bobby full of cookies. They'd been very helpful; Jeff would be glad to return the favor.

Jeff parked a few meters back and got out. "Hi, Will, having trouble with the new Bronco?" He started to offer his help, but something in the older man's face tripped up his tongue.

Even now, in April, Will's face and neck above his jean jacket bore a deep red farmer's tan. A green cap emblazoned with a brand of herbicide shaded his cold blue eyes. It reminded Jeff unpleasantly of the mirror shades his brother had used to hide his drug-dilated eyes. Dangerous, unstable Todd, from whom Jeff had never known whether to expect a slap or a smile.

False impression, of course. A trick of the setting sun.

"No trouble here," Will said.

"Good, good." Embarrassed that his help wasn't needed, Jeff looked away and noticed a green John Deere tractor. "Having a look at the fields then? Is it seeding time yet?"

"Next month. The ground's too wet."

"Ah." Jeff was about to make his excuses—Well, gotta run, see you later—when he saw the hole in the ground beside the Bronco. It was square and deep. A pile of turf and a spade lay beside it in the ditch.

Will was not having a look at the fields.

Jeff's eyes snapped back to his neighbor's face. The natural, normal thing would have been to ask what Will was doing, digging so close to the phone line. Jeff didn't ask, obeying the iron rules learned in his childhood. "Nice weather, huh?" He started to edge away.

Will didn't smile back. He moved his solid bulk between Jeff and the hole, like a linebacker blocking Jeff's view. "Why don't you go back to town?" he said gently. "The phone lines are down."

The phones lines hadn't just gone down, Will had cut them on purpose. Jeff knew it, and Will knew he knew it, but Jeff affected surprise. "Are they? Well, that's someone else's problem. It's not my shift. I'm going to drive home now. Penny gets miffed if I let supper get cold." That was a lie. Penny was an indifferent cook, and she'd planned to make hot dogs tonight so, if she and Bobby were hungry, they didn't have to wait for Jeff to get home at seven-thirty.

Will didn't seem to hear him. He stared off into the distance as if seeing ghost ships in a clear blue sky. "Sometimes things aren't always what they seem. Sometimes people aren't what we think they are."

You sure as hell aren't. "Really?" Jeff said politely.

"Sometimes," Will said, "the face we see is just a paper mask hiding a demon."

Will had lost it. Jeff felt his stomach curdle. "I have to go now." He stepped back, feet sinking a little into the soft earth. He wanted desperately to be back on solid pavement.

Will's hand shot out and grabbed his shoulder. Despite his sixty-some years, his grip was strong, his piercing gaze that of a fanatic. "How well do we really know the people around us? Even those closest to us. How well do you know your wife, Jeff? Do you know what lies beneath her mask?"

Jeff didn't like his mention of Penny. He started to warn Will to back the hell off, but the words rusted in his throat when he saw past Will into the Bronco's darkened interior. The setting sun provided just enough light to make out the crouched, silent figure of a man inside.

Jeff did not ask who the man was.

Jeff did not ask why the man was hiding.

Jeff most emphatically did not ask why the man in the back of the Bronco held a hunting rifle, the black muzzle pointing straight at him.

"I think you've been drinking a little too much," he said, even though Will's breath carried no whiff of alcohol. "You were digging too near the phone line and had a little accident. Everyone has an accident now and then, so I'm going to go home now, and we'll just pretend this whole conversation never happened."

"Go back to work, Jeff." Will almost seemed to be pleading. "You don't know what's beneath the mask."

"You sure are a kidder," Jeff said, although he couldn't have felt less amused if his house had just burned down.

The sun glared in his eyes, and a blackbird called from the windbreak as he slowly walked back to his car, expecting with every step for a bullet to hit him between his shoulder blades and sever his spine.

• 2 •

The wind shook the trailer.

Inside, April Jongkind shivered. There was something a little spooky about being alone in a trailer on an isolated farm during a storm. Well, not exactly alone. She was baby-sitting, but her charge, Kristy, was asleep, as befitted ten-year-olds at quarter to ten at night, and April felt restless. Bored.

Not that she had any right to complain. She'd jumped at Sharon Hillock's weekend job offer. She'd been so desperate for an excuse not to go to her aunt and uncle's twenty-fifth anniversary supper and dance she would have taken a job rock picking.

Normally, April enjoyed baby-sitting, and Kristy was a favorite — a bright kid who would play cards for hours and didn't whine at bedtime — but today Kristy's endless questions had irritated instead of amused her.

April stared moodily out the darkened living-room windows. Rain splattered the panes, and the wind's howling suited her frame of mind. She'd been feeling rather howly herself for the past four months, since New Year's, and she didn't like it. She was not by nature a moody person or even a very serious one.

She liked little kids and dancing and volleyball, and, while her job as a clerk at Macleod's Hardware wasn't thrilling, she didn't mind it. Although she'd been thinking about going off to university in the fall—she'd been out of high school for two years—it wasn't career angst that was keeping her from her aunt and uncle's anniversary celebration.

Gavin Lindberg was.

Well, that wasn't fair. It wasn't as if Gavin had put a gun to her head and said "Don't go." Gavin didn't even know she existed; he didn't know any girl existed except Bethany Mills. It was her own stupidity that was keeping her from dancing the night away.

The truth was she would rather have hot nails driven into her stomach than watch Gavin slow dance with her beautiful blond cousin Bethany.

The wind gusted, buffeting the trailer. April jumped at a sudden, banging noise. She tried to convince herself it was nothing. Trailers made all sorts of eerie noises in storms. Creaking and . . .

Bang!

The noise was coming from the direction of the built-on porch. Was someone knocking? She would have noticed headlights if anyone had turned down the driveway. Who could it be at this time of night?

Someone whose car ran out of gas a mile down the road. Now go answer it.

She walked into the porch and peered out the darkened window. There was definitely someone standing out there. Obeying an instinct she didn't understand April yanked opened the door, and a man half lurched, half fell over the threshold.

In the instant between when he pitched forward and she caught him, she recognized him. Gavin Lindberg.

Staggering under his deadweight, April quickly lowered him to the floor. "Gavin!"

But his eyes did not open, and her only answer was the enraged shriek of the wind. She struggled to support his torso while closing the door. The wind cut off, and she studied the unconscious man at her feet.

Why was he here and not at the anniversary dance with Bethany?

He was pale and wet—and there was a bullet hole in the shoulder of his navy blazer.

He's been shot! Practical matters stifled her other concerns. Gavin was hurt. He needed her. Small bits of first-aid training come back to her. *Stop the bleeding. Apply pressure to the wound.*

She ran down the short hallway, yanked open the closet door, and grabbed a pile of linen. Pillowcases would work the best, she decided, dropping the sheets and hurrying back. Her fingers still clutched the corner of one, and a white fitted sheet billowed out behind her, skimming along the linoleum floor.

She slid to a stop in her stocking feet and dumped the linen by the porch entrance.

What else?

She scooped up one of the pillowcases and dashed to the bathroom. After soaping her hands, she shoved disinfectant, Band-Aids— could one use Band-Aids on a gunshot wound?—and some cotton balls inside the pillowcase.

At the porch entrance she spun around, almost losing her balance, and ran back to the kitchen. A moment's rummaging in the junk drawer produced a pair of scissors and some masking tape, then back to Gavin.

He hadn't moved. April fell to her knees beside him and emptied the contents of the pillowcase on the floor.

The blazer would have to come off. April hesitated for a moment, then used the scissors. Trying to wrestle it off his shoulders would be awkward and might hurt his wound. Besides, sporting a bullet hole, the blazer was no longer fit to wear.

Snip, snip. Carefully, April pulled back the navy material. It stuck to the wound, but she worked it loose without causing more bleeding. Underneath he wore a blood-splotched white dress shirt, which she also cut and peeled back. The wound she revealed both relieved and frightened her.

It was smaller than she'd feared and bled little. When she slid her hand beneath his inflamed shoulder she felt a hole on the other side. She wouldn't have to dig out the bullet as she'd read in her dad's

Westerns. Thank God. It had also missed his lungs. Gavin wouldn't die, coughing up bubbles of blood.

Disinfectant next. April decided against the cotton balls and poured the stuff on. It would probably sting like crazy, but Gavin was unconscious. Besides, disinfectant had to be better for wounds than the whisky they used in Westerns.

Some disinfectant trickled down his chest, and she sopped it up with her sleeve. It suddenly struck her that she was touching Gavin Lindberg's chest, and her stomach fluttered. He had little chest hair, but he wasn't skinny, just lean and — What was wrong with her? He was unconscious, for heaven's sake!

April packed the wound with cotton balls and taped the folded pillowcase over it. Next, she rolled Gavin onto his side and cut off the rest of his shirt. The detached sleeve sagged down to his elbow.

The wound widened to the size of a dime on the other side, jagged edges signifying the exit wound. Gavin had been shot from the front. April dribbled on more disinfectant and bandaged up this side, too.

She sat back on her heels, surveying his bloodless face. Now what? *Get him warm.*

The built-on porch wasn't heated, and the floor was covered only by a rubber mat. She had to get him into the trailer and under some blankets. She hesitated, leery of simply dragging him. She didn't want to strain his wound.

"Gavin, wake up." She shook him. Awake he could walk down the hall to a bed. But his eyes remained closed.

What if he never woke up?

Fear brought April to her feet. She looked around the built-on porch in desperation. It was a bare room, taken up mainly by coats, shoes, and a big freezer, but there were a few bits of clutter. Her gaze lit on Kristy's red wagon, then discarded it. Trying to move Gavin in it would only end with the cart tipping.

Her eyes fell on the fitted sheet abandoned on the floor, and it gave her an idea. She spread the sheet out over the kitchen floor, then stepped down into the porch, put her arms around Gavin's waist, and dragged him backward until his upper body toppled sideways. She paused, straightened him, then lugged him the remaining foot to the porch entranceway.

Lifting him from the waist up the small step proved impossible, so she grabbed him under the arms. A groan escaped him, but his eyes stayed shut. Hastily, April set him down on the sheet. She let his upper body fall back before lifting his long legs and arranging the bunched linen under him. Then she took two handfuls of sheet and heaved.

For a string bean, he was heavy. April panted as she dragged him the length of the hall. The ride had been smooth, though; Gavin made no noise indicating pain. If not for his shallow breathing, she would have thought him sleeping peacefully.

The sheet tore halfway inside the carpeted master bedroom. April took one look at the queen-size bed and acknowledged there was no way she could get him up on it. Instead she stripped the bed of blankets and, by rolling Gavin onto first one side and then the other, placed the puffy blue comforter under him.

With troubled eyes she rolled him onto his back. Was his breathing more regular?

His skin still felt cold, so April covered him with another blanket. *Treat all injured for shock.* She elevated his feet with two pillows to increase blood circulation to the head.

Done, she sat back for a moment and studied him. Tenderly, she brushed back a lock of wet brown hair. She felt fiercely glad she'd been here, baby-sitting, that she'd cared for him not Bethany.

A small noise from the doorway attracted her attention. Kristy stood there in a pink nightgown, rubbing her eyes. "What's happening?"

"Nothing." April steered Kristy back to her bedroom. "You're having a dream. Go back to sleep."

Kristy started to protest, but a yawn almost split her face in two, and she allowed herself to be tucked back into bed. April closed the door behind her.

A quick check on Gavin to see if he was still okay. Still breathing. Still unconscious.

April hovered, anxious, for a minute then returned to the kitchen.

Soup, she decided. Something easy to eat and easy to make. She'd just put some water on to boil when headlights arced across the ceiling.

Kristy's parents. But they're not supposed to be back until Sunday. Then she saw the flashing red-and-blue lights of a police cruiser.

Then and only then did she realize just how strange her actions for the past half hour had been. She'd acted quickly and efficiently, stopping the bleeding and getting Gavin inside the trailer. Not once had she wondered how he'd been wounded. Not once had she thought to call an ambulance. Or the police.

• 3 •

"He's not real. He's just a dream. He can't hurt you."

The raw sound of her own voice pulled the woman known as Genevieve from her sleep.

Shivering, her cheap cotton nightgown sticking to her back, she sat up. She half expected to see the man from her dream, the man with the knife, but the pale wash of moonlight through the upstairs window revealed only her own empty bedroom.

"You're alone. You're safe."

Her words lacked conviction. They lingered in the air along with the stale odor of sweat, a disturbing aftertaste of terror. Genevieve's hands fisted in the bedclothes. Damn it, her days of feeling weak and frightened were supposed to be over. She'd spent the last seven months painstakingly building a new life for herself; one episode of a recurring dream shouldn't shake her to the core.

She didn't turn on the light. If she did, it would be an admission that she was afraid of him, afraid of a dream. So she sat alone in the dark, even when the house groaned like a colossus waking from a thousand-year slumber and black shadows piled in the corners like dirty blankets.

Her pulse galloped like a skittish horse, and she wanted to run — *No. I'm stronger than that.* To prove it she lay back down and kept her eyes closed even after the dream started to play in her mind again, like footage from a car crash on the evening news too horrible to look away from.

THE DREAM ALWAYS begins the same way, with the door.

[*It is an ordinary screen door, but to Genevieve it might as well be the door to Hell itself, carved deep with blood runes and rimed with frost. Behind it lies her nightmare. Each time she tries to stop herself from going in. Each time she fails.*

[*She bursts through the door and down a flight of stairs into a basement den. Blue china plates line the mantel above an ash-cold fireplace, and clocks nest on every available surface—shelves, cabinets, the floor—old clocks, antiques with round faces and Roman numeral eyes that peer up at her like owls.*

[*In among all the clocks are three people, a woman and two men. For an instant they don't move, frozen in a strange tableau as if posed by some insane department-store decorator.*

[*Then the grandfather clock in the corner sonorously begins to strike.*

[Bong. Bong. Bong.

[*Each strike shivers through Genevieve as if the clock counts damned souls instead of hours. Time resumes, lurches forward.*

[*The woman sprawls backward on the pale rose carpet, one hand grasping the couch, the other clutching the ruins of her throat. Blood spurts through her fingers, staining her white silk shirt crimson.*

[Bong.

[*Spatters of blood lie like dew on her black velvet trousers. Short blond-silver hair caps her head, and pearl drops glint at her ears. Her pink-outlined lips part on a gasp. She is dressed to go dancing. Dining.*

[*She shouldn't be dying. Her green eyes roll up in her head: she chokes. Her hand tightens on the cushion, then falls away.*

[Bong.

[*Stricken, the first man watches his wife die. He grips a brass poker, but does not raise it. His face turns gray, old in an instant, seventy instead of fifty.*

[Bong.

[*He falls without a scream when the knife plunges into his neck. It sticks there, black handle slick with blood, while he bleeds to death. He speaks, gurgling horribly, "Ruoon Naiee."*

[Run, Mary! Run! *Genevieve tries to obey, but her legs are lumps of wood, nailed to the floor.*

[Bong. *A second clock on the mantel chimes, and a cuckoo bird pokes its head out of a third, sounding a discordant chorus.* Cuckoochimebong.

[*The second man steps into her field of vision, moving with the efficient grace of an athlete as he leans over the fallen man.*

[Cuckoobong.

[*His hair gleams midnight black, his eyes electric blue. A smile of pleasure transforms the hard planes of his face into a pure, cruel beauty as he retrieves his knife. It comes loose with a wet, sucking sound, and the dream — shimmers, fragments —*]

The dream always begins the same way, but each time it ends differently.

[*The dead man and woman vanish. The sofa and fireplace become blue sky and yellow-green grass. Only the murderer remains, standing over a young blonde.*

[*Once she might have been pretty, now she lies like a broken doll. The wind whips blond hair into her face, casting a silken veil over her shattered cheekbone. The fine strands catch in a drop of blood in the corner of her mouth, and a dark red stain covers her heart.*

[*The Selector wipes the knife on his T-shirt, leaving guilty smears on the white fabric.*

[*"Hello, Mary." His voice purrs pleasure, and his blue eyes are intense. Intimate. "I've been waiting for you. I know how you like to watch me work, culling the herd."*

[*The herd. Unwillingly, Genevieve looks down at the dead girl. The very beautiful, very human, dead girl.*

[*The Selector nudges the body with his toe. "Pretty, isn't she? A perfect specimen on the outside: blue eyes, long legs, lush breasts, hair like spun gold. I had hopes for her, but she disappointed me. Do you know she actually expected her beauty to protect her?" He laughs low in his throat, sharing a joke. "As if I were so weak I could be swayed by the lures of the flesh." He shakes his head. "Stupid, Inferior."*

[*Genevieve shrinks back. She, herself, is merely pretty. How would the Selector judge her?*

[*"But enough about my day. Let's talk about you. Tell me, Mary"—his voice is smoother than honey—"are you still with that poet man of yours?"*

[*Superstitiously, Genevieve doesn't answer. It disturbs her that he remembers Matt is a writer from her last dream. Which is silly. The Selector is a figment of her imagination: he knows everything she knows.*

[*She takes a deep breath and repeats the words she once read in a book. "This is just a dream. It cannot harm me. I am in control, and I have the power to stop or redirect the dream as I choose. On the count of three the dream will end, and I will wake up.*

[*"One."*

[*"Do you like poetry, Mary?" His thumb idly caresses the knife, not even noticing when the edge draws blood. "I can write poetry, too. Listen."*

[*"Two." Oh Christ, she wants to wake up.*

[*"Twisting the knife that kills/I revel in the blood that spills!"*

[*"Three!" she shouts.*

[*But her dream refuses to shatter, caging her with industrial-strength steel.*

[*Smiling, Selector walks toward her. He holds the knife casually at his side, but Genevieve is not fooled: he's stalking her as a tiger hunts its prey, muscles moving sleekly, eyes avid, waiting for her to make a break to the left or right. "Tell me something else, Mary. Tell me where you live so I can kill you."*

[*In spite of Genevieve's best intentions, she backs up. A pulse hammers in her throat.*

[*Grass tickles her bare feet, and she makes herself stand perfectly still. Running will only make the tiger pounce. "This isn't real. I'm dreaming."*

[*"If it isn't real, then it won't matter if you tell me, will it?" He presses closer, until he stands directly in front of her, so close she can feel his body heat. She quivers, painfully aware that only the thin cotton of her nightgown covers her nakedness. "Come on, give me a hint," he coaxes, as if asking what she'd bought him for his birthday.*

[His thumb strokes down her cheek, once, twice, rubbing over her lower lip in a mockery of a lover's caress. The knife in his fist shines dull silver, the blade only inches from her dazzled eyes. "Are you on the coast?" A lock of raven hair falls across his blue, blue eyes.

[For a terrible instant, torn between attraction and fear, she wants to tell him, wants to please him and make him happy so that he will smile at her forever. After all, he's just a dream . . .

[She opens her mind just a crack. Fast as a striking snake, the Selector rams his foot in the door and wedges it further open. Pushing. His hand seizes her chin, holding her head still so he can probe her soul. "No, not the ocean, a lake. One of the Great Lakes. Which one? Come on, you little bitch—"]

AND THEN SHE'D woken up, proving it wasn't real, that the Selector was just a dream. A very unpleasant dream, certainly, a nightmare, but nothing to cause this gut-wrenching fear.

Not even if she had let slip that she lived by Lake Michigan in that last instant.

• 4 •

Jeff drove. He was whistling "Jingle Bells," but he didn't know it. He didn't know he was speeding either. He should have noticed: at 115 km/h the station wagon bounced from washboard to washboard and skidded in the loose gravel that had replaced pavement two miles back.

His foot didn't touch the brake till he turned down his own driveway.

Prior to his marriage, Jeff had never lived in anything but run-down apartments with rusty curtain rods and toilets that didn't flush right. The simple white bungalow he and Penny lived in usually gave him a feeling of deep satisfaction mixed with mild worry over the large mortgage Penny had coaxed him into.

Today Jeff felt neither the well-being nor the worry. He parked by the swing set and got out of the car before it stopped moving.

He stepped over his three-year-old son's toys in the entranceway and went to find Penny.

He found her in the kitchen, standing on a chair, getting something down from the top cupboard shelf. Jeff didn't tell her to be careful. He didn't say anything, still whistling.

"Hi, Jeff." She flashed him a brilliant smile. "Hold the chair. I can't quite reach the coffee can."

Jeff didn't ask her why she put the coffee can there if she couldn't reach it. He gripped the back of the chair. "I ran into Will Halvorsen today."

"Where?" Penny stretched, caught the tip of the coffee can, and spun it forward so she could get a better grip.

"On the road." Jeff stared straight ahead, remembering Will's cold eyes.

The coffee can landed on the counter with a *thunk*. Penny stepped down from the chair and began to rummage in the bottom cupboards.

"There was something wrong with Will today," Jeff told the back of his wife's head.

Cans appeared on the kitchen floor like mushrooms springing up. Soup, pineapple, tuna, and peanut butter. "What was wrong?" Penny asked.

"He had a new Bronco, and it was in the ditch."

"Help me put the cans in the box, will you?" Penny's flushed face emerged from the cupboard, her short dark hair standing up in sweaty peaks.

Jeff neatly stacked cans while Penny shoved them in as quickly as possible. "He kept talking about masks and demons, and he'd dug a hole in the ground."

"Bobby, don't," Penny called over his shoulder. "Leave your toys in the box."

Jeff didn't glance at his son. Desperately, he tried to tell Penny what had happened, what had been so *wrong* about Will Halvorsen and his new Bronco. "There was a hole in the ground," he started again.

"What for?" Penny wedged the last can into the box and folded in the top.

"He'd dug up the phone line. On purpose."

"That doesn't sound like Will." Penny got up and dusted off her white maternity jumpsuit. "Can you carry this for me?" She hustled Bobby down the hall before Jeff could reply.

Jeff packed the box down to the porch where he found Penny busy putting Bobby's chubby arms in a red jacket. Bobby refused to let go of his toy truck. "Vroom, vroom."

"Penny."

"Just put it down there," Penny said.

"Vroom."

Jeff put it down. "Penny, are you listening?"

"Of course, I'm listening." Penny zipped up Bobby's jacket, then sat Bobby down on the step and stuffed his feet into Velcro runners. "You met Will Halvorsen on the road. His new Bronco was in the ditch." One shoe on. "He acted strange, and he'd dug up the phone line." Two shoes on. "Did I miss anything?" She tousled Bobby's brown hair.

"Vroom."

She hadn't missed anything. "No, but—" He broke off when she started down the basement stairs. He frowned, then followed. Something very strange had happened to him, and she wouldn't stay still long enough to listen.

"Penny," he said, and the words that had stuck in his throat earlier burst out, "there was a man with a rifle in the back of the Bronco. I thought he was going to shoot me."

That got a reaction. Penny turned, green eyes huge with fear. Her hand clutched the banister—for a moment—then she continued down the stairs.

Angry, Jeff followed. He found Penny by his workbench with its scattered gadgets. She held yet another cardboard box. "Which ones do you want to take?"

"I nearly got shot, and that's all you can say?"

Penny looked up, and he saw the tears in her eyes. "I love you, Jeff. Tomorrow I'll probably get all shaky about what happened today, but right now it's more important to get you and Bobby and the food in the car before Will gets here and kills us. Now which inventions do you want to bring?"

"You want to leave, too?" Jeff was astonished. He'd been trying so hard to explain what had happened on the road with Will so she wouldn't object to driving into town tonight.

He felt cold every time he remembered the cut phone lines and the way Will had ranted about masks and demons. And Penny was pregnant right now, so damn vulnerable it made him nervous just to see her climbing on chairs.

"You really want to leave?" he repeated.

Penny nodded.

Exquisite relief washed over him. He'd been afraid she would frown and protest the whole way. He took the box from her and set it on the floor. "To answer your question, I don't want any of my gadgets, just my tools." There weren't any gadgets he couldn't rebuild, but his tools would take time to replace.

He swept up his set of tiny screwdrivers and dumped them in the red toolbox Penny had given him for his last birthday. A socket set, pliers, wire strippers, clamps, and black electrician's tape soon followed. Working quickly, he cleared his workbench and flipped the locks on his toolbox. At the last second he included the mini–grappling hook he'd been thinking about. "Done."

"Good." Penny shooed Bobby up the stairs, leaving Jeff to trail behind again. She had her blue jacket on by the time he got to the top, and she held the door open for him.

"Are the keys in the station wagon?"

Jeff shook his head. Out here in the country Penny had gotten in the habit of leaving the keys in the ignition, but Jeff hadn't been able to break the training of a lifetime. He pulled his key ring out of his pocket and tossed it to her.

Penny popped the tailgate and waited for him to push the toolbox in. "There's a lot more stuff in the house."

She wasn't kidding. Besides the box of cans, she'd packed a cooler full of drinks and perishables, a box of Bobby's toys, three suitcases bulging with clothes, her baby bag, two sleeping bags, a first-aid kit, and a big box crammed full of "couldn't-leave-behinds."

"We don't need all this stuff. We're only going to be gone a couple of nights." Jeff grabbed the two most necessary items, the suitcases. Bobby struggled with an overnight bag.

"Are you sure?" Penny asked.

Suddenly, Jeff wasn't. "How long do you think we'll be gone?"

"I don't know." She looked nervous. Hunted. "Two weeks. A month. Maybe forever."

"Forever?" Jeff stopped dead.

"Maybe." Penny looked him in the eye. "I'll explain later."

"Later?" Jeff echoed. "No, explain now. You're not making sense. All we need to do is lie low somewhere for a couple of days until the police arrest Will."

First you lose your house . . .

"And why would the police arrest him?" Penny asked quietly.

"Shit." Jeff dropped the suitcases. "Where's my head? I should phone the police." For years the police had been the enemy, but he was a law-abiding citizen now; he deserved protection. Penny and Bobby deserved protection.

"The phone's out, remember?"

Jeff halted halfway to the house. "Damn. He's cutting us off from help." Will knew Jeff didn't have a cell phone, had heard him complain about them a few months ago.

"Please, Jeff. We have to go now."

Jeff picked up the suitcases. "We'll go to the police station in town. We're not leaving this house forever. We have a mortgage to pay."

Penny said nothing, neither agreeing nor disagreeing.

Despite Penny's no-lifting and Bobby's "help," Jeff loaded the station wagon in record time. He picked his son up with one arm and the last bag with the other. "Here's some luggage we forgot."

Bobby giggled, unfrightened by their talk of leaving. The only thing Bobby couldn't bear to leave behind was his imaginary playmate, and she traveled with him everywhere.

A moment to fasten his seat belt and start the station wagon, and they were off. At the end of the driveway Jeff suddenly realized he had no idea where to go.

Penny did. "Go left."

Jeff obliged. Will Halvorsen lived a mile down the road to the right on a farm like a fortress guarded by a phalanx of steel granaries and a double windbreak of spruce and maple. His Bronco had been in the ditch five miles farther down the road. Unfortunately, town lay that way, too.

Thinking of the Bronco, Jeff depressed the gas pedal. He'd just pushed the wagon up to fifty when Penny told him to slow down.

"Why?"

"We have a stop to make. Turn in the next dirt driveway."

"Yes, ma'am."

If Penny noticed his sarcasm, she did not show it, face intent on the woods.

"Se-ket hideout, se-ket hideout!" Bobby bounced up and down in his seat.

Jeff raised an eyebrow at Penny as he put the station wagon in Park. What secret hideout? *He* didn't know anything about a secret hideout.

Penny opened her door. "Bobby, stay in the car; we'll be right back."

"Why?"

"Because I said so." Penny slammed the door shut.

Jeff wondered if she'd say the same thing if he asked why, too.

He followed her outside. This clearing was legally on the quarter section that came with their house, but Jeff had never stopped here before. Whatever the driveway had once been for was long gone; he saw only weedy grass, thornbushes and anthills before the land sloped down to a sluggish creek, dammed by some industrious beavers.

Penny ignored the clearing, heading for a thick stand of poplars. She followed a deer track for a few yards, last year's leaves and dead branches cracking underfoot.

"It should be underneath that spruce tree. See the board?" She kicked the leaves away.

Jeff moved the plywood board aside, revealing a hollow partly formed by tree roots and partly dug out by his enterprising young wife. Inside lay another first-aid kit, more canned food, a coil of rope, matches, a gasoline can, and a revolver.

"We might need the gas." Penny stooped to pick it up.

Jeff remained half-crouched. So many shocks had hit him today he'd missed a lot of things right under his nose.

Penny had been packing before he got home, before he'd told her about Will Halvorsen.

And this, this took the cake. How long had the secret hideout been here? He and Penny had only moved here five months ago, and she'd seemed to like Will Halvorsen as much as he had.

But this spoke of weeks of preparation. The food would have been easy enough to sneak out, but the gasoline and the gun, when and where had she gotten them? And why? For God's sake, why?

"How long have you been planning this?"

This time Penny didn't evade his question. "How long have I known we would someday be in danger? I knew before I met you. Actually" — Penny smiled again, bright and vivid — "that was the only thing I knew about you when we met. That and that I would marry you."

• 5 •

Bethany's scream pierced the layers of unconsciousness protecting Gavin's mind.

He jerked upright and raised his hands defensively, warding off a danger that wasn't there. The movement sent a shock of pain through his shoulder, and his left arm flopped uselessly.

He'd been shot. He remembered that.

A prickle of danger that made him straighten in time to see a strange man holding a gun. A hammerblow of pain as a bullet ripped through the muscle of his shoulder, the gunshot cutting off the echoes of Bethany's last scream like the blade of a guillotine. Incomprehension, stumbling backward. Then his mind shut down, and he ran.

More gunshots and whipping branches . . . He must have fled into the forest. Strange, he didn't remember. He must have been shell-shocked by Bethany's—

—death—

—her scream—

No! Gavin grabbed at his crushing guilt and grief. *You don't have time for that now: you're in danger.*

Concentrate.

Ruthlessly, Gavin ordered his thoughts the way he did his legal notes. Priority number one: where was he?

A crack of light from a doorway to his right illuminated a large square shape to his left. A bed. He must be in a bedroom. *Oh, you're a wonder, a real Sherlock. Whose bedroom, you ass?*

Cool air struck his chest as he pushed aside the blanket. His wound had been bandaged, and his blazer and shirt removed.

Clenching his teeth against the pain, Gavin rolled onto his knees and edged the door open. A linoleum hallway greeted his eyes, and he heard voices.

In frozen silence, he pulled back into the protective shadows and listened.

"—heard any strange noises or seen anybody lurking around the yard?" a man asked.

"Just the wind," a girl replied. "Why?"

"We're looking for a man, a suspect, last seen heading into the woods a few miles from here. He's about twenty, Caucasian, brown hair, brown eyes, five-eleven. He was last seen wearing a white shirt and blue suit jacket."

Great. The only thing they'd missed was the zit on his nose.

He would have to make a break for it out the window. Only the shape he was in they were sure to catch him halfway through with his butt in the air.

"Brown hair, brown eyes," the girl repeated. "If I see anyone matching your description I'll call you."

If I see . . . Gavin stilled. Didn't she know he was in the bedroom?

"Why are you looking for him?" she asked.

"We have reason to believe he murdered a girl."

Now, Gavin thought sickly, *she'll tell them now.*

"Believe?" a second man interrupted. "Hell, we're dead sure he killed her. I found him standing over the body."

Looking down at Bethany, dead in the grass. Blood still warm when he fumbled for a pulse . . .

"Whose body? What girl?" the girl asked sharply.

"We're not allowed to say—" the first man started.

"Bethany Mills," the second policeman confided. "His girlfriend."

"Oh, my God. Bethany's dead?" Her voice hitched.

"Maybe you'd better sit down," the first policeman said. A chair scraped back. "Did you know her?"

A long pause. "I—I knew her from school. Poor Bethany. This is horrible."

Horrible. *Tangled blond hair, dead staring eyes . . .*

Gavin forced the memory away and listened, nerves raw.

She cried, but still didn't give him away. Maybe she really didn't know he was here.

Yeah, maybe he'd been taken in by a bunch of kindly elves, who knew how to bandage up gunshot wounds.

"Are you going to be all right, Miss? Maybe you'd like to come back to the station with us?"

"No." The girl blew her nose. "I can't. I'm baby-sitting. Kristy's asleep, and I don't want to frighten her. We'll be safe enough here in the trailer if I lock the door behind you. He's probably long gone by now."

"If he isn't, we'll catch him," the first policeman assured her. "We have dogs searching the woods, but the rain is confusing the scent. If you hear anything, just call us."

Dogs. Swell. Gavin had an immediate vision of a slobbering hundred-pound German shepherd. He had a feeling he'd lose a tussle with a puppy just now.

"We have other farms to visit," the second policeman said impatiently, and they left. Gavin heard gravel crunch as they drove away.

Painfully, he pulled himself back against the wall as the girl's footsteps came down the hall.

She didn't hesitate, but went straight to his room and opened the door. "You're awake." No screams, no gasps of horror, no fleeing in terror.

Shadows obscured her face; her voice sounded husky and unfamiliar.

"Why didn't you report me to the police?"

She said nothing.

He knew he should be grateful to her for saving his hide, but he found himself perversely angry at the danger she'd put herself in. "We're all alone here in this trailer. I could murder you, and no one would even hear you scream."

"You won't murder me."

Her confidence made him want to shake her. It was the same kind of confidence that had gotten Bethany killed. "You don't know that; you don't know me."

"You may not know me, but I know you." Her words sent a small shock wave through him. "Your name's Gavin Reed Lindberg. You have a bachelor of commerce degree and are taking first-year law at the University of Calgary. You get good grades, you grew up in Vancouver . . . and you loved Bethany."

That her information was correct only frustrated him.

"How are you feeling?" Her voice was dove-wing soft.

"Like someone just scraped me off the bottom of his shoe. How do you know I loved Bethany?" Past tense. That hurt.

"You were cold earlier, in shock. Are you getting a fever?" Her hand reached for his forehead.

He knocked it down and sucked in a breath when a bolt of pain from his shoulder punished him. "Pay attention. You're alone in a trailer with a murder suspect. You should be worried about your health, not mine."

She glared at him. "Stop trying to frighten me; I know you didn't kill Bethany. Now let me feel your forehead."

Stumped, Gavin leaned back against the wall and allowed her to press her cool hand against his skin. "Are you aware you've committed a crime? You could serve two to five years hard time for harboring a fugitive." He wasn't sure about the numbers, but they sounded good.

"Well, you're a little hot, but not burning up. I'll get you some Tylenol for the pain, and, hopefully, that should take care of the fever, too."

Gavin's shoulder burned, but he closed the pain off, focusing on the girl. "I give up. Why don't you turn on the light so I can see who I'm talking to?"

Light flooded the room.

Blinking rapidly, Gavin studied his rescuer. She was on the short side and had a round face with a cute snub nose and freckles. Permed, light brown hair bobbed around her chin. Her blue eyes were tear-swollen, but her gaze was direct and honest. Under her jeans and ratty purple sweatshirt her body looked compact and athletic.

She was a stranger.

But she knew him. "How do you know me?"

She looked uncomfortable. "I saw you at the New Year's Eve Dance."

He had a brief memory of a girl in blue velvet, rolling her eyes and laughing at her escort's preoccupation with—Bethany. New Year's had been their last perfect day together. After that she'd become bored with him, slipping farther and farther away.

The remembrance made his voice harsh. "You took one look at me and immediately thought, 'What a nice guy. I bet he could never commit murder'?"

"You loved her."

"So? Haven't you ever heard of crimes of passion?"

She flinched, but held her ground. "Look, don't you think we have more important things to talk about?"

"Like what?" Gavin couldn't think of anything.

"Like how to smuggle you through the police roadblocks before Kristy's parents come home on Sunday."

CHAPTER 2

• 1 •

[*Anxiety. Confusion.*]

Jeff's emotions pushed at Penny like a bulldozer. She wanted to hug him, but they didn't have time.

"I don't understand." Jeff looked dazed by the bizarre turn his evening had taken when he stopped by Will Halvorsen's Bronco. "How could you know about the danger before you met me?"

"I'll explain everything as soon as we're in the wagon. I promise." At that point she would have promised the moon just to get him out of there. Will could be approaching this very minute.

She could tell Jeff didn't want to wait, but after a tense second he picked up the rope and the jar of matches. Penny hurried after him, carrying the gun and the gas.

Bobby's brown eyes widened when he saw the revolver. He recognized guns from television, but Penny doubted he understood their deadliness. "This is not a toy," Penny lectured. "It's very dangerous, okay?"

Bobby nodded solemnly. "Kisty says don't touch." But his eyes followed the gun as she placed it in the glove compartment, and she could feel his curiosity. He'd inherited Jeff's love of gadgets, along with his dark hair and brown eyes.

Speaking of Jeff . . .

[*Curiosity. Fear. A touch of anger.*]

Penny distracted him before he could demand an explanation. "We need to decide on a route."

"There's only one road that connects to the highway," Jeff said. "We have no choice, we have to take it."

"What about the elevator road?" Penny asked.

Jeff shook his head. "It doesn't go anywhere. It loops around and rejoins with the secondary road before the railroad tracks where Will is. He'll see us. Unless," Jeff added thoughtfully, "we park a quarter mile back and wait for Will to drive by before rejoining the road to town."

It was the best choice. Jeff started the engine even as Penny nodded in agreement. Once they hit the road, Penny could hold him off no longer.

"Now would you mind telling me what the hell is going on?"

Penny took a deep breath. She'd never liked keeping secrets from him—had wanted to tell him the truth years ago—but that didn't mean she wasn't a little apprehensive about his reaction.

"Do you remember the club I belonged to at university? The Kithkin Klub?"

"Sure. What does that have to do with this?"

Penny ignored his question. "It wasn't an ordinary club. We didn't all cook or swim or ride horses. We had very little in common—on the surface. So why did we all decide to join the club?" she asked rhetorically.

Jeff watched the road carefully as they passed Will Halvorsen's farm, but Penny sensed she had the rest of his attention. "I joined because my mother made me promise to apply. I didn't understand why, but I went to the meeting anyhow.

"When I got there I struck up a conversation with Carrie and found out her parents had made her come, too.

"The girl in charge passed around five-page-long application forms. Carrie and I couldn't believe it, but we'd both promised, so we filled it out.

"It called for an in-depth personal history, brothers, sisters, parents, birthplace, schools, etc., plus a few rather strange questions. Have you ever had a narrow escape from death or injury? Have you ever done something inexplicable that turned out to be a good thing later on?

"When I handed it in the girl said I had to go through Initiation next. I was nervous—you hear so many things about frat and sorority initiations—but she said all I had to do was go through a series of doors, and if I picked the wrong one the doorknob would give me a small jolt of electricity.

"They put me in a room with five doors. I picked the third one and opened it. No jolt. But all four of the other doors were rigged with joy buzzers. That worried me. Not just one chance in five of getting a jolt, but one chance in five of *not* getting a jolt. I went through five sets of five doors without getting buzzed once. I couldn't believe my luck."

"I'll say," Jeff agreed. He signaled for the turn onto the road leading to the grain elevator. "Those are pretty high odds. Let's see. Five to the fifth power . . . six-twenty-five times five . . . about a one in three thousand chance."

"A minute later, Carrie followed me out. She hadn't gotten buzzed either.

"The next boy was furious. He'd gotten zapped all five times and swore he'd never come back to this stupid club again. I had a few mixed feelings myself, but when I was accepted, I decided to go back. Carrie went with me.

"At the second meeting we found out the purpose of the Initiation. It separated the wheat from the chaff." Penny wet her lips nervously, but she couldn't keep him in the dark forever. "Those of us who didn't get buzzed were psychics."

[*Surprise. Disbelief.*]

"Psychics?" Jeff stared at her. Gravel skidded underneath the station wagon's tires. "You're a psychic?"

"Yes." Penny rushed on before he could protest. "All Kithkinners have the danger instinct."

"The what?" Jeff turned back to the road.

"The danger instinct. It's a survival mechanism. If something bad is going to happen, we avoid it. It's a low-grade gut feeling we're usually not even aware of. It's as though"— Penny struggled for a metaphor—"there are two paths, but you know one's bad so you take the other one."

"Maybe it's just luck," Jeff suggested. He still would not look at her.

"One in three thousand odds," Penny reminded him. "Anyhow, the danger instinct is just the beginning."

[*Apprehension.*]

She wished he would look at her. Was he afraid of her now? She decided to get the worst confession out of the way. "Most Kithkinners have additional Talents. My Talent is empathy. I can tell you're feeling very apprehensive right now and wondering if I'm crazy."

"No shit." Jeff gripped the wheel hard.

Penny tried not to feel hurt by his negative reaction.

From the time she was eight Penny had been aware her empathy gave her an unfair advantage over everyone else. It let her glimpse people's secrets. She'd known when her mom was upset but pretending to be happy. She'd known her best friend Delilah secretly loved math despite all her grumbling.

And she'd known her grade three teacher, Ms. Peterson, had a crush on the principal, Mr. Kent.

When she'd innocently revealed as much she'd created a hullabaloo that had ended with Ms. Peterson in tears and Mr. Kent embarrassed. When her beloved teacher had resigned halfway through the school year, Penny had been guilt-stricken.

Childishly, she'd sworn never to reveal anyone's secret again. She'd invented a set of rules for using her Talent "for good, not evil."

However, Penny was not above using her empathy to decide on the best tack to take with individuals. Jeff didn't want to talk about her empathy, so she dropped the subject. "Anyhow, one of the other psychics, a Seeress, told me that she saw great danger in my future. She said if I followed her advice, I would survive it. I made the cache in the woods that she suggested, but otherwise forgot about her prophecy until this afternoon, when I felt the danger approaching."

"How can you *feel* danger approach?"

Penny bristled a little at his phrasing, but it was a fair question. "I usually take Bobby for a walk after his afternoon nap. Today I felt like going for a second walk after supper. I decided to take some juice along. Then I grabbed some cookies in case we got hungry, even though we'd just eaten. Then I took some bandages in case

Bobby fell. I'd packed him a suitcase when I suddenly realized how strangely I was behaving—how strangely my danger instinct was making me behave.

"All I could think about was leaving the house. Only you weren't home yet." Remembered panic made Penny dig her nails into her palms. She'd started packing as a way to keep herself from making endless trips to the window to watch for the station wagon. "When you drove into the yard, I stood there and just shook for a moment."

"You seemed fine when I came in."

Penny laughed. "Jeff, darling, how would you know? You were so shocked you didn't even tell me not to climb on chairs. I kept you busy packing so you wouldn't see my face."

"I wasn't that far out of it," Jeff protested. Penny raised an eyebrow, and he conceded, "Well, maybe a little."

"Maybe a lot. You'd just come face-to-face with a gun held by someone with Will Halvorsen, a man you liked and respected."

Jeff frowned. Penny thought he intended to protest again, but she was wrong. "So you just sensed general danger. You don't know why Will Halvorsen wants to kill us?"

Penny shook her head, suddenly solemn. "I have no idea. I don't know what we're running from," she added, "but I do know where we're running to."

"Great," Jeff said, patently not meaning it.

"The nearest web house is David Calder's," Penny said. "He lives on an acreage by Chinchaga."

"Web house? Is he a Kithkinner?"

"I'm not sure. The Kithkin Klub formed twenty years ago so the children of the Futurists could meet one another. David Calder might be older than that."

"Okay, this is close enough." Jeff slowed the station wagon to a stop and pulled over onto the gravel shoulder. They were about a quarter mile away from the turn back onto the secondary road. "You and Bobby stay in the car. I'll walk down and see if Will and his friend are still there."

"I'm coming with you." Penny opened her car door. "Bobby, you stay in the car." She pushed down the automatic door lock.

Jeff frowned, and Penny felt his disapproval, but he knew her well enough not to argue.

Pregnancy made Penny too breathless to talk and walk at the same time. Both the extra weight she was carrying and her cramped lungs slowed her down, but Jeff kept pace beside her as they followed the windbreak down to the secondary road so the poplar trees shielded them from sight.

When they reached the ditch, Jeff bent down into a crouch and motioned her to do the same. "They're still there," he said.

Penny raised her head far enough to see the blue Bronco for herself. Jeff pushed her back down. "What are they doing?" She caught herself whispering, even though they were much too far away to be heard, her danger instinct prickling.

"Will's driving the tractor," Jeff reported. "The field is pretty wet, he's churning up ruts—Oh, shit."

"What?" Penny asked, but in a moment she saw for herself.

Will had fastened chains from his tractor to a spot three-quarters of the way up the power pole. As they watched, the powerful John Deere tractor began to pull.

• 2 •

"No," Gavin said for the fifth time. "Negative. Not a chance."

April listened to his refusal with growing impatience. Gavin was proving to be about as flexible as the Rock of Gibraltar. "But—"

"Maybe she doesn't understand English," Gavin said to the ceiling. "How about French? *Non.* German? *Nein.*"

"Why not?"

He turned from the ceiling to her, brown eyes intense. "I won't let you risk your life for me."

"Driving you for an hour isn't going to kill me," April pointed out, through gritted teeth.

"It could land you in jail if the police caught us." That settled the argument as far as he was concerned. "I'm putting you in danger just sitting here." He pulled himself to his feet.

The force of the storm lashed rain against the window. The trailer's tin walls seemed suddenly frail, easily overturned, a toy to be picked up and tossed around by the banshee wind. It was a bad night to travel anywhere.

April seized on the excuse. "If you walk off into the forest, the police will find you, and the first thing they'll ask is, 'Who bandaged your wound?' "

"I'll tell them the elves did it."

April smiled, but the situation soon sobered her. "You won't have to tell them anything. All they'll have to do is look at the pillowcase. They'll match the flower pattern to the Hillock's linen." She used all the arguing skills she'd honed against her three brothers. "I'll be safer if we follow my plan and get you out of the area."

Gavin looked frustrated. Her brothers usually did, too. "You know most people would be glad to see me go. They'd be pushing me out the door, screaming for the police. Why are you so determined to help a total stranger? A murder suspect?"

Because I think I might be in love with you. April bit her tongue to keep the words inside, arguing sternly with herself. It wasn't love that she felt. How could it be? She didn't know Gavin.

It was attraction. A crush, not love. But. But. But she'd had crushes before in high school, boys she'd blushed over, and they hadn't felt like this. They hadn't been this . . . intense.

When she first saw Gavin on New Year's Eve all the breath had slammed out of her body as if she'd flubbed a volleyball dive.

She'd known, of course, that her cousin Bethany had a new man who'd come up to spend the holidays with her family, but she'd felt nothing but mild curiosity over how long this one would last until she saw him.

She'd been dancing with Shane and having a good time. Then Shane had stepped on her foot, and she'd followed his glazed gaze over to her cousin's bare shoulders. She'd been a little exasperated because Shane was her date, but only a little because as far as she could tell *every* guy drooled over Bethany, even short, fat, bald, married men. April had long ago decided it was some kind of male reflex programmed into their genes, and no use blaming them.

She'd been about to step on Shane's foot to regain his attention when she'd seen Bethany's dance partner.

He'd been looking their way, probably warning Shane off, and their eyes had met.

Gavin had looked away at once, pulling Bethany closer, but April had stopped dead, staring. Just like that, she'd fallen.

The crazy thing was, compared to Bethany's usual type, Gavin wasn't even that good-looking. Not that he was a troll, he was just average: brown eyes, plain haircut, and a skinny bod. Her eyes saw that, but the rest of her insisted he was Tom Cruise and Brad Pitt rolled into one.

What her eyes had also seen all too clearly was that Gavin was in love with Bethany. And that Bethany was not in love with him.

Bethany had liked him, even clung to him a bit because that was what Bethany did, but she hadn't loved him any more than she'd loved any of the other guys she'd dated.

Men fell in love with Bethany, not the other way around. She smiled, and they melted. April had never been able to figure out just what had made Bethany beautiful instead of pretty, but she had been beautiful. And nice. That had been the worst thing about Bethany Mills: you couldn't hate her.

After stepping on Shane's toes twice April had excused herself, saying she felt ill. Shane had believed her. She'd almost believed it herself staring at her white reflection in the washroom mirror.

You're being stupid, Jongkind. People don't really fall in love at first sight. Besides, he's fathoms deep in love with Bethany, probably sleeping with her. Beautiful Bethany. You can't compete with her any more than Mom could compete with Aunt Kimberly. Save yourself some heartache and forget about him.

She'd given herself the same pep talk for three months. It hadn't helped. Several times April had caught herself cold-bloodedly making plans to wait until fall and go to the University of Calgary, which Bethany and Gavin both attended. By fall she'd been sure Bethany would have broken up with Gavin—Bethany had gone through men like other people went through Kleenex—and April could catch Gavin on the rebound.

But now Bethany was dead.

"Why?" Gavin asked again. "Why are you helping me?"

April didn't answer. "The longer you stall, the harder it's going to be to get around the roadblocks."

Gavin looked mutinous. He looked good, too, broody and hand-some. April's eyes kept dropping to his bare chest. She swallowed a sigh and made her voice tough. "Look, Gavin, do you want the police to catch you or not?"

A pause, then a sullen, "No."

Thunder cracked open the sky. She didn't even flinch, intent on convincing Gavin. "You have to be out of this area by daylight. Far, far away. The only way you can do that is by car. Unless you steal a car and leave a theft trail, you need someone to drop you off. That's me. You have no choice."

"You're not going to give up, are you?"

She shook her head.

He sighed. "All right, with one condition. Since we're probably going to share the same cellblock for the next ten years, I'd sort of like to know your name."

"April Jongkind." Flushing, she walked over to the closet and fished out one of Brent Hillock's blue flannel shirts. He had five of them and wouldn't miss one. "Here." She tossed it to Gavin. "Put this on." They had to hurry.

Awkwardly, he eased his injured shoulder into the sleeve. He only got it halfway up before he had to stop, teeth clenched in pain.

April helped him into the shirt. She didn't tell him if he couldn't even dress himself, he needed her help. The point had made itself.

Buttoning his shirt made her nervous. To cover up she got down to practicalities. "Do you have any money?"

"Fifty bucks," Gavin said instantly.

April called his bluff. "Good. I'll need ten bucks for gas."

Gavin opened his mouth, caught flat-footed. He'd been so sure she'd offer him money. "You little brat. You win. I don't have my wallet with me."

She forced him to take $30 of her $35, but he insisted it was a loan. "I'll pay you back with interest. Double what the bank pays." He was honest to a fault.

How could the police think he'd murdered Bethany?

Tears threatened again, so April busied herself, first getting some Tylenol for Gavin to swallow, then making bologna sandwiches.

A spectacular stroke of lightning and a crash of thunder came from outside. April was amazed Kristy hadn't woken up again. Her hands stilled. "Kristy."

"What?"

"I forgot about Kristy, the girl I'm baby-sitting. What are we going to do about her?" She would only be gone a couple of hours. Kristy would probably sleep through the entire trip, but she had a certain responsibility to Mrs. Hillock.

"Baby-sitting? You mean that wasn't just a lie you told the police?" Gavin looked appalled.

" 'Fraid not. We'll have to take her with us," April decided. "I can't leave her alone when there's a murderer on the loose."

"So you're going to take her on a car ride with a suspected murderer? That makes sense," he said sarcastically.

"Yes." April didn't realize how strange her answer sounded until she'd said it. Embarrassment sharpened her voice. "You didn't kill Bethany, but somebody else did—and somebody shot you."

"What makes you think the police didn't shoot me?"

"They didn't describe you as wounded and dripping blood." April slapped a slice of bread on top of the bologna.

Gavin was silent, thoughtful.

"A good thing, too, because I'd left the bandages sitting out." April bit her lip to stop chattering. Was that a dog barking in the distance? How close were the search parties?

She thrust the sandwiches into Gavin's hands and hurried to wake Kristy. She found her snoring in bed, her covers yanked up to her chin. April stopped dead. Kristy always slept curled up on her side, and she never snored. Kristy was faking.

Damn. So much for Kristy sleeping through the entire journey. After a moment's thought April decided things might work better this way. "Kristy, you're going to start sleepwalking."

Obediently, Kristy got up and lurched across the room, eyes screwed shut, arms held stiffly in front of her like Frankenstein's monster.

April fought back a giggle. "Kristy is leaving her room."

Kristy swerved right and would have crashed into the bookcase if April had not steered her away. "Kristy's sleepwalking down the hall to the kitchen."

Gavin blinked. Twice.

"Be quiet, Gavin," April stage-whispered. "Kristy's sleepwalking."

"Of course. What was I thinking?"

"You know it's a funny thing about sleepwalkers," April announced. "Sometimes, even though they're sleepwalking, their eyes are open."

Brown eyes sprang open.

"Sometimes, they'll even talk to other people and not remember it when they wake up."

Gavin looked at April as if doubting her sanity.

Kristy smiled at Gavin. "Hi."

Gavin ignored her, speaking to April, "Are you sure this is a good idea?"

April wasn't sure, but she couldn't leave Kristy behind. "Kristy's dreaming," she said lightly. "She dreamed she saw you earlier, too."

"I dreamed you were bleeding." Kristy showed her dimples.

The worry-frown on Gavin's face deepened.

April sensed objections coming and headed them off at the pass. "Don't worry. Even if she wasn't dreaming, Kristy wouldn't tell anyone."

"Can I tell Bobby?" Kristy beseeched.

April melted. Kristy's brown eyes reminded her of Gavin. "You can tell Bobby, but no one else."

"Well, that makes me feel much better," Gavin said.

April grinned. "Bobby's her imaginary friend."

Kristy closed her eyes, the way she always did when "talking" to Bobby. She wouldn't blab the secret out loud.

"Talk to him later," April said firmly, steering Kristy down the hall. "Go get dressed."

While waiting for Kristy she hastily threw the sandwiches, some more bandages, and the Tylenol in a grocery bag with a couple of cans of pop. Even though the police had been and gone, she kept lifting her head to check for flashing lights outside. A little voice in her head said, *"Hurry, hurry."*

April hurried. She handed Kristy her coat, eased an old jean jacket over Gavin's arms, and hustled them out the door. Cold rain pelted her face, but exhilaration filled her. She was with Gavin, and, better still, he needed her. Really needed her the way no one ever had before. If not for her Gavin would—

—be under arrest for Bethany's murder. Guilt blindsided her. How could she be thinking about Bethany's boyfriend when Bethany was dead? What kind of sick—

"Please tell me this isn't your car." Gavin's voice derailed her train of thought. He stood on the bottom step, gloomily studying her green Chevy. "Tell me you have Corvette or a Trans Am hidden in the machine shed."

"Not a chance. Don't worry, Rustbucket runs all right." She rapped the wet hood. "When he wants to."

"What year is it? Nineteen thirty-eight? The trunk's rusting out," Gavin said critically, head hunched against the wind and rain.

"Be grateful," April said, opening the trunk. "Those are your air holes. Climb in."

• 3 •

For the second time that morning Genevieve found herself standing outside in the dewy grass, pickup keys in hand, without quite know- ing how she'd gotten there.

She'd had a craving for ice cream and had decided to drive into town to get some.

At six in the morning. For breakfast.

A minute ago it had made perfect sense. Only the fact that dawn was just breaking, and the store wouldn't be open for several hours yet, had stopped her.

Half an hour ago she'd remembered that her library books were overdue and rushed out to the pickup so she could return them in the overnight drop and avoid incurring seventy-five cents' worth of fines.

Both reasons were ludicrous. They camouflaged the true reason she was standing out here again without even a jacket: paranoia.

In her dream last night the Selector had found out she lived near Lake Michigan, and she was afraid he would find her. Never mind the fact that the Selector didn't exist; part of her was terrified. Was certain that if she didn't leave right now, this instant, he would find her, and she would be the one left bleeding in the grass.

Genevieve clutched the keys so tightly they left imprints in her palm, willing herself to think of sanity. Of Matt. Holding a picture of him in her mind like an icon—brown hair, warm smile, and intelligent gray eyes behind gold-frame glasses—Genevieve walked back to the two-story house.

To distract herself she made a huge breakfast: ham and mushroom omelets, toast, hash browns, and freshly-squeezed orange juice. The smell of it pulled Matt downstairs, but his appreciative comments died when he was reaching for his second piece of toast and he got a good look at her face.

"You had the dream again last night, didn't you?"

Bitterly, Genevieve reflected that in the seven months since she'd come to live in his house as his research assistant/chauffeur Matt had had plenty of opportunity to learn the signs of a bad night.

She tried to make light of it. "What? I can't cook breakfast without having had a bad dream?"

Matt didn't smile in return. "Don't pretend, Genevieve."

The smile slipped off her face and fell into the Grand Canyon. "Please, Matt. Let me handle this my own way."

"I know you can handle it, that's not the point."

Could she handle it? Genevieve thought that was debatable. Sometimes it hit her like a hangover; she'd be quiet in the morning and back to normal by noon. Sometimes Matt could joke her out of it. And sometimes, like today, the dream would play over and over in her mind until she forced it out with mindless physical labor—

scrubbing the floor until her body was covered in sweat and her hands were raw.

Matt kept telling her housecleaning wasn't in her job description. She did it anyway. Anything to drive away the images—

[*Spatters of blood lie like dew . . .*]

"The point is you don't have to handle it alone," Matt said earnestly. He reached across the table and held her cold hand. "You can ask me for help."

Genevieve had never intended Matt to know about her dreams at all, but he'd found her crying one night. She refused to tell him anything about them beyond the bare fact of their existence. Some burdens had to be borne alone.

"Please don't shut me out," Matt said quietly. "Too much of your life is already closed to me. Because of your amnesia."

It always came back to her amnesia. "I'm sorry, Matt." It hurt her to hurt him like this, but she couldn't tell him about the dream. Couldn't tell him about clocks and blood and murder.

[*The knife plunges into the older man's neck . . .*]

Genevieve shuddered, and Matt gripped her hands harder, centering her for a moment.

"It might do you good to talk about your dreams," Matt suggested, not for the first time. "If not to me, then to someone else. It doesn't take a degree in psychiatry to figure out that your dream has something to do with your past."

"No." Genevieve rejected the idea out of hand. "I know you only want to help, but—no."

Matt smiled wryly. "My motives aren't entirely unselfish. You know I want to marry you."

She nodded. He'd proposed at Christmas, almost breaking her heart.

"And you still refuse to marry me without knowing your identity?"

It was a question. Genevieve swallowed and answered, "Yes."

Matt sighed. "I wish you'd believe me when I tell you that your past doesn't matter. I love you."

He struck a nerve. "How can you say that?" Genevieve asked passionately. "You don't know who I am. I could be anyone."

Matt's lips twitched. "If you're trying to tell me you're a Mafia hit woman, I don't believe you. You're an amnesiac, not an escaped criminal. Stop treating yourself like one."

"I could be married." She made her words hit like stones. Saying no to his proposal had been hard enough at Christmas. She couldn't bear to have this argument again.

"I'm just as afraid of that happening as you are, sweetheart, but let's be logical. You didn't have a ring."

"I didn't have a wallet either. Do you think a mugger would miss a ring?" she asked woodenly.

"You're young. Dr. Brannigan estimates around twenty-three. You're probably not married," Matt said.

"People get married at eighteen all the time."

Matt produced the most conclusive bit of evidence yet. "If you're married, why hasn't your husband filed a missing persons report? If you were my wife, I would move heaven and earth to find you."

Genevieve had no answer.

"It's been seven months, and your memory hasn't returned yet. What if it never does? Are you going to remain single forever?" Matt asked.

Genevieve bit her lip.

He gentled his voice. "I'm not asking you to marry me tomorrow. I'm asking you to stop drifting and think about the future. Set a time limit of six months — or a year, for that matter — and make a decision then. Do more newspaper interviews to discover your identity. Tell me you don't want to be tied down so young, or you're not sure if you really love me. Just don't use your amnesia as an excuse. I can take anything better than hanging around in this limbo." He left the table.

Genevieve scraped the uneaten food on their plates into the garbage. Saturday was technically her day off, although Matt did not keep regular office hours. She usually spent the day doing laundry or watching TV. Today she found herself pacing, going from window to window. Watching. Waiting for the Selector to show up.

Waiting for a nightmare.

Crazy.

Desperate, she went upstairs with the vague idea of doing something mechanical like dusting or vacuuming.

She wasn't surprised when she found herself packing. Emptying drawers, neatly folding clothes.

She wasn't going anywhere, there was no reason to flee, but the action calmed her, and, so long as she knew she was humoring herself, what could it really hurt?

She didn't own a suitcase, so she shoved the clothes into two duffel bags.

Once she'd emptied the dresser drawers, she pulled out the top one and peeled off the white envelope taped to the end. She opened it up and counted off fifty green twenties. One thousand dollars, cash.

Fingers shaking, she stuffed the money into her pocket. If the Selector was real — even though he wasn't — she didn't want to be caught on the run without a purse.

Like last time . . .

Genevieve shied away from the thought. She got up again and started pacing, trying to ignore the constant nagging voice in her head telling her to leave now, save herself, forget about her clothes and her money or anything but getting out of this house, this death trap.

Maybe she should go to Matt. She'd upset him with her refusal to talk. He'd been right. It wasn't amnesia that was keeping them apart. She desperately wanted to tell him about her dream, explain why she couldn't marry him.

Soak up some of his strength like a parasite.

She leaned on Matt enough as it was. He deserved someone who could share his dreams. She had only nightmares.

If they were ever going to build a future together, she had to stand her ground, not run. Vanquish the dream.

But, oh God, it was hard. Like standing on railroad tracks while a train hurtled toward her. Telling herself it was a ghost train, that it would pass right through her, but able to feel the rumble of the steel rails beneath her feet and hear the scream of the whistle —

Doubt suddenly assailed her. What if it wasn't a ghost train?

Didn't it make more sense to leave until the feeling faded, just in case? It was her day off. She could tell Matt she was driving into town for some groceries. After all, she could always come back.

For the third time that morning, Genevieve found herself outside. This time she was sitting behind the wheel of Matt's 4×4 before she stopped. Frustrated tears pricked her eyes, and she impatiently blinked out her green contacts.

You can't have it both ways. Either you're in danger or you're not. If you're not, there's no point in leaving. If the danger is real . . .

If the danger was real, she would be leaving Matt to face it alone.

The knowledge hit her like a kick in the gut. Matt. She scrambled out of the pickup, allowing her paranoia full rein. She was getting the hell out of here, and she was taking Matt with her. She'd make up some excuse and hustle him into the pickup.

The relief that should have come when she caved in didn't arrive. Two steps inside the side door nausea cramped her stomach.

Through the window she saw an old yellow car turn down their driveway.

She was too late. The danger had arrived.

• 4 •

With a great *crack!* the power pole splintered in half like a matchstick. The top half fell, and the two power lines it carried snapped like threads. The dangling ends whipped back, then spooled to earth in a shower of yellow sparks, narrowly missing the John Deere tractor.

Jeff studied the still-snapping live wires with a sick feeling in his gut. Will Halvorsen had taken out both power and phone. The sun had almost set. If they'd been at home, they'd have been without communication in the dark, helpless.

Penny's hand found his, and the two of them watched in silence as Will and his partner spoke briefly, then split up. The partner got into the Bronco, reversed onto the road, and whipped down it at great speed.

Jeff held Penny's head down, huddling in the ditch, as the Bronco went by, throwing gravel from its back tires. A stone stung Jeff's back, but the Bronco didn't see them and kept going.

Jeff glanced up and saw that Will had the tractor on the road, mighty engine going at full throttle. But its top speed was 35 km/h, and from its high cab Will would have a good view of the ditch where he and Penny were hiding.

The John Deere had eight wheels the height of a man. Jeff had a nightmare vision of Will spotting them and turning the juggernaut toward them, running them down. He tensed, about to pull Penny up into a run and make a break for the station wagon.

"No!" Penny said over the roar of the tractor. "We're safer if we don't move."

Jeff wanted to argue, but then it was too late, the tractor too close.

"We'll be okay. He won't see us—Oh!" Penny gasped.

"Penny?" Jeff turned to his wife while the tractor went by. "What is it?" A cold lump settled in his stomach. "Is it the baby?"

She clutched his hand with bruising strength, her face chalk white. "N-no . . . I can feel . . . his hatred . . . choking me." She bit her lip.

Jeff watched helplessly, held in place by the tractor passing by on the road. Penny's breathing came in gasps until the black wheels had taken Will twenty meters away, then she collapsed backward in the wet grass. "He's out of range now. I'll be okay in a second."

Jeff wasn't sure he would be okay. "What happened?"

"My empathy Talent." Penny smiled wanly at him, still shockingly pale. "Sometimes it can be more of a hindrance than a help."

Jeff dropped the subject. The last thing he wanted to think about right now was whether or not his wife had psychic powers.

The green tractor continued to toil slowly up the road. It was unlikely that Will would look back now and see them, but Jeff waited until the tractor was a mile down the road before standing. "Stay here. I'll go get the station wagon and pick you up."

Penny nodded, which worried him even more. He ran.

When he reached the station wagon, he spared only a moment

to reassure Bobby before starting the engine and going to pick up Penny.

She got in quickly, and, hands slippery with sweat, Jeff turned onto the secondary road and floored it. He divided his attention between the tractor in the rearview mirror and Penny. Even if Will saw them, Jeff could easily outrun the tractor, but a lot of farmers had two-way radios in their cabs. If he contacted the driver of the Bronco, it would be another story.

The station wagon gathered speed, each second increasing their chances of escaping unseen. The tractor vanished behind a small rise, but Penny's pallor remained. He tried to distract her. "You said the Kithkinners were the children of the Futurists. Who are they?"

"The Futurists?" At first Penny was slow to respond. "That's just what the psychic community calls itself."

Jeff waited until she continued.

"Each Futurist lives in a different part of the country, making up the points of a web." Penny regained the color in her cheeks. "That way, in case of emergency, everyone knows one other point on the web and can go there for help."

The web sounded a little more serious than a bunch of people bending spoons. Just what exactly was Penny involved with? "Do these emergencies happen often?"

"Not anymore. The Futurists first formed as a defense system against the old man, but he's dead now."

"What old man?" Jeff checked the mirror. The reflection of the sky on the pavement made the road look like it was dissolving, but there were no signs of pursuit.

"I don't really know." The admission seemed to surprise Penny. "I've only heard him referred to as 'the old man.' He died before I joined the Kithkinners."

Jeff's distrust of strangers reasserted itself. "If Will Halvorsen has nothing to do with the psychics, then why should we go to a web house?"

"Because," Penny said, and then stopped. "Because a web house is unknown. I've never met David Calder. There is no connection between the two of us, so Will Halvorsen will never guess to look for us there. Besides, how do we know Will Halvorsen has nothing to do with the Futurists? All we know is he's trying to kill us."

"Will's flipped his lid. When he finds us gone he'll just pick another victim; he won't chase after us."

"No." Penny touched his arm. "You're wrong. He's trying to kill Bobby and me. He doesn't care about anyone else. He just wants us dead."

Instinctively, Jeff glanced at the backseat, where his son sat. Bobby looked wide-eyed, sensing something wasn't quite right even if he didn't understand their words.

"How do you know that?" Jeff braked at the intersection with the main highway. Draketown, where he worked, lay fifteen minutes to the right; Chinchaga, two and a half hours to the left.

"I *know*." Tears shone in her green eyes. "My Talent is empathy. When Will passed by, his hatred almost smothered me, like being sucked down into quicksand. He intends to kill us."

Jeff remembered her reaction and reluctantly decided she'd felt something. You couldn't fake pallor like that, but he didn't want to admit that Penny might be a psychic. Jeff liked things he could take apart and put back together; he didn't trust vague feelings.

"You've been closer to him before, why didn't you sense the hate then?"

"He didn't hate us earlier. I don't know why he does now. I know it doesn't make sense, but it's the truth."

Thinking about it gave Jeff a headache. "We should go to the police."

"The police would laugh at us. Will Halvorsen is on the hospital board. Everyone knows him. Filing a report will only slow us down." Her face twisted. "Every minute counts. The farther away we are, the safer we are. The safer Bobby and Damaris are."

"Damaris?" Jeff asked, startled. "Who's Damaris?"

Penny's face softened into a smile. Her hand curved over her protruding stomach. "Our daughter, Damaris."

Jeff felt stunned. "A girl? You're sure?" They wanted a girl.

Penny nodded, and Jeff smiled in pure delight. He was going to have a daughter.

If Will Halvorsen didn't kill mother and child. Jeff had seen a few victims of violent death during his less-than-ideal childhood, and his mind conjured a picture of Penny with her skull crushed in, sitting in a pool of her own blood, flies buzzing around her head, crawling across her cheek... The image sent an atavistic chill over him. *Never,* he swore silently. No matter how slight the chance of Will killing Penny, he would not risk it.

He wouldn't let his mother's curse come true.

He'd last seen his mother three years ago. Bobby's birth had given him such a rush of optimism and hope that he'd gone to visit her. To try and see if they could have some kind of relationship. Even then he must have known better because he'd brought her money, five hundred dollars he'd saved for a trust fund for Bobby. The few times she'd been happy to see him in his childhood were when he brought her money—or booze.

He'd tracked her down to an ugly, one-room apartment. The dump could have been the clone of any of the ones he'd grown up in. Water stains on the wall, overflowing ashtrays, empty bottles everywhere, unwashed dishes in the sink.

She'd worn a low-cut dress and stunk of cheap perfume. She'd been drunk, of course. He'd recognized the signs from his childhood and calculated that while she was mean drunk, she wasn't yet at the violent stage.

She took a swig from an open bottle of rye, wiped her mouth with the back of her hand, and said, "So you're back. Wanting a place to stay, I suppose."

"No, Ma," he said calmly. "I have my own house now." He told her about his job and Penny and Bobby, hoping, foolishly, that she would be happy for him. Proud. But she just sat there, bloodshot eyes simmering with malevolence, until he finished his little speech. Then she let go with both barrels.

"You make me sick. You think you're so great, think you're better than your brother, but you're not." She walked right up to him, tottering on her ridiculously high heels, spraying spittle in his face. "You'll lose it all. *First your house, then your wife, then your son, then your life.*"

He'd walked away from his mother without a backward glance.

"Kisty thinks we should go to the spiderweb," Bobby said.

Jeff smiled gently down at his son's serious face. "I guess I'm outvoted. To the spiderweb we go." It scarcely mattered where they spent the weekend so long as it wasn't at home. He turned west toward Chinchaga.

Five minutes later his grin faded. Penny kept turning to look behind them, checking for the Bronco.

Jeff didn't like to think about what a chase would entail. He tried to keep the station wagon tuned up, but it was ten years old, and the Bronco was brand-new. The once-pleasant straight lines of the highway took on the sinister appearance of a trap. No place to turn off, no place to hide. In the maze of a city he had confidence he could lose a pursuer. He knew Calgary like the back of his hand. Hadn't he lost Todd there once when Todd came after him with a baseball bat?

What would he do if the Bronco followed them? The man in the back of the Bronco had had a rifle, and he had noth—

Penny had a gun. She'd put it in the glove compartment.

"Where did you get the gun?"

"A store. I have a license."

"Then why hide it in the woods? Why didn't you tell me about the cache or any of this?"

"It's not my secret alone to tell, and I didn't think you'd believe me."

Jeff wasn't sure he believed her now, but he didn't admit it, insisting, "You should have told me."

How well do you know your wife? Will Halvorsen had asked. *Do you know what lies behind her mask?*

Jeff would have sworn he knew everything about Penny, that she was too open even to wear a mask. It disturbed him to discover how wrong he'd been.

To be fair, he'd kept secrets from Penny, too—was still keeping them—but he couldn't help being a little upset. "How long ago did this Seeress tell you about the danger? I would have appreciated a little advance warning."

"Five years ago."

Jeff laughed in relief. "Five years ago? Isn't that a little like saying it'll snow during July and claiming you're right when it snows in November?"

"She was dead right about her first prediction: I did marry you," Penny said.

"What a risk. Five years ago we were dating."

"Five years ago we *started* dating. I hadn't even met you when I saw the Seeress. She told me to marry an engineer named Jeff."

Jeff snorted. "I'm a lowly Telecommunications Engineering Technician with a degree from SAIT."

"But I met you at a University Engineering party. There were only two Jeffs at the party, and only you had a mustache. With a little detective work, Carrie and I found out your name and contrived to meet you."

The bottom dropped out of Jeff's stomach. His ears rang. "Let me get this straight." He had a death grip on the steering wheel. "You're telling me, on the basis of some old woman's crackpot vision, you cold-bloodedly decided to meet and marry me?"

Penny winced, but all Jeff registered was her reluctant voice saying, "Well, yes, it was kind of calculated at first."

"*Kind of* calculated?" Jeff burst out, before clamping his mouth shut.

A terrible fear sank its talons into his flesh.

What if she had married him, not because she loved him, but to fulfill some prophecy?

His intellect rejected the idea. He and Penny had been married for close to four years. They had a child. They'd made love hundreds of times; she couldn't have been lying all those times.

Could she?

She hadn't told him about the Futurists.

His mind struggled to point out that a lie by omission was quite different from an outright lie—

But he kept remembering how astonished he'd been when they met, how awed that someone as pretty and popular as Penny Gillis could be interested in him, and he kept hearing his mother's voice: *"You're no good for nothing, just like your father."* She'd told him that so many times, he'd grown up believing it. Only Penny's love had convinced him he wasn't destined to be a failure.

But she might not love him, after all.

Despair and fear tore through him.

"It was a game," Penny said desperately. "A peek at my future husband. It stopped being a game when I met you."

He wanted to believe her, wanted to believe she couldn't have married someone she didn't love, but he had to ask. "Why did the Seeress tell you to marry me?"

She smiled uncertainly. "She said you would invent something that saved my life."

And there it was. A reason to marry.

All his life the people he had loved, his mother, his brother, had used him for what he could do for them. And now Penny was saying she had done the same thing. His heart felt as if it were freezing, cracking in half.

"Jeff? What is it? I can tell you're upset."

Of course, she could. She was an empath. She knew how he felt, had known all along he loved her . . .

She put a hand on his arm. "Jeff?"

He couldn't bear to be touched with the revelation still so raw; he shook her hand off. "Do you do it through touch? Does it help you read my mind?" he asked viciously.

Her mouth dropped open, stunned. Hurt and reproach filled her eyes. "That isn't why I touched you. How can you suggest such a thing?"

"Okay," Jeff said, "I won't." He clenched his jaw, but nothing could stifle the howl he felt inside.

Ma had gotten the last laugh after all.

• 5 •

Gavin swore silently, sweating, as the Rustbucket bumped over yet another pothole. The Tylenol hadn't helped much, and his shoulder twanged like an out-of-tune guitar at the slightest jar. The potholes were murder. He'd almost passed out several times from the sheer pain.

The rest of his body was accruing a few bruises as well from being bounced around so much. The inside of the trunk was cramped and, rusty air holes or not, very dark. Someone with more imagination might have compared it to a coffin, but, as his teachers had often lamented, Gavin didn't have an imagination. He didn't see the point. Wasn't reality bad enough? He had a gunshot wound that rendered him all but helpless and would probably get infected. He was hiding in the trunk of a car, gulping down carbon monoxide, and the police were hunting him for Bethany's murder—

Don't think about her.

He thought about the pain in his shoulder instead as they jolted over more bumps. The Rustbucket didn't have any shocks, and he was developing a pathological hatred for gravel roads. To think he'd once complained about Vancouver streets. Unfortunately, a back-road route was necessary: the police would have roadblocks up on the highway.

Gavin breathed through his shirt. Had they passed the roadblocks yet? About twenty minutes had passed, but April had promised to drive no faster than 60 km/h. No telling how far they'd come.

The Rustbucket braked suddenly. He banged his head, but barely noticed, gasping from the pain in his shoulder. Jesus. How could one tiny bullet hole hurt so much? Couldn't April have slowed down gradually?

They'd stopped. The motor turned over once, then died. The sudden silence made Gavin's ears ring. Where had they stopped? Past the roadblocks—or at one?

His shoulder throbbed.

A car door slammed. Footsteps.

April, Gavin told himself, but he pushed himself farther back into the trunk just in case, scrunching up his long legs, although the police would have to be blind not to see him.

A key rasped in the lock. The trunk opened. "Gavin?" April whispered. "Are you there?"

"No, I'm on a beach in California, and this is all a dream." Gavin uncurled himself and began the awkward process of getting out; he banged his shin on the spare tire and jarred his shoulder. Only the cold rain on his face kept him from blacking out.

"Here, lean on me." April slipped an arm around his waist. Her strength surprised him. Although her head barely reached his shoulder, she was sturdy. Solid. She helped him into the front seat of the car. Kristy was sleeping under a blanket in the back. "I think we're past the roadblocks. I'm going to try the highway."

Gavin nodded and closed his eyes, listening to the whisk of the windshield wipers. He felt a rush of gratitude toward her. April's willingness to help a murder suspect still appalled his legal mind, but if not for her he'd be in jail, a sitting duck for the real murderer.

"Always advise a fugitive to turn himself in," he remembered his Criminal Law professor saying. Gavin broke out into a cold sweat just thinking about following that advice.

He hadn't seen the face of the man who had shot him, but he'd noticed the uniform.

A policeman had shot him.

At the time he'd assumed the policeman had mistaken him for Bethany's killer and was trigger-happy, but April had said that his police description did not include a bullet wound, which raised more ominous implications. Had the policeman killed Bethany and then shot Gavin to get rid of a witness? It seemed crazy on the face of it—probably the police had just forgotten to tell April to be on the alert for a wounded man—but Gavin had deliberately not told April who shot him in case the knowledge was dangerous.

Gavin brooded over the problem as they drove into the night, gradually outdistancing the thundershower and coming closer to their destination.

They crossed a set of railroad tracks and came upon a bunch of vehicles with flashing yellow lights. Adrenaline jumped in Gavin's veins until he realized it was the power company working on a downed line and not a police roadblock.

"We're almost there," Gavin told April five minutes later. "It should be the next house on the right." He'd only been to Penny's house once, but he had a good memory for directions.

The Rustbucket dipped down a small hill. The headlights hit a darkened driveway—and drove on past.

"You just passed it."

"I know." She sounded calm, amused. "Safety precaution: we don't want anybody remembering a late-night visitor at your friend's place." There was an overgrown driveway at the top of the hill. She turned far enough in that they weren't easily visible from the road, parked, and killed the lights and motor.

"Thanks." Gavin felt incredibly awkward sitting there in the dark. How could 'Thanks' possibly express the enormity of his debt? "I owe you one," he tried again. "I owe you ten." He chucked her under the chin. "I'll never forget you."

He had one leg out of the car when headlights topped the first hill.

"Shit!" April said. "Quick, close the door. Slide over and kiss me."

Gavin understood her plan at once. He scooted over and kissed her.

He listened for the car with both ears. His eyes were closed as if in passion, his good arm around her. If anyone spotted the car, they would just see some teenagers out necking, not fugitives on the run.

Their noses bumped and instinct made him angle his head more to the right. Her lips parted slightly, warm and sweet. Good. Bethany had always tasted of lipstick—

And where the hell was the car?

The vehicle should have passed them by now. Gavin opened his eyes; April peered back at him. "They must have turned off," he said. But the only turnoff was Penny and Jeff's.

"I don't like this," April said uneasily.

"You're not the only one." A strand of her hair brushed his lips, and he let go so fast his arm gave him a speeding ticket. "It's after eleven o'clock—a bit late to go visiting. The house lights are off.

Penny and—I mean, my friends—are probably already in bed."
Damn. He'd made a point of not telling her the names of the friends
with whom he planned to take refuge.

April pretended not to notice his slip. "Well, the only way to find
out what's happening is to go take a look." She got out of the car
and started locking the doors.

Gavin quickly got out on his side. "What are you doing? Your
part's over. Get back in the car and take Kristy home."

"Kristy's asleep. She'll be fine for a few minutes."

"What if she wakes up? She'll be alone in the dark." Gavin
warmed to his argument. "She—"

[*AaiieeeeeeeeeeeeeEEEEEeeeeeeeeeeeeeeeeeeee!*]

The scream sliced into his head, almost driving Gavin to his
knees. He put both hands over his ears, welcoming the pain in his
shoulder because it drowned out the terrible sound of Bethany's
scream, Bethany's voice pleading for his help.

[*Gavin! Gavin, help me! Noooooooooooooooo!*]

Help he hadn't been able to give—

The shriek tore at his mind, reopening wounds barely scabbed
over.

Shut up! You're dead, I can't help you! Shut up! His heart
pounded; he heard April ask, "Are you okay?"—he'd never be okay
again—but all his concentration was centered on one thing: pushing.

He pushed back Bethany's soul-tearing scream, closed his eyes to
the sight of her bloody body, bit his tongue on the taste of lipstick.
He couldn't help her. The only thing he could give her was justice.
He would find her murderer and see that he was punished.

"Gavin?" April tentatively touched his arm.

"I'm okay," Gavin lied, focusing on the rounded oval of her face.
The wind and his hands had mussed her toffee-colored hair into an
attractive tangle. "Let's go." He plunged down the hill, no longer
interested in arguing.

They cut across the yard, walking in wet grass instead of on
crunchy gravel. They crossed a bare patch—Penny's garden, Gavin
supposed. He had trouble picturing Penny doing something as mun-
dane as gardening, but guessed she'd simply thrown her great enthu-

siasm into it as she had earlier, knitting baby clothes for Bobby. Penny always kept busy with something.

As they stealthily approached the back of the house, the wind stirred a stand of poplars, and the air was full of rustling branches and strange, grotesque shadows. Suddenly reluctant to take another step, Gavin caught April's hand and tugged her into a crouch. Together, they crept forward and peeked around the corner.

The thin moonlight allowed him to make out a blue Bronco. "Penny and Jeff own a station wagon," he whispered.

"The cupboards and the closets have been cleaned out," someone said. A man's voice, angry and petulant. "They're gone and not expecting to be back soon. I told you we shouldn't have waited until dark."

"And I told you we couldn't risk being seen at the scene of a crime by anybody passing by," a second man replied. "It was your job to watch the road. They shouldn't have been able to get past you without being seen."

The first man took the rebuke in silence, then said, "What do we do now?"

"Find them," the second man said, his tone so cold a chill slithered down Gavin's spine. "Find them and kill them before the Demoness spawns another child."

CHAPTER 3

• 1 •

Matt Rutledge stared at the blinking cursor on his word processor. He hadn't written one word in half an hour, and his mind was tangled on Genevieve, not the problems of his Civil War characters.

He hated the way her recurring dream turned her back into the woman he'd found on his doorstep seven months ago, a bewildered stranger in a kelly green sweater with curly dark hair and tearful green eyes.

Green eyes full of secrets, his writer's mind had supplied. They'd held panic, too, when she'd said, *I don't know who I am.* A purple bruise had marred her temple.

When she'd asked if he knew her, he'd been forced to say no.

"I woke up in a ditch a couple miles down the road. I don't have a purse, but I found this in my pocket." She produced a crumpled newspaper clipping of his ad for a research assistant/chauffeur. It was the only clue they'd ever found to her identity.

He would never forget the extraordinary courage with which she'd faced losing her memory. She'd cooperated fully with the police and hospital authorities, not once giving in to tears, and when, two weeks later, the newspaper stories, sessions with Dr. Brannigan, and an investigation of missing persons failed to turn up the smallest clue, she'd still smiled gamely when Matt dropped by the hospital to ask if she had any plans.

"That depends. Is that position still open?"

Matt had interviewed several qualified applicants, but he'd said yes without a qualm. "If you need it, it's yours." He knew she needed it.

"I want it, but it hardly seems fair to you. I don't have a résumé. I don't even know if I can be a research assistant or drive a car, but I must have or I wouldn't have clipped the ad, right?" Her smile had wobbled a little.

"I'm sure you'll do fine," Matt said.

Matt couldn't drive because of his epilepsy, so her driver's license was of primary importance. She retook her driver's exam, and Matt arranged for her to be granted a temporary driver's license until either her memory returned or the police discovered her identity.

Together they had picked out her name: Genevieve, because they both liked it, and Kelly because of her sweater.

Her research skills had turned out to be minimal, but she was a fast learner, and they worked well together researching his Civil War novel. He enjoyed her company immensely.

He'd fallen in love with her long before their first kiss.

Each facet of her personality, once revealed, became a precious piece of a complex puzzle. Her soft heart. Her appalling taste in soap operas and weepy romances. Her passion for chocolate. Her habit of keeping a "cash stash" instead of a bank account.

She had a mischievous child's sense of humor. She tied his socks together, ambushed him with water pistols and, two weeks ago on April Fool's Day, she'd used the search and replace function on his word processor to substitute Cinderella and Prince Charming for the names of his two protagonists. She'd laughed herself almost sick at the expression on his face.

Despite her everyday good spirits, Matt was well aware of the deep currents lurking beneath the surface.

He'd formed numerous theories—each worse than the last—about the trauma that had made her prefer to live her life in limbo rather than remember. As a result he'd been rather cautious the first time he kissed her, but his fear had proved to be groundless. Genevieve had turned in his arms with a sigh and wrapped her arms around his neck.

Matt had let her set the pace for the physical side of their relationship, and they hadn't progressed much beyond kisses and tickling skirmishes. He'd thought time was on his side, but now he wasn't so sure—

The doorbell rang. Seizing on the excuse, Matt got up to answer it.

He stumbled over two duffel bags in the hall. *That's odd.* He was reaching down to look inside them when the doorbell dinged again.

He straightened and started toward the kitchen door.

"Don't!" Genevieve's voice, frantic and sharp.

Matt scanned her pale face as she ran toward him, but could find no obvious injury. "What's wrong?"

The doorbell pealed again, their visitor impatient.

"Don't answer it!" She gripped his arm.

"Okay," Matt agreed, trying to calm her down. "Who's there?"

She ignored his question. "Is the door locked?"

Matt stared. "No." This wasn't the city. He only locked the place when he left on an extended trip.

"Shit," Genevieve said. Genevieve never swore. There was something different about her face, too . . .

"Stay here. Let me handle this."

Before Matt could object, Genevieve rounded the kitchen corner. Handle what? Who was at the door? He hesitated, then hung back. He had a hunch this had to do with Genevieve's amnesia, and he might learn more out of sight.

"Let me in," a strange man said. "I know you're in there."

"Go away," Genevieve said.

A masculine chuckle. "Is that any way to greet your long-lost husband?"

Shock robbed Matt of breath. He'd been so sure this couldn't happen. *So sure, because he couldn't bear it.*

"—never saw you before in my life," Genevieve said shakily.

The knot in Matt's stomach eased, only to pull tight again a few seconds later.

"But you have amnesia, don't you, Mary darling?" The man made an insult of an endearment. "You don't remember anything."

Matt felt a rush of dislike. If he'd just found his lost wife, he would have pleaded for her to remember, not bullied.

"I don't know you. I want you to leave."

The door rattled. "Not a chance, Mary dear. Where's the poet man? Upstairs poeting?"

"He's not here," Genevieve lied. "He's out walking."

"Good." The screen door crashed open, and Matt whipped into the kitchen just as Genevieve took refuge behind the island counter.

"Who is this? What's going on?" He moved between Genevieve and the stranger.

The scruffy little man surprised him on several levels. Matt wouldn't have cast this man as Genevieve's husband. He was older, not younger, than Matt's thirty-two, and his work shirt and jeans were blue-collar redneck, not university graduate. He was unshaven, and grease had made a permanent home under his fingernails.

He ignored Matt, his flat black eyes fastened hungrily on Genevieve. "I'm Mary's husband, poet man."

The naked contempt in his voice unnerved Matt. The man was smaller than Matt and had a beer belly. Why was he so confident? Did he have a knife or some friends waiting outside? "Genevieve, do you know this man?"

Genevieve shook her head. Her hands shook, too.

She's lying. Matt felt sick. She wouldn't be so afraid otherwise.

"Jenny-vive. Is that what you're calling yourself now, Mary?"

"That's the third time you've called her Mary," Matt said, stalling.

"Mary Dunstan was her name until she married me. Now it's Mrs. John Crabtree."

"No!" Genevieve said, breathless. "I've never seen him before in my life."

"Well, I remember you." Crabtree smiled, exposing cigarette-yellowed teeth. The incongruity of the pair grated on Matt again.

"I've got your driver's license." Crabtree produced a card from his back pocket. Matt watched his hands closely. "Brown hair, blue eyes, age twenty-three, sure sounds like you to me." Crabtree tossed the card on the table.

Matt's heart, which had leapt at the words *blue eyes*, plummeted to his socks when he saw the photo. He recognized Genevieve—or Mary rather. Mary Dunstan. "This license says Mary Dunstan, not Crabtree."

Crabtree leered. "We were newlyweds."

"Do you have a marriage certificate?" Matt felt sick, asking. Marriage certificate or not, he wouldn't let Genevieve leave with this man. Genevieve loved him.

Mary, his mind insinuated. *How can you be so sure of her love when you didn't even know her name?*

"Of course I have one." The black eyes flickered. "But I don't need proof. Mary remembers her husband, don't you, Mary?"

Genevieve said nothing, neither confirmation, nor denial.

"Genevieve doesn't recognize you, and, even if you are her husband, she doesn't have to go anywhere with you. I'm going to have to ask you to leave."

Crabtree's expression shifted into genuine ugliness. "Out of my way, poet man. Mary's mine."

Matt shook his head, trying to remember what little he knew about street fighting. His friend Ian, the sheriff, had demonstrated a couple of tricks for him once. Ian had claimed half of fighting was keeping yourself balanced and your opponent off-balance. Matt put his weight on the balls of his feet and waited for the knife to appear. Waited for the three burly reinforcements.

"Last warning, poet man. Give me the girl, or I'll kill you." Crabtree sounded utterly confident.

Genevieve pressed something into Matt's hand, and he held up the long knife she'd used to cut ham that morning. "Stay back," he warned.

Crabtree didn't even pause. He lowered his head like a bull and charged. At the last moment Matt tossed the knife away rather than skewer him.

He's insane. Matt thought, as Crabtree's head drove into his stomach and smashed him against the kitchen counter. Grunting, Matt grabbed a handful of Crabtree's dark hair. He pulled Crabtree's head up and split his lip.

Crabtree rocked back on his heels. A snarl twisted his face, but he gave no outcry, fighting in eerie silence.

His foot lashed out with its heavy work boot. Pain exploded in Matt's kneecap, and his leg gave way, slipping sideways. As he fell Crabtree hit him in the stomach, once, twice, the blows as rhythmic and powerful as a man swinging a sledge. Matt curled up in a ball on the floor, unable to breathe.

Crabtree could have finished him off easily with a kick to the head, but he shrugged Matt aside and turned cold eyes on his real prey, Genevieve.

"No." Matt's mouth shaped the word, but he lacked the breath to speak.

"Mary." Crabtree smiled with bleeding lips.

Genevieve stood stock-still, trapped on the other side of the counter. "Stay away from me."

Matt tried to rise, but his knee collapsed like a lawn chair under a three-hundred-pound man.

"You should have run when you had the chance." Crabtree advanced another step. "I—"

Genevieve snatched a frying pan off the stove and hit him on the side of the head.

Crabtree staggered backward into a chair, overturning it, and crashing into the table. Breakfast dishes went flying, bowls and cutlery ringing against the floor. He was down.

Matt painfully pulled himself to his feet. Needles of fire pierced his skin when he put any weight on his knee, but his concern was all for Genevieve. "Are you all ri—?"

He never got to complete the question. Genevieve's eyes widened, and he saw that Crabtree was back on his feet. Weaving, but upright.

"Mary." A flap of scalp hung slightly sideways, and blood ran down his face, but Crabtree kept coming. This time he didn't try to go around the counter; he lunged over it, hands outstretched—

Face white with determination, Genevieve hit him again. The frying pan clanged against his skull. Crabtree collapsed with a sick thud, sliding off the counter and onto the linoleum. This time he didn't move.

Genevieve gripped the frying pan as if she couldn't believe what she'd done. Matt couldn't believe it either. His gentle Genevieve, animal-lover-who-couldn't-hurt-a-fly, had just walloped her "husband" over the head with a skillet. Twice.

Matt made himself look at the man on the floor. Crabtree wasn't dead, he saw with relief, just unconscious. And likely to stay that way for a while. But then, he couldn't believe the man had gotten up the first time. Crabtree's face was a bloody mask.

"We need to call an ambulance." Matt was surprised to find his voice still worked. "And the police."

"No!" Genevieve's eyes looked wild and—blue? "No police. Not yet."

"Why not?" Matt stilled as another thought struck him. "Do you know Crabtree?"

She didn't answer, didn't look at him, head down. She walked down the hall into the living room; Matt limped after her. "I have to leave. I'm sorry, Matt, but if he found me once, he'll find me again. You can call the police after I'm gone."

She couldn't leave. "No. You can't—" Matt gave a short involuntary scream as the muscles in his throat and then his entire body, convulsed.

• 2 •

Matt's eerie cry made Genevieve turn, just in time to see him topple over, like a tree chopped down at the base. His head just missed the coffee table, before hitting the carpet.

He lay with his back arched, rigid and tense.

Tonic.

He was having an epileptic seizure.

Genevieve hurried over to help him, pushing him onto his side away from the coffee table and inserting a sofa cushion between him and any sharp edges. She unbuttoned his Western shirt and removed his glasses, working quickly, racing the coming clonic phase, which would soon follow the tonic, motionless, phase.

When she finished, she stepped back, feeling helpless. Matt's arms muscles stood out in thin cords, contracting.

How long had he been tonic? She glanced at her watch. Grand-mal seizures averaged around three minutes. Much longer and Matt risked entering the state of *status epilepticus*, which could cause death.

Don't think about it.

She'd done all she could. He would probably be bruised from the unnatural fall, but he couldn't hurt himself too badly on the carpet. The loosened clothing should keep him from choking.

Not that Matt was breathing right then. During the first tonic phase, he could not breathe, his muscles locked.

Come on, come on, Genevieve urged silently as Matt's face flushed first red, then turned blue. Still that locked agony.

Then Matt's arm jerked. As if that were a signal his whole body began to thrash and dance as though connected to a strong electric current. Clonic phase. During it Matt could breathe — irregularly, as his muscles alternately contracted and relaxed — but he could breathe.

Genevieve let out her own breath, but kept biting her lip. Matt had told her he experienced little pain — he was unconscious and would not even remember the seizure afterward — but her eyes said differently.

Her eyes saw Matt's head striking the floor, his arms thrusting outward as if to ward off an attack, his legs kicking, and even his mouth opening and closing.

How much longer? Shouldn't the three minutes be up yet? Genevieve's eyes skidded to a stop on her watch. Only a minute and forty seconds had ticked off.

Thump, thump. Matt's head hit the carpet with chilling regularity. *What if he gives himself a concussion? He could —*

I should turn around now.

A bloody hand grasped the kitchen doorjamb, leaving red streaks on the white paint. Genevieve turned cold with horror as the knuckles flexed and a black head moved into view.

Crabtree. Oh, God. In her concern for Matt she'd forgotten all about Crabtree.

Disbelieving, Genevieve watched Crabtree pull himself upright. Her last blow had broken his nose and caved in his right cheekbone, making one side of his face sag. Blood streamed from the gash on his forehead, dripping off his eyebrows, and Genevieve glimpsed white bone where a flap of skin had peeled back.

He should have been unconscious or crawling on the floor, blinded by blood and pain. He shouldn't be walking toward her, crazed black eyes fixed on her face and knife in hand.

Genevieve retreated a step. The frying pan was back in the kitchen. If she turned to grab a lamp, Crabtree would be on her in an instant, knife plunging deep—

Only it wasn't really Crabtree, had never been Crabtree; it was the Selector stalking her.

The knowledge came from deep down, instinctive and unshakable. It didn't matter that Crabtree looked nothing like the man in her nightmare. It was him—he'd called Matt poet man, had known her true name.

"Come to me, Mary. I've got your room all ready for you," he crooned.

Matt's hand hit her ankle, and she stumbled. She twisted to avoid stepping on Matt, and the back of her knee hit the coffee table. She fell backward, screaming. Her shoulder sank into the couch cushion on the other side of the table, and her hip connected bruisingly with the floor.

Crabtree smiled, gliding closer. "Mary . . ."

Matt's leg drew back and kicked Crabtree in the kneecap.

Genevieve scrambled furiously out from underneath as Crabtree fell forward. His knife tore open the blue sofa cushions instead of her soft flesh.

She snatched up the lamp and threw it, but the cord was still plugged in, and it fell short, smashing against the coffee table instead of Crabtree's head.

Crabtree shrugged the white lampshade aside and got to his feet. "Got your room all ready . . ."

Matt's thrashing body lay between her and the kitchen. That left the staircase. If she could just make it to one of the bedrooms and lock herself in . . .

Her hip hurt, but she made herself ignore it, running up the stairs.

She'd reached the top when a hand grabbed her ankle, pulling her down, slamming her knees into the stairs. Genevieve's foot lashed backward, driving into Crabtree's face. He let go.

Sobbing, chest heaving, Genevieve pulled herself up using the banister and dived into Matt's bedroom. She slammed the door, putting all her weight behind it, but it didn't close all the way. She shoved harder. Why wouldn't it close?

Disbelieving, she looked up and saw four bloody fingers wedged into the doorjamb. Crabtree's fingers. "Oh, God, oh, please, no." She threw herself against the door—once, twice—grinding the bones, but Crabtree didn't let go, didn't cry out even though his fingers must be broken.

He chuckled instead. "Let me in, Mary."

She pushed harder, but he pushed back, and her feet began to slide along the hardwood floor.

• 3 •

Matt's head hurt. He felt exhausted and very groggy. His eyes wanted to close, but he knew he shouldn't let them.

Sleep would feel so good right now . . . No, mustn't sleep. Matt squinted. Carpet fibers pressed into his cheek. Gray carpet. He was lying on his living-room floor near the coffee table, and he could smell the sour odor of his own sweat. He must have had an epileptic seizure.

God, his head hurt. And his neck muscles when he lifted his head.

Genevieve . . . the thought flitted through his mind, igniting a tiny spark of urgency. He forced his eyes open again. The room looked blurry. Smudged, as if he were looking not at his living room, but at a watercolor painting of it.

A lampshade lay on the carpet beside him.

Matt scowled. That didn't make sense. Things seldom made sense right after a seizure; his brain needed time to unscramble even after his brain waves stopped spiking.

With one hand he felt his face; he wasn't wearing his glasses.

Genevieve must have taken them off. Last time he'd had a seizure Genevieve had been there when he woke up, holding his hand. Where was she?

Maybe she left with her husband, he thought muzzily.

Husband?

That shocked his mind back into gear, and a scream from upstairs kicked recent events back into place.

Genevieve's husband. Fight. Knife. Frying pan. Genevieve insisting she had to leave. Genevieve!

Matt got up in a single movement and almost fell down in the next, his hurt knee giving out.

Another scream, shorter this time. Cut off.

"Genevieve," his voice rasped. He grabbed the stair railing. Pulled himself up three steps at a time. Pain in his knee.

A crash from one of the bedrooms. His bedroom.

Last step. In the hall. Bedroom door closed. He staggered into it, and it flew open, caromed off the wall and back into him.

Two figures lay locked together on the floor, Genevieve on the bottom. Both her hands struggled to hold off the knife. She looked up when the door banged open, but Crabtree didn't, every muscle straining toward one goal: Genevieve's death. The knife scraped down her neck, drawing blood.

Matt didn't think. He snatched up a chair and brought it down hard on Crabtree's back.

Crabtree collapsed heavily on top of Genevieve. The knife went through the collar of her shirt, pinning her to the floor.

Matt swung the chair again, overbalanced, and was carried along with its momentum. He and the chair hit Crabtree together, falling in a terrible tangle.

Matt's head grazed the side of the dresser, and his abused muscles made him slow to get up, but Crabtree was even slower. Unconscious. Matt heaved Crabtree off Genevieve.

She moaned, struggling to sit up, but prevented by the knife in her blouse. Unsteadily, Matt pulled it out and examined her for injuries. Her lip looked puffy, and her throat bled, but lightly. She looked beautiful to him. Matt drank in the sight of her heart-shaped face, her scraggly dark hair, her blue eyes . . .

Blue eyes, just as Mary Dunstan's driver's license claimed.

Matt didn't care. "Are you all right?" He forced the words out of his too-tight throat.

Genevieve threw her arms around his neck, shuddering. Matt squeezed her hard enough to crack her ribs. She was alive.

Before he could draw in more than a breath of gratitude, Genevieve pulled away. "We better tie him up."

They used four of Matt's ties to bind each hand and foot to a bedpost. Genevieve obsessively tightened each one twice. Considering Crabtree's resurrection, Matt couldn't blame her.

Crabtree looked like death, but Matt felt no inclination to bandage him up. Let the bastard wait for an ambulance. He'd tried to kill Genevieve.

"Let's go downstairs." He put a hand on Genevieve's shoulder, steering her away from Crabtree.

In the living room he seated himself in the overstuffed armchair. It felt good to sit down. He was exhausted, but grimly aware he wouldn't be able to rest for a while. He put on his glasses and picked up the phone. "I'd better call Ian."

"I have to leave," Genevieve said abruptly.

"What?" Matt's false calm shattered. He dropped the phone back into its cradle. "You can't leave."

"I have to." Genevieve spoke rapidly. "I can't stay here. It's not safe. You can't stay here either. You mustn't be here when he comes."

"He?" Matt picked up on the word. "Do you mean Crabtree?" And the question he'd feared to ask: "Is he your husband?"

"Not Crabtree. Someone else. Come on." She grabbed his hand. "I'll drive you to town. You can stay with Ian. I'll take Crabtree's car."

Matt resisted. "What are you talking about? I'm not going any-where."

"You have to." Genevieve spoke through white lips. "He'll kill you if you're here when he arrives. The poet man. He'll kill you just to see my face when he does it."

Her hysteria alarmed Matt. "He who? Crabtree's tied up. He can't hurt us. You're safe, Genevieve." He stroked her hair. When he thought of how close she'd come to dying . . .

"I'll never be safe," Genevieve said vehemently. Or did Mary speak? Had there ever been a Genevieve? "Never. And now you're in danger, too."

"From what?" Matt asked, exasperated. "Crabtree's tied up. Ian will put him in jail."

"You don't understand. Crabtree isn't the threat, it's who he rep-resents." Genevieve tugged at Matt's hand. "We have to get out of here now."

"No, I don't understand," Matt agreed. Did she know Crabtree? He couldn't believe she was married to him, but she knew more than she'd told Matt. More than an amnesiac could know. "I'm not going anywhere until you tell me what's going on."

Genevieve laughed a little wildly. "I wouldn't even know where to begin."

Blue eyes full of secrets. He tried to make things easier for her. "Begin when you got your memory back."

"Oh no." Genevieve sat down on the couch, face tragic. "It's worse than that. I never got my memory back because I never lost it in the first place."

• 4 •

Demoness? The word tilted April off-balance. She'd half expected the men to be RCMP officers searching for Gavin. What was going on? Were they wackos? Nobody believed in demons nowadays, did they?

Cold-voice believed it.

A chill shivered through April that had nothing to do with the dew soaking the knees of her jeans or the frost in the air. She would have traded Cold-voice for a dozen policemen.

"We'll do a quick sweep of the yard. You go that way, I'll go this way. Don't shoot Jeff if you can avoid it—it's the Demoness and her brat we want. Try not to shoot me either, okay?"

If his partner noticed Cold-voice's sarcasm, he didn't say so.

Gavin tugged at her arm, and April followed him into the denser shadows behind a lilac bush near the corner of the house.

Footsteps scuffed on gravel, and a flashlight beam swung closer.

Evil thickened the air. *Demons* . . . April stayed very still, trying to exhale quietly. It shocked her that even now she was conscious of Gavin's body beside her, of his warm breath stirring her hair.

The flashlight beam played across the south side of the house where someone had planted tomatoes in plastic margarine containers, tripped across the slowly greening grass of the lawn, caressed the string fence around a flower bed, and slashed back to the house where April and Gavin huddled.

Like hide-and-seek in the dark, only the other team was armed with guns and flashlights.

April remembered playing hide-and-seek with her brothers and cousins. Bethany had hated the dark, and the guys had always found her first, but April had loved it. She'd moved through the night like a ghost, pretending she was the Invisible Woman. She was always the last found.

God, don't let me be found now.

The torch picked out individual leaves on the lilac bush then moved down and touched April's purple running shoe.

[*Nothing but grass here. Grass.*]

Gavin gripped her elbow cruelly tight. A long second passed, then the man moved on, examining the west side of the house and the garden with his flashlight.

He hadn't seen her.

It didn't seem possible. Perhaps he was only pretending, waiting for his friend to join him so they could attack together.

"See anything?"

"Not even a rabbit," Cold-voice said. "Let's go."

Even after they walked back to the driveway and got into the Bronco, April could not relax. They were playing a mind game, fetching another gun.

A motor revved. Headlights traced the length of the gravel driveway.

When the Bronco turned left, away from the Rustbucket and Kristy, April collapsed bonelessly in the grass. *You really outdid yourself this time, Jongkind. Some evening: a handsome gunshot man, a murder and a police blockade, now demons.*

She was afraid, so she made light of the incident. "Well, Gavin, I don't think your friend's are home. Where should we go now?"

" 'We'?" His head snapped around. " 'We' aren't going anywhere together. You and Kristy are going to drive home." He pulled her to her feet and herded her back toward the Rustbucket.

April blinked. "You really mean for me to leave you here, in the middle of nowhere, wounded and on the run?"

"Yes."

"At least let me drive you into town."

"I'll be safer away from people."

"You don't know that. The police might have arrested another suspect."

"Christmas might come twice a year, too." Gavin stopped beside the Rustbucket. "Look, April, I'm really grateful to you for helping me. You have my undying gratitude forever, but—"

"Good," April said crisply. "You can repay me by listening to the radio news with me. They do the news every half hour on the half hour. Ten minutes won't make much difference at this point."

She could see that Gavin wanted to argue, but guilt trapped him. "Ten minutes maximum." He opened the passenger door.

April checked to make sure Kristy was still asleep, then turned on the radio. A blast of country music hit them, and she hastily turned down the volume.

"Do you have any family you'd like me to get a message to?" she asked.

"My mother, but—"

"Wait! Let me guess. It's too dangerous."

"It is," he said firmly.

The night turned the car into a warm dark cocoon. April sat beside him, listening to the love ballad on the radio and thought how funny the situation was in a bittersweet, typically April Rae Jongkindish way.

She was parked in a dark car with the man she loved—but who loved her dead cousin—listening to romantic songs on the radio—while waiting for the police report. All the scenario needed was for Kristy to wake up, and Gavin to tell her she was a real pal.

"You know, April, I wish I could have met you under different circumstances. I bet you're one hell of a good friend."

"I wish I'd met you earlier, too." *I wish you had met me instead of Bethany,* she thought, and hated herself for it. Hot tears ran down her cheeks; she breathed through her mouth to keep from sniffling.

Another song began on the radio, and Kristy muttered in her sleep, "Last born speaks . . ."

"April? What's the matter? Are you crying?"

Not much point in denying it. "Yeth." She sniffed and wiped her cheeks.

"It's okay," Gavin said, his voice hoarse and unsteady. "I can't believe she's dead either." All the grief he'd bottled up poured out. "I loved her . . . I loved her so much." He squeezed her hand, and April squeezed back.

She felt no jealousy, only a desperate need to comfort him. His pain was hers, like holding a handful of slivers, but the pain was a kind of closeness, too, so she embraced it.

"I heard her screaming . . . I biked as fast as I could, but I didn't get there soon enough. I can still hear her screaming," Gavin confessed rawly. "She's calling to me for help . . . but I . . . can't . . . help her."

April made shushing noises and stroked his hair.

She looked over his shoulder and saw Kristy's wide-awake eyes. She tried to smile reassurance.

A second song began, ended, and the news came on.

"Police are still looking for Gavin Lindberg in connection with the murder of a young woman in Huld."

Gavin pulled back from her.

"A second tragedy struck Huld tonight when a trailer burned to the ground. A ten-year-old girl and her twenty-year-old baby-sitter perished in the fire. Arson is suspected.

"Elsewhere in the world, leaders in Iraq have . . ."

"I don't believe it." Gavin looked stunned.

"A ten-year-old and a twenty-year-old. They mean Kristy and me. The trailer burned down." April felt as if the world were cracking around her. First Bethany's murder, now this.

"The police suspect arson. Shit!" Gavin's eyes bugged. "They'll think I did it! Three murders."

"April, I'm scared," Kristy said from the back.

"Climb over and sit beside me." April cuddled Kristy's thin body to her side. God, if she'd left Kristy behind . . . she would be dead now.

"The Hillocks! They'll think—" she stopped suddenly, aware of Kristy's big eyes. "And my parents." Her parents would be frantic. And Jerry, Allan, and Dean, her lughead brothers. They would kill her when they found out she was alive. "I've got to get to a phone."

"Yes." For once she and Gavin agreed. "I'll get out, and you drive home at once."

Stricken, April turned to Gavin. "If I go home, they'll ask where I was."

"You'll be an accomplice." Gavin whitened. "I *knew* I shouldn't have let you help me. Tell them I kidnapped you."

"No. You're not a kidnapper, and I won't say you are one." April cast around for ideas. "I'll tell them a noise scared me so we left. . . . No, that won't work." An hour she could explain away, but not two.

Two hours had seemed like nothing when she volunteered to drive Gavin to his friend's house. She'd thought to be back long before anyone noticed her absence. "Damn the trailer for burning down."

"For being burned down. Arson, remember? I'm a suspected arsonist," he said glumly. "This is going to look wonderful on my résumé."

April frowned. "But why would someone burn down the trailer?"

"To get the car probably," Gavin said morosely. "The police will think I stole it."

"That's not what I meant. I know you didn't torch the trailer. Why did the arsonist do it?" Did it have anything to do with Bethany's murder, or was it just a coincidence?

"The bad guy wants to kill me," Kristy said.

Gavin and April stared at her, astonished. "What bad guy?"

"The man who killed my parents," Kristy replied, brown eyes scared, but sincere.

"But your parents are alive. They'll be back from their trip Sunday," April said.

Kristy shook her head. "Not those parents. The ones before. The bad guy killed them, and then Mom and—Mr. and Mrs. Hillock adopted me."

The day just got more and more bizarre. "Why does the bad guy want to kill you?"

"He wants to kill everyone."

"This isn't getting us anywhere." Gavin scowled. "We have to decide what to do next."

Kristy's face puckered up. "You're supposed to listen to me. 'Last born speaks, who listens seeks, to free the one who cried.' "

Gavin ignored her. "April, you and Kristy should go back. Tell the police I kidnapped you."

April knew pleas for his own safety wouldn't move him. "The first thing the police will ask me is: where did you drop him off? Why didn't you phone the police right away?"

"You heard about the trailer fire on the radio and rushed home," Gavin suggested.

April crushed that idea. "I rushed through two towns without stopping to phone my parents or notify the police? The police won't buy that.

"Do you have any idea where your friends might have gone so I could take you there?" April saw Kristy open her mouth and hastily covered it with her hand.

"Not really. Penny would have gone to the nearest—But I don't know where it is. Chinchaga, Freelan, even back in Huld where we started."

Kristy pushed April's hand aside. "Chin-chaga. Let's go to Chin-chaga."

"Got it!" Gavin said. "Tell them I kidnapped you, dropped you off in the middle of nowhere, and left with the car. You and Kristy spent the night sleeping in a shack then started walking the next morning. You found the car with a flat tire a mile down the road, changed the tire, and drove home. It's perfect! The police will be looking for me in Huld while I'm really miles away."

He was going to win this argument—unless she cheated.

"Kristy," she said casually. "Grab Gavin's arm." She shifted into Drive and jammed down the gas pedal.

By the time Gavin reacted, Kristy had hold of his injured arm and they were back on the road. He tried to jerk free and gasped with pain. April winced, but didn't slow down.

"What the hell do you think you're doing?" he said murderously.

April concentrated on the car's climbing speedometer: 60, 70 km/h. Much too fast to jump. "I'm driving you to Chinchaga, and I'm not stopping until we get there."

• 5 •

Will Halvorsen's stomach churned with fear. He could taste acid in the back of his throat, and he had to keep wiping his hands on his jeans to keep them from slipping off the steering wheel.

The Bronco's headlights carved a tunnel through the total darkness caused by the power outage. He concentrated on driving straight down the middle of the narrow gravel road, but the activity wasn't enough to keep his fear at bay. He had failed. He had let the Demoness escape, and now the Voice would be angry with him.

Will feared the Voice almost as much as the demons.

He knew he shouldn't—the Voice was good, and the demons hideously evil—but he couldn't help it. When the Voice discovered his failure it might hurt his head again, and Will didn't think he could endure the pain a second time.

He'd first heard the Voice this afternoon when his neighbour, crazy Corny Tobert, dropped by. Janet didn't like Corny in her kitchen, so Will had been standing on the cement pad of his garage, listening impatiently to Corny's confused tale of talking to God.

The mad light in Corny's gray eyes made Will uneasy, but it was also oddly compelling. He experienced a sudden vertigo just before the Voice spoke his name.

[WILL HALVORSEN, YOU MUST OBEY ME.]

Shocked, Will grabbed hold of the doorknob for support. He didn't catch much of what the Voice said after that until it ordered him to kill Penny and Bobby Lacrosse. Taken in by the Demoness's human disguise, he was horrified.

He refused.

He dared to refuse the Voice.

The Voice smote him.

Pain spiked through his skull and drove him to his knees. He tried to scream, but the Voice froze his vocal cords.

Afterward, Will couldn't be sure how long he'd battled the Voice. An eternity, it seemed. He vaguely remembered looking up at Corny's face once and thinking how much he despised the man, then the pain rose another notch, and his vision closed off until there existed only agony and the bludgeoning thunder of the Voice.

[OBEY ME!]

The pain crucified him, but Will clung to his defiance, even as the Voice stormed his mind's last stronghold.

[OBEY ME OR DIE!]

Never, Will thought, as life faded, faded . . .

When he regained consciousness Corny was bending over him, a strange look in his eyes.

[YOU HAVE PASSED THE TEST,] the Voice said.

The pain was gone. Before Will could form any thought beyond simple relief, the Voice explained. The woman he knew as Penny Lacrosse was not a woman at all, but a demoness. She and her son were bent on great evil in the world of mortals. Thinking herself safe, the Demoness had become pregnant—and temporarily vulnerable. The Demoness must be killed now, before she came to term, and the hell-spawn child before his powers matured.

Before the new child hatched and dined on human flesh.

[*I AM FROM THE SAME PLANE AS THE ONE FROM WHICH THE DEMONESS ESCAPED. IT IS MY TASK TO BIND HER ONCE HER MORTAL BODY HAS BEEN DESTROYED.*]

Head throbbing, Will tried to protest that demons didn't really exist, but the Voice battered away his logic. It showed him pictures, terrible pictures, of the Demoness that slobbered and schemed behind Penny Lacrosse's warm smile.

The Demoness had coveted the house she now lived in, so she had cold-bloodedly murdered the previous owner.

Nat Spenrath had not been mauled by a bear as everyone supposed. The Demoness had chomped off his arm with casual, inhuman strength, then stood and licked her lips with an obscene pink tongue as Nat died of shock and blood loss.

Nat had been his best friend and his neighbor for close to twenty years, and the grief of his death last fall was still raw. He should have known. Hadn't he told Janet at the time that Nat was too smart to have gotten so close to a grizzly bear before making sure it was dead? He should have known.

Will's stomach heaved, and the pictures the Voice was showing him mixed with old, half-forgotten memories of his own.

Campfire tales his cousin had whispered late at night when only a few red-orange flames staved off the blackness . . .

The Demoness devouring a plump black-and-white tomcat in one gulp, like the cherry off a sundae. Will had presumed the cat had just wandered off.

Pictures of scaled, sharp-clawed demons torturing a sinner from a lurid book about Hell he had once seen . . .

The Demoness with her hands on Janet's neck, about to break it with one quick snap, when Will returned home unexpectedly.

A fever-induced hallucination of a pair of red eyes peering out from his closet. He'd tried to tell his mother about the eyes, pointing to the closet, but she'd misunderstood and OPENED THE DOOR WIDER . . .

Green scaly skin and glowing red eyes now colored his memories of Penny Lacrosse. The Demoness had obscured his vision, but the Voice wiped away the cobwebs, and he saw clearly.

Seeing, he believed.

Believing, he had no choice but to act.

Will didn't understand why the all-powerful Voice had chosen an old man and an idiot for his task, but it didn't matter. They had been chosen. Unlike Corny, Will had no taste for killing, but he understood the necessity of it.

For necessity's sake he had slipped two sleeping pills into his wife's coffee. He did not want Janet involved in this. He'd seen her to bed, claiming he wanted to finish reading the newspaper by candlelight.

He hated lying to her. She'd been his wife for thirty-seven years, stood beside him in thick and thin, raised his children, but this burden he could not share with her. She liked Penny Lacrosse and adored Bobby. When he recalled the times Janet had baby-sat the hell-spawn creature, his blood ran cold. Their grandchildren had played with it. To protect his family, he would do whatever was necessary, including lying to his wife.

Will Halvorsen always did what was necessary.

He'd learned that lesson during the blood and muck of the Korean War, and he had never forgotten it. They had pinned a medal on him after the war, but Will had always felt it undeserved. When the enemy shot down his friend within fifteen yards of safety, Will had had no choice but to run back and get him. Simple. Necessary.

Likewise, he had been fully prepared to enter the Lacrosse house tonight and kill the Demoness in her human disguise. He wouldn't have liked it — he'd never shot a woman, only soldiers in the war — but he would have done it. He would even have killed the child, Bobby, although he feared the boy's innocent-looking brown eyes might have caused a fatal hesitation. He would probably have turned that duty over to Corny and, if necessary, the killing of human Jeff Lacrosse, too.

That part of the plan bothered Will, but he saw no way around it. Jeff loved his wife and child, ignorant of the demons within. How could he know? The outward mask of a warm, loving woman was perfect.

He'd hoped taking out the phone lines would keep Jeff late at work as well as prevent the Demoness from calling for help, but it hadn't worked. Still, he'd stopped Corny from shooting Jeff on the road, and part of him had been relieved to find that Penny Lacrosse had already fled when he and Corny arrived.

The Demoness, he reminded himself, the Demoness had fled.

"Where are we going?" Corny asked him for the twelfth time.

Will's hands tightened on the steering wheel. "Where does it look like we're going?"

Corny leaned forward. He wasn't wearing a seat belt, and Will fought a sudden urge to slam on the brakes and send Corny crashing through the windshield. "Looks like we're going down the elevator road."

"Then that's where we're going, isn't it?" Will asked sarcastically. He'd never liked Corny, but before all this he'd tolerated the man. Was Corny worse or was the change in him? The thought frightened him.

The Bronco neared the grain elevator, and Will eased up on the gas, his foot fumbling for a clutch pedal that wasn't there. He was driving Corny's Bronco, and the damned thing was an automatic. The power was still out, so there were no yard or house lights to make things easier. The best he could do was slow to a crawl and try to pick out vehicles in the Bronco's headlights.

Squinting, he made out the reflected taillights of the elevator man's pickup and car, but no third vehicle. No station wagon. Of course, if Jeff had parked behind the house, he would have no way of knowing, but Will thought it unlikely. The Lacrosses were new here. The only neighbors they were really close to were himself and Janet.

Will drove on to the next farm anyhow. When the Voice demanded to know what had happened, Will wanted to be doing something constructive.

Exhaustion dulled his senses. He was too old to be out driving around in the dark searching for demons. He should be at home, in bed with his wife.

[*WHERE'S THE DEMONESS?*]

Will's hands jerked at the wheel. The power steering responded faster than his old pickup, and the Bronco's tires slipped out of their gravel-free tracks, veering toward the ditch.

Spring runoff had eroded the ditches into miniature canyons, and Will swerved wildly. The Bronco skidded in the gravel, and he slammed on the brakes. His left foot pumped uselessly on an invisible clutch pedal. Corny slid off his seat and banged his head on the dash, but, unfortunately, didn't die. The Bronco jerked to a stop, the nose pointing toward the ditch.

[*IS SHE DEAD? DID YOU KILL HER?*] The Voice either didn't notice his near miss or didn't care.

Heart banging like a tin drum, Will put the Bronco in Park. He lowered shaking hands into his lap. They were strong, callused hands, which had handled horses and tractors with equal competence, but they shook now out of fear of the Voice. He braced himself for his punishment.

He did not have long to wait. The Voice reached in and tore the answers from his mind in great chunks.

[*YOU LET HER ESCAPE!*]

Will hunched over, his hands covering his ears to try and block out the Voice. But the Voice could not be shut out because he spoke from inside Will's head.

[*YOU SHOULDN'T HAVE WAITED UNTIL TONIGHT TO KILL HER. HOW DARE YOU PUT YOUR OWN SAFETY AHEAD OF THE HUMAN RACE? YOUR LIFE IS NOTHING. NOTHING! I HOLD IT IN THE PALM OF MY HAND.*]

Pressure on his head, like a giant squeezing juice from an orange. Will screamed, but made no sound. He no longer had control of his own body. His jaw clamped shut, and his teeth sawed savagely on his lower lip. Blood filled his mouth.

Corny watched with avid interest, hands stroking his rifle.

Finally, the vise eased. Moaning, Will heard the Voice speak, oozing satisfaction.

[GOOD. NOW DRIVE TO CHINCHAGA. THE DEMONESS WILL HAVE FLED TO A FRIEND OF HERS, ONLY SHE DOESN'T KNOW HER DEMON-FRIEND IS DEAD. DRIVE.]

Blood running down his chin, a painfully wide-awake Will Halvorsen drove. He'd learned his lesson. He would not fail again.

• 6 •

"David Calder?" the man at the door repeated. "You're looking for David Calder?"

"Yes. I take it he moved?" Penny couldn't prevent a little crawl of fear. The man wore a corona of uneasiness.

"How well do you know David Calder?"

"He's a friend of my mother's," Penny said. "She asked me to look him up." The lie was a bit thin—who dropped in on strangers at midnight?—but the man seemed to buy it.

[Relief followed by regret.] "I'm afraid I have some bad news for your mother. David Calder committed suicide four months ago."

Suicide? Penny spent the next few minutes on automatic, saying how awful, her mother would be sad to hear it, she should be on her way now. The door closed, and she headed back to the station wagon.

She had insisted on going in alone in case Mr. Calder had company, but she had not anticipated this. Where were they going to go now? Her shoulders tensed, dreading having to tell Jeff.

He hadn't wanted to come here. He hadn't said a word, but she'd felt his reluctance dragging like an anchor. Jeff hadn't said much of anything since she explained about the Futurists, but she could feel his emotions like a splinter under her skin.

[Fear. Pain. Despair.]

Penny's empathy depended on three things. Physical distance, strength of emotion, and how close she felt to the other person.

She seldom picked up on strangers' emotions unless they stood right beside her or experienced cataclysmic grief, anger, or pain. With casual acquaintances such as Will Halvorsen, her range normally extended to about ten feet. Even his unusually strong hatred had faded within twenty feet.

But Jeff was the closest person to her on earth. And she'd been sitting right next to him, bearing the full brunt of his distress.

His pain was making her frantic. She could understand why he was upset that she had known about the danger for five years and not told him, but not why the knowledge he would one day save her life had devastated him.

She'd asked him what was wrong several times, but he'd clammed up on her. "Nothing's wrong." She couldn't even joke him out of it. He refused to talk to her.

Wouldn't let her touch him.

She'd broken the Futurists' greatest law by telling him about her psychic powers, and now he wouldn't let her touch him.

He thought she was a freak.

A demon.

You don't know that. You sense emotions, not thoughts. But the pep talk didn't work. She felt like crying, but if she started, Bobby would, too. If Bobby's psychic Talent had been empathy, he would have bawled the whole trip.

Fumbling with weariness, she opened the car door and awkwardly lowered herself inside.

"Well?" Jeff asked.

Tersely, she explained about David Calder's suicide.

"Great," Jeff said sarcastically. "What a wonderful help your spiderweb is."

At the moment Penny couldn't have agreed more, but she felt obliged to defend the Futurists. "Maybe they don't know he died."

"Then they should." Jeff put the station wagon in reverse.

"Where are we going?" Penny asked apathetically.

Jeff hesitated, studying her. Concern replaced his buzzing emotions. "It's midnight. You and Bobby are beat. I'll find us a motel, and we can decide what to do in the morning."

Penny considered protesting—a motel wasn't much of a hiding place—but felt too tired to make the effort. "Fine." She leaned back against the seat and closed her eyes. Her back ached.

Jeff helped her out of the car after checking into the motel. His tender care brought her perilously close to tears. He did still love her, he did.

Damaris squirmed and stretched, making Penny's abdomen bulge. At eight months the fetus already projected vaguely formed feelings, and Penny knew her daughter had just woken up and felt sleepy. Penny put a hand over her womb and hummed soothingly. Jeff wouldn't let her carry a suitcase, so she woke Bobby and led him inside.

He was cranky, so Penny hummed louder. She had sung the same song to Bobby when he was a baby, and it usually calmed him.

" 'Firstborn hooks,' " she sang, easing off his Velcro runners. " 'Sister looks, and sees deep inside.' " Jacket next. " 'Mary dreams, Brother screams, he hears one who's died.' " Bobby yawned and lifted his arms so she could pull off his T-shirt. " 'Eileen learns, Peter burns, in ice he hides.' " Pants off. " 'Last born speaks, who listens seeks, to free the one who cried' . . ." She put his arms and legs into pajamas.

Bobby's head lolled, but when she stopped singing he opened his eyes. "Do it 'gain. Kisty likes it."

Smiling, Penny did an encore. The third time Bobby's eyes stayed closed. She tucked him under the covers and kissed his chubby cheek.

A frown pulled Jeff's eyebrows together. His curiosity tugged at her. "That song, what is it?"

"Just a lullaby. My mother sang it to me."

"A lullaby? It's in a minor key. And those lyrics—'Mary dreams, Brother screams'—don't sound lullabyish."

"And 'When the bough breaks, the cradle will fall' does?"

Jeff shut up, and they got ready for bed.

Although they shared the double bed, Jeff tried to put as much distance between them as possible, turning his back to her.

Penny didn't let him get away with it. She pretended she couldn't feel the storm of hurt and betrayal coursing through him, pretended this night was just like any other night. "I'm cold. Hold me." She took ruthless advantage of the insight her empathy gave her. Jeff loved her, and he would not stand idly by when she was in need for even the smallest thing.

Reluctantly, Jeff turned over and put his arms around her, holding her against him spoon-fashion. The contact made Penny bite back a gasp. It was like an electric current connecting. His hurt was so strong.

There was no use asking him again what she'd done. He'd only freeze up on her. If Bobby hadn't been in the same room, she would have made love to him, instead she reinforced the bond between them in the strongest way she could. She took his warm hand and placed it over her womb.

Damaris responded with a tiny push. "Feel that? She's stretching. I've been picking up more emotions from her every day."

A pause. "What's she feeling?"

"It's hard to describe. Warm and floaty and sleepy." Penny interlaced her hand with Jeff's and brushed the scar caused by Bobby's C-section. "Sometimes she gets cranky. That's when she moves around the most. She's pretty cramped."

[*Awe. Love.*] Jeff's pain didn't ease completely, but his arms tightened around her, and they slept together as a family.

CHAPTER 4

• 1 •

The Selector opened one of Crabtree's eyes and peered around. The room looked blurry, bloodshot and uneven. His right eye wouldn't open.

Probably crusted over with blood, the Selector decided indifferently. He didn't care if Crabtree bled or hurt. He considered rupturing a blood vessel in Crabtree's eye for today's fiasco, but shelved the idea. First he had to figure out if Mary had escaped or if he could still spring his second trap. Fun could come later.

He made Crabtree turn his head to the side. Pain drilled into his temple, and Crabtree whimpered. The Selector suppressed the troublesome nerve endings, and the pain stopped. He'd once done that to a man with a shattered thighbone, and the man ran on the leg. He'd never walked again, but for a time he'd run. The Selector had the power to do that.

He had the power to do many things.

Except, it seemed, to kill Mary Dunstan. Crabtree had come so close he'd smelled the fear-sweat collecting underneath her arms and breasts, so close he'd breathed her very breaths, held her on the cusp of death and stared deep into her terrified eyes as her struggles ebbed, ebbed—

—so close only to fail again.

To fail because of this miserable heap of flesh. Savagely, the Selector commanded Crabtree to move, neurons firing bright sparks in the darkness.

Crabtree's body heaved, but did not get up. It was like sending an electric current through a dead frog, the Selector thought in disgust. Mary had tied down Crabtree's hands and feet. He supposed he couldn't expect her to forget *twice*.

But then Mary had made a lot of mistakes this round.

She shouldn't have been here when Crabtree arrived. She should have fled last night when she first felt the danger.

Why hadn't she? Had her danger instinct deserted her? She would be easy pickings if it had.

Crabtree licked his lips and tasted salty blood. The Selector liked the taste; he forced Crabtree to bite his lip and make it bleed harder. He felt some of Crabtree's pain, but sometimes he liked that, too.

The Selector rewound Crabtree's memories to his arrival. Mary hadn't wanted to open the door. There had been no surprise on her face, only dread.

So why hadn't she run? If not before, then when Crabtree's weak body had lain unconscious?

The poet man. Crabtree's lip curled up in a sneer. She loved the poet man. The Selector remembered the man's thrashing arms and snickered. A poet *and* an epileptic. Mary could sure pick 'em.

Although the poet man had been surprisingly persistent, getting up again to knock out weak Crabtree. [*Weak.*] He stopped shunting away the throbbing pain in Crabtree's skull.

Crabtree's good eye overflowed with tears, and the Selector's disgust increased. He disliked using tools this weak, but Crabtree had been the only one close enough to Mary's hideout to make it before she fled, and, with himself in charge, he hadn't expected much trouble from frightened-of-her-shadow Mary or her poet man. Who would have expected a woman to fight him?

He made one last effort to escape with Crabtree's body. He failed. Again. The Selector did not like failure; he loathed it.

He lit out with all his fury on the only being within reach, the tool he no longer needed. The weak tool who now cried like a puling baby.

Time to set the second trap.

[*Crabtree?*]

[*Yes?*] The man's whimpering ceased. His body tensed.

[*Nothing,*] the Selector said gently. Then he formed great steel claws and ripped them across Crabtree's brain.

• 2 •

Crabtree's scream jerked Genevieve to her feet like a puppet attached to a child's marionette strings.

The sound was unearthly, all but inhuman. A cry of agony. Unbearable in its fear of death and its greater fear of pain.

Matt, who had been staring at her in shock after her revelation that she had never had amnesia, hurried up the stairs. She followed, hand skimming the smooth wood of the banister.

"Jesus Christ." Matt stopped in the doorway. "I'll go call an ambulance." He turned and went back downstairs.

Genevieve stepped into the room, drawn by a sick sense of horror and the stirrings of pity. The blows she'd landed with the frying pan had destroyed Crabtree's face. His eyes peered out of a mask of blood, glazed and stupefied with terror. He screamed hoarsely, vocal cords worn thin.

"Shh," she said gently. "The ambulance will be here soon." She touched one of his bound hands, instinctively offering the comfort of human contact. Crabtree wasn't the enemy anymore—

The screaming stopped.

The sudden cessation of sound jangled Genevieve's nerves; she started to pull back, but Crabtree's fingers tightened unexpectedly. Cruelly.

"*Mary.*" The glazed look vanished like a shutter sliding across a camera lens. A bloodshot eye rolled over to look at her. "Such kindness toward someone who tried to kill you." The husky, ruined voice mocked her. "Such sweetness. Do you weep sugar tears?"

His face held the gray pallor of a corpse, and his fingernails were already blackening, but he hung on to her with the strength of armies. "Sweetness won't save you, nothing will. You're mine, I—"

The hand spasmed under hers. Dull, animal pain replaced the intelligence in his face.

"The claw—the—" Crabtree spoke through mashed lips. Shuddered. Died.

Very carefully Genevieve pulled her hand away. Once she would have wept, but too many nights and nightmares had passed since then.

She went down to the living room and found Matt speaking into the phone. "Yes, I need an ambulance. My address is—"

Genevieve depressed the receiver, severing the connection before he could identify himself. Red Squirrel was too small to have a 911 service. "He's dead," she said before Matt could ask her why.

"Shit." His hand gripped the phone. "Guess I'd better call Ian."

"No." Genevieve held down the receiver while Matt stared. "I can't take the time to fill out a police report. I have to leave now. Give me a couple hours head start, then call Ian. Stay with him tonight. I don't have time to explain, but there are men coming after me. If you get in their way, they will kill you."

She expected Matt to ask her what the hell she was involved in, if it was criminal, if the Mob was after her. Instead he said, "If you're leaving, I'm going with you."

"No." Just the thought of it filled Genevieve with horror. If he went with her, she would be responsible for his death.

"That wasn't a request," Matt said firmly. "Unless you plan on knocking me out—which is a rather tricky procedure outside of TV, by the way—it's hard to judge the correct amount of force to do the job without causing serious damage—you're stuck with me."

He didn't understand. "If you come with me, you'll be arrested for murder." Or killed. Or both.

Matt didn't blink. "Sounds like fun. Whose murder?"

"Crabtree's."

"That was self-defense."

Genevieve wasn't even sure it had been that. *The claw* ... "But we won't be here to explain that to the police. A couple of hours from now one of the men who are after me will go to Ian in concern for their friend, Crabtree, and report that he was searching for his missing wife. They'll describe me. Ian will be forced to come out here, and he'll discover the body."

"Clever," Matt said. "Explain to me again why we should leave without reporting Crabtree's attack to Ian."

"Time. If I'm still here when the men looking for me arrive, I'll be wearing a bullet hole right here." Genevieve tapped her forehead.

That shook him, a little. "How much time do we have before these killers arrive?"

Genevieve considered. Her need to leave was gaining force, but not yet frantic. "An hour, maybe two."

"Great. That gives us enough time to dump the body."

Genevieve blinked. Before she could ask what he was talking about Matt raced ahead.

"The Sheriff's Department will look for blood and fingerprints. Everything Crabtree touched will have to be washed down. The bloodstains won't come out of the sheets; we'll have to burn them. And the floor will have to be vacuumed for hairs. After we move the body, of course—"

His detailed plan made Genevieve give a short laugh.

He looked at her.

"Nothing," she said. She still didn't want him to come with her into greater danger, but if he had to, his plan made sense. "Let's do it."

She opened the cupboard with the cleaning supplies and produced two pairs of rubber gloves, buckets, sponges, and Mr. Clean.

Matt waited until they were at work, she cleaning the outside of the side door and he the inside, before hitting her with a gentle question. "So you never had amnesia?"

"Never." Genevieve's hand paused, but only for a moment before continuing to wipe down the doorknob. "I'm sorry for lying to you, Matt. But when I saw your ad I was on the edge of a nervous breakdown. I hadn't eaten or slept in days, and I had no money. The job sounded perfect, but I had no I.D., and nobody I dared use as a reference. Pretending to have amnesia went with the bump on my forehead and solved all my problems, so I did it." It was a relief to confess her sin.

"But why? Why didn't you have I.D. or money? Were you running from Crabtree? Was he" — Matt choked over the question — "an abusive husband?"

"No. At least, I don't know. He wasn't my husband; I never saw him before in my life."

Matt frowned on the other side of the door. "Why would a total stranger try to kill you? And how did he get your driver's license?"

"I don't know." Done with the door, Genevieve picked up the bucket of sudsy water and moved into the kitchen. Crabtree had fallen there. She could see the bloodstains. "I'll do the floor, you pick up."

Matt righted the overturned table. "How did you lose your driver's license?"

"I didn't lose it. My purse just got . . . left behind." The bloodstain did not want to come out.

"How? I have two sisters," Matt said. "They treat their purses like a third limb."

"I didn't have time to retrieve it from the front of the restaurant when two men showed up, asking for me. I left out the back door as fast as I could."

"What two men, if not Crabtree?" Matt put a broken plate in the garbage.

"I don't know. I never saw them before in my life."

From Matt's expression he was finding it harder and harder to believe her. "Then why did you run away? Maybe they were just customers."

"Maybe." Genevieve threw her sponge in the bucket and started helping Matt pick up.

"So why did you run?" Matt asked.

"I don't know." She met his disbelief with frustration. "And no, that's not a cop-out. I really don't know. I might as well have amnesia because I don't have a frigging clue why any of this is happening to me.

"I've been on the run for close to three years now. How long have I been here? Seven months? That's the longest I've lasted anywhere. Usually after one or two months I just run—get up and leave in the middle of the night."

"What happens every few months?" Matt asked. "The dream?"

"Yes. Afterward I have a panic attack. I become paranoid and get the craziest feeling that if I don't leave immediately, I'll die. The longer I stay, the worse the feeling gets, as though someone's holding a gun to my head. The pressure just builds and builds until I give in and run like a coward."

"And that's what happened this morning? You had a panic attack?"

Genevieve nodded. She threw the cutlery in the sink and ran water over it.

"But this time you didn't run."

"I intended to. Only Crabtree showed up first."

Matt frowned. "And as it turns out you had a good reason to fear Crabtree."

"Yes." The kitchen was done. Genevieve moved into the living room.

Matt watched her pull the vacuum cleaner out of the closet, but stopped her before she could turn it on. "You haven't told me everything yet. Talk to me. Tell me how it all started, and maybe we can figure it out together." He touched her cheek. "Trust me with your secrets."

Genevieve stopped and kissed his hand. "I will," she promised. "But not now." Her need to leave was escalating. *Train bearing down* . . . The bloody body on the bed could so easily have been hers.

Matt nodded. They went back to the grim business of cleaning up all traces of Crabtree's presence.

An hour later she was desperately glad to be on the road, although she would have felt a great deal happier if she hadn't been driving Crabtree's yellow car with Crabtree's battered body stowed in the trunk.

The black pickup she was following seemed to crawl, miserably slow, a worm crossing the road. "Hurry up," she said, even though she knew Matt was right not to attract attention by speeding, knew driving was dangerous for him even at low speeds.

An epileptic required a doctor's certificate declaring him seizure-free for a year to obtain a driver's license. Medication helped cut down his seizures, but had not eliminated them. He'd had one in November as well as the one today, and stress only increased the chances of his having another one.

Ahead Matt turned down a graveled side road with large DO NOT ENTER signs. The owner of this piece of property resided here only during hunting season. He wouldn't return until fall.

The side road led to a driveway about a hundred yards farther in, and they parked there behind a large stand of pine trees.

Matt joined her outside as she inserted the key in the trunk and turned. She glanced around uneasily before reaching inside the tarp-lined trunk to grasp Crabtree's ankles with her gloved fingers. If someone saw them now, they'd go to jail.

Matt took Crabtree's shoulders, hefting. Handling the corpse, sticky with drying blood, was creepy, but Genevieve gritted her teeth and did it. No tears, no screams. She'd changed so much since first going on the run.

Matt looked a little pale, and both of them were happy to set Crabtree down at the car door. Stuffing him inside and forcing his already stiffening joints to bend made Genevieve's stomach heave. She was touching a dead man. . . .

Crabtree's open eyes seemed to stare at her. Accuse her. The Selector had killed him because of her.

Genevieve stepped back, slamming the door. She couldn't think that way, or she'd go crazy. The Selector was responsible, not her.

"Give me the keys," Matt said.

She shook her head and went around to the passenger-side door. She and Matt had already had this argument at the house. She'd pretended to agree, driven by an intense need to get out of the house, but she hadn't given up yet.

"Genevieve!" Matt put his hands on the doorframe before she could close it. He looked frantic.

"Remember that scene in your book where Samantha locks James up rather than let him take on the soldiers while he's too wounded to fight?" Genevieve asked him.

The expression of Matt's face clearly said he knew where she was going with this argument and he didn't like it.

"You just had a seizure; your reflexes aren't one hundred percent. It can't be you, so it has to be me."

"When James gets out he wants to kill her for putting herself in danger like that." Matt was silent for a second, then he handed her the flat slab of sandstone they'd selected when they discovered Crabtree's car didn't have cruise control. "Be careful."

She nodded, then leaned over and started the engine for the corpse.

The already-warm motor came to life at once, and she shifted into gear, gingerly edging Crabtree's right foot away so she could reach the gas. Backing out of the driveway was terribly awkward and made even more grisly by the fact that Crabtree kept leaning against her shoulder. It was important that Crabtree's body not be wearing a seat belt so he slumped forward, horribly slack, a deadweight — very, very dead.

She aimed the car straight down the gravel road toward the BRIDGE OUT sign. According to Matt, the sign had been put up three years ago when the bridge washed out and the owner decided not to repair it since it discouraged trespassers. Steering with one hand and manipulating the accelerator with her left foot, she reached over and picked up the sandstone. She removed her foot and laid the stone in its place.

The Chevy roared once, shifting gear, and began to pick up speed.

Genevieve pulled her leg free and put her hand on the handle of the passenger-side door, nerving herself to jump.

Crabtree fell sideways, and his mouth lolled against her shoulder, like an infant gumming for milk.

The movement was so lifelike Genevieve was fooled for a moment. She keened in the back of her throat and pushed back, shoving at his arm, his lank hair, trying and trying to get him off her. Slowly, like a pendulum, his weight shifted the other way, and he fell against the door.

The car was up to 30 mph, creek dead ahead.

Before she had a chance to consider if staying in the car might be safer, her reflexes pushed her toward the door. Already unlatched from her previous effort, the door swung open, and she fell out.

Her head tucked automatically in the way her fifth-grade gymnastics teacher had taught her, and she hit the gravel and rolled. Rocks scraped her forehead and one forearm, but she didn't feel it, lying winded on her side near the ditch.

The Chevy was still picking up speed when it hit a pothole. The corpse bounced against the window; the passenger door flapped open, then banged shut just before the car shot out over the non-existent bridge. A whale-size splash rose up.

Sensation began to return to her body; her skin stung, and she felt wet blood on one arm as she sat up painfully.

"Are you all right?" Matt ran up to her.

She managed to nod and hold her arm at the same time. "I'm okay."

Matt didn't quite believe her, but after a quick look see he went down the creek bank to retrieve the rock.

Genevieve just sat there, limp as a noodle, and watched two vehicles raise dust on the main road. They seemed not to notice her sitting there in the ditch. *But how can I tell? Maybe the drivers saw, but won't think anything of it until the skeleton is discovered in the fall.*

She could do nothing. If they had seen, they had seen. The thought gave little comfort, and a minute ticked by in an agony of tension.

Finally, Matt emerged from the creek, dripping, and they hurried back to the pickup and the protective stand of trees.

Genevieve nearly tore her shirt in her eagerness to get it off. It had Crabtree's blood on it, the taint of a dead man. She was barely conscious of her partial nudity as she rooted around for a top in her duffel bag. "I want to get out of here so bad it isn't funny."

Matt looked pale, but he scared up a grin as he changed into dry clothes. Genevieve caught flashes of his tanned, lean body as she yanked a blue T-shirt over her head. "You think I want to stick

around? I couldn't *teleport* out of here fast enough." He tossed his
wet gloves onto the seat. "I don't think I'm cut out to be a criminal."

"Me either." Genevieve shuddered as she slid into the driver's seat
of the pickup. Matt had left it running, and she shifted into first.
The pickup lurched forward three feet, then stopped. Grimly, she
shifted back to neutral and restarted the engine. This time she made
it onto the road.

A mile later, Matt got rid of the sandstone slab. One more stop
back at Matt's house to burn the bloodstained clothing and quickly
hose down the tarp. Back in the pickup, Genevieve tromped down
on the gas pedal. She felt like a prisoner escaping from a dungeon
just as the gate came down.

• 3 •

Someone had stolen their cache of arrows.

Peter Chambry stared down at the empty hole in the ground,
hands clenched into fists. "They're gone," he told his best friend, Al
Ghostkeeper.

"But it took us all week to make them," Al said in dismay. A slim,
lithe boy with straight black hair and brown skin, he edged forward
to take a look himself. "D'ya think Larry took them?"

"Yes," Peter said shortly, trying to control his temper. Al's older
brother Larry was always taking their things. Not that he wanted
them—he made fun of their "toys"—he just liked to be mean.

One of these days, Peter would get his revenge. He wouldn't be
twelve forever. Someday he'd be just as big as Larry at sixteen.

"Let's have a slingshot contest then," Al said, the missing arrows
already forgotten. He was used to Larry taking his stuff. "Loser pays
a forfeit."

"All right," Peter said slowly, but he didn't find it as easy to let
go of his anger as Al did. Lately whenever he got mad it was like a
flame burning inside of him, an itchy heat that invaded his fingers
and made him miss his first shot. He banked his anger. Froze it.

With his anger transformed into cold concentration, Peter hit the next four targets. Al hit his usual three out of five.

"You always win," Al said good-naturedly. "Name the forfeit."

"Trade jackets," Peter said instantly, much of his anger evaporating like steam. Al had a real buckskin jacket, complete with fringes to slough off the rain. Peter shrugged out of his own bright blue nylon jacket—a present from his grandma. He'd told her it was the wrong color—how could you blend into the trees wearing blue?—but his mother made him wear it anyhow.

His mother didn't really approve of all the time Peter spent in the woods. She was always nagging him about wearing sunscreen or encouraging him to join an organized outdoor sport, like soccer. Other parents tried to drag their kids away from their TVs, but Peter's mother had bought him Nintendo for Christmas to try to keep him inside.

Similarly, Al was welcome to stay over at Peter's house anytime, but his mother always found some excuse to prevent him from staying at Al's. The Ghostkeepers didn't actually live on Silverwood Estates, but in a cabin tucked farther back in the woods across a ravine. Peter's mother, who sold real estate, called the cabin a "firetrap." She liked it even less when Al's mother let them tent out in the woods.

Peter's dad had once explained to Peter that his mother was a little overprotective because Peter was an only child and adopted, which didn't really make sense to Peter, but he was used to his mom's weird behavior. He'd simply gotten in the habit of not telling her everything he and Al did. The arrows, for instance, would have upset her.

"What do you want to do now?" Al asked, scuffing at some dead leaves with a moccasined toe. Peter would have asked for the moccasins, but his feet were bigger than Al's. "Wanna play fort?"

"Nope." Peter grinned. "I've got a better idea. Let's build a trap so the next time your dorky brother tries to steal our stuff, he'll get caught and hang upside down until we let him go."

"Yeah!" Al gave him a high five. "We won't let him go until he promises never to touch our stuff again."

"Until he gives us his Swiss army knife!"

"Until he promises to do my chores." The promises they planned to extract from Larry got wilder as they hurried to Peter's house to get Peter's illustrated hunting and trapping library book.

They started to run. Peter slowed only when they reached the log across the ravine. The log was quite wide, and they'd examined it for dry rot, but his mother would still have a cow if she found out he crossed it instead of the wooden bridge a half mile away. The ravine was quite deep and Peter and Al often pretended it was the Grand Canyon with the mighty Colorado rushing along the bottom instead of a little trickle that only flooded during spring runoff. A fall into the ravine would mean a broken arm at the very least. Peter put one foot on the slightly rounded surface of the log, hesitated, then removed it.

"Whatcha waiting for?" Al stepped lightly onto the log and started across.

Show-off. Peter could walk across with his arms held out for balance, but he dared not run the way Al did. Al had perfect balance.

"See, it's easy." Al stopped in the center of the log, as comfortable as if he stood on a concrete bridge. "Peter is a chicken. Peter—"

It was the last word he ever said. An arrow—their arrow—flew out of the bushes on the other side of the ravine and hit Al in the chest.

Surprise and pain widened Al's brown eyes. As if in slow motion, Peter saw him windmill his arms. Lose his balance.

Fall.

• 4 •

Penny woke with a dry mouth and a pounding heart from a dream. It was an old dream, familiar, but never any less chilling, of being tied down and tortured.

She even knew what caused it: an incident when she was five years old, the first time her empathy Talent had manifested. Her mother had taken her to visit her grandmother, who was in the hospital recovering from pneumonia, and on their way out their path had crossed the permanent care ward.

One of the women inside had developed a tolerance for morphine and was sweating out the pain, waiting for her next dose. She must have been suffering from a stroke or paralysis because she couldn't communicate with the doctors to tell them what she needed. The pain made her want to die, and she'd come to think of the nurses who rationed out her living death as fiendish tortures.

Her intense physical pain and turbulent emotions had totally overwhelmed the little girl Penny had been. She'd thrown a screaming fit in the green-tiled hallway—*screaming as the woman wanted to but couldn't*—fingers clawing the slick, black surface of the floor—*locked inside the pain*—until her horrified mother hauled her away by the ear.

The crucifying pain had faded once they left the building, but by the time Penny was old enough to explain to her mother what had been wrong, the woman had either died or been moved. Penny still felt guilty over that as well as a dread of hospitals and an exaggerated fear of pain.

She gritted her teeth and forced herself to visit the local hospital every month just long enough to make sure none of the patients were suffering in terrible silence, and then she fled with her tail between her legs.

The only time she'd been hospitalized herself was to give birth to Bobby. She'd been downright grateful when the doctor said Bobby was a breech and she would have to have a Caesarean section instead of giving birth the natural way. The *extremely painful* natural way.

C-sections were no walk in the park, but at least—

Damaris kicked fretfully.

Penny put her hand on her stomach, started to make soothing sounds, then abruptly realized the dream alone hadn't woken her. Nor was it the usual pressing need to change position or visit the bathroom. Her sense of danger vibrated like a tuning fork.

She sat up, eyes straining against the dark. Her outstretched fingers brushed a lamp, started to turn it on, then stopped.

Will's found us. Or he's about to.

By feel Penny located Jeff's watch on the dresser table and pressed the light button: 3:48 A.M.

Three and a half hours' sleep. Not great, but better than nothing. Penny reached out to shake Jeff awake then stopped, remembering his skepticism toward her psychic powers. She wanted to have something a little more concrete than a "danger feeling" before she woke him.

Silently, Penny rolled out of bed and waddled toward the half-light filtering through the brown curtains. Awkward with her extra bulk, she knelt by the window and twitched back the bottom corner of the curtain. She looked out and froze.

Separated only by the windowpane was a man.

Penny forgot to breathe, certain he would see her, but all his attention was trained on the crack between the curtains.

The dim light prevented her from making out his face, but he looked too thin to be Will Halvorsen.

"Find anything?" a second man called to the first.

The first man turned away from the windowpane, and Penny glimpsed curly blond hair and a homely, narrow face. He looked familiar, but she couldn't name him.

"Too dark to tell. Could be them. Want me to find out?" He hefted a rifle.

Damaris pummeled the walls of her womb. *Danger.*

She received an unwanted flood of empathic emotion from him. [*Excitement. Hunger. Bloodlust.*] He licked his lips.

"Don't be stupid," the other man told him. "And quit waving that damn rifle around. You want someone to call the police?" He tried to wrest the gun away.

Disgust from him for his partner and distaste for the job at hand. No bloodlust. For the fiftieth time Penny wondered why Will Halvorsen wanted to kill her.

"Fine, keep it then." Will released the rifle. "Just go back to the Bronco. It's their station wagon. All we have to do is wait for them to leave in the morning."

The rifleman didn't move. "Be easier to kill 'em now while they're asleep."

Penny tensed. If he saw her, he'd shoot through the window as casually as stomping a bug.

"Are you crazy?" Will hissed. "We don't know for sure who's in that room. Innocent women and children could be killed!"

"The Voice wouldn't care."

Will's face became very cold. "You son of a bitch. If you kill one innocent person—and for now that includes Jeff Lacrosse—I will personally hunt you down like a rabid dog. Got that?"

The rifleman shifted, and Penny feared there would be mutiny and murder on the spot. Apparently Will had the same thought. He spoke rapidly:

"You're not only crazy, you're stupid. If we shoot the wrong people, the Demoness will escape, and we'll be arrested. Do you want to explain to the police that sweet-faced Penny Lacrosse and her cute little boy are really Demons from Hell?"

[*Black hate and shuddering fear.*] Demons. Will Halvorsen thought she was a Demoness. He wanted to kill her and Bobby but not Jeff.

Freak. Demon. Witch.

Her kind had been called all that, but they were supposed to be living in more enlightened times now.

"The Voice will explain." The rifleman sounded the tiniest bit uncertain.

"And what do you think the Voice will do if the Demoness escapes again?"

Silence. Penny breathed carefully, straining ears and senses. Uneasy fear emanated from both of them. Whatever the Voice was, they feared it.

"I'll wait in the Bronco." The rifleman moved away.

When their footsteps faded Penny used the windowsill to pull herself upright.

She stared at Jeff's motionless body, amazed. All that danger, and he still slept like a baby. No, not like a baby, Penny corrected herself as Damaris kicked, like a nonpsychic. Defenseless.

A fierce surge of love overcame her, and she lay back down beside him. Dear Jeff. She kissed his shoulder. Let him sleep a while longer.

Asleep he wasn't in pain.

Her gaze roamed the room, checking off exits. The window and door both faced the parking lot. The bathroom had no window. The adjoining door led to another motel room, another window and door facing the parking lot.

Another trap.

Disguise was impossible, and a diversion would require other people.

If David Calder were alive, she could have phoned him for help. That was the purpose of the web. Damn it, she should have been given another contact when he died. As it was the closest Kithkinners she knew were the Millses, three and a half hours away in Huld.

Penny spent the next hour recalling relatives and old school friends. No good. Neither she nor Jeff came from this area originally, and none of their new neighbours would believe Will Halvorsen capable of murder.

In the hours before she woke Jeff at six, Penny came up with only one halfway viable plan. Only one number to call.

"Jeff. Jeff, wake up." Penny shook his shoulder.

She was mildly surprised when Jeff's eyes popped open. It usually took ten shakes and a mixture of bribes, kisses, and threats to pry one eyelid open.

When he dived off the bed and came up holding a gun her heart nearly stopped.

He pointed it at the room in general, not at her, but Penny still couldn't believe what she was seeing. He'd slept with the gun under his pillow.

"What are you doing with that? I thought you left it in the car."

Jeff looked at her as if she were stupid. "A hell of a lot of good it would do us there if Will found us."

That reminded her. "Will did find us. He's outside."

"Outside?" Jeff tensed. "How the hell did he locate us so fast?"

"I don't know, but he did."

"Shit." Jeff's hand tightened on the gun. "Turn on the light. I can't see a damn thing."

"Put that down. And the light stays off—I don't want Will and his buddy to know we're awake."

Jeff lowered the gun. "His buddy? The rifleman?"

Penny nodded. "He and Will arrived around four."

"Four?" Jeff tore his eyes from the door and looked at Penny. "But it's almost light out."

Imperturbably, Penny continued, "They stood outside our window for a few minutes, but they couldn't tell if it was us in the dark, so they decided to wait until morning. Will recognized the station wagon, so he knows we're here somewhere. He's hearing voices." She relayed their conversation.

"He's schizoid. Damn. If I could just get five minutes alone with his Bronco . . ." Jeff grimaced. "There's no help for it: we'll have to call the police."

Penny stared at him, then collapsed into giggles.

"What's so funny?" Jeff asked, but a small grin now shaped his mouth. His mustache twitched.

"Just that I should have woken you up at four. It took me two hours to come up with the same plan: phoning the police. An anonymous tip about his rifle pal should detain him long enough for us to drive away."

"Drive away, where?" Jeff's jaw hardened. "I have to work Monday morning. Let the police take care of Will, we'll go home."

Penny felt chilled. "No." She hastened to justify her gut reaction—her *psychic* reaction. "Will's too smart to give himself away to the police. They'll just delay him; he'll keep chasing us. Our only chance is to go to Calgary and get help from the Futurists. We can't go home, Jeff. Not yet." Maybe not ever. Penny thought sadly of her newly planted garden.

Jeff stared at her, yesterday's pain and fear stealing back. And that puzzling hint of despair . . . "You win. Get Bobby up, I'll phone."

She nodded and crossed over to Bobby's cot. "Rise and shine," she started, then noticed Bobby's wide-open eyes. Poor kid. The danger instinct had robbed him of sleep, too. With Damaris and her own instincts blaring, she hadn't noticed Bobby's fear.

"It's okay, Bobby." She hugged him and tried to distract him. "Why don't you talk to Kisty?" That always cheered him up.

Bobby's face remained clouded. "Kisty says I have to be quite so the bad guys won't hear me."

Well, that one had backfired on her. She should have known if Bobby was in danger his imaginary friend would be, too.

"She says if I'm really quiet I can be Batman next time even though it's her turn," Bobby continued, but Penny had ceased listening.

Underneath Jeff's hand the telephone rang.

• 5 •

"Come on, come on, pick up the phone." Gavin listened to the phone ring a fifth time. He felt conspicuous standing in Chinchaga's one and only phone booth, half a block from the motel where both the blue Bronco and Penny's station wagon were parked. Like a giraffe hiding behind a fig leaf.

Six rings. Seven.

"Pick it up, Penny," Gavin said into the mouthpiece. "Pretend you're telepathic instead of empathic. A little voice in your head says pick up the phone."

Eight rings.

A click and a man's voice, "Hello?"

"Hi, Jeff, this is Gavin Lindberg. I have to talk to Penny."

"I'm afraid you have the wrong number," the man said.

The motel clerk hadn't had any Lacrosses registered. Gavin had tried Penny's maiden name, Gillis, on impulse, but not a smidgen of doubt crossed his mind. "Damn it, Jeff, this is important! There are two demon-hunters outside your motel. Let me talk to Penny."

A pause, then Penny's voice, "Gavin, is that you?"

"No, it's the Easter bunny." Gavin leaned against the phone booth wall, eyes flicking over to the Bronco. No movement. "Are you and Jeff and the kid okay?"

"We're fine. Where are you calling from? More to the point, why are you calling? Jeff and I have our hands full right now."

"I know." Gavin grimaced. "Blue Bronco with a couple of demon-hunters. I'm calling from down the street. Chinchaga only has one phone booth." He stopped rambling. "As to why: Bethany's dead. Murdered."

"Oh, no." Penny's soft gasp of horror barely carried over the telephone line. "I'm so sorry."

"The police think I did it. I headed for the only web house I knew—yours. When we got there we found the Bronco—the same Bronco that's parked by your heap of a station wagon. What were you thinking, Penny? Staying in a motel?"

"My web-house contact is four months dead," Penny said crisply. "And apparently my instincts let me stay in a motel so you could phone and yell at me. Never mind. Jeff's going to give the cops an anonymous tip, and we'll escape while Will answers questions. After that, Calgary. Sound okay?"

"Anything short of incarceration sounds great to me. Do you have room for three more in your station wagon? Our car is going to turn up on police hot sheets anytime now." April couldn't return now and not be implicated in his escape. She'd lost her chance being stubborn last night.

He and April had discussed leaving Kristy behind as the police would hardly arrest a ten-year-old, and her parents would be frantic, but Kristy had refused. "The bad guy will get me. He burned down the trailer."

Gavin's reassurances that the bad guy was after him not her hadn't worked. Her lower lip had stuck out stubbornly. "If you leave me behind, I'll tell the police who you're with." And so they were three.

"Three—? Never mind, you can explain later. We can fit three more. Where do you want to meet?" Penny asked.

Gavin had never been in Chinchaga before and had no idea what there were in the way of landmarks. "What about at the 1 km services sign west of town? We'll have to ditch the car first. Give us twenty minutes, then call the cops."

"Can do. See you in half an hour." The line hummed in his hand.

After another glance at the Bronco, Gavin exited the phone booth. He hurried down the street, deserted at this hour of the morning. The lack of witnesses should have relieved him, but he felt exposed instead.

The Rustbucket was parked by the CIBC on the main drag. April opened the door for him. Her tense expression told him that she, too, had felt like a sitting target.

"Well?" A catnap had removed some of the pallor from her face, but Gavin was still glad she wouldn't be driving much longer. Beside her Kristy looked pale and scared and wide-awake.

Gavin tried to sound confident. "Jeff's going to tip off the cops about the demon-hunters and slip away in the confusion. We ditch the car and meet them at the 1 km sign west of town."

"Abandon the Rustbucket?"

Could she actually be attached to the thing? "If someone steals it, they'll regret it." Gavin backed down under April's loyal glare. "I mean, the police are probably looking for it. The car's likely to get home before you do."

"True." April shifted into gear: she'd kept the motor running in case they needed a quick escape.

They left the Rustbucket in a farmer's field, behind a stand of willows, and walked back toward town, keeping to the ditch. Two vehicles passed them, but no one stopped.

They'd almost reached the sign when a brown station wagon pulled up. "Hop in." Penny smiled through the open window.

"Hurry," Jeff said. He didn't smile.

Bobby was in his booster seat in the back, so Kristy scrambled into the front seat between Jeff and Penny, while Gavin and April squeezed into the back. Gavin was still shutting the door when Jeff hit the gas. Gavin had just opened his mouth to do the introductions when someone else stole his thunder.

"Hi, Kisty." Penny's three-year-old son beamed at them. Chocolate crumbs decorated his chin, and his grimy fingers clutched an Oreo. "I got cookies for breakfast."

• 6 •

After a moment of electric silence, everyone tried to speak at once.

"Kristy?" April said.

Penny and Jeff echoed her. "Kisty?"

"Bobby? Your imaginary friend is Bobby Lacrosse?" Gavin stared at Kristy.

Kristy smugly accepted an Oreo from her "imaginary" friend. "I told you he was real."

"And Bobby's imaginary friend is real, too." Penny slumped back in her seat.

"That's impossible." Jeff gripped the steering wheel.

"Well," April said wryly, "that will bring the total up to three impossible things before breakfast. Do I qualify for an Oreo? I'm starved."

"Of course." Peny passed her the bag.

"Thanks." April grabed three and handed the bag to Gavin.

He stared at her instead of opening it. "We just find out two kids who we thought had imaginary friends are telepathic, and you want an Oreo?"

"I'm hungry."

"She probably hasn't eaten in hours while you've been dragging her all over the country." Penny smiled at April. "There's bread and jam in the back if you can dig it out."

"Telepathy?" Jeff sounded fearful. "It's just a coincidence the names are the same."

"I didn't drag April anywhere; *she* dragged *me*."

"Nice to meet you, April." Penny shook hands. "I'm Penny, and this is my husband, Jeff."

"Hi." April spoke through a mouthful of cookie.

"Just a coincidence," Jeff repeated. He made the turn onto Highway 2 South and merged with the traffic flowing down to Calgary.

"Cookie." Bobby leaned sideways toward Gavin.

Gavin absently gave him one, eyes trained on Penny. "Did the decoy work?"

"The police looked like they had a few questions for Will Halvorsen. If he doesn't have a rifle permit, he's as good as jailed."

"He probably does," Jeff said. "A lot of farmers have squirrel guns or hunt deer in the fall."

"And now he's hunting demons," Gavin said grimly. "Just wait till he discovers his quarry has increased to three."

Penny looked disappointed. "April's not then?"

Not what? April wondered, when Gavin shook his head.

"Too bad." Penny sighed. "When you said you had help I presumed you meant Futurist help."

"April helped because she says she knows I didn't do it." Gavin sounded disgusted.

"Well, you didn't," Penny pointed out. She looked straight at April. "Thanks for helping Gavin."

"No problem." April blushed under Penny's perceptive gaze. She tried to throw her off the track. "Bethany was my cousin."

"Your cousin?" Gavin said, shocked.

"Yes." April knew she didn't look like Bethany—blond and beautiful—but his astonishment was hardly flattering.

Gavin exchanged looks with Penny. "It's possible," he said. "April, are you a university student?"

"No, I plan to enroll in the fall, but I haven't decided on a career yet."

"Her mother might not have told her about the Futurists yet," Gavin said to Penny.

"Did your mother ever mention a Kithkin Klub?" Penny leaned over the seat.

"My brother, Dean, belongs to them. Why?"

"The Kithkin Klub is a cover for a group called the Futurists," Penny explained. "Futurists are psychics, and the talent tends to run in families. If your brother is a Futurist, it's likely you are, too."

April blinked, not quite believing what she was hearing. "A psychic? You mean like crystal balls, seeing into the future, all that jazz? I can't do anything like that."

"But you do have the danger instinct," Gavin said, brown eyes intense. "You overrode all my objections and left the trailer before it burned down. You must have sensed danger."

April had been trying to save Gavin, not herself, but since she didn't want to explain her motives, she changed the subject. "What does that have to do with demon-hunters?"

Gavin spelled it out for her. "Will Halvorsen thinks Penny and Bobby are demons, but not Jeff. If his grudge is against psychics, he'll try to kill you, too. Your life is in danger because of me."

April quickly denied the guilt she could hear in his voice. "You haven't endangered me."

Penny supported her. "If this truly is an attack on all Futurists, April would be in danger at home, too."

A chill slid down April's spine. *All* Futurists. "My mother and brothers. They're in danger."

"Bethany's parents, too." Gavin swore. "The next town we stop and phone."

"No," Jeff said grimly. "No stopping until Calgary. We may have only a fifteen-minute head start on the Bronco."

"But my mother!" April said.

"Your mother wouldn't want you to get killed protecting her." Jeff kept his eyes on the road. "If your mother's a psychic, she can protect herself. Bobby and Damaris can't. I'm not stopping until we hit Calgary."

Dead silence. They rocketed along at the posted speed limit of 110 km/h. They couldn't stop Jeff without risking an accident.

April wanted to protest that the demon-hunters might not know their destination, but couldn't get the words out. The demon-hunters had picked Chinchaga with little difficulty.

Penny broke the silence. "Gavin, why don't you tell me the long version of what happened? April, feel free to interrupt if he misses anything."

Gavin's expression became shuttered, bleak. "Yesterday, during her parents' anniversary dance, Bethany said she had to drive into town to buy some strawberries, that the caterer didn't have enough leftovers to put out snacks at midnight. Bethany said she wouldn't be long and there was no point in me coming with her. I should have insisted." Regret weighted his voice.

"I'm Batman," Bobby said, but quelling looks from Penny and Kristy shut him up.

Gavin didn't notice, deep in his memories. "I wanted to go, but she teased me about getting as possessive as Ron."

"Who's Ron?" Penny asked.

"Bethany's ex-boyfriend. She broke up with him because of his jealousy, so I couldn't insist on going, could I?" Gavin appealed to them.

"Of course not." April had seen Bethany tie too many guys in knots not to appreciate how well she did it.

"The dance music was giving me a headache, so I borrowed a bike and went for a ride. A mile down the road I heard her scream." Gavin closed his eyes.

April frowned. If Gavin had biked a mile down the road, Bethany should have been miles away in her car. How could he have heard her?

"I fell off the bike. I couldn't get up, the screaming hurt my head so much. I just sat there holding my ears while Bethany died."

"You didn't kill her, Gavin," Penny said sharply. "You weren't anywhere near her when she died. You heard her *psychic* scream, didn't you?"

"Yes," Gavin rasped. Tears shone in his eyes. "I heard her *psychic* scream. My goddamn *psychic* Talent let me hear her scream"—the tears fell then, and April felt her own cheeks getting wet—"and *scream* while I was too fucking far away to save her. She was dead by the time I arrived."

Kristy and Bobby started crying, too. April kissed Bobby's forehead and smoothed his hair, wishing she dared comfort Gavin.

Penny, green eyes full of empathy, reached out to Gavin. "I know your Talent must seem horrible. To be unable to help first your father's cancer and now Bethany, but it's not your fault. And your Talent did save someone. You saved me from drowning when that undercurrent grabbed me.

"And I'll tell you something else: it would have been my own fault if I had drowned. I knew swimming in the river was dangerous, but I went swimming anyhow. Bethany must have known she was heading for danger."

Gavin stubbornly shook his head. "Bethany didn't want to die."

"Of course not," Penny said impatiently. "Her murderer is to blame for her death. Not Bethany and not you."

Gavin's features hardened. "I'm going to get that bastard."

April believed him. "Did you see who did it?"

"Maybe." Gavin roused himself. "A police officer shot me. I suppose he might have thought I killed Bethany, but later the police described me down to my clothes and never mentioned a bullet wound."

"Wait just a damn minute," Jeff said. "Do you mean the police think you're the murderer?"

"Yes." Gavin looked surprise. "Didn't Penny tell you?"

Penny winced. "I guess I forgot to mention that."

"I guess you did," Jeff said, face grim.

April had the uncomfortable feeling if Jeff had known he would never have picked them up. In an effort to break the tension she took over the story, adding in silly descriptions of how heavy Gavin had been and how he'd berated her for hiding a murder suspect.

Penny was amazed. "You save his life, and he lectures you?" She stared at Gavin. "You should have been down on your knees thanking her and pleading your innocence."

April grinned. "Oh, he didn't get around to telling me he was innocent until a couple hours later at your house. I had a hell of a time convincing him to let me drive him there. He wasn't lying. I did drag him along, not the other way around."

Gavin looked sheepish.

"The only reason we're here is because Gavin wanted to warn *you*," April added.

"Ha," Penny said. "I knew about the danger long before Gavin did." She launched into an explanation of what had brought Jeff and her to Chinchaga: her own sense of danger, Jeff's encounter with

Will Halvorsen on the road, their flight, David Calder's suicide—

"At the time I thought it was just bad luck, but now I'm not so sure."

—the motel, and the whispered conversation about the Voice and demons Penny had overheard.

"Demons." April shivered.

Jeff snorted. "The man's psychotic."

"The man with the rifle just wanted to kill," Penny agreed, "but Will honestly believes we're demons. Something's made him psychotic. I've been near Will before, and I've never picked up anything like this. Will Halvorsen liked me. He thought Bobby was cute. It just doesn't make sense."

"Does hatred ever?" Gavin asked. "The Futurists wouldn't exist if not for some crazy old man who hated and feared us enough to try to destroy us, and now the cycle's starting all over again."

Penny put a hand on her swollen stomach. "You're right, bro, we have to stop it."

"Bro?" April riveted on one word. "Gavin's your brother?"

Jeff twisted around, surprised. "You don't have a brother."

Penny laughed. "I don't know if I do or not. I'm adopted, remember? So's Gavin. The only thing we know about our birth parents is that they were psychics, too. When we became friends in the Kithkin Klub we decided to call one another brother and sister since we'd never had any siblings. For all we know, we could be related."

"You could have told me," Jeff grumbled, but to April's eyes he looked more relieved than mad.

Penny's green eyes danced. "I could hardly have used Gavin to make you jealous enough to propose if you'd known I thought of him as a brother."

April looked from Gavin to Penny. "You don't look like brother and sister to me. If I'd had to pick two of you, I'd have said *Kristy* and Gavin," she joked.

"Well, Gavin's my brother, too," Kristy said offhandedly. Everyone stared. "He's 'Brother screams, he hears one who's died.'" She faced Penny. "I guess you're 'Sister looks, and sees deep inside' since you aren't Mary. And I'm 'Last-born speaks.'"

• 7 •

"Damn."

Will Halvorsen swore when the police car turned into the motel parking lot. He swore again when the Demoness and her family dashed from their motel room to their station wagon. She must have called the cops.

He turned to say as much to Corny and saw the man sighting down his rifle at the Demoness. "Don't be a damned fool!" He knocked Corny's rifle up. "The police are coming. Stow that thing in the back."

For a second, Corny pointed the rifle at *Will's* chest, but then some modicum of sense filtered through, and he climbed into the back.

Will's heart thundered, and sweat sheened his skin. He'd always viewed his partner as — unstable — but for an instant he'd seen something else in Corny's eyes. Madness.

Dear God in heaven, demons *and* madmen. His galloping heart could not take much more of this.

The police car stopped beside the Bronco as the station wagon pulled out of the parking lot. An armed RCMP officer got out of the car.

Will rolled down his window. "Good morning, Officer. Can I help you?"

The station wagon turned onto the highway going east out of town.

"Get out of the vehicle. Keep your hands visible at all times." The officer speaking looked nervous and young, the mustache he was trying to grow little more than peach fuzz. His partner was older, running to fat, his heavy-lidded eyes giving the impression of sleepy boredom.

"Whatever you say, son," Will said reasonably. "I ain't gonna argue." He released the door handle, put both hands on the rolled-down window, and got out. "What's this all about?"

The young officer relaxed at Will's nonthreatening demeanor. "We're checking out a complaint made by one of the motel residents about a blue Bronco and two armed men who've been peeking in motel windows."

Damned Demoness. Will hid his anger with a smile. "A Peeping Tom, you mean? I promise I'm not the type."

"The man seemed more worried about being murdered in his bed than an invasion of privacy." The officer's frame straightened. "Are you carrying a gun or concealed weapon?"

"Lord, no." Will tried not to overact his surprise. "Do you want to search me?"

The officer nodded. "Please spread your arms and legs and lean against the Bronco."

Will did as he asked. The young officer patted him down while his older partner held his gun. "He's clean. Any weapons in the Bronco?"

There was the kicker. "Just my jackknife and Corny's rifle." He struggled to sound casual.

The two cops exchanged glances. "The complaint mentioned a rifle. Who's Corny?" the younger one asked.

Will thought fast. "My neighbor. We stayed up all night watching for a pack of wild dogs. We came into town for breakfast, but the motel cafe isn't open yet, so Corny went to sleep in the back." Will prayed Corny heard him and lay down.

He should have known better.

"What's going on?" Corny appeared at the passenger-side window. Carrying the damned rifle.

The older cop took a step back, blinking. The nervy younger one spoke. "Put the gun down immediately. Weapons must be properly stowed in a gun rack when in a vehicle. I'm going to have to ask to see your FAC registration. Do you have a license for your rifle?"

"Yes." Corny looked sullen, but then Will couldn't remember seeing him otherwise.

Will began to think they might pull it off and get out of there only fifteen minutes behind the Demoness. He was wrong.

"Yes, I have a license," Corny repeated. Will's insides froze. Madness shone in Corny's eyes. "I have a license from God. He tells me who must be killed." Corny swung the rifle up, firing.

The younger cop recoiled, blood blossoming from a hole in his chest. Face bulging with shock, the older cop fired spastically, hand shaking. Bullets whined off the metal sides of the Bronco.

Belatedly, Will threw himself facedown out of the line of fire.

Rifle shots. Sounds of alarm from the motel. The booted toe of the young officer filled Will's vision. It was black and shiny, without so much as a scuff mark. It never moved.

Several feet away Will could see the muzzle of the officer's handgun. Slowly, crawling on his belly and sweating, Will reached for it. Shots barked overhead, and the older cop screamed in pain. Will kept his gaze directed at the gun. He tried not to look at the dead officer as he carefully pried the Smith & Wesson out of his grip, but he couldn't help one glance.

The officer's mouth and eyes lay open in an expression of shock. Up close, he looked even younger to Will. Barely shaving. Although he knew, logically, that the officer must be in his twenties, Will couldn't rid himself of the thought that he had grandchildren as old as this boy. Just a boy, and now he was dead, and it was Will's fault. What would Janet say?

The shooting stopped.

Will pulled himself up and looked at his partner.

Corny smiled, eyes bright and insane. Blood streamed from his forehead where a bullet had creased him, but the wound was superficial. Corny would live.

The two policemen were dead.

Will lifted the gun, aiming carefully because he might only get one shot. Finger on trigger—

[*STOP!*]

A star-flash of pain made him drop the gun. Flames seared his mind. Pain gripped his chest much like the heart attack he had suffered two years ago. And the Voice. Overpowering. Loud and AWEful.

[*FOOL! CORNY DID MY WILL. THE MEN HE STRUCK DOWN WERE IN LEAGUE WITH THE DEMONESS. HE HAS UPHELD ME; YOU HAVE SHAMED ME WITH COWARD-ICE!*]

Pain forced Will to his knees. Nausea, sharp and bilious, rose up within him, and he vomited. The Voice pushed down on him, thundering in his ears, shaming him, showing him the error in his thinking until he groveled on the pavement, weeping over his failure, his doubt of the Voice. He pressed his face into the vomit to show his unworthiness; he was less than dog puke.

The Voice became impatient; it prodded Will to his feet with threats and blasts of pain. Will picked up the gun and stumbled into the Bronco's passenger seat.

Still no movement on the street or from the motel, certainly none from the dead cops.

Corny drove, screeching tires like a maniac and cutting corners so close Will fell off his seat. His breath came in pants, and his face was a cardiac patient's purple, but Will Believed again. He had strayed, but the Voice had shown him the truth.

All those who opposed him were demons.

CHAPTER 5

• 1 •

"Last-born what?" In the rearview mirror Jeff saw Gavin turn toward Kristy. "What are you talking about?"

"I think I know." Penny recited the lullaby that had bothered Jeff so much the night before. "It's one of my few memories of my real mother. If Kristy's right, we have a brother or sister for every line."

" 'Brother screams, he hears one who's died,' " Gavin said through white lips. "That could be me. I heard Bethany scream."

" 'Sister looks and sees deep inside' could be my empathy." Penny sounded excited.

"I hate to interrupt the family reunion," Jeff said sarcastically, "but one verse of a song doesn't make you an instant family. Wouldn't the lines apply to a lot of psychics?"

He excepted an argument, but instead five heads turned as one and looked out the back window.

"Uh-oh," Bobby said.

One glance told Jeff what the problem was. The blue Bronco, three cars back in the right lane. "Shit!" He ignored the 110 km/h speed limit on the four-lane and floored the gas pedal, increasing speed from 115 to 135 km/h and maintaining it despite ominous groans and shudders from the chassis.

"How did he catch up so fast?" Penny twisted in her seat to watch.

"Either he didn't talk to the police very long, or . . ." Gavin glanced significantly at Kristy and Bobby.

Jeff had no more trouble finishing that thought than Penny and April. Or the police were dead.

"Maybe the police are after them." The worried look on April's face gave lie to the optimism of her words.

Chinchaga had a population of fifteen hundred. There couldn't be very many cops stationed there. It would take time to organize a pursuit. In the meantime they were on their own.

He switched into the left lane to pass a sporty white Probe. "Put your seat belts on. Someone call out reports if the Bronco gets closer or changes lanes." At this speed, if Will shot out a tire, they would skid and crash.

"How fast are we going, or do I want to know?" Gavin asked.

Jeff had inched it up to 140 km/h, passing the sports car. He didn't reply, trying to control the wobble of the station wagon. Why hadn't he listened to Penny and bought a nice new car with air bags instead of relying on his tinkering skills to keep this old heap running?

Because he hadn't wanted to go into debt, that's why.

And now his cheapness might get Penny and Bobby killed.

"They're passing a red van," April reported.

Up ahead a boxy red Sprint and a silver Taurus drove side by side, blocking both lanes. "Damn, damn, damn." Jeff stamped on the brakes. The speedometer needle dropped back to 120 km/h. He rode hard on the Sprint's bumper, honking his horn.

"The Bronco just passed another car. He's closing the gap."

The Sprint realized Jeff's problem and sped up. It edged ahead of the silver car with agonizing slowness.

"Eight seconds behind us," April said. Everyone else kept quiet, thank God. The rattle of the station wagon was loud enough. It took him a moment to identify the other sound as his own mad whistling.

The station wagon drew level with the Taurus, but remained trapped behind the laboring Sprint.

"One car behind."

No time. He pulled onto the left shoulder and began passing the Sprint. Though paved, the shoulder was corrugated; it made a terrible whining noise under the tires as a warning to drivers. It was also barely the width of a car, and, at high speeds, passing on the shoulder was rather like doing flips on a narrow balance beam. Too far to the left and his tire would slip off the edge of the pavement and pull them into a skid. Too far to the right and the station wagon would scrape paint off the Sprint.

"Vroom?" Bobby said doubtfully.

Penny was more vocal. "What are you *doing*?" She clutched the dash with both hands.

Jeff caught a glimpse of the Sprint driver's openmouthed stare before she got the hint and dropped speed. He swerved into the opening. "Didn't I ever tell you about my former career as a juvenile delinquent?"

Even in the middle of the chase Jeff felt a grim desire to shock his wife. To test her love.

"Where's Will?"

He spared a glance at the rearview mirror, even as April said breathlessly, "He just passed the sports car. He's going to try to pass the other two on the shoulder."

The Bronco was gaining.

Jeff gritted his teeth and forced the station wagon back up to 140 km/h, desperate to widen the gap or at least maintain his lead. The shakes jarred his bones, and the engine sounded as if it might disintegrate into a heap of rust at any moment. The Reliant was trying its heart out, but its puny four-cylinder engine was no match for the Bronco.

That left only one thing in his favor: driving skill.

He had the experience of three high-speed car chases under his belt. His longest one had taken place on the six-lane Deerfoot Trail at four in the morning. If the police hadn't radioed ahead and got a second car to lay down a tack sheet that ripped his tires out from under him, they wouldn't have caught him.

Of course, the Porsche he'd been driving hadn't hurt.

Jeff tore past a Honda Accord while searching furiously for an opportunity to turn his skill to his advantage. A shallow, grassy ditch served as a median between the four lanes. He could cut across it and join the flow of traffic going north, but the station wagon was built a lot lower to the ground than the Bronco. He might scrape bottom and leave half his motor behind.

What he really needed was a driving maneuver that would crash the Bronco, while leaving the station wagon unscathed.

"Everybody duck! He's getting out his rifle!"

Honking madly, Jeff swerved in front of the Accord. A shot rang out. Brakes screeched, and the Accord 360'd off the road and into the ditch.

Now only highway separated the Bronco from its quarry.

Like the answer to a prayer a green sign loomed ahead: HWY 27, OLDS, THREE HILLS, NEXT EXIT.

"Go right!" Penny grabbed his arm, and they veered right just as another rifle shot cracked out.

They nearly hit the ditch before Jeff wrenched the car back under control.

More traffic approached, a green van in his own lane, but Jeff dared not pull into the fast lane to pass because the Highway 27 overpass was quickly approaching. He stamped the brakes hard, cutting speed to 110 km/h.

"The gun!" Suddenly galvanized, Penny fumbled with the glove compartment. She ducked, and a bullet punctured the back and front windshields where her head had just been. A crack spread across Jeff's line of vision, a silver, twisting river, Draco's spine, but the safety glass didn't shatter. The wind added its own shriek to the car's groans and Bobby's cries.

A second green sign flashed past. HWY 27 WEST OLDS, and an arrow.

Penny handed Gavin the gun.

"Where's the safety?" he asked.

"Give me that." April grabbed it. "You can't move your left arm, and you've probably never fired a gun in your life."

Jeff drove past the turnoff. Under the overpass.

"Have you?" Gavin demanded.

"My brother's BB gun."

Third sign. HWY 27 EAST, THREE HILLS. EXIT RAMP, 30 KM/H.

Jeff took it at 80 km/h. April fired just as he jerked the steering wheel hard to the right. Her shot went wild. Kristy screamed as he headed up the tight spiral of the clover leaf. The steep curve made his arms ache, and he veered dangerously close to the guardrail, sides almost kissing, but he managed to hold on until they reached the top and straightened out onto the overpass.

Try that, you bastard. Jeff listened for the crash that would tell him Will's reflexes hadn't been fast enough to allow him to take the curve.

"For God's sake, Jeff, if we wanted to die, you could just stop and let Will shoot us." Gavin gripped the back of the seat.

Jeff ignored him. "Did the Bronco make it?"

"Yes," April said after a pause, "but he's fallen behind."

"Then we do it again." Before Gavin could protest, Jeff swung onto the down exit ramp labeled Highway 2 North. He took his foot off the accelerator, but didn't touch the brakes, steering with ruthless concentration.

There was a small merge lane at the bottom, but Jeff didn't merge. He intended to take the Olds cloverleaf back up, cross the overpass again, and spiral back down to Highway 2 facing their original direction.

That was his intention.

"Look out!" Penny screamed and pointed.

The blue Bronco roared toward them, coming the wrong way down the Olds exit. Will must have bumped across the median, cutting him off instead of following blindly.

Jeff swerved left without shoulder-checking and nearly sideswiped a blue Dodge Aries. With a screech of brakes, the Aries steered left and *did* sideswipe a motor home. The two vehicles tangled briefly, then slid into the ditch.

Jeff pulled as far left as he could, desperate to get around the blue Bronco. This close he saw that Will wasn't driving, the rifleman was. The Bronco shot forward, attempting to ram the station wagon. Jeff squeaked by and nailed the gas pedal to the floor. It would take the Bronco precious seconds to get turned the right way on the road—

Bang! A gunshot blew out their rear tire.

The back of the station wagon swung hard to the right, fishtailing, while the steering wheel pulled left, burning through Jeff's palms. The whole vehicle fought him, skidding sideways while he pumped the brakes and steered right, flat tire thumping, kids screaming—

—and they hit the ditch, plowing toward a small creek before finally sliding to a stop fifteen meters away.

The car was skewed so that the nose faced east instead of north. "Get out and stay low," Jeff told Penny. "Maybe we can catch a ride with a motorist going the other direction." All traffic had ceased flowing north.

"Too late." Penny caught his hand. The Bronco stopped twenty meters down the road, and its two occupants spilled out, rifle at the ready. If they tried to cross the ditch, they would make perfect targets. They had no choice but to hide behind the car and pray April's gun could hold their assailants off until the police arrived.

Jeff kept a wary eye on Will Halvorsen and the skinny rifleman as he unbuckled Bobby's safety harness. The blond man looked familiar, but Jeff couldn't make out his face.

Two more shots from April, both misses. "How much ammunition is there?"

"Just what's in the gun. Six shots." Penny swayed on her feet.

Fear and rage gripped Jeff. He couldn't believe this whole thing was happening. Couldn't believe his family was going to be murdered in broad daylight with dozens of motorists passing by. This kind of random violence only happened in big cities.

But it wasn't random. Will Halvorsen had selected his victims deliberately.

Will could speak of demons all he liked, but Jeff knew who was shooting at defenseless women and children and unborn babies, and he had his own opinion of who the demons were.

Exposing only the top of his head, Jeff peeked over the window's edge. Will and the blond man appeared to be arguing. The blond man won, wresting the rifle from Will's grip. Confidently, he walked toward them.

Tense, Jeff waited for him—or April—to shoot. He glanced at April, but she held her fire. With only three bullets left she had to be sure of hitting her target.

Strategically it made sense, but Jeff's insides knotted as the rifleman came closer, closer . . . close enough for Jeff to recognize him. Narrow, homely face, scruff of blond whiskers, smiling mouth and mad eyes . . . Corny Tobert. Crazy Corny with his penchant for shooting ducks or deer or anything that moved. Jeff instantly wished it was someone else, *any*one else.

"Shoot him," Penny whispered. Her nails dug into the muscles in his shoulder. "He's insane. I can feel . . . he wants to kill."

The madman stopped ten meters away. "Come out, come out, wherever you are."

Jeff flattened.

Two gunshots in quick succession. Gunshots from April.

Jeff risked a quick glance up — and ducked again as a bullet twanged into the side of the car. Corny's left arm hung uselessly, but he still stood, smiling madly.

Whap! Another bullet whined off the metal framework.

A return shot from April . . . "He's down." Her voice cracked.

Jeff had no sooner drawn a breath of relief when he heard Will's voice. Will, who had circled around while Corny approached, now pointed a 9mm Smith & Wesson at Penny. "I only want the Demoness and her hell-spawn offspring."

Jeff moved like lightning, throwing himself between Will and his pregnant wife. His eyes flashed to Bobby, heart shuddering in gratitude when he saw Gavin shield Bobby and April, Kristy. In relief his anger flared. Demoness? Hell-spawn offspring? How dare Will call his son hell-spawn offspring? "There are no demons here."

The only man Jeff had ever counted as a neighbor stared at him with cold eyes. "They're not worthy of your protection. They've deceived you into thinking they're human, but they're demons." He seemed very lucid, as if every word he said was logic instead of madness.

Penny clutched at Jeff's shirt, helpless.

"Take another step, and I'll shoot." Hysteria tinged April's voice as she aimed the pistol at Will. At five feet she couldn't miss.

"If you could, you would have already." Will's expression didn't even flicker. "Give up, Jeff. Move or I'll have to kill you." His hand trembled. "The Voice won't care if I kill you, and it's very hard to resist the Voice . . ."

Penny tried to edge away, to sacrifice herself, but Jeff held tight to her waist.

"You're insane! There are no demons."

A bullet thudded into the sod by his left foot. "Please move," Will said. His eyes looked distracted, as if he wrestled with an inner voice.

The Voice. "The Voice is lying to you!" Jeff yelled as another bullet parted the grass. "A demon has possessed *you*, making you commit murder!"

Will hesitated.

"My wife is not a demon!" Jeff sensed he'd gained some sort of advantage, but had no idea how to keep it. "Penny is not a demon! She's my wife, and I love her." Oh, that would impress a madman. Desperation made him go on. "She's only twenty-five years old, for Christ's sake. Bobby's only three."

Tears blurred Jeff's vision, making him think he could see tears on Will Halvorsen's cheeks, too.

"They're demons," Will said, but he seemed unsure of himself.

"Human!" Jeff bellowed back. "Human. If she was a demon, don't you think she would have nuked you by now?"

"Human?" Horror replaced the coldness in Will's eyes. "Not demons?"

Hoarse and relieved, Jeff nodded.

"But then . . ." Will struggled in the grip of some terrible truth. "But if they're not demons, then neither were the policemen."

Jeff said nothing. He became aware of Bobby and Kristy sobbing, of passing cars. His gaze remained fixed on Will's face.

"Corny shot them." Will's skin turned ashen. "My God, he *murdered* them—" He broke off on a sharp scream.

Penny realized what was happening first. "The Voice!"

Gavin lunged forward, making a grab for the gun.

Too late. Two emotions, two people, warred in Will Halvorsen's face. Hatred and horror. "Lindberg. I'll kill you yet," the voice snarled just before the hand pulled the trigger and blew away Will Halvorsen's head.

• 2 •

The Selector reeled across the hotel room clutching his head. He fell to the floor and lay there for a moment, stunned. His fingers felt his skull beneath his thick black hair, but his mind didn't believe it.

His mind insisted his head had been blown off.

[*Pain. Blood and destruction.*] It had been all over in an instant for Will Halvorsen.

The Selector had barely escaped down his line. He'd had to leave his hook behind, and a diamond-bright aftershock of pain had followed him.

[*Bullet biting the brain, splatter of blood, recoil of thunderous noise . . .*]

The Selector moved his hands over his scalp, fingers seeking, but not finding. No sticky blood, no hole where gray matter leaked out.

Sitting up, he cursed Will Halvorsen. The man had looked inferior, an old farmer with a sagging belly and blurred vision, but his strength of will had been that of a young bull. The Selector had had to strip the man back to his childhood to find something he hated enough to kill. What had taken thirty seconds with Corny had taken fifteen brutal minutes with Will Halvorsen.

In his youth Will might have been worthy of becoming a Selector.

People came in three types in the Selector's experience. The weak, the eager, and the strong.

The weak were easily mastered, but required constant supervision. Instead of rejoicing in the Selector's glorious purpose, they whined and cried and selfishly tried to save their own skins. Crabtree had been weak.

The eager needed little instruction. A small nudge here, an adjustment there, and they would kill. But killing was all they could do: they couldn't think. Too often they killed the wrong people. The Selector cared little for the inferiors' slaughter, but the results inconvenienced him. Eagers never lasted very long. They kept getting themselves arrested or killed like Corny.

Corny had accepted the Selector's word he had a mission from

God without a qualm. Will Halvorsen had had to be ripped apart to find a chink in his armor, and then hammered at repeatedly to make the lie stick.

The lie had crumbled within a day, disintegrated in the face of Jeff Lacrosse's foolish defense of his wife. Corny would have blown the man to bits, but Corny was eager, and Will was strong. Strong enough and stupid enough to overthrow the Selector's mastery not once, but twice. Ordinarily, the Selector would have taken personal control after Will tried to shoot Corny, but he'd been occupied with Mary. His trigger had pulled him back into Will's head just as Will shot himself rather than kill a couple of inferiors.

The Selector didn't understand the strong.

Sometimes he felt like the only human being in the world capable of clear thinking. All the answers were so obvious.

The human race had been allowed to breed rampantly for too long. All the natural checks and balances once imposed by disease, war, and predators were gone.

Medicine kept alive those who were meant to die. Mental incompetents were allowed to live and even procreate instead of being drowned at birth. Paraplegics who should have had the decency to commit suicide ran around in wheelchairs and demanded special parking slots. And everywhere you looked there were old people, so-called senior citizens, hanging on to life like parasites, sucking the economy dry instead of making way for the next generation.

Instead of a man earning the right to pass his genes on in combat or by fighting off a lion, he took university courses and opened up a McDonald's.

Bombs killed indiscriminately instead of encouraging individual glory.

Snot-nosed children laughed at tigers in cages and truly thought themselves superior.

The human race had become soft and weak.

Only a radical purge by the few remaining purebloods could save it now. That was the purpose of the Selectors.

Even as a child the Selector had understood the necessity. He'd killed his first man at age seven, a betrayer.

Of course, the man had been tied to a chair, but he could still remember the way the mercenary's curses had turned to pleas, the sweat that suddenly sprang up on his forehead when he realized he was staring into the face of death in the guise of a seven-year-old boy. The Selector would never forget the heady rush of superiority and the pure physical joy of killing: the meaty thunk of the knife when it finally slipped in between the third and fourth ribs, the convulsive heave of a dying heart and the gout of blood.

He'd asked Nigel if he could do it again. Nigel had smiled and ruffled his hair. "Of course."

The next man had only been sleeping, not bound. After that, the Selector graduated to drunks and tender children.

For years Nigel had Selected the targets; this one a betrayer, this one a Jew or a black, this one a slut or a coward, and the Selector had killed for him, a weapon.

How astonished the old man had been when his turn came and he was Selected for destruction.

In his childhood Nigel had been strong, a god. But old age had weakened his body and softened his mind, making him a pushover for a little charm. He'd started to fret about little things like laws and evidence.

Since that day the Selector had killed whenever he wanted, however he wanted.

For the moment his prey were the Futurists.

The psychics were the most dangerous of all because they didn't look like inferiors; they had the blood of gods in their veins, but they had tainted it, warped it with cowardice.

Infuriatingly, their disgusting flaw made them harder to kill. If there was one escape, one thousandth of a chance for life when he had painstakingly closed off all other exits, they would take it. Unerringly.

Take Peter, for instance. Yesterday the Selector had thought the boy dead at the bottom of a ravine, but upon closer questioning he had discovered his minion had killed a different boy.

Or Mary. The Selector had every intention of taking Mary. He'd been hunting her for three years, and his hunger for her blood had acquired a keen edge.

• 3 •

While Matt gritted his teeth and held on, Genevieve made the ten-minute drive into Red Squirrel in six minutes flat.

"What now?" she asked, as they entered the town limits.

Matt had thought it all out. "The bank first. We need cash— checks and credit cards leave a paper trail. Then you go to the grocery store while I fill my epilepsy prescription. After that we hit the Sheriff's Department."

"The sheriff's?" Genevieve repeated.

"Yes," Matt told her, his mind already running ahead to possible problems. "We need a cover story. I'll tell Ian we're getting married in Las Vegas and ask if it's legal for amnesiacs."

Genevieve frowned. "What's he going to say when you come back, still single?"

"Well, we could actually get married," Matt teased her. "Otherwise, I'll just say you changed your mind."

Instead of smiling, Genevieve looked shattered. "You'd still marry me? Right now? Without hearing the whole story?"

"Yes," Matt said simply. "Any way I can get you."

"Then I accept."

She stunned him. "Genevieve!" He couldn't get another word past his tight throat. He took out the square box he'd shoved in his pocket at the last minute and slid the emerald ring she'd refused last Christmas onto her finger. "It doesn't match your eyes anymore."

"I don't care." Genevieve touched his cheek. "I love you, Matt." They kissed for a long, sweet moment before a car's horn and reality intruded. Crabtree.

After running their errands, Genevieve parked in front of the sheriff's office. "Do you want me to come with you?"

"Yes." Matt hesitated. "But let me talk to Ian first."

Red Squirrel Sheriff's Department was a small two-man operation, only ever really busy during tourist season. Matt went up to the red-haired man behind the desk. "Hi, Ian."

"Matt!" Ian pretended to hide behind his *Fish & Game* magazine. "Don't tell me you're writing another police script."

"Nope, better. I'm getting married."

The magazine dropped. "The hell you say!" A smile cracked Ian Dempster's freckled face. "You finally talked Genevieve around, huh? Congratulations!" He jumped to his feet and pumped Matt's hand.

"Thanks."

"So you came here to check and see if it was legal, right? Well, rest easy. So long as neither party is married, it's legal."

"Good," Matt said, and meant it. "But there's something else I'd like to talk to you about."

"Oh?"

"It's about Genevieve. She's getting bits of her memory back. A man came to the house this afternoon, claiming to be her long-lost cousin."

Ian's eyebrows shot up. "Did Genevieve recognize him?"

Matt nodded grimly. "She thinks he's the one who stole her wallet just before she got amnesia."

"A thief?" Ian frowned. "Why would a thief come back?"

"I haven't told you all of it yet. I was upstairs when he arrived, and the first thing I heard was Genevieve's scream. He had a knife at her throat and was trying to drag her outside. Genevieve stamped down on his instep, and I clobbered the bastard with a frying pan."

Ian looked angry and hard, no longer an amiable fisherman, but a lawman. "I hope you hit him hard."

"He went down like a ninepin." Matt didn't mention that he hadn't stayed down.

"Where is he?" Ian started to move out from behind the counter.

"Gone." Matt's disgust wasn't faked. "Genevieve and I went to call you, and I had one of my damn epileptic seizures. Genevieve didn't want to leave me, and he got away."

"Are you okay now?" Ian asked in concern. He'd witnessed one of Matt's attacks on a fishing trip and had confessed afterward he would rather have had a shoot-out with an armed robber. You could shoot armed robbers; you couldn't do anything about epileptic seizures.

"The usual headache. I'm fine, just angry with myself for not tying him up."

"It's not your fault you had an attack."

"Yeah, well," Matt said, unconvinced, "it's too late to change things now."

"Let me write out a complaint, and I'll find the s.o.b. if he's still in the area."

"Please, but we won't be around to press charges." Ian looked up in surprise, and he explained, "I'm worried. What would a thief want with Genevieve? It doesn't make sense—*unless someone else is looking for Genevieve and is offering a reward.*

"Now maybe this is just my writer's imagination, but I don't like that idea one damn bit. You don't hire thugs to hunt down your amnesiac daughter. Something else is going on, and, until Genevieve gets her memory back, we can't tell the good guys from the bad guys."

Ian nodded thoughtfully. "So where are you going?"

"Las Vegas. The sooner Genevieve is legally tied to me the safer I'll feel. We'll honeymoon in one of the places Genevieve has partial memories of and try to prod those memories into returning fully."

"What about the thief?"

"That's what I wanted to ask you about." Matt leaned forward. "Could you do a police check on him? He said his name was John Crabtree. He looked like a real sleazeball, and he might have a previous record. I'd like some more information about what we're up against."

"It's worth a try." The pen moved to paper. "Description?"

Matt quickly described both Crabtree and his car. "I think I broke his nose with the frying pan, so you might try the hospitals."

"Okay." Ian passed the clipboard and paper over to Matt. "Let's see if Genevieve can add any more details. Genevieve," he raised his voice, and beckoned.

Genevieve came over, smiling nervously. "Hello."

"Hi, Genevieve," he said easily. "I just need you to read over Matt's description of your attacker."

She accepted the clipboard. "Sounds right. You've forgotten his age, though. His hair had some gray. He looked about thirty-five or forty." She pushed back the clipboard.

Ian didn't take it, frowning. "Funny, I could have sworn you had green eyes."

Matt's heart leapt into his throat.

"I do," Genevieve said cheerfully, with none of the hesitation Matt had dreaded. "These are colored contacts. You're very observant. It took Matt five hours to notice."

"Did not," Matt said without heat. "I just didn't mention I'd noticed until five hours later."

"Right," Ian said, his frown a vanished memory. "Well then, I'll wish you two luck, and, since I'll miss your wedding, I'll kiss the bride now." He kissed Genevieve's cheek and shook Matt's hand. "Have a safe trip."

"Thanks, Ian." Matt lifted a hand on his way out. "I'll call you later."

Outside the sunshine seemed brighter. Matt smiled for what felt like the first time in years.

In contrast, Genevieve looked strained. "We have to get out of here."

"We're going," he soothed.

Genevieve took his words to heart. It was fortunate Ian was sitting behind his desk and not out on patrol because she pushed the pickup up to 65 mph well within town limits. She relaxed slightly once they hit the highway. "So where are we going anyway? Shall I head for Vegas?"

"No. Vegas is just a cover. For now, just head for Detroit."

"Why Detroit? Why not New York? It's a bigger place to hide."

"Detroit is closer, and it has a university library."

"Why do we need a library?"

"For information, of course," Matt said lightly. "What kind of research assistant are you, anyway?"

"A fake one, remember? What kind of information do you think we'll find in a library?"

"Who the Selector is, hopefully." Matt paused. "If he's real or not."

"You mean if I'm paranoid or not," Genevieve said quietly. "Fair enough. I wasn't sure myself until this afternoon. But I still don't understand how a library will help us."

"It might not. It will depend how much you can remember from your dreams, and if we can corroborate it. There are some things I'm still not clear on." Translation: there were huge gaping holes in her story.

Genevieve nodded. A mile flew by in silence before she spoke: "My name used to be Mary Dunstan. A plain, serviceable name for a rather bubble-headed girl."

• 4 •

April turned quickly, shielding Kristy from the sight of Will Halvorsen with the top of his skull blown out. She wished someone had been there to shield her, too.

She was intensely grateful to Jeff when he stripped off his jacket and threw it over the remains. Only Kristy's arms, so tight and trusting round her neck, locked the scream in her throat. "We're safe now," she kept repeating to Kristy in the hopes of convincing herself. "It's over."

"Are you all right?" After covering up the second man, Gavin approached April and Kristy.

April nodded. Over his shoulder she saw Penny and Jeff rocking their crying son. "What about everyone else?"

"They're fine."

Gavin didn't look fine to April—his skin had a greenish cast. Wordlessly, she held out an arm, including him in their hug. After a second's hesitation he clutched her back with his good arm. The pressure felt good. April closed her eyes.

"Is everyone all right?" Penny's anxious voice intruded.

Reassurances followed. No one had been hurt. Every time April thought of what might have happened—and what had—she shivered uncontrollably. Shock, she supposed. Unbidden, her eyes wandered over to the second man's body. Long, skinny arms and blue-jeaned legs stuck out like spindly spider limbs from underneath Brent Hillock's jean jacket.

She'd killed a man . . .

"I've got to go," Gavin said, jolting April. "The cops will be here soon."

"Hurry," Jeff said just as Penny said, "No, you can't."

If Gavin stayed, he would be arrested. "I'm coming with you." April didn't want to be separated from him.

"Oh no, you're not," Gavin said. "Not this time."

"He can't go." Penny glared at Jeff. "Too many witnesses saw a second man at the scene. We'll make up a story—pretend Gavin's my brother Tom Gillis . . ."

April put her hands on her hips. "I am going, and you can't stop me."

"He has to go," Jeff said harshly. "Most of the witnesses only caught glimpses driving past." He gestured toward the highway, where traffic had picked up again. "The police have his photo by now. They aren't stupid, you know. If he stays, we all go down. Even April will raise questions."

"See! Jeff thinks I should go." It felt strange to agree with Jeff when he was so hostile toward Gavin, but April couldn't afford to squander her advantages.

"I'm coming, too," Kristy chipped in.

"No!" Four adults blasted her in unison.

Kristy pouted.

"You can be my niece," Penny placated her.

April locked eyes with Gavin. "You don't have a choice. With your shoulder you couldn't stop Kristy, much less me."

Gavin looked torn for an instant then nodded. "All right, let's go."

"Not so fast." Penny grabbed his sleeve. "We need to decide on a rendezvous in Olds. We'll meet you at Kentucky Fried Chicken, okay?"

Jeff scowled, but sirens in the distance cut off any further discussion.

As April hurried after Gavin she heard Jeff say to Penny, "Just look pale and shaken. You're in shock. You just shot a man, shot Corny Tobert."

Was that his name? Corny had been crazy, and she'd killed him. Aimed at his heart and squeezed the trigger . . . "I think I'm going to be sick."

Gavin took her arm. "Try to hold on until we reach the creek culvert. We can hide there."

April made it, but just barely. She crawled a few feet into the culvert and barfed on the corrugated metal floor. She felt sweaty and gross, watching her vomit mix with the small trickle of water in the culvert. What glamor. Bethany would have fainted and been carried to safety in Gavin's arms.

She squashed that thought. She'd decided back in high school that there was no point in being jealous of her cousin. She was a better dancer than Bethany and a better athlete. Bethany couldn't have hit a volleyball to save her life, and for all her beautiful smiles she'd had the sense of humor of a pot of marmalade.

Bethany would never have had the nerve to shoot—

She'd just killed a man. It didn't seem possible, so April said it out loud. "I just killed a man." The culvert threw her words back at her, *just killed a man.*

"It was self-defense," Gavin said, voice pitched low to avoid echoes carrying. Gavin, the lawyer-to-be. "No jury would convict. It was him or us."

"I know," April said, and she did. "I always knew I could, you know. Kill someone. I hate it in the movies when the girl has the gun and the villain says, 'You won't shoot me. You haven't got the nerve.' and the twit doesn't. I knew I'd kill him. Bang." She shuddered, remembering the way the gun had bucked in her grip and the red hole in Corny's chest . . .

"You were very brave. You saved our lives." His good arm slipped around her, and they leaned back against the curved wall.

"I know." But April kept seeing Corny's face. He'd looked so surprised, astonished, as if he'd been wearing bulletproof armor and couldn't be killed. "It was too easy. It's too easy to kill a human being."

"Don't think of him as human. Think of him as a rabid skunk."

April tried to, but still felt glad for the distraction of approaching sirens. The cavalry had arrived.

"Do you think they'll find us?" She cuddled back against his chest. Still that mindless tug of attraction . . .

"I doubt it," Gavin said. "My danger instinct isn't goading me. Is yours?"

April considered the matter. "I don't think so."

They fell silent, listening as the sirens gave one last wail. Car doors slammed, and a policeman yelled, "Drop your weapons!"

"The gun's on the ground," Jeff called back. "The men who attacked us are dead."

Corny . . . April covered her ears.

"I'm sorry, April." Gavin's whisper in her ear raised goose bumps.

"It's not your fault. I'll be okay. Only, would you mind talking about something else?"

"Sure." Gavin cleared his throat. "Nice weather we've been having, isn't it?"

April choked with laughter.

"Sorry, I'm a terrible conversationalist. I regularly bore goldfish to death."

She laughed harder and got the hiccups. "I meant—" Hic. "—tell me about yourself." Hic. "What do you like to do in your spare time?" Hic.

"Read Westerns, watch hockey, study. Read history books, watch the news, study. Law students don't have much spare time."

April was thrilled: they both liked to read Westerns. And even though volleyball was her sport, she usually watched hockey playoffs. "Why do you want to be a lawyer?"

"Truth, justice, the Canadian way." He shrugged. "I know lawyers are only supposed to only be interested in money—half the people in my class think they're going to star in *L.A. Law*—but I don't even want to practice criminal law."

"What then? Family law?"

"No. I like the big issues. The constitution, apartheid, the environment . . . stuff like that. Criminals are boring. It's usually pretty damn obvious if they're guilty. I don't have the stomach to defend most of them, and prosecuting them would be too bleak." His face hardened. "Except for Bethany's killer. I'd make an exception for him."

"How do you know it's a him?"

Gavin stared hard at the culvert wall. "Bethany was getting phone calls."

"Threats?"

"Not exactly." He paused. "She was flirting with the caller. Bethany told me it was her friend Carrie, but I know it was a man. She only smiled that way, all secret and mysterious, for guys. I think she went to meet him, and he killed her."

"She was seeing someone behind your back?" April was shocked.

"It's not what you think," Gavin defended Bethany. "She wasn't cheating on me, because there was nothing to cheat on. Bethany didn't really date me."

"What?" *What, what* echoed the culvert. April winced at the noise and lowered her voice. "What do you mean you didn't date? I saw you together at the New Year's Eve Dance." Had seen them dancing close and been consumed with jealousy, certain they were sleeping together.

He grimaced. "I was her cover. Ron broke her heart, and she needed some space to recover. So she went out with me, nice nonthreatening Gavin."

"She used you." April balled her hands into fists. She'd known Bethany was selfish, but this went beyond hiding the last piece of a jigsaw puzzle.

Gavin wouldn't hear any criticism against his beloved; he shook his head. "She asked me to be her friend. She needed some time, and she knew the other guys wouldn't leave her alone if she was single. I was the one who mucked everything up by falling in love. I think I lasted an entire week."

For Bethany a week without succumbing was a world record. "You weren't in love with her before?"

"I was attracted to her. I mean, I'm not blind. But we were so different. . . . Bethany always had to be going somewhere, doing something. I'm more likely to stay up to 4 A.M. finishing a paper than partying. Ron Revarc was more her type. A perfect prince."

"He sounds like a toad to me, and Bethany must have thought so, too, or she wouldn't have broken up with him," April said stoutly.

Some of the yearning left Gavin's eyes. "God, I'll never forget the night they broke up. It was at a party, and Bethany was teasing me about needing 'lawyer' glasses, when he grabbed her arm and called her a flirt.

"Bethany told him his jealousy had ruined their relationship. She said she hadn't been flirting with me—"

Oh yeah? April had seen guys trip all over themselves for a smile from Bethany. And Bethany had known exactly what effect she had.

"—but since they'd broken up, she could flirt all she liked. Then she kissed me." Gavin's face held bemused wonder at the memory. "Ron looked like he was going to have a stroke. He kept saying she was his, they were perfect together. I thought he was going to rip my head off when I stepped between them. When we left he called after her, 'Don't go,' and she nearly stopped. She nearly went back to him."

"Then she was stupid. He sounds obsessed."

"You don't understand. They were perfect together. God and goddess. A head above us poor mortals."

April was fed up with Ron's virtues. "What would Ron have done in the shoot-out just now? Would he have shielded Bobby with his body?"

Gavin snorted. "Ron had what the Futurists call the Shine. In five minutes he would have charmed the gun right out of Will's hand and had Will thank him for the privilege."

"But would he have risked his life? Put his body between a bullet and a little boy?"

"Nooo . . ."

"I thought so." *And you can damn well bet Bethany wouldn't have.* Bethany would have hidden behind Gavin. She and Ron did seem well matched. Why couldn't Bethany have stayed with Ron and left Gavin alone?

Not that Bethany's leaving him alone would have guaranteed his interest in April, but at least she wouldn't have had to compete with a ghost—a beautiful, tragic, fragile flower who had "needed" Gavin's protection.

Outside car doors slammed as the police car and ambulance drove away. April and Gavin waited ten minutes, then crawled out of the culvert.

The station wagon still sat there, sagging in the corner with the flat tire. "They'll probably send a tow truck for it," Gavin said.

"Yeah." April brushed off her jeans. "Let's go." Traffic whizzed by on either side of them, not stopping. "So tell me," she said as they began to walk toward Olds, "do you like to dance?"

• 5 •

Penny yawned. Her eyelids felt weighted by tombstones. They'd been inside the police station for two hours, and the nightmare tension sustaining her had been replaced by bone-sucking fatigue.

She leaned back against Jeff's shoulder and closed her eyes. In the five minutes before the police arrived they'd gotten their stories straight. She'd shot Corny, not April. She'd wiped the gun of fingerprints and imprinted her own. They were driving their niece, Kristy, back to Calgary.

Jeff identified Will and Corny as neighbors and related the story of the cut phone line. Penny invented a threatening phone call just before the phone went out. "We decided to leave for Calgary a little early and stay in a motel in Chinchaga." She recounted seeing the men at the window and calling the police. "We weren't sure how long they could be held, so we left as soon as the police drove up."

Penny had been arrested, but the police officer had assured her that it was just a formality. "Those bastards murdered the two officers investigating your complaint this morning." The constable's jaw clenched in fury. "Once the prosecutor gets all the facts he'll drop the charges."

Penny massaged her forehead. "I keep thinking about his poor wife. This is going to hit Janet so hard. She's been so nice to me — so was Will for that matter until he started raving about demons. It makes me wonder if maybe he had one of those brain tumors. Something that made him crazy. Tell Janet that at the end he seemed to realize what he'd done. He killed himself so he couldn't kill us."

"I'll tell her." The officer left them to sit and wait while he filled out forms. Bobby and Kristy played tic-tac-toe. Two hours shuffled by like convicts in a chain gang.

"Tired?" Jeff asked the top of her head.

"Exhausted." Penny cuddled closer. Since the shoot-out Jeff had been unfailingly protective, sticking close to both her and Bobby. His love was balm for her shattered nerves.

If only she could shake the terrible premonition that Will's and Corny's deaths weren't the end.

She didn't want to think about it. She concentrated on Jeff's fingers stroking her hair instead. It felt so good. . . .

JEFF WOKE HER an hour later. "Time to go. Our car's been fixed, and we've been released."

On impulse she kissed his lips. The intended peck turned into a warm exchange.

"What was that for?" he asked a moment later, bemused.

Penny's eyes misted. "For never, ever, even once thinking I was a demon."

Jeff gifted her with a slow, wide smile. "I don't think you're a werewolf, either. Do I get a kiss for that, too?"

"If you want one," Penny said softly, tipping her head back in invitation. His mustache tickled her lips, and his arms slowly tightened around her. She felt his love like the heat of the sun, reveling in it. Will was dead, everything was going to be okay. . . .

Then something drew across the face of the sun like an eclipse, darkening with fear, and Jeff drew back. "We should go," he said roughly.

Penny blinked back tears, trying to calm down as they left the building. Something was wrong, yes, but it wasn't as if Jeff had stopped loving her.

Maybe she should just leave things alone, give him time to adjust to the revelation that she was a psychic. She felt uncertain and didn't like the feeling. Usually her Talent enabled her to say the right thing in any situation, but this time her own emotions blinded her.

"I'm hungry," Bobby announced. He hadn't had anything to eat since his breakfast of Oreos, and it was close to twelve.

Looking at him, Penny felt cold fingers clutch her heart, remembering how close she'd come to losing him. *The Demoness and her hell-spawn child* . . . "We'll eat soon," she promised.

Jeff scooped Bobby up. "How do hamburgers sound, sport?"

"Yeah, yeah!" Bobby nodded his head enthusiastically.

Penny glanced at Jeff sharply. "They don't serve burgers at Kentucky Fried Chicken."

"Maybe I don't feel like chicken."

Penny stopped walking. "We're going to KFC's."

"No, we're not." [*Unbudging stubbornness.*]

Kristy looked uncertain. "But isn't that where . . . ?"

"Yes." Penny's gaze didn't leave Jeff's face. He knew it was the rendezvous.

Jeff looked around quickly—[*nervousness and fear.*] "Not here." He unlocked the station wagon.

Penny strapped Bobby into his booster seat, then clambered into the front and slammed the door. "You know damn well we have to go to KFC's to meet Gavin and April."

"We don't have to go anywhere, especially with a murder suspect. I couldn't believe it this morning when he said the police are after him. How could you do something so stupid?"

[*Distress from Bobby. Anxiety from Kristy. Anger and fear from Jeff.*]

"Gavin did not kill Bethany." She dealt with that issue first. "I could read his emotions, and I swear to you, he's innocent."

Jeff surprised her. "I know that—no killer would have shielded Bobby. The point is, the police are after him. We're accomplices for helping him. Do you want to give birth to our daughter in a jail cell?"

Penny didn't, but she didn't admit it. "I had to help him. He's my brother. He was in danger."

"Will's dead now. And Gavin's not your brother."

"Just because Will is dead doesn't mean the danger's over. Remember the Voice he heard? Until we find out who or what the Voice is, we can't be safe. We have to go to Calgary."

"Why?" Jeff asked, so bluntly Penny was stymied. Why were they going to Calgary? Suddenly it didn't seem like such a good idea. . . . Her danger instinct kicked in.

She ignored it. "We have a moral responsibility to warn the other Futurists about the Voice."

"The only responsibility you have is toward Bobby and the baby."

He meant it. He had no qualms about leaving the Futurists to their fate.

Penny's chin lifted. "They need to be warned."

"So phone them."

Penny considered the idea, noting the relief that accompanied it. Not go to Calgary . . . But it wouldn't work. "They won't believe me over the phone. I have to talk to the Council."

"Forget it. We're not going."

Pigheaded, stubborn man. Admittedly, he just wanted to protect them, but still. She tried a different approach. "The Futurists can protect us. We'll be safer there."

He raised an eyebrow. "Like the web house? That much safer?"

His sarcasm silenced Penny, and Bobby filled the gap, "Hungry."

"If you're not going to Kentucky Fried Chicken, I'll go alone." Kristy put her hand on the door handle.

"Park it, kid." Jeff scowled. "April and Gavin should never have brought you along in the first place. Your parents must be frantic."

"I can't go home without telling them about April and Gavin," Kristy said.

Jeff didn't look like he cared.

"If Kristy goes home or Gavin gets caught, we're implicated," Penny pointed out. "If he hangs around Kentucky Friend Chicken all day, someone might notice him."

Jeff wouldn't look at her, wouldn't admit she was right.

She brought out the big guns. "He saved Bobby's life."

Jeff flinched then started the engine. "You win. But when we get to Calgary the debt's paid."

• 6 •

April's hands shook as she placed a call to her parents from a pay phone outside of Kentucky Fried Chicken. She didn't dare risk calling collect, so she'd converted some of their precious money into quarters.

She hoped her father didn't answer. He knew nothing of the Futurists. After he got over his happiness at her being alive he would demand an explanation.

One ring. Two.

"Hello?" Luck was with her. Her brother Dean answered.

"Dean? It's April. I'm alive, and so's Kristy—"

"April?" Dean interrupted, his voice joyous and incredulous. "April, is that you?"

April found herself crying. "Yeah, it's me."

"Thank God. Jesus, April we thought you were dead. Where the hell have you been?" And in the same breath. "Never mind. You can tell me later. I have to tell everyone the good news."

"Wait! Don't call them yet. Is anybody else there besides family?"

"No," Dean said, surprised. "The neighbors all went home, leaving their casseroles behind. Not," he accused, "that anyone is hungry."

Guiltily, April acknowledged he had a right to feel angry. "I'm sorry, Dean. I wanted to call earlier, but things have been rather—hectic."

"I'm getting Mom and Dad," Dean announced.

"Does Dad know about the Futurists? My explanation has an awful lot to do with them."

A pause. Then, "Tell me." Unspoken, but implied, were the words *this had better be good.*

April told him, words spilling out in a rush. "It isn't a coincidence Bethany died on the same day the trailer burned. Bethany and I are both Futurists. The little girl I was baby-sitting is a Futurist and Gavin Lindberg is a Futurist." She held the phone away from her ear, anticipating an explosion.

"Gavin Lindberg?" the phone squawked. "Bethany's killer? Christ, tell me you're not with him, he didn't kidnap you?"

"He didn't kidnap me, and he didn't kill Bethany," April said firmly.

"But you are with him?" Dean was well into his big-brother act now. "Tell me where you are, and I'll come pick you up."

April had been prepared for this demand. "I can't."

"Are you being held hostage?"

April fought back a giggle as she looked through the window and saw Gavin gloomily drinking coffee and hiding behind a potted plant. "No, I'm not being held hostage."

Dean swore. "No, you're just alone somewhere with a murderer. Nothing to worry about," he said sarcastically. "Dad—"

"*Shut up!*" Her brothers tended to steamroller over her if she didn't shout. "You're in just as much danger as I am. Gavin didn't kill Bethany, but somebody else did."

She softened her voice. "Think about it, Dean. I'm a Futurist. Would I go anywhere, willingly, with a murderer? Gavin's innocent. I swear."

"Maybe so," Dean conceded reluctantly. "But I'm still going to pick you up. Where are you?"

"You're not thinking, Dean. If I come home, I'll get arrested as an accomplice. I can't come back until Gavin's name is cleared."

"And when will that be? The police are looking for Gavin; they're not looking for anyone else."

"I know. That's why I need your help. To prove he's innocent."

She gave him the facts as fast as she could, finishing with: "Someone's out to get the Futurists. Dean, promise me you'll be on your guard. And warn Mom, Allan, and Jerry. The Millses, too."

"Yes, okay." Dean sighed. "God, what a day. First Bethany . . . and on Aunt Kim and Uncle Luke's anniversary, too."

"Yeah, I know." April felt tears gathering in the corners of her eyes. "Tell everyone I love them and I'll try to call again—"

The line beeped twice, telling her to insert more coins, then went dead.

Slowly, April hung up and went back inside. She and Gavin each drank two more coffees before Penny and her family showed up and got into line at the cash register. Kristy waved.

"About time," Gavin grumbled, but April could see the relief in his eyes.

"Let's get something to eat," April suggested. Her stomach growled. All that exercise had made her hungry. *Exercise* . . . She remembered Corny and changed her mind.

Dinner was strained. Jeff concentrated on his chicken as if the lost treasure of the Incas lay buried under the Extra Crispy skin. Penny spoke of the police station in whispers, and Bobby smeared ketchup all over his face.

"You look cute dirty," April told him. "I probably look like a disaster."

"Actually," Penny said, "you do. You can use my butane curling iron. I'm probably a sight myself." She grimaced.

"You look cute dirty, too," Jeff assured her, in a rare instance of good humor. "Must be that big stomach."

Penny poked him before taking Bobby's hand and leaving the table.

"Two quick things," Penny said when they reached the washroom. Her green eyes met April's in the mirror. "Are you in love with my brother?"

April almost dropped the curling iron. All her snappy refusals died in her mouth. She nodded miserably. "At first sight."

"Tough, isn't it?" Penny said sympathetically. She wet a paper towel and sponged off Bobby's face and hands. "And up against Bethany, too. I remember from university how Bethany smiled, and the guys fell down like ducks in a shooting gallery. It was her psychic Talent, that instant dazzle."

Another woman entered the washroom, and Penny took Bobby into one of the cubicles. April went back to curling her hair. She was hair spraying it in place when the other woman left.

"Last thing," Penny said. "Gavin broods too much. It's our job to distract him, okay?"

April nodded.

They were moderately successful, keeping the conversation general and not touching on Bethany's murder. They were discussing the lullaby when they entered Calgary and Gavin swore.

"What's wrong?" April asked, envisioning more horrors.

"Professor Murdoch's Torts final is Monday. It's worth fifty percent of our mark, and I'm going to miss it." Gavin sounded horrified. "My study notes are in Huld."

April laughed out loud in relief. Gavin looked offended.

The Kithkin Klub was situated in the upper floors of the Cambrian Building and looked more like a lawyer's office than a university club, April decided, studying the oak-paneled walls. It came complete with a haughty receptionist who guarded its hallowed doors.

Gavin and then Penny, both members, were allowed in, but the cool courtesy came to a jarring halt when Penny mentioned Jeff and Bobby.

"I'd like to request that my husband and son be admitted entry. My son Bobby has already shown signs of possessing the danger instinct, and Jeff knows about the Futurists."

"You told him?" The woman acted as if Penny had sold military secrets to Iraq. "A nonpsychic?"

Jeff's face darkened; Penny remained calm. "I would have preferred to tell him sooner, but I obeyed the will of the Council until it became essential that he know." Jeff looked mollified. "If anyone objects, they can talk to *me* about it."

The receptionist pursed her lips. She clearly wanted to refuse them entrance, but whoever she spoke to on the phone overruled her. "Please, take a seat, someone will be down shortly." She turned to April with icy eyes. "And are you also a nonmember?"

Gavin smiled encouragement at April.

April felt her heart melt. Not that it was ever much harder than taffy concerning Gavin. She straightened her shoulders. "My name is April Jongkind. I would like to apply for membership. My brother Dean is a member." She waited while the receptionist typed in the right keys and a form printed out.

"And would you also like to apply?" the woman asked Kristy sarcastically as she handed April her form.

"Oh, no." Kristy smiled sweetly. "I'm just here to visit my grandmother, Portia Carver."

The receptionist's lipsticked mouth dropped open.

"Portia Carver?" Penny repeated, voice cracking. "Grandmother?"

Gavin looked just as surprised. April watched their reactions, puzzled. Who was Portia Carver?

The receptionist's voice cut like a whip. "Miss Jongkind! The form must be completed alone. Please sit over there."

April flushed. As if she would cheat! She sat down to take the test.

The questionnaire was long—long and boring. But when she handed it in the others were still waiting for her.

A thirtysomething man with curly golden-brown hair had joined them. He wore a lightweight suit, but no tie. His white shirt was open at the throat revealing tanned skin and a gold necklace. Penny had evidently briefed him on the situation because when the receptionist tried to prevent April from entering—"She hasn't been Initiated yet"—he countermanded her.

"After what this young lady has been through, the test is a mere formality." He clasped both her hands in his. "Welcome to the Kithkin Klub, April. I'm Travis." His smile held the heat of a summer sun.

April blinked under the lethal dose of charm. He was out of her league, Bethany's type, not hers. Gavin was the only man they had ever agreed on. April glanced at Gavin and saw him frown.

"Let's get going," Gavin said.

Travis shrugged. "This way." The six of them followed him into a large well-furnished office. He perched on the edge of his desk, crossing one perfectly creased gray pant leg over the other. "What can I do to help you?" The sun shone on Penny.

She did not smile back. "Two things. Gavin's been shot; we need a Futurist doctor to look at his wound."

"Can do." Travis nodded. "We have several on staff who'll keep things quiet and unofficial. What else?"

"I'd like you to call an emergency meeting of the Council and Portia Carver."

Travis raised an eyebrow. "My dear, you don't ask much! Portia Carver will come *if* she wishes, not because someone demands. Even if," he inclined his head toward Kristy, "this girl is her granddaughter."

Penny's expression didn't change. "The Council exists to protect the Futurists. The Futurists are in danger."

"Danger?" Travis scoffed. "You've been through a horrible experience, my dear, but the man is dead. There's no need to cry wolf because of one lunatic."

"Two lunatics," Penny corrected grimly. "Two lunatics who called Bobby and me 'demons' and tried to kill us in plain sight of half a dozen motorists. Some other lunatic tried to burn Kristy and April to death. And someone *did* kill Bethany Mills and shoot Gavin. All within the space of one day. Doesn't that tell you anything? Can't you feel the danger coming?"

Travis looked uncertain, a touch afraid.

Suddenly, abruptly, so was April. Throughout the whole trip she'd been telling herself they'd be safe once they got to Calgary. *Safe.* But the air felt oppressive and stale. She had a panicky urge to flee. Had the danger followed them?

"Now call that meeting!" Penny ordered. Even pregnant she looked formidable.

Without a word Travis began to dial.

part two

Knowledge

CHAPTER 6

• 1 •

Mary Dunstan had been the name on the driver's license. Matt nodded, then caught himself. Bubble-headed?

Genevieve smiled sourly, as if sensing his doubts. "Aunt Dorothy called me a frivolous butterfly. She would dolefully shake her head at me, but I knew I could twist her around my finger."

Well, that hadn't changed, Matt thought, as Michigan greenery flashed by outside the pickup windows. Genevieve could wrap him around her fingers.

"She wasn't really my aunt," Genevieve continued. "She adopted me when I was a toddler, and she was in her forties. She told me once she'd felt too old to be called Mama, and too young to be Grandma so she'd settled on Aunt.

"I was spoiled. Not so much by Aunt Dorothy as by life. I was pretty and popular, good at sports, better than average at art and music. I got effortless B's and C's at school. I probably could have gotten A's if I'd buckled down like Aunt Dorothy told me to, but my social life kept me much, much too busy." Genevieve mocked herself. "I didn't know what I wanted to be so I took a couple years of college, bachelor of arts, just putting in time. My sole worry was that my college boyfriend would forget me over the summer."

Matt tried to picture Genevieve's life as she was describing it and failed. The Genevieve he knew was hardworking and responsible. What had made a Genevieve of Mary?

"I never finished my degree. On May 27 I had the dream. God" — she let out a sharp expulsion of breath — "that sounds so commonplace. So ordinary. Everyone has dreams. If I say nightmare, a little more of the feeling creeps through: I had the nightmare for the first time."

Matt felt the hairs lift on the back of his neck. He remembered the night he'd heard Genevieve crying and had gone to see what was wrong. She'd been drenched in sweat and had woken with a scream on her lips. She'd nearly clawed his eyes out. Only his glasses, unthinkingly put on when he got up, had saved him. Everyone did not have dreams like that.

"No, that's still too soft." Genevieve struggled to express the terror of her dream. Her blue eyes turned almost black with the remembrance. "A nightmare is something you wake up from, realize it was just a dream, and go back to sleep, the nightmare forgotten by morning. This dream was different."

"How?"

"It was . . . real. I know it sounds crazy, Matt, but I swear it was real. As real as you and I sitting here. As real as this pickup." She rapped the dashboard with a knuckle. "*Real.*"

"Tell me." Matt listened in silence while she told him about a basement full of clocks, a dying couple, and their murderer.

"I must have made some kind of noise because he turned suddenly and saw me. Up until then it was one of those dreams where you're invisible, a spectator. But he saw me, and he was so surprised he jerked the knife out of the older man's neck and walked toward me. 'Who are you?'

"I was so scared I didn't think not to answer. I told him my name.

" 'Hello, Mary Dunstan,' he said, and he smiled at me — this wonderful, dazzling smile — he smiled, and said, 'I'm the Selector, Mary. I select who lives and who dies.' Then he tried to kill me, and I woke up."

So it was a dream. While Genevieve had been talking the dream she'd painted had seemed real. Vivid. Solid.

Genevieve wasn't finished. "Two days later, on a whim, I decided to go to a dance in another town. Once I got there I didn't want to leave. I phoned Aunt Dorothy and told her some lie about my friend being too drunk to drive. That was the last time I talked to her.

"I had the dream again that night. Only the dream changed halfway through. Instead of the strange man and woman, someone else was lying on the floor. Someone I knew." Genevieve clenched her hands on the steering wheel.

Matt touched her shoulder compassionately. "Your aunt?"

She nodded. "She lay facedown at the bottom of the stairs, as though she'd been caught trying to climb them. Her hair was in the ugly plastic curlers I always teased her about, and her nightgown was hiked up around her thighs.

"You would have to have known Aunt Dorothy to understand, but she was a very dignified woman. She would have hated dying in her curlers. Being found that way. Photographed by the police. Somehow that was almost worse than her death.

"I screamed when I saw her, and the Selector turned toward me. 'I've been looking for you, Mary. Are you really here this time?' He tried to stab me again, but his knife passed right through me as if I was a ghost.

"When I woke up I realized it had been a dream, but I was so scared I phoned Aunt Dorothy anyway.

"A man answered, and said, 'Hello?'

"I thought I'd dialed the wrong number. I started to hang up, but he asked, 'Is this Mary?' I said yes and asked who he was.

"He didn't answer." Genevieve's lower lip trembled. "He said, 'Where are you? Your aunt is worried about you.'

"I didn't tell him, thank God. I asked to speak to my aunt, and he said—" Genevieve licked her lips. "He said, 'Don't be silly, Mary, you know your aunt can't come to the phone right now. She's dead.' "

Matt flinched.

"I couldn't believe Aunt Dorothy was dead." Genevieve's eyes shone with tears. She stared straight out the windshield. "She was such a good woman, a little stiff maybe, and not much for hugs, but I grew up knowing I was loved. She gave me a home, and he killed her for it. No other reason. Just because she was home, and I wasn't.

"I dropped the phone. I remember it bouncing up and down at the end of the cord. That's when I had my first panic attack. I didn't call the police or stop and think, I just ran. I ran as hard as I could for a week." She closed her eyes, hands clenched into fists. "When I ran out of money it occurred to me that maybe I should make sure the dream really had happened."

"And had it?" Matt had ambivalent feelings about whether or not he believed her. Dreams coming true were the stuff of fiction, but he trusted Genevieve.

"Yes. Aunt Dorothy was dead. Killed wearing her curlers just like I dreamed, but the Selector didn't do it. The police arrested someone else, Dan Quillon, a middle-aged man who looked nothing like the Selector."

"Any chance they arrested the wrong man?"

"No. They caught him red-handed. Literally." Genevieve's mouth turned down. "Blood on his clothes. Knife in his glove compartment. All the forensic evidence. There's no doubt about it: he killed her, not the Selector.

"Aunt Dorothy's murderer was in jail. There was no reason why I couldn't go home, but I didn't. Couldn't. Just the thought of it made my skin crawl. So I stayed where I was, got a job doing dishes."

"Whenever Aunt Dorothy wanted me to do chores I always had some homework to do, but right then I was so damn grateful to do dishes I almost cried."

She paused before continuing and passed a slow-moving motor home. "I had a savings account, but I didn't take any money out. Didn't phone any of my friends or my boyfriend to let them know I was all right. Just hid from a man who doesn't even exist. That's all I've been doing. Hiding. Until the next dream comes.

"I thought they were just panic attacks, but Crabtree called me Mary and you poet man, just like the Selector does in my dreams. Crabtree proves that the Selector is real and he's chasing me. Sooner or later he'll catch me. I wish you'd let me drop you off somewhere. Being with me puts you in danger."

"I don't see why," Matt said lightly. "It sounds like your dreams give you plenty of warning."

"They give me warning," Genevieve agreed. "Me and nobody else. The instinct that warns me I'm in danger only cares about me. It's very selfish."

"Selfish?" The word bothered Matt. Genevieve was one of the least selfish people he knew.

"Oh, yes, very selfish." Shadows crowded Genevieve's blue eyes. "My selfishness killed Aunt Dorothy."

"Don't be ridiculous," Matt said. "The Selector or Dan Quillon killed her, not you. If you'd been home, you probably would have died, too."

"But I wasn't home, was I? I had a panic attack that afternoon and begged Aunt Dorothy to let me go to the dance. As soon as she agreed all my worry lifted. Vanished. I trooped merrily off and left Aunt Dorothy to face the killer alone."

"You didn't know it was real. You thought it was just paranoia. How could you have known?" Matt argued.

"And after Aunt Dorothy died? I knew then, but I nearly did the same thing to you this morning. I caught myself sitting in the pickup with the keys in the ignition. I almost left you to face Crabtree alone."

"But you didn't. And you won't," Matt said firmly.

Genevieve still looked troubled. "I wish I could be as sure as you are."

Matt steered the subject back on track. "How often do you have the dreams? Is there a pattern to it? Do you always have a panic attack after it?"

"If there's a pattern to it, I haven't noticed. I don't have a date circled on my calendar or anything. As for the panic attacks—I used to get them after every dream, but after the fifth time I started to get smart. If I don't talk to the Selector and tell him where I am, he can't find me right away.

"In the seven months I've been working for you I've had four dreams. In the second last one he found out you wrote poetry. Last night he found out I lived by Lake Michigan."

"Found out?" Matt picked up on her ambiguous choice of words. "Did you tell him?"

Genevieve shifted uncomfortably. "Not in words, but if I even think about telling him I . . . open up, and he can . . . grab at my thoughts. Glean little bits of information."

"And while the Selector gets information from you have you ever gotten anything back from him? A real name and address would come in handy," Matt joked.

"Nothing like that." Genevieve shivered. "Just a sense of evil. He kills people with knives because he likes the blood. He—he hates me."

"What does he look like?" Matt asked quickly. He fired a bunch of neutral descriptive questions at her, putting her at ease even as he slowly gathered information.

The Selector had blue eyes, a square chin, and short dark hair.

She guessed him to be in his mid-twenties.

He was muscular and had large hands.

He almost always wore jeans and a T-shirt, usually white, sometimes red.

The places where she'd seen him kill varied widely, as did the ages of the victims.

Except for her dreams she had never seen the Selector. He always sent his minions after her.

"Minions?" Matt asked.

"You know. Like Crabtree. If someone calls me Mary, it means the Selector sent him. The Selector's the only one who calls me that anymore. I haven't used my real name for a year."

Matt paused. Her real name. "Would you like me to call you Mary?"

"No. No, please don't. He's ruined it for me, destroyed my name." Her mouth twisted. "I never liked it anyhow. It was too plain, too boring."

"I think every kid thinks that," Matt said easily. "I remember trying to make my parents call me Matthew in high school. But somehow Matt just stuck."

"Call me Genevieve," she said firmly.

"Genevieve," Matt repeated. "Okay, let's go back to your dreams. Now you said your dreams about the Selector have a high degree of reality—that they do in fact come true—"

"They don't come true," she interrupted. "They aren't prophecy dreams. They happen as I watch."

"Well, I suppose that's just as believable as seeing into the future." Matt was careful to keep his tone even. "More believable in some ways. All right. So if your dreams are real, there are a whole lot of unsolved murders out there. The police must be looking for the Selector, too. If we can find out who he is and tip off the police, they can arrest him."

"I don't think it will be that simple." Genevieve looked doubtful. "But okay, how do we find out his name?"

"First we find out if the murders have happened, then we look for links between the victims. Motive, means, etc. But that's if the murders have happened."

"Aunt Dorothy's dead."

Matt gentled his voice. "Yes, but since someone else was arrested for her murder, we still don't know if the Selector exists. The police could have arrested the wrong man—we don't know. We need more proof—that means information about the other murders. Let's start with names and dates."

Matt rummaged around until he found a pen in the glove compartment. He clicked the ballpoint. "You said your first dream was May 27, 1998. And an older man and woman were killed?"

Genevieve nodded jerkily.

"Any idea where the murder took place? What city? What time? Their names? Something we can do a newspaper search for."

"I've watched them die a dozen times," Genevieve said, "but I don't know their names. I can tell you they were killed in their basement, and that's about it. Oh, and they had a collection of antique clocks. How's that for a clue?"

"If they had clocks, then you know what time the murder occurred."

Her mouth fell open.

"You said you had this dream a dozen times. Where do the hands on the clock point?"

"Nine o'clock, or a few minutes to. Only a few of the clocks had started to strike."

"And what time was it when you woke up?"

"Eleven. Aunt Dorothy was just going to bed."

"Then the murder occurred two time zones west of you," Matt deduced. "Where did you grow up?"

"Iowa." Genevieve stared at him. "God, Matt, I had no idea I knew the time of the murder."

"Just call me Sherlock," Matt said lightly. "The name of the city would still help. Let's skip your aunt for now. What was the next dream you had?"

For the next hour Matt took careful notes while Genevieve talked, reliving her dreams. When she finished he was astounded. "Twenty-eight. You've seen twenty-eight murders in thirty-five months. No wonder you were on the edge of a nervous breakdown. Most hit men don't kill that often."

"He isn't a hit man. He calls himself the Selector because he selects who lives and who dies. Hit men kill people marked for death by other people."

"Any idea why he's selected you?"

She shrugged. "I don't think he thought about that much. I witnessed a murder, so he has to kill me."

"Witnessed? Hardly. You had a strange dream. No court of law would accept it as evidence."

Genevieve looked startled. "You're right." Her mouth turned down. "He probably just decided I was inferior and deserved to die—though from what I've seen there aren't very many people who meet his criteria. The girl I saw last night was beautiful, and he still killed her. He called it 'culling the herd.'" She was silent for close to a minute. "He's a monster."

• 2 •

Gavin paced the length of the waiting room for what felt like the hundredth time. The tetanus shot the doctor had given him made his shoulder feel even sorer.

Jeff glared at him in irritation. Gavin glared back. Twice Jeff had asked him to stop pacing. Twice Gavin had asked Jeff to stop whistling. Gavin never wanted to hear "Jingle Bells" again as long as he lived.

"What's taking them so long?" Gavin growled. The Council had been meeting for an hour.

Kristy looked up from her Find-a-Word puzzle. "They're probably dithering. Mother said they do that a lot."

Travis drew himself up, taking umbrage at her remark, before remembering she was only a child and it would be undignified to argue with her.

"And Grandmother Portia hasn't arrived yet," Kristy added.

"Chairwoman Carver rarely attends Council meetings," a dough-faced matron informed them. She was wearing a horrible puce jacket and skirt, and if she was capable of any expression beyond disapproval, Gavin had yet to see it.

He turned away from her and went to sit by April. "How are you doing?" The receptionist had called her out of the room half an hour ago to take the Talent test, and she'd only just gotten back.

She shrugged. "Okay, I guess. Some of those questions were pretty weird."

"So are some of the Talents." To distract himself Gavin started explaining the various categories. "Besides the danger instinct there are nine categories. I have Psychic Agony. When someone I love is in agony, I can sense it. You're much better off without that Talent, believe me."

April squeezed his arm in sympathy.

[*AAAIIIIIIIIIIIIIIIIEEEEEEEEEeeeeeEEEE!*]

The scream rang through his mind as if Bethany was right there in the room, shrieking in his ear. If not for April's total lack of reaction, Gavin would have thought she was really there, begging and pleading and screaming.

[*Gavin, please, you've got to help me. Oh, pleeeeaasee . . .*]

He was going crazy. Bethany wasn't screaming anymore, she was dead, and she'd never called his name anyway only screamed and screamed as if being eviscerated alive —

"Gavin?" April's voice, concerned.

[*Bethany screaming*—]

NO! Lock it down. Grieve later: concentrate on April, on the concerned look on her face. Gavin didn't want to talk about his flashbacks, so he made himself keep talking about the Talents.

"Penny's an Empath. She can sense other people's emotions. A nice Talent, that; it's hard to pick a fight with Penny. Actually, Penny has one and a half Talents. She also has Genetic Instinct, which means recognizing your mate when you meet them. Penny says she knew as soon as she saw Jeff that she loved him. Who knows?" Gavin tried to sound cheerful. "Maybe that's your Talent, and you just haven't met the right guy yet."

His attempt flopped. April blushed, and Gavin doggedly went on to the next category. "Then there's Luck. Bethany's dad has it. Their instinct goes beyond which door *not* to pick and tells them the *best* one to pick. They usually make a killing in the stock market."

April nodded. "Uncle Luke always wins at poker. It drives my dad nuts."

"Never play cards against someone with Luck." The chance to lecture relaxed something in his chest. "And be careful around some-one with the Shine."

He'd been meaning to warn April about this since Travis fawned over her hand. "Shiners can charm birds out of the trees. They can date any girl they want, and they know it. They've been smothered with attention since birth, so they're bound to be a little selfish. They forget other people can be hurt."

April gave a funny little smile. "Everyone else is in love with them, but they never seem to love anyone else."

"Exactly." Gavin beamed. She wouldn't be taken in by some Shin-ing charmer and have her heart broken like Bethany.

Bethany's heart wasn't broken anymore, her body was.

[*Gavin, help me!*]

Gavin jerked his attention back to April. Lock it down. "Then there are the three types of visions. Ghosting, which doesn't neces-sarily deal with true ghosts, just scenes from the past. Penny and Bethany's friend Carrie has it, and she freaks out at the scene of old car accidents.

"I don't know anyone with the other two. Prophecy is a vision of the future, and Viewing is a vision of the present." Gavin tried to remember what he'd been told about that dubious Talent. "They're supposed to occur in dreams a lot."

" 'Mary dreams,' " April quoted.

"Yeah." Gavin counted in his head. He'd listed eight Talents so far. "Then there's Illusions, and that's it. For the known ones at any rate," he amended with a quick glance at Kristy and Bobby. They were the only two telepaths in the fifty-year history of the Futurists.

"What about hooking and burning?" April asked.

At first Gavin didn't know what she meant, then he remembered the lullaby, which had been discussed to death during the drive to Calgary. "Firstborn hooks" and "Peter burns." He shrugged. "I don't know. Maybe Peter's just very angry, and Firstborn's a fisherman." Even as he said it Gavin didn't really believe it. April didn't look convinced either.

Gavin got up to pace again. Jeff started another chorus of "Jingle Bells." Kristy chewed on her pencil. Bobby sucked his thumb. April gazed out the window. Travis picked lint off his slacks. The matron flicked through a *Bride* magazine. Into this atmosphere of restless waiting Portia Carver exploded like a bomb.

Gavin knew of her only by hearsay, but he recognized her immediately.

The Founding Lady of the Futurists commanded attention. At— what? Sixty-five? Seventy?—she was still attractive, her face mostly unwrinkled. Her eyes were a clear piercing green, Penny's inheritance. Her white hair was braided into a coronet around her head, and she wore a navy jumpsuit with military-style epaulets.

As he looked at her, Gavin's mind stumbled. Grandmother? The word didn't fit.

Around the room the others reacted to the Chairwoman's presence. Travis smoothly got to his feet, ingratiating smile in place. The matron dropped her magazine and stood. Jeff and April watched warily, but such was the power of Portia Carver's presence they, too, stood.

Only Kristy seemed unimpressed, casually closing her puzzle book.

"Well, Travis?" Portia Carver smiled. "What's all this about an emergency?"

"News of three separate attacks on Futurists," Travis summarized. "A Kithkinner, Penny Lacrosse, is talking to the Council now."

"Penny Lacrosse, formerly Penny Gillis?" Sharp green eyes kindled.

"You know her?" Travis asked, surprised.

"Of course she does." Kristy stepped forward. "Penny's her granddaughter."

The regal head turned. "Hello, Kristy. Are my daughter and son-in-law with you, or did they abandon you like all the rest?"

The cruel thrust took Gavin aback. Kristy's assumed poise fled. "You don't know?" Her childish voice rose to a shriek. "You don't know what happened to them?"

Gavin stepped forward, but April beat him to her, putting her arms around Kristy.

Portia Carver backed up a step, her forehead wrinkled in displeasure. "What is the child going on about?"

"They're dead!" Kristy yelled, face red with fury. "They died three years ago, and you didn't know!"

For an instant Portia Carver stood very still. Then she turned to Travis. "Take me to the Council."

Her hand trembled on Travis's arm, but Gavin saw no tears in those hard green eyes, no grief on that unlined face.

• 3 •

Quillon Charged in Dunstan Murder. When the headline flashed by, Matt slowed the speed of the microfilm reader and backtracked. He and Genevieve were at the Kresge Library at Wayne State University in Detroit doing research.

Reading through the newspaper account of Dorothy Dunstan's murder and Dan Quillon's arrest, Matt quickly found out that

Genevieve was right: there had been overwhelming forensic evidence against Dan Quillon. How could anyone be so stupid as to just keep the murder weapon in his glove compartment?

Stupid or very arrogant.

He almost would have wondered if the mysterious Selector had framed Dan Quillon, were it not for the report of the trial several months later. Dan Quillon had pleaded not guilty by reason of insanity and talked about a "Voice" in his head. The court had sentenced him to life in an insane asylum.

Even more disturbing than the Voice was Dan Quillon's confession halfway through the trial that he had murdered Mary Dunstan and buried the body. Prior to that he had insisted he knew nothing about Genevieve's disappearance and the testimony of one of her friends that she had been at a party in a nearby town at the time of the murder had supported him.

Although hardly a saint—his wife had left him because of repeated alcohol abuse—Quillon had been leading a fairly quiet life for four years before Dorothy Dunstan's murder, attending AA meetings and holding down a job as a bus driver.

Bus schedules had shown that Mary had taken the bus he regularly drove several times a week. The prosecutor had speculated that Quillon had fixated on the pretty college student and had killed Dorothy Dunstan while in a rage over not finding Mary.

Aside from the bus route Quillon had no connection to either Mary or her aunt.

When questioned as to why he'd suddenly confessed, Quillon had said, "If the Voice says I did it, I must have." He claimed not to remember where he'd hidden the body.

Chilled and uneasy, Matt walked away from the microfilm reader until he could see Genevieve standing at a blond wood computer workstation, searching for articles on the first murder she had witnessed. She looked reassuringly alive, if a little thinner than the smiling graduation photo in the newspaper. Why the hell would Quillon confess to a murder he hadn't committed? Was he really insane, or was the Voice linked to the Selector somehow?

Matt printed out a negative to positive copy of the trial article and hurried across the brown tweed carpet to join Genevieve. "Take a look at this."

She read silently, only her sudden intake of breath alerting Matt that she'd just read about her "death." "I don't understand."

"Me either." Matt changed the subject. "Find anything?"

Genevieve shook herself and turned back to her computer. "Maybe. I started out with (Murder or kill?) and (husband and wife) and (stab? or knife or cut?) limited by the date, May 27, 1998, and I pulled up ten articles. I'm just going through them. So far nothing jibes." Genevieve clicked on the next article.

Matt read two accounts of couples being murdered over her shoulder before they hit one that looked promising. "There." Genevieve tapped the screen. "Their throats were cut." The other two couples had been stabbed in the chest or the back. "And look here, it says they were killed in the basement of their home in Spokane, Washington. Michael and Terisa Richmond." They read the full-text of the article in silence. The police had no suspects and were leaning toward an interrupted burglary scenario.

"I think it's them." Genevieve printed the article before going on to the next one. None of the remaining four was correct in all of the details.

"Michael and Terisa Richmond," Genevieve said aloud. "I'm glad I finally know their names. I've seen them so often, watched them die . . ."

Matt squeezed her shoulder. "Do a new search using their names. See if anyone was ever arrested."

(Michael or Terisa) with Richmond, Genevieve typed in. The machine hummed, then said: 1 article. Genevieve called it up, but it was the murder one they'd already seen.

"Try a nickname, like Mike," Matt suggested. "Or another way of spelling Terisa. The i is a little unusual."

(Michael or Mike or Terisa or Teresa or Theresa) with Richmond. 1 article.

"Damn."

"Keep trying," Matt said, moving to the computer station next to hers. "I'll search for one of the other murders."

He and Genevieve tried various searches on different indexes for two hours, but pulled up either nothing or over fifty articles. Genevieve didn't remember her other dreams as well because she'd only had them once, and many of the dates on them were only approximate.

"I was trying to forget my dreams, not make a diary of them," she'd said.

The fatigue and strain on her face worried Matt. "It's getting late." The sun lay on the horizon. "Why don't we find a motel and something to eat?"

"Sounds good. I'm starved."

Matt picked an independent motel instead of one of the big chains and got a double room under a false name, paying in cash.

Surprisingly, Matt found himself a little nervous, hauling in their luggage after supper. Although Genevieve had lived in his house for seven months, they'd never shared a room.

"I'm going to take a shower," Genevieve said without looking at him. She vanished into the bathroom.

Matt found himself holding his breath, listening to the small sounds of Genevieve taking off her clothes and then starting the water running. His always vivid imagination tortured him.

To distract himself he went to the phone and dialed Ian's home number. He didn't want to talk to Ian at the station just in case he was now wanted for murder.

Ian answered the phone on the third ring. He barely let Matt finish saying hello. "Matt! I've been waiting for you to call. I've had one hell of an interesting afternoon, thanks to you."

Matt tensed. Had Crabtree's body been discovered?

Ian kept on talking. "I checked out Crabtree. You were right, he does have a record, but get this: both of his priors are for something that happened last night. Before that he was as clean as a whistle. Then he gets one speeding ticket at 3 A.M. and a second at 4:30 A.M., only this time he didn't stop. He ran the cop off the road. The cop took his license plate and got his name that way. I talked to him this afternoon, and he was still mad as hell."

"No doubt." Matt sat down on one of the double beds.

"Anyhow," Ian said, "I got Crabtree's home address and phoned his house. I spoke to his girlfriend. She was absolutely frantic—"

Girlfriend. Matt's stomach plunged. He hadn't thought of a girlfriend. And Crabtree was dead, had died in Matt's own bedroom. . . .

"—said she'd expected him home at 6 A.M.—he works the night shift at a bottle factory—so she got worried and called his boss. Turns out Crabtree just up and walked off the job at 1 A.M."

Matt wondered what time Genevieve had woken from her dream.

"He caused a big pileup at the factory, wrecked one of the machines. The foreman wants to press charges—"

Matt interrupted. "He just up and walked off mid-shift? That's odd. Was he talking to someone, or did he get an important phone call?" From the Selector.

"Not as far as I know. Anyhow, that isn't the oddest part. Not an hour after I get off the phone some guy shows up claiming he's Crabtree's brother-in-law. Says his sister is worried sick about the guy and the last they heard Crabtree was heading for Red Squirrel to talk to some poet fella, Matt something or other. He actually wanted me to get a warrant to search your house!"

"Oh?" Matt's throat felt tight. He and Genevieve had tried to clean up all the bloodstains and fingerprints, but a good forensic team would still find traces of hair and fingerprints in Matt's bedroom.

Ian continued, oblivious. "I told him his theory was real interesting seeing as how I had just talked to Crabtree's girlfriend on the phone, and she didn't think he was married."

"What did he say to that?"

"Nothing much. He blustered a little, but I'd caught him out, and he knew it. I told him Crabtree was wanted for assault and several lesser charges, and that I would spend my time looking for him, not harassing honest citizens." Ian hesitated. "I didn't tell him you were out of town. He looked like a bit of a bruiser. I thought he was going to take a swing at me, but Kowalski wandered over, and he left."

"Thanks, Ian. This is sounding worse and worse. You take care, all right? Whatever they want with Genevieve they seem to want it bad. I don't think they'll quibble over murdering a law officer."

The shower stopped.

Matt's heartbeat picked up, even as he coached himself to be patient. Both he and Genevieve had been through a lot of emotional upheavals in one day. Crabtree's attack, his epileptic seizure, Crabtree's death, and the truth about Genevieve's amnesia. The barrier of Genevieve's secrets had been broken; she'd accepted his proposal. How could he ask for more?

He couldn't, but that didn't stop him from wanting more.

His fists clenched as he remembered the knife scraping down her neck. He'd nearly lost her today. He needed to reassure himself that she was alive and unhurt. He needed to hold her, to breathe in the warm scent of her skin, to feel her body pressed against his.

She'd nearly died, and the Selector was still out there. Matt was grimly aware that they might not survive their next encounter with the Selector.

More than her body, he wanted—no, needed—her trust.

"Don't worry about me," Ian said cheerfully in Matt's ear. "You just take care of Genevieve and have a good honeymoon. Can you give me your phone number in case I need to get in touch with you?"

The door opened with a soft click, and Genevieve stepped out amidst a cloud of steam.

Her hair curled in damp tendrils around her face. She was wearing a white terry-cloth robe, loosely belted at the waist, that displayed an enticing amount of cleavage.

Genevieve caught his gaze, then gracefully shrugged out of the robe and stood naked before him, her expression both shy and proud.

She was beautiful. Matt got to his feet without conscious volition. He realized he was still holding the phone, that Ian was waiting for an answer, but he couldn't remember the question. "I'll call you back later." He started to hang up.

But Ian's voice suddenly changed, turning the fire in Matt's veins to ice water. "Where did you hide the body, poet man? I need it to make the charges stick."

• 4 •

Penny's temper simmered. For the last forty minutes she'd sat and listened to the Council discuss earthshaking matters like: should Kithkinners be tested for Talent before the age of sixteen? should the membership fee be raised from $7 to $10? By the time someone finally introduced New Business she was boiling.

She stood up. All eyes flashed to her face, then dropped to her stomach. Fighting back a blush, Penny launched into her story.

They were strangers, difficult to read, tiny hard kernels of personality. She fed their faint curiosity first, then played to their instinct for danger. She'd reached her arrival at David Calder's when the Council doors opened.

What little momentum she'd gained drained away. With flickers of relief and respect, the Council stood to welcome Portia Carver.

Portia abandoned her escort and walked to the head of the table. She gestured for everyone else to take a seat. They sat, leaving Penny the only one standing. Portia inclined her head. "Please continue."

Penny started her story over from the beginning, trying to rebuild some tension. Portia Carver listened intently, but Penny sensed an underlying hostility that made her nervous.

"All the attacks were aimed at Futurists," Penny finished. "I believe they all have some common cause rather than individual lunatics."

Silence from the Council.

Portia Carver leaned forward. "And do you have any idea what this common cause might be?"

The lullaby didn't apply to Bethany or David Calder. "No."

"Do you have any idea who these hypothetical killers might be?" [*Hostility like leaping flames.*]

Penny's temper went back on simmer. Hypothetical? "No, I hoped the Council might know."

Portia attacked. "Why would the Council know? This is the first we've heard of this conspiracy of organized madmen. The term is an oxymoron."

"Hitler's army consisted of organized madmen." A hit, a mental flinch from Portia. Penny pressed on. "Organized madmen are the reason the Futurists exist. Some crazy old man wanted to wipe us out."

Green eyes flashed. "The 'crazy old man' as you call him has been dead for four years."

"So?" Penny shrugged. "Maybe his son decided to take over the family business."

"Nigel Carver had no sons." Portia made each word a deadly blow. "He had one daughter. Your mother."

Your mother. Penny clutched the table as Damaris auditioned for the Rockettes. Her mother the crazy old man's daughter? Portia Carver, founder of the Futurists, the old man's wife? Her grandparents?

Green eyes moved in for the kill. "For the past twenty-five years your mother insisted the Futurists were in danger. She married a non-Futurist and falsified her name. She scattered her children across the country to 'protect' them. If anyone was crazy, it was she.

"And now here comes one of her children, also married to a non-Futurist, claiming the same things. Well, I'm sick of it! The danger does not exist!" Portia Carver stood, thumping the table. Monarchs could also be tyrants. "I've kept the Futurists safe for the past fifty years, and they'll stay safe for fifty more!"

The Council applauded thunderously. Portia Carver sat down.

Penny shook. "I'm sorry you feel that way, Grandmother, but closing your eyes won't make the danger go away." She walked toward the door.

Portia Carver wouldn't let her have the last word. "Nigel Carver is dead! Dead, do you hear me? *I heard him die.*"

Penny kept going. Pushing through the doors into the waiting room was like exiting a gas chamber into clean air. Jeff took one look at her face and went to her side. Gavin, April, and Kristy gathered around, looking anxious.

"Well?" Gavin asked.

Penny shook her head, leaning gratefully into Jeff's supporting arm. "They don't believe me." She felt blank, exhausted. "Portia Carver doesn't want to believe it, and, therefore, neither will the Council."

Gavin scowled. April bit her lip. Only Kristy seemed unsurprised. "She never listens to anyone."

Penny focused on her. "What do you know about Portia Carver?" Did Kristy know about the crazy old man?

Jeff glanced around. "Listen, why don't we talk about this somewhere else? Who's ready for an ice-cream cone?"

Penny's gaze touched the middle-aged woman pretending to read a *Bride* magazine and nodded. "Let's go."

Bobby woke up cranky, but the promise of ice cream hushed him. A five-minute drive to Dairy Queen, a brief bathroom break while the others ordered their cones, and then they all sat down on plastic chairs. The perfect place for a clandestine meeting. Penny stifled a crazy laugh; what they had come to talk about wasn't funny.

"Portia let something slip at the meeting. The name of the crazy old man who tried to kill off the Futurists."

"Who?" Gavin asked. He didn't know.

"Nigel Carver. Portia's husband. Our grandfather."

"Ah, jeez." Gavin slumped back in his chair. "I should have stayed a pitiful orphan."

Penny wasn't watching him. Her eyes were on Kristy, on Kristy's lack of reaction. "You knew, didn't you?"

Kristy nodded. "My first mother told me."

"Enough secrets, Kristy," Gavin said. "Talk."

"I'll talk," Kristy told them loftily. "You just make sure you listen. 'Last born speaks, who listens seeks, to free the one who cried.'" She checked to make sure she had their attention, then paused to lick her cone.

"Okay, the history of the Futurists and Portia Carver. After World War II Nigel shows up on Portia's doorstep. Says he knew her brother, he died bravely, blah, blah, blah. Portia is very poor, and she falls in love with him. They get married, and he takes her to a better life in America. They have a daughter—our mother."

"When Mom was three, she starts screaming and refuses to get on a horse because she knows she'll get hurt. Nigel puts her on the horse anyway. She breaks her arm, and Nigel freaks out and tries to kill her."

Penny stopped licking her cone. Kill her? Kill his three-year-old daughter?

"Portia stops him, and he attacks her. Says she's breeding coward-ice into the human race. He swears to wipe all cowards off the face of the earth."

Crazy. Damaris kicked.

"Portia runs away with our mother. She decides psychics are an improvement and gets her relatives to form the Futurists. Nigel tries to kill them. The Futurists move to Canada and set up the web. Except for a couple of times Nigel never finds them again. The end." Kristy hastily licked her dripping cone.

"Portia swears up and down Nigel's dead. Says she heard him die." Penny frowned. "That's weird. She didn't *see* him die, she heard him."

"Not if you have my Talent." Gavin grimaced. "I hear, I don't see."

"The hag!" April burst out suddenly. "The hag! That's what you meant, didn't you, Kristy?"

Kristy nodded, grief welling up on the verge of tears. Penny didn't understand.

April explained. "Psychic Agony. Portia heard Nigel dying: she still *loved* him, but she didn't know Kristy's parents were dead. She didn't hear her daughter die."

Penny added her own bit of proof. "When she spoke to the Coun-cil she sounded as if she hated out mother. Maybe she blamed her for turning Nigel against her."

"How could she love someone who tried to kill their daughter?" Gavin asked, revolted.

Penny shrugged. "How can all those women profess to love the husbands who beat them?" Penny remembered something else that had been bothering her. "Kristy, Portia said our mother was crazy.

Was she? I mean, according to the lullaby she had seven kids. Did she give them all up for adoption? Why keep having them, only to give them away?"

"She wasn't crazy," Kristy said defensively.

Penny sensed pain on Kristy's part. She had been older than the others had when she'd been adopted; the rejection had hurt more. "Then why?" Penny asked.

"I'm not sure." Kristy looked down at her hands, then up again. "It had something to do with a vision of the future she'd had. She said once that she'd made a terrible mistake, that she'd been too weak to do something she should have, and bad things were going to happen because of what she'd done. She said everyone in the lullaby had to be born in order for things to be put right again. She said"—Kristy's voice became very soft—"that she was sorry and that she loved all of us very much. She wouldn't have given us away if keeping us hadn't been too dangerous."

There was silence around the table for a moment until Jeff shifted and broke it. "So what now?"

"Portia isn't going to help us," Gavin said. "We might as well leave." Nods of agreement around the table.

"I think we should stay a little longer," Jeff said unexpectedly.

This from the man who hadn't wanted to come to Calgary at all? Penny started to object, but Gavin beat her to it.

"Why?" Gavin demanded. "There's no help for us here. They don't believe us."

Jeff's defenses rose like the drawbridge on a castle. "There might not be any help, but there is information. I don't know about you, but I don't intend to be on the run for the rest of my life. I have a job and a mortgage to pay off. Right now the enemy knows a lot more about us than we do about him. He knew who you were, that you were all Futurists. He knew where to find you. He knew about the web houses. Don't you see? *He's a Futurist himself.*"

• 5 •

"Who is this?" Matt asked sharply. "What have you done to Ian?"

Just like that Genevieve knew what had happened. A coldness that had nothing to do with her nakedness sliced through her. She grabbed the phone out of Matt's hands. "Hello?"

"It's good to hear your voice, Mary," the Selector said, using Ian's voice. "I usually have to kill someone before you'll talk to me."

Fear and anger leapt and guttered inside her like a candle flame, one waning while the other waxed. "What have you done to Ian?"

The Selector laughed, and the difference between Ian's normal warm laugh and the one Genevieve now heard was like the difference between water burbling over rocks and a knife grinding against a whetstone. "You know perfectly well what I've done. I've turned your sheriff into my hunting dog. He's not a very good dog—he needs lots of supervision—but he'll do." His voice deepened. "Where are you, Mary?"

"Let Ian go." Genevieve's grip tightened on the receiver.

"Now why would I do that?"

Genevieve saw a chance and took it. "Let Ian go, and I'll tell you where I am."

Matt sucked in a breath, but Genevieve's whole attention was focused on the phone. By the Selector's pause she knew she'd surprised him.

"An interesting proposition. But how do I know you'll tell the truth?"

"If I lie, you'll find out soon enough and reclaim Ian."

"True," the Selector said. "Very well, I accept. Where are you?"

Genevieve opened her mouth, but no sound came out. Every instinct inside her screamed not to tell him. Every *selfish* instinct. "What's your name?" she asked instead.

"You know my name. I am the Selector."

"Your real name."

"The Selector is my real name, my true name. You're the only person alive who knows who I really am." His voice resonated with the deep loneliness of the only human being left alive on the planet.

Genevieve stifled a pang of pity. The reason he was lonely was because he killed everyone who came within arm's length.

"You're cheating." Her skin chilled to ice. "What name do you go by in the real world?"

"I go by many names. Dan Quillon, Ronald Carver, John Crabtree, and Charles Mathieson to name a few," he said impatiently. "If we're asking questions, it's my turn now, Mary. Why do you want to know my name?"

She dared not lie. Genevieve's nails dug into her palms. "So we can turn you over to the police and have you arrested."

"You intend to hunt me?" Mirth vibrated in his voice. "What an — amusing idea. The poet man thought of it, didn't he?"

"Yes." Somehow talking with the Selector, their plan didn't seem very smart. It seemed downright dumb, like trying to catch a tiger with bare hands.

But it was working, in a fashion. The Selector's arrogance had given her two more names to work with. "Where were you born?"

He laughed, a full-throated chuckle that almost made Genevieve want to smile and laugh with him. "Wrong question, Mary. I don't know where I was born. I never bothered to find out. You should have asked where *you* were born. Or who your parents are. Wouldn't you like to know? The fat broad who brought you up swore she never told you."

Genevieve's outrage over his reference to Aunt Dorothy smothered under a mounting wave of dread. "What do you mean? How do you know who my parents are?"

"Unh-uh." The Selector clicked his tongue at her. "You already asked your question: it's my turn. Have you married the poet man yet?"

"No." Genevieve didn't like the turn of conversation. She started to ask another question, but the Selector overrode her.

"Good. You don't belong to him. You're mine." Possession rang in his voice.

"No." Genevieve could barely breathe; she felt as if she were drowning in an ocean of black crude. "I'm not yours. I'll never be yours."

In a crystal moment of clarity she realized that this was what she had fought against all along. Attraction. Possession. Not death. After the first few dreams he'd stopped trying to stab her, but her terror had risen like mercury on a hot day. The real danger had been that she might willingly give herself to the Selector.

She'd always told herself she hadn't made love with Matt to protect her lie of having amnesia, but suddenly she wasn't so sure it had been a pair of green contacts keeping them apart.

"You're mine, and you know it."

Genevieve fought him with every weapon she possessed. "No, I belong to Matt, and he belongs to me."

"Have you slept with him?"

She wanted to lie. She tried to lie, but the word wouldn't come out. She felt so cold. "We're in room 307 of the Sleepytime Inn in Detroit. Now leave and let me talk to Ian."

"I'll let him go as I promised, but he may not want to speak to you." The Selector chuckled maliciously.

"Why?" Genevieve demanded, instantly suspicious.

No reply. The Selector was gone.

Genevieve flinched as the phone on the other end was dropped on the floor. "Ian? Ian, can you hear me?"

Matt started to come close, but she waved him away, listening as hard as she could. What had the Selector done to Ian?

Fumbling on the other end. Raspy breathing. "Gen'vieve?" Ian's voice was slurred.

"Ian, are you all right? Is the Selector gone?"

"Run." More labored breathing. "Don't let . . . him catch you. Run."

Genevieve felt tears start in the backs of her eyes. "We will. But what about you? Should I call you an ambulance?"

A long pause. "No," Ian said at last. "I'm dead already. Gut shot. Wouldn't tell him Vegas. . . . Hurt me, shot me in the stomach. Didn't tell. . . . Then, the claw. Told him then. Screamed it. Ears bleedin'."

"I'm so sorry," Genevieve whispered, eyes closed. Ian was a good man, and he was dying because of her.

"Not yer fault. Tell Matt." His breathing grew heavier, more ragged. "Kill da bastard fer me."

"I will."

In. Out. In. Out. Gasping. "Can't see. It's all red . . ." His voice was a bare whisper.

Ian was dying, but it might take a while. Time Genevieve didn't have. "He'll be coming soon." Guilt twisted her insides. "I have to go."

"Yess," a hiss of agreement. Ian was too much a friend to ask her to risk her own life to comfort him in his last minutes.

Gently, as if she could somehow touch Ian through the medium of sound waves, Genevieve hung up the phone. He would die alone and in pain.

In that moment she hated the Selector with a virulent force that even Aunt Dorothy's death had not engendered.

"What happened?" Matt asked, face anxious. "Did he let Ian go?"

She nodded, eyes closed. The Selector had followed the letter of their agreement. It was her own fault for not spelling things out more carefully.

"Thank God," Matt said.

She couldn't bring herself to tell him his praise was misplaced. Not now. Not yet.

"Right then." Matt rallied himself. "The Selector knows where we are. We have to get out of here."

He was right. Even now Genevieve could feel the danger gathering itself, coming closer. Tension invaded her muscles. But there was something she'd started that she wanted to finish. Something she should have done a long time ago.

"Not yet." Taking her courage into her hands, she reached up and unbuckled his belt.

Matt stilled. At her touch all the hairs on his body stood on end and desire dilated his eyes. He wanted her, but he hesitated, holding on to sanity a moment longer. "Do we have time?"

Danger rushing towards them on slick rails.

Ian dead or dying.

Genevieve had lived on the edge of death too long to waste time wailing and gnashing her teeth over something she couldn't change. She couldn't save Ian, but she could make love to Matt. "I need you," she told him. The words had never been truer. She lay back on the bed, open to him, and he followed her down, crushing her with his weight. He kissed her with hard passion, and she responded gratefully in kind.

"Why?" he asked, coming up for air. She knew what he was asking. Why now and not later when they could take their time, be tender?

Her hands tangled in his hair. No more lies. "Because I love you. Because I'm not going to let the Selector come between us anymore. Because I don't want to die with regrets. And because I want to hurt the Selector for what he's done to us, done to Ian and Aunt Dorothy. This will hurt him. Okay?" She arched her body into his.

"Okay," Matt gasped. The fire took them both.

• 6 •

Jeff and Gavin were elected to go to the Kithkin Klub to do some computer digging into the Futurist killer and other brothers and sisters from the lullaby while April, Penny, and the kids went shopping.

Gavin didn't want to return to the Kithkin Klub. Their rudeness and refusal to help made him want to shun them in turn, but Jeff was right. They needed information.

The lure of finding Bethany's murderer dangled like a carrot in front of him.

He had plans for the bastard. He wanted justice for Bethany, and if he couldn't get it from a trial, judge, and jury he'd get it another way.

But first he had to get access to confidential computer records. If he had the Shine, it wouldn't be a problem. Travis or good ol' Ron would have the receptionist begging him to have a cup of tea while she looked the information up for him.

A college-age girl had replaced the haughty receptionist and, while Gavin didn't exactly charm her, she happily gave them direc-tions to the computers. "All Kithkinners have access to the database." Gavin had been prepared to claim that Jeff was an Empath he knew, but the girl just waved them on.

"That was almost too easy," Gavin said, sitting down in front of a terminal. He and Jeff were alone, the only people with nothing better to do on a bright Saturday afternoon.

"Yeah," Jeff agreed. "So much for narrowing down the suspects. If I could get in, so could anyone."

"Leave the suspects to me," Gavin said. Justice. "You try to find the rest of the family."

Jeff nodded, and they got to work.

First, Gavin decided to get a firmer fix on when the killing started. Once he had a date he could start looking for new members who'd joined around the same time. One new member in particular who stalked them as a cat among pigeons.

Typing awkwardly with one hand, he opened up the Members database and called up Bethany's record. He breathed a sigh of relief. The database had fourteen fields, including birth and death dates, membership dates, parents, addresses, and telephone numbers.

Although he'd resisted getting a full-time job in the hotel his dad had managed, preferring McJobs, which didn't carry the taint of nepotism, Gavin had pitched in behind the desk enough times to know his way around dBASE.

Gavin collated a set of all the Kithkinners who had died in 2001: 32 out of 8398. Suddenly realizing the 8398 represented the total number of members since the founding of the Futurists fifty years ago, Gavin made another set, this time of all the dead excluding the 32 from the current year: 3102 out of 8398.

Gavin jotted the number down and subtracted: 32 dead out of 5296 members. Approximately 6 out of 1000. Under the national average, but not exceptional.

He checked how many died in 2000 for comparison and got a similar number, 29. He scowled. This wasn't working. Maybe he should leave . . . No! Justice, he reminded himself. But he'd been so certain 2001's number would be significantly higher than 2000's.

Maybe the murders had only begun in the last month, and the numbers hadn't been affected yet. . . .

Gavin cursed. The last month. Sometimes his brain didn't work. This was only late April of 2001. Thirty-two deaths in four months *was* significantly higher than 29 deaths in twelve months.

Gavin checked 1999. Twenty deaths that year, a considerable drop. He did a month by month check of 2000. One to two dead each month until November. Five that month and eight in December.

Three extra deaths in November. On a hunch Gavin called up the five records and printed them. Jeff glanced up at the printer's sudden activity, but said nothing. The inkjet printer seemed very loud in the silence.

Scanning the columns Gavin saw one of the deaths was of a seventy-seven-year-old Futurist. Presuming she'd died of old age, that left four possible murders.

Of the four deaths left, three of them had occurred in the last week of November. A chill prickled his scalp: the killing had started then.

He started a new search. He wanted a list of Kithkinners who had joined from September to December 2000. The computer coughed up thirty-four names. He pressed the print button.

"Find something?" Jeff asked.

"A list of suspects. How are you doing?" Gavin looked over his shoulder while waiting for the printer to finish.

"Not so good," Jeff admitted. "Portia Carver is listed as having one daughter, Terisa, but there's no record under Terisa Carver." Kristy had known their parent's first names, Terisa and Michael, but not their last name. "Penny's record gives the Gillises names, and then says adopted. I've been going through the records looking for adoptees within a certain age span. One possibility so far."

"Sounds good," Gavin said.

Jeff grimaced. "*Your* record only lists the Lindbergs, and Kristy doesn't have a record."

"Keep trying," Gavin said, but his concentration had been broken. The room felt too hot. Too quiet. The filing noises in the next room had stopped. Secretary gone for her coffee break, Gavin presumed. He wouldn't mind going for coffee about now. A breath of fresh air would be nice.

He made himself sit down again. Justice.

He tapped in a few letters and paused. God, he hated this building. Penny and April had been smart not to come back. If Jeff hadn't suggested coming here, they could have been out of the city by now.

Gavin started to sweat, his mind teetering on the edge of some unpleasant discovery. Only Jeff had wanted to come. Gavin had accompanied him out of a sense of duty to Bethany's screaming ghost and because one Kithkinner was needed to go to get them inside the building.

One Kithkinner . . .

None of the five psychics had wanted to return.

Stones of silence weighted the high-rise, as if everyone had decided to go on coffee break at the same time. All the psychics had left.

"Jeff!" Gavin stood up so fast his chair rolled three feet on metal wheels.

Jeff looked up, surprised.

"Print your list, and let's get out of here. Something bad is going to happen." Gavin folded his own list and shoved it inside his coat while Jeff gaped. He grabbed Jeff's shoulder. "On second thought, let's just get out of here."

For a second Jeff balked, then followed. "What's going on?"

"Don't know," Gavin said, already halfway down the hall. "Danger."

He hesitated half a second at the elevators then veered toward the stairwell. They were twenty-two floors up, but it felt right. He broke the glass on a emergency alarm in case there were any nonpsychics in the building.

The shrilling of the fire alarm jangled Gavin's nerves. The danger felt close, overpowering.

He and Jeff pounded down three flights of stairs. Gavin kept his hand on the rail, hugging the inside track and using the rail to pivot where the stairs switchbacked. Jeff shadowed his heels. If Gavin stumbled, Jeff would fall, too.

Gavin didn't stumble. The movement made his injured shoulder feel like a giant was trying to rip his arm out of his socket, but he gritted his teeth and kept running. As they neared the eighteenth floor, two people burst into the stairwell and started down. The fire alarm had saved someone.

Saved them from what? Gavin ignored his mind's question. It didn't matter. Right now the only important thing was to get out of this building. Get to safety.

Get the hell out of Calgary.

• 7 •

Gavin didn't realize who was running in front of them until Portia Carver tripped. She cried out as she fell four steps onto the landing in between the sixteenth and fifteenth floors.

Close on her heels Gavin grabbed the railing to stop. Jeff barreled into him, and Gavin's feet shot down two steps. He banged a shin and wrenched his shoulder. Red agony flared in front of his eyes. For a second he feared he would pass out from the pain, but his danger instinct forced air back into his lungs, cleared his vision just in time to see Portia's companion vanish down the next turn.

Pain contorted her face as she sat up. Her mouth moved, but Gavin couldn't hear her over the harsh Klaxon of the fire alarm. It scarcely mattered.

Jeff pulled her to her feet. Portia's face turned the color of old milk, but she did not faint. "My ankle!"

Jeff put an arm around her waist and helped her down the stairs. Gavin walked behind, unable to help.

Hop, step, limp. Hop, step, limp. Their hellishly slow progress maddened Gavin. His danger instinct urged him to overtake them, but he restrained it. How would he face Penny if he lived and Jeff died?

Jeff stopped on the fifteenth floor. "We'll have to take the elevator! This is too slow."

A twinge of unease struck Gavin, but the only other choice was to abandon Portia in the stairwell.

He held the door open for them. Portia limped through, face grim but game.

The Cambrian Building was organized in a series of squares with the elevators, washrooms, and a second set of stairs in the center column and offices forming a larger square around it.

Gavin jabbed the down button between the two elevators. To his relief, the button lit up. He knew you weren't supposed to use the elevators during a fire, but he couldn't remember if that was in case of electrical failure or just to reserve their use for the handicapped and the firefighters.

Portia pushed Jeff's hands away. "I can take care of myself from here."

"Be my guest." The fire alarm drowned Jeff out, but Gavin thought he saw Jeff mouth, "You old biddy."

Gavin's gaze returned to the elevators like a compass needle swinging toward magnetic north. He jabbed the button again and wished fervently for a panel to tell him what floor the elevators were on.

Two interminable minutes passed. Were the elevators moving or were they sitting on the bottom floor?

"What the hell?" Jeff said. He put his hand on a white cord running around the elevator bank and traced it around the corner.

The down arrow lit.

"Jeff! Come back, the elevator's coming!"

The alarm shrilled furiously. Had Jeff heard him?

"Jeff!"

" — right there," Jeff called.

The elevator doors opened.

Portia limped inside. Gavin followed and put one hand on the door to keep it open, torn between fear for Jeff and a dreadful tearing need to *hurry*.

"Jeff!"

"Thirty seconds and not one more," Portia said fiercely.

Her danger instinct must be riding her just as hard as his. Whatever was going to happen would happen *soon*. "Jeff, get the hell over here!"

Thirty seconds.

Portia jabbed the CLOSE DOOR button just as Jeff dashed around the corner.

The doors started to close, jerked open again when Jeff crossed in front of the light sensor, then closed a second time. Portia had already pressed M for main, but she hit it again in a fury of impatience.

"Bomb," Jeff gasped. Gavin didn't think he'd heard right, but Jeff immediately repeated himself. "There's a bomb in the stairwell. The white cord is called det cord . . . it's explosive and someone's packed it with plastique for good measure."

Worse than fire. A bomb.

Jeff consulted his watch. "We have three minutes and forty-five seconds by the clock."

Compulsively, Gavin watched the floor panel light flicker slowly down. Fourteen . . . thirteen . . . He timed the floors. About four seconds per floor. A little under a minute to reach the lobby and two minutes forty-five seconds to get out before the building collapsed around their ears.

If no one else was using the elevator, and it didn't stop on any of the other floors. *If* there wasn't an electrical failure.

"If you knew it was a bomb, why didn't you disarm it?" Portia asked.

"I'm an engineering technician, not a demolitions expert," Jeff said irately. "It could have been booby-trapped and triggered an immediate explosion."

Tenth floor.

The elevator was faster than the stairs. So why had both his and Portia's first choice been the stairs?

Ninth floor.

Because the elevators would blow first, dummy.

Eighth floor.

The three of them were silent, dividing their attention between the descending floor numbers and their watches. Three minutes and fifteen seconds now.

It would be close, but Gavin figured they would make it. Portia would have to limp real fast on her ankle, but he would elude the enemy for—Gavin counted—the third time in twenty-four hours.

Bethany was the only one who'd died so far. Everyone else's danger instinct had allowed them to slip the noose. It didn't pay to hunt Futurists as their enemy would soon learn—

Oh shit. Their enemy already knew because he was a Futurist himself.

Fifth floor.

Gavin suddenly noticed that he and Portia were both standing against the sides of the elevator, leaving Jeff, the nonpsychic in the middle. In the line of fire . . .

He punched the second-floor button.

"What are you doing?" Portia screeched.

Gavin cut her off. "The bastard knows we're coming. He's laid a double trap. There'll be someone with a gun waiting for us at the bottom."

A second's silence.

Fourth floor.

"And how will stopping help?" Portia demanded. "There's no way off the second floor. No pedway and all the windows are too thick to break."

Third floor.

"It'll confuse him. He'll think we got off and watch the stairs instead." Maybe. The stairwell was only a few feet away, more likely the gunman would cover both at once, but at least it was a chance.

Second floor.

The elevator stopped and the doors slid partway open. Portia stabbed the CLOSE DOOR button. Gavin pushed her hand away and pressed OPEN DOOR. "No! He has to notice that we've stopped."

Precious seconds bloomed and withered away. Gavin's heartbeat sped up, sweat greasing his skin. Bomb ticking down. Two minutes fifty-five seconds now.

Mouthing curses, Jeff hopped on one foot and took off his shoes as the doors finally closed.

"Take one." Jeff handed him a hard-heeled dress shoe. "Use it as a missile."

Gavin took it. Portia had abandoned her heels in the stairwell, and he wore rubber-soled sneakers. He made himself stand in front of the doors. "I go first. You've got Penny and Bobby to think about."

Ping! Main floor.

The elevator dipped, then settled.

Door sliding back . . . Gavin exploded through the narrow opening, crouched low to avoid being hit. He saw the bodies at the last moment and scrambled to avoid stepping on them, off-balance. The gunman had been guarding the stairs, but he was turning now—

Gavin hurled the shoe. It flipped once in the air and hit the man bang in the forehead. He flinched, but didn't drop the gun. Despite the red mark on his forehead he smiled as he swung the gun over. "Good-bye, Lindberg."

The killer was a short, bald man in a navy pin-striped suit. He was going to get shot by a banker, for crying out loud.

Jeff's second shoe knocked the gun out of the bald man's hand, and in the next instant Jeff tackled him to the floor.

The gun skittered across the tiles. Portia efficiently scooped it up and aimed it at the man's head. Not so much as a wisp of hair had escaped her iron braids in all the fuss.

"Let's go!" Jeff hauled the bald man to his feet and shoved him ahead of him, twisting his arm behind his back. "Go, go, go!"

The bomb.

Gavin started to run for the doors. He got four steps before he remembered the bodies. His danger instinct screamed at him as he turned back.

His stomach heaved when he recognized Travis, lying facedown in a pool of blood. The coed receptionist sprawled not far away. At first glance she appeared unharmed, but when Gavin hurried over he saw a small black hole in her forehead. She'd never fill in for anyone again. Movements frantic, he turned Travis onto his back. Gaping eyes. Blood like a bucket of paint. Three chest wounds.

Get out of here!

Three paces from the doors, the bomb went off.

A flash of light lit the stairwell, and Gavin dived through the glass doors as the concussion of air blew out all the windows.

He went down on one knee on the sidewalk, then was up again and running. Pain knifed through his shoulder, but his instinct kept him moving.

Metal shrieked and groaned behind him, steel girders snapping like pretzels, as the thirty-story building collapsed in on itself in a terrible, loud sliding roar.

On the plus side, the fire alarm finally stopped.

Gavin fought a weird urge to laugh as a sofa tumbled past, splintering on the sidewalk a few feet away. Dust drifted down from above, powdering his hair. He caught up with the others and pushed them forward.

Police and firemen met them in the parking lot. The firemen, after a brief, curious look, went on. They had other priorities.

"What's going on?" one policeman asked.

Portia stepped forward, speaking crisply. "My name is Portia Carver. Someone planted a bomb in the building. When we escaped in the elevator this vermin"—she glared at the bald man—"was waiting for us at the bottom. He killed my assistant Travis Monteith and a secretary with this gun." She shoved the weapon at them. The policeman had no choice but to take it. "Lock it up and take it out of my sight."

Bemused, the police officer took custody of the prisoner.

The bald man found his voice. "I'm not a criminal. The bitch held a gun on me, not the other way around. If you want a criminal"—the poisonous eyes narrowed—"arrest *him*." He tried to point, but the officer deftly cuffed his wrists. "Arrest Lindberg. He murdered his girlfriend—"

Portia Carver slapped him across the face. "I will hear no more such slander! Murdering vermin have not the right to speak!" She inclined her head stiffly to the police officer in charge. "I will go down to the station to make a statement within the hour. In the meantime, I suggest you see if there are any more gunmen hanging around."

The police officer flushed, but she strode away before he had a chance to mutter an order. Gavin and Jeff hastily followed.

Gavin felt the beginnings of respect for his grandmother. He had an inkling now of the force of personality that had shaped the Futurists.

Out of the policemen's hearing, Portia turned razor green eyes on them. "You were right," she said in clipped tones. "I was wrong."

It was as much of an apology as they were likely to get. She swept on to more important subjects. "I'll put things back together here, but you must leave at once." Her gaze nailed Gavin. "Go!"

Jeff looked outraged and all too willing to leave. She hadn't even thanked them for saving her life.

Gavin locked eyes with his grandmother. "The enemy is a Futurist. He has to be, to know so much about our weaknesses."

The warning cost him dearly.

A hand clapped him on the shoulder, and a policeman said, "Gavin Lindberg, you're under arrest for the murder of Bethany Mills."

CHAPTER 7

• 1 •

Two fire trucks blocked the station wagon's approach to the Cambrian Building.

"Fire!" Bobby bounced in his seat. "Fire, fire!"

April's heart jumped into her throat. She craned her neck, expecting to see flames licking at thirty-story windows. What she saw was worse.

Where the Cambrian Building had once scraped the sky beside the pointed silhouette of Husky Oil, there was a notch in the horizon. The entire building was gone. No, collapsed, into the dusty mess and debris the fire trucks had cordoned off.

Traffic had stopped. Penny parked right there in the street. "Jeff," she whispered, her face dead white.

April opened her door. "Come on." She struggled to think through her fear. "Jeff was with Gavin; his danger instinct should have gotten them out of there."

"Yes, of course," Penny said blankly. "My empathy . . ." She hurried toward the remains, leaving April to take charge of the kids. Kristy's hand felt cold in hers.

A crowd of onlookers had gathered. Penny fought her way to the front, but was stopped by a fireman. An ambulance siren wailed as two paramedics hustled a body on a stretcher inside.

Penny stepped toward the stretcher, then stopped as someone shouted, "Penny!"

Jeff waved to them from across the parking lot.

April searched frantically for a second person at his side, but didn't see Gavin. She turned away from Penny and Jeff's passionate embrace, unable to watch.

"I'm never letting you out of my sight again." Penny buried her head in Jeff's shoulder.

April looked around wildly. Gavin had to be here somewhere. He'd been with Jeff, and Gavin had the danger instinct. He had to be alive.

"A bomb exploded," Jeff was saying.

"Where's Gavin?" April interrupted.

"He's been arrested. Whoever set the bomb left a double trap. Make that a triple. He set up an ambush at the bottom of the stairs. Gavin and I took him out, but when we handed him over to the police he identified Gavin."

Arrested, not dead.

Relief swelled, then leaked away. Gavin would be a sitting duck in jail. "We have to get him out."

"Yes," Penny echoed. "If I go down to the station and identify him as my brother Tom Gillis—"

"They'll know you're lying," Jeff finished. "Haven't you ever heard of fax machines? The police will have his picture by now."

Silence.

"We'll have to break him out of jail." Kristy stuck out her lower lip, determined.

"Batman! Batman!" Bobby ran in circles, arms held out.

"How?" Penny asked in despair. "We'll have to wait and post bail."

Jeff tensed to object, but April beat him to it. "No. That will take too long. I don't know how we'll break him out, but I know who does." She fixed her eyes on Portia Carver and started toward her.

Penny took one step to follow, but Jeff caught her. April heard them start to argue in the background.

Portia was talking to two of the Councillors, an elderly man and a disheveled woman. April ignored both of them. Her eyes met Portia's green fire. "Gavin's been arrested," she said starkly.

"So?" Portia raised one eyebrow.

April's temper flared. "He's your grandson."

"A grandson I never met before this afternoon," Portia pointed out. "In any case, I do not play favorites. All of the Futurists are under attack, not just Gavin." She turned back to the elderly man. "The backups for our membership list are at my house . . ."

April stared at her, furious. "Don't you understand? He'll die in jail."

Portia's head swung around; she glared. "He'll only die if you fail to rescue him. Why are you bothering me? I'm the Chairwoman. I can't take time to rescue individual people. You'll have to do it yourself."

"How? I don't have any connections. You do."

"You don't need connections. You need an Illusionist."

One of the Talents. Yes, illusions would be useful in a jailbreak. "And where do I find an Illusionist, pray tell?"

To her immense annoyance Portia laughed, the sound surprisingly rich. "That's right, you didn't stay around long enough to get the results. You are the Illusionist, my dear."

• 2 •

Something was bothering Genevieve, Matt was sure of it. Something above and beyond the fact that the Selector was hot on their trail.

Two hours had passed since Genevieve had told the Selector where they were. Since then they had driven across the Canadian border and registered under false names at another cheap motel. Genevieve said that they weren't in immediate danger, but her shoulders remained tense and knotted.

Matt opened his mouth to ask her what was wrong, then closed it. It would be better if she broke her habit of distrust voluntarily. He decided to give her until morning to tell him what was wrong. In the meantime he tried a gentle prompt. "You haven't told me what the Selector said to you on the phone. Did he answer your questions? You asked him his real name."

"He said his true name was the Selector, but that he used many aliases, Crabtree and Quillon among them. He gave me two new names to work with: Ronald Carver and Charles Mathieson."

"Great." Matt memorized the names. "What else did you ask him?"

"I made a mistake. I asked him where he was born, but he said he didn't know."

"He probably lied."

"Maybe, but I don't think so." A cute little frown wrinkled Genevieve's forehead. "The Selector is a pretty straightforward thinker. 'I'm going to kill you, Mary.' Not a lot of subtlety there." She hesitated, looking haunted. "He said he knew where I was born, who my real parents are."

Was that all that was bothering her? "Of course," Matt said calmly. "If you think about it so will you." He'd had his suspicions for a while.

Genevieve thought about it, staring at the blank TV. Realization touched her face. "Michael and Terisa Richmond, the murdered couple."

"I'm afraid so," Matt said. "Do you remember anything about your birth parents?"

"Nothing," Genevieve said, then stopped, frowning. "Maybe. When I try to picture my mother I hear this song in my head. A lullaby."

"Try to sing it," Matt suggested. A lullaby wasn't going to be much help, but one memory might trigger another.

" 'Firstborn hooks.' " Genevieve paused. "That may not be right. It doesn't really make sense."

"Keep going," Matt urged.

" 'Firstborn hooks, Sister looks, and sees deep inside, Mary dreams' — I remember that line especially because it had my name in it. My mother would always touch my nose when she sang it."

Matt abruptly started paying more attention.

" 'Brother screams, he hears one who's died. Eileen learns, Peter burns, in ice he hides. Last born speaks, who listens seeks to free the one who cried.' That's it."

"Can you say it again for me? I want to write it down."

Genevieve obliged, and Matt stared down at the scribbled lyrics for a long time. "Bingo," he said softly.

"What is it?" Genevieve asked. "Do you recognize it?"

"No—not that having some poems published makes me a world expert—" Matt added, "but I think this was written by your parents, Genevieve. I think this is a clue."

"A clue to what?"

"A clue to your family."

"I don't have a family." Genevieve frowned.

"I think you do. Listen to the lyrics: Firstborn hooks, last born speaks, sister looks, brother screams. I think every line refers to a different child. Your mother taught it to you; you're mentioned in it by name 'Mary dreams,' therefore they're your brother and sisters."

"Mary is a common name," Genevieve said.

"Yes," Matt agreed. "It's the 'Mary dreams' part that is the most convincing. It's too much of a coincidence that you also have very unusual dreams."

"But how would my mother have known I would start having unusual dreams?"

"Maybe you had them as a child and don't remember. Or your psychic powers are genetic," Matt said.

Genevieve stared at him. "Psychic powers? I don't have psychic powers."

Her shock amused Matt. "You see things in dreams that are happening somewhere else, and you can sense danger coming. If those aren't psychic powers, what are?"

"Uh," said Genevieve.

"Anyhow," Matt moved on, "it's a theory that I think is worth looking into. If the Selector is hunting you down because you are Michael and Terisa Richmond's daughter, one of the other children might know why or be able to tell us who the Selector is."

"If the Selector hasn't killed them already," Genevieve said glumly.

"There are six other children mentioned in the poem. Surely one of the others has survived—"

"Six?" Genevieve interrupted. "You're saying I have six brothers and sisters?"

"Unless I counted wrong." Matt went over the sheet in his hands again. "No, there are seven lines counting yours."

"Six." Genevieve looked stunned.

"Yeah. It's too bad more of them aren't mentioned by name. It's going to be hard enough to track down an Eileen and Peter Richmond—that's assuming Richmond is their last name," Matt thought aloud. "They could be adopted as well, or Richmond might be an alias—"

"I can find them," Genevieve said. Her face was pale but determined.

Matt stared at her. "How?"

"I can dream about them. I did it once by accident. I was thinking about some of my old friends, feeling homesick and wishing I could just see them all once more, and that night I dreamed about them. I always meant to try to dream about the Selector, but I never had the guts actually to do it. I just kept lying to myself and pretending he wasn't real." Genevieve shivered. "I'm such a coward."

"You're not a coward," Matt said sharply. He hated it when Genevieve put herself down. "Dreaming about the Selector would be a very dangerous thing to do. You said he keeps trying to kill you and that he can read your mind."

Genevieve didn't look convinced. "But I might learn something, too. I found out more talking on the phone to him yesterday than I did in the three years before that."

Alarm shot through Matt. Crabtree had almost killed Genevieve. He did not want the Selector to get another shot at Genevieve under any circumstances. Dreaming about him was too dangerous. He wouldn't let her do it.

Let. Matt bit his tongue. This was Genevieve's battle, not his. She knew the risk better than he did, and it would do her good to start viewing her dreams as a tool instead of a source of horror. All he said was: "Why don't you start off with one of your brothers and sisters, until you know for sure it works?"

"Good idea." Genevieve relaxed. Matt could tell that she didn't really want to dream about the Selector. She lay down on the double bed, fully clothed.

He squeezed her hands. So cold. "I'll wake you if you look disturbed."

She nodded and closed her eyes.

"Will it keep you awake if I phone Ian?" Matt asked.

She didn't open her eyes, but her body tensed. "Yes. Sorry."

He could call Ian later. Matt got out pen and paper instead and tried to work on his novel, with little success. He was too conscious of Genevieve, of her chest rising and falling. He knew the exact moment her breathing evened out and she slept.

• 3 •

"Tell me you're not seriously considering going on a jailbreak," Jeff said ominously to Penny. Didn't she realize how vulnerable her pregnancy made her? She couldn't even run.

Her chin lifted. "Gavin's my brother. I have to help him."

"Your first responsibility is to Bobby and Damaris."

"I'm not abandoning Bobby or Damaris," Penny said gently, "but I won't abandon Gavin either."

Her words triggered an avalanche of guilt. Gavin had saved Bobby's life and now his, and Jeff had repaid him by pretending not to know him when the police came. "I didn't abandon Gavin. If I'd spoken up, I'd have been arrested, too."

Penny studied him with dawning awareness. "So you just stood there and watched him get arrested?"

Hot anger melted his guilt. "If I didn't go to jail for my brother, why in God's name would I go to jail for yours?"

"Your brother?" Penny looked confused. "You don't have a brother."

Jeff cursed his tongue. "Not anymore."

Penny stared at him as if she didn't know him. As if he were gutter slime. His stomach twisted. He was gutter slime. He'd spent five years pretending he wasn't, but the stink of the slums never wore off.

"You stopped having a brother when he went to jail?"

Jeff heard the same condemnation in her voice he'd heard in his mother's. *"You're no good for nothing. Lying to the police. Letting your brother go to jail. You ain't my son no more, and he ain't your brother!"*

"Let me tell you something about brothers since you're so damn eager to acquire one." His throat felt tighter than a rubber band. "Blood relation doesn't mean a thing. My brother was a thief and a murderer. I stole, too, but I drew the line at scarfing old ladies. Todd wanted me to give him an alibi for the police. He killed her for her Canada Pension check and a fake pearl necklace." Jeff was breathing hard, glaring at his wife.

"Oh, no," she said.

"Oh, yes," Jeff said grimly. Things like that didn't happen in her world. He'd seen the house she grew up in and the white picket fence that had kept her safe. Penny had fallen out of her share of trees, but her adopted mother had always been there to kiss the hurts better.

"What happened when you refused to be his alibi?" Penny hadn't a single doubt of his refusal.

Jeff had had a few doubts. When Todd had pulled the knife he'd almost changed his mind.

"Jeff?"

His lips twisted. "Remember when we compared scars and I told you I'd gotten mine falling out of a tree, too?"

He didn't have to spell it out for her. Her face whitened. Her obvious concern over a scar that was seven years old touched him. Penny was the only one who had ever cared if he was hurt or cold or hungry—

April jogged up, breathless. "Portia won't help, but she says I'm an Illusionist and can do it myself."

"We'll help," Penny volunteered.

There she went again. "No, we won't. Will's shooting this morning is still big news, we can't risk being connected with Gavin. If they find out he was with us, the self-defense ruling might be overturned."

"He's my broth—" Penny stopped at the expression on Jeff's face. "Please understand, I have to help him. I won't be able to live with myself if I don't."

Do you think I'd be able to live with myself if I let you do this and you got hurt? Jeff asked silently.

Frustrated, he grasped at straws. "What about your other brothers and sisters? The killer will be after them, too."

"We don't know where they are."

"We do now. I found a record of another adopted Futurist in the right age range with the right name while hunting through the Futurist database. Peter Chambry in Thunder Bay, Ontario."

"Peter burns . . ." Penny whispered, quoting that stupid lullaby again.

Jeff didn't believe in the thing himself, but he'd do anything to get Penny out of town. Ontario sounded nice and far away.

"His line is the last before Kristy's," Penny said thoughtfully. "He can't be very old."

"All the more reason he needs our help," Jeff lied.

April looked anxious, but said firmly, "I never expected you to help with the jailbreak. If this illusion thing works—and I'm having trouble believing it will—then it will probably work best on one, at the most two, people."

"All right." Penny nodded slowly. "We'll go to Ontario, and you follow."

"How will I find you?" April asked.

"Phone—no, that won't work." Penny frowned.

"I'll stay with April and tell her," Kristy said. "Bobby and I can talk together no matter how far apart we are."

• 4 •

A black police officer handcuffed Gavin and shoved him in the backseat of a police car with the killer.

The man didn't look like a killer. He looked innocuous: just some middle-aged, ineffectual executive with a potbelly showing under his rumpled business suit. A jury would never convict.

The businessman smiled, and it was like a shark fin cutting through the calm waters of a duck pond; Gavin could see the killer underneath, cold and repellent. "Hello, Lindberg. If I'd known it was you, I would have shot through the elevator doors. How's the shoulder?" Before Gavin could respond, he slammed into Gavin's left side.

"Hey now, none of that." The black policeman glared at them through the steel mesh while his partner started the car.

Gavin swallowed a childish urge to say, "He started it." Pain streaked through his shoulder like fire.

The killer slammed him against the door. Gavin shoved back, but the handcuffs hindered him.

"I said stop it!"

"Whatcha gonna do, nigger, shoot me?" The killer straightened away from Gavin.

A dark flush mantled the cop's cheekbones, but he kept his temper. "Now what would be the point of that when you're already going to be locked up for the rest of your natural life?"

The quiet reminder depressed Gavin, but the killer laughed. "You can't touch me."

The cop's lips tightened, but he turned away, not wanting to be drawn into the fight. After all, the person being beaten up was a murderer. No great loss.

The killer lunged forward, but this time Gavin was ready: he raised his feet and kicked.

He bloodied the killer's nose, and the sight made up for jolting his shoulder.

The killer blinked, his eat-shit grin missing. He tried to wipe his nose, but his handcuffs prevented him so he sniffed instead. "Hey, I'm bweeding."

"So you are," the policeman faced forward again, disgusted.

Alarm filled the killer's eyes. He looked harmless and frightened. "Why ab I handcuffed?"

Neither cop answered so Gavin did. "You set off a bomb in the Cambrian Building and shot the Kithkinners trying to escape."

The man's eyes bulged. "What?"

Gavin sighed. He wouldn't convict either. "What's the last thing you remember?"

The businessman's brow wrinkled. "I wuth shaving, when . . ."

"Did you hear a strange voice in your head?"

"Yeth!" The man looked surprised. "Howb did you know?"

"Lucky guess," Gavin said grimly. "What did the Voice say?"

The black policeman turned around again, listening.

"He said—he said—*fuck off, Lindberg!*" He head-butted Gavin, catching him hard on the chin.

Gavin fell back against the side door, banging his head on the window. He drew up his knees just as the killer threw his weight against him.

The driver hit the brakes, and both Gavin and the killer flew forward, imprinting chicken wire on their faces. "Stop it!"

The killer seemed to subside, but Gavin soon found out he'd only switched physical violence for verbal taunts. "Just wait till we're alone in jail, Lindberg. I'll cut you up, just like I cut—"

He stopped delicately, allowing Gavin to fill in the blank. "Just like you cut Bethany?" Tears of rage sheened his eyes. "Are you the bastard that cut Bethany?"

The killer smiled. Sharks circling . . .

Gavin kicked the killer hard in the kneecap, but the man just laughed, the Voice speaking, "Charles Mathieson was in a board meeting when Bethany died. He has an airtight alibi."

The second policeman was watching now, too, in the rearview mirror.

Gavin couldn't bring himself to care. He hunched into the corner, legs drawn up protectively.

When the police car arrived at the station, the police escorted Gavin and the killer out of the car separately.

"He really hates you," the black policeman commented.

"I know," Gavin said shortly.

"Any idea why?" The question sounded casual, but a shrewd intelligence gleamed behind the officer's eyes dark eyes. He knew something was wrong.

Gavin hesitated, then shrugged. He wanted to trust the policeman, but he feared his fair hearing would grind to a halt the moment he mentioned psychics and demons, and he didn't want to implicate April or Penny.

While contacting the police in Huld about Bethany's murder, the police locked Gavin up in a holding cell.

Gavin paced the small space. Now what? He had faith that Canada's justice system wouldn't convict an innocent man. The wound in his shoulder would prove that something was wrong with the Huld cop's story. If he made it to trial. A very large if. One that increased when the killer was installed in the cell next to him half an hour later.

"You look good behind bars," the killer mocked. "You'll look even better in a casket. Of course, you'll be a bit crooked because they'll have to reattach your head after I tear it off."

Something evil lurked in that smile, a dark shape twisting below the water.... Gavin backed away until his shoulders touched the iron bars on the opposite wall.

"Gotcha," said the man in the next cell, and strong hands seized his throat.

• 5 •

[A *pitch black room. Crying.*

[*Genevieve turned in a circle, searching for the source of the sound, but couldn't see anything.*

[*The crying continued, softly, heart-wrenchingly. It sounded like a child, which puzzled her. She'd been trying to dream about Firstborn hooks. Firstborn should be older than she was.*

[*Although the Selector was the only one who'd ever been able to see her when she dreamed, Genevieve couldn't help speaking. "Who's there?"*

[*Only the same unnerving weeping answered her.*

[*A child was in pain; she had to help it. She tried again.* "Don't be afraid. My name's Genevieve. Where are you?"

[*Soft sobs. Genevieve tried to follow the sounds, approaching the corner where they seemed loudest.* "Don't be afraid, I won't hurt you."

[*No response, just steady weeping. Genevieve took a step closer, and suddenly her eyes adjusted to the gloom. She saw a small boy, huddled in the corner, crying.*

[*She knelt beside him. He didn't notice her, weeping.*

[*He looked about four years old, with blond hair and scrawny arms hugging his knees. It took Genevieve a moment to realize the darker spots on his arms were bruises, not shadows.*

[*She checked her first instinct to hold the little fellow and comfort him. Even if she was able to touch in the dream state, he probably feared everyone bigger than himself.* "Hello, there," *she said instead.*

[*His hands rubbed the tears from his eyes. Dark bruises ringed both his eyes, and his mouth looked fat and puffy.* "Won't cry," *he muttered.* "Won't cry. Only baby, weak girls cry."

[*Genevieve's heart ached for him, and her blood boiled. How dare someone beat a four-year-old for crying!*

["*The Selector never cries,*" *the blond boy said, startling Genevieve badly. She'd just decided this dream had nothing to do with Firstborn or the Selector.*

["*Never cries. Never gets hurt. Won't cry. Won't cry.*" *The blond boy rocked back and forth, reciting a litany.* "Won't cry. Bad boy Ronnie, for crying." *He hit himself.* "Bad boy Ronnie, for crying. Won't cry." *But his tears continued to fall like steady rain. He slapped his cheek.* "Bad boy . . ."

[*Genevieve couldn't bear it any longer. She reached out to stop him—and her hand passed right through him.*

[*The boy stopped hitting himself and started singing, his voice high and off-key.* "'Firstborn hooks, Sister looks—and sees deep inside' . . ." *He stopped rocking and faded away.*

[*Genevieve was alone in the darkened room.*]

She woke.

"Well?" Matt asked, anxious. "How did it go?"

"I'm not sure," Genevieve said slowly, sitting up. "I think I might have just dreamed about a ghost." She told Matt about the dark room and the crying boy. "If that was Firstborn, he died before he could grow up. He couldn't have been older than four."

"I'm sorry."

Matt's condolences startled her until she realized part of her was grieving. Bad boy Ronnie for crying had likely been her older brother.

Genevieve blinked. "Well, that was inconclusive. I guess I should try again." She looked at the poem and picked "Peter burns" at random.

• 6 •

Peter Chambry was in bed, but not asleep. Faintly, downstairs, he could hear his parents talking. He couldn't make out their words, but he knew what they were saying. What they'd been saying all day with their sad, watchful eyes.

They were worried about him.

Peter knew it, but couldn't seem to make the effort to ease their fears. He spoke when spoken to, ate what his mother put in front of him, went where he was told, but he wasn't there. Not really. He was deep inside himself.

His parents had taken him to a doctor today. A head doctor. They hadn't told him that part; Peter had figured it out.

He had answered the doctor's questions politely.

(Did he know his parents were worried about him? Yes, he did.)

(Did he know why his parents were worried? They're worried because I haven't been myself since Al Ghostkeeper died.) He'd said that without flinching, without once looking into the woman doctor's kind eyes.

(Did he want to talk to her about Al's death? No, he didn't.) A brief stab of pain, remembering his best friend's laughing face.

(Al's death hadn't been his fault. Yes, he knew that, too.) Not his fault, but someone's fault. Peter didn't say that aloud. The adults called it an accident, death by mischance.

The doctor called his parents back in. Nervous, both of them, his mother teary-eyed. Her tears disturbed him, but the feeling was dim and distant, like a shout underwater, and he said nothing. He obediently went into the waiting room. (He's in a state of denial.)

Muted anger. Peter wasn't in denial. It was the adults who denied everything, refusing to listen.

He'd told the police about the arrows Al's brother Larry had stolen, but after Larry's employer gave him an alibi they had kindly wrapped him in a blanket and given him hot chocolate. Peter had been assured over and over that Al's death was not his fault. That they knew Peter had not meant to hurt Al.

When Al's mother and grandfather arrived he'd tried to tell them he hadn't shot Al, but they hadn't listened either. Al's mother screamed at him, calling him a murderer. The policemen had had to hold her back.

Desperately, Peter turned to Al's grandfather—he and Al had sat at the old man's feet for hours, listening to his tales—surely he would listen. But Al's grandfather had looked pale and shaken and old. He'd patted Peter's shoulder, but all his attention had been focused on the body of his grandson and his weeping daughter.

He tried once more with his parents. "I didn't shoot Al."

"We know you didn't mean to, honey." His mother had hugged him. "Don't worry, no one's going to put you in jail."

They didn't listen, so Peter had retreated into himself, carefully hiding the rage in his soul. He'd frozen it, but it was still there, waiting to be used.

Underneath the sheets, Peter bared his teeth in a snarl. Since the police weren't even going to try to catch Al's murderer, he would.

• 7 •

She was going to break Gavin out of jail.

She was out of her tiny little mind.

Portia had been confident that April could save Gavin on her own, but, in spite of entrusting Kristy to Portia's care, April didn't like the Chairwoman very much. Portia was too concerned with the Futurists as a whole to worry about individual members, including her grandson.

Gavin meant more to April than he did to Portia; Portia didn't love him.

April's score on some test didn't make her an Illusionist. Neither did the three quick trial runs she had practiced on Penny, Jeff, and Kristy.

April stared harder at the brick building across the street. The police station. She'd gotten directions and a van from Portia; the rest was up to her.

One of the questions on the Futurist Talent test had been, *Are you good at hide-and-seek?*

The question had reminded her of that awful moment in Penny and Jeff's yard when Corny's flashlight had touched her foot. It hadn't been luck that Corny hadn't seen her; she had used her Talent. With Penny and Kristy watching critically, April had struggled to re-create what she'd done, pinned against the wall, Gavin breathing beside her. She'd kept very still, pretending she was invisible.

It had seemed to work. Both Penny and Kristy had claimed that she'd vanished, and Jeff had closed his eyes and shaken his head.

But that had only been for a moment. Breaking Gavin out of jail would take at least fifteen minutes. Could she hold her invisibility that long? What if someone bumped into her?

So pretend to be a cop. Just move. Gavin needs you.

Determination etched on her face, April crossed the street. If her disguise didn't work she'd probably be asked a few questions, but not arrested. If she failed, she could try again.

Inside the building she saw people lined up in front of a policewoman's counter. April carefully studied her uniform—beige shirt, black pants with a red stripe—and the policewoman herself—dark hair rolled into a neat bun, coffee-colored skin—then closed her eyes and tried to craft an illusion of the Filipino policewoman in her mind.

When the image was as perfect as she could make it, she glanced

down and saw both her jeans and the illusioned black pants, super-
imposed over the first image.

The sensation was odd, heavy, rather like donning a full suit of
armor.

"Hey!" A child of ten saw her and pointed. His distracted parent
turned toward April—

Heart thumping, she pushed through some half doors marked
AUTHORIZED PERSONNEL ONLY as if she had every right to be there.
As if she were the policewoman behind the counter.

[*Beige shirt* . . .]

No one raised the alarm, but once inside April discovered she
didn't know where to go. Where was the jail? Was it even in the
same building?

Keep moving. She walked briskly down the hall and found herself
in a large noisy room, filled with desks, cops, and criminals being
booked.

Gavin wasn't there.

"Hey, Navarre!"

One of the cops was shouting at her.

"Nice shoes, but I don't think the captain's going to like them."
He laughed.

April glanced down and saw that she had forgotten to extend the
illusion to her feet. He could see her purple runners.

She almost lost the whole thing right there. No. [*Coffee-colored
skin, dark hair rolled in a bun* . . .] She hung on by an act of will
and hurried off down the nearest corridor. Ahead of her a black
policeman was escorting a short man in a business suit.

Were they going to the jail cells? Gavin might be there.

[*Dark shoes* . . .]

Sweat began to run down April's face. The armor grew heavier
with each step, and her temples throbbed. She must not let the
illusion waver. [*Red-striped pants* . . .]

The businessman ahead pretended to stumble, and his escort
yanked him back in line. The businessman saw her following them
and said something obscene. "Sow," he added for good measure.

Sow meant female pig. He thought she was a cop. April smiled widely. The businessman scowled, confused, then turned away again.

To play it safe, she lagged behind. She rounded the next corner just in time to see them passing through some kind of security check.

Damn! She could Illusion a policewoman's uniform, but not a voice or identity badge.

Making a snap decision, April discarded the first illusion and imagined herself invisible. She charged down the hall. Maybe she could sneak through the gate with them. . . .

The cop and the businessman turned in surprise.

April opened her mouth to make some excuse, but the cop looked right through her. She breathed carefully; every exhalation sounded as loud as a blacksmith's bellows to her ears, but he still didn't see her, hear her—Of course! Her footsteps. Apparently, illusions were strictly visual.

The black cop shook his head and turned back toward the gate. On tiptoe, April followed.

The gate started to buzz shut, and she hastily squeezed through. Her arm grazed the businessman's sleeve.

"Hey!" He jerked around. Off-balance, April hit the wall. [*Invisible. Transparent.*] Instead of wearing armor, April felt as if she were being pressed flat between two glass slides. Hardly able to breathe. Lack of air made her dizzy.

"What is it?" the cop asked, tightening his hold.

"Someone touched me," the businessman said.

The cop grunted. "Yeah, well someone's going to push you if you don't get moving."

After another wary glance over his shoulder the businessman started walking again. April stayed still and invisible. If a policewoman suddenly materialized, the cop would wonder why he hadn't heard the gate buzz.

Breathing shallowly, she waited until the cop locked the businessman up and buzzed back outside before easing around the corner out of sight of the gate. Should she go back to her policewoman disguise? Or stay invisible? She didn't want the woman she was impersonating to get in trouble, but she would attract attention talking to Gavin, invisible.

Her diaphragm struggled under an immense weight, as if pushing mud instead of air.

What about the security cameras? Would her illusions show up on film? She had a sinking suspicion a camera would see the truth. It didn't have a mind to fool.

One thing at a time. She hadn't planned farther ahead because she hadn't really believed she'd make it this far.

A soft metallic clang.

April forced in another lungful of jellied air, listening.

A faint gargling sound, as if—as if someone were choking.

She couldn't know what the noise meant, but part of her did anyhow. It was Gavin. She dropped the deadweight of her illusion and sprinted around the corner.

She spied him instantly in the third cell, pressed back against the bars by the brawny arm encircling his throat. "Stop!"

His attacker looked up and grinned, showing a battered face and two missing teeth. "Make me stop."

For a second, April hesitated. What could she do? They were inside the cells; she was outside, and she didn't have keys.

Gavin clawed feebly at the arm.

Her illusions. This time she didn't bother with the red-striped pants; she drew an illusion gun and pointed it at the attacker. "Let him go!"

The attacker blinked bruised eyes, but his grip did not loosen. "You must be the baby-sitter. I've got a bone to pick with you once I finish with shithead here." He shook Gavin like a rag doll.

He was as crazy as Will and Corny. "Is that it?" she asked through tears and rage. "Are you hunting demons? I'll show you demons!" She launched a fanged, red-eyed monster at the killer, claws extended.

He staggered backward, both hands raised to protect his face, and crouched against the cement wall until he realized the so-called demon had passed through him without so much as scratching him.

April quickly constructed a new image, lifting heavy building blocks with her mind. [*Demon licking his chops, grinning at the attacker, as he advanced step by step, one three-clawed foot after the other.*]

The attacker pushed himself to his feet. "An Illusionist." His Irish accent matched his red hair. "You won't fool me a second time." He stretched a hairy arm through the bars and grabbed Gavin's wrist.

In despair, she let the demon disintegrate. "Gavin!" The other prisoners were screaming and yelling, but April didn't see, didn't hear. "Gavin, wake up!"

His eyes opened slowly, dazed. He tugged weakly against the hand dragging him closer.

[*A tiger springing, jaws spread wide enough to swallow a house. A silver-tipped grizzly bear, standing on his two hind legs, taking swipes with his mighty paws.*] April threw all her waning strength into the efforts with no avail. Gavin flinched, but the attacker just laughed.

"Nice try, baby-sitter, but why spend your efforts trying to save a wretch like him? Lover-boy here has already lost one girlfriend this week."

Gavin sat up, pulling harder. He gasped and wheezed, unable to get his breath.

April screamed because she couldn't think of a damn thing else to do. She screamed in rage and helplessness; she shook the iron bars. It couldn't happen this way. She'd just met Gavin. He couldn't just die right in front of her eyes.

Like hauling in a fish, the attacker used his beefy arms to pull Gavin closer, grabbing first his elbow, then his shoulder. Gavin's shoes scraped across the floor.

The gate buzzed open, and two cops rushed in, weapons drawn. "Quick! He's killing him!"

The cops didn't ask who she was or what she was doing there. "Drop him!" the black cop shouted.

Large hands with fingers the size of sausages closed around Gavin's throat.

"Stop or we'll shoot!"

Fingers pressed into flesh.

Bang! The blond cop fired, and a bullet flashed off an iron bar.

He put up his weapon, the danger of ricochets too great.

"Open the door!" April tugged uselessly on the iron bars.

Gavin's face turned an unhealthy color. Dying.

The cell door opened. April lunged inside, grabbing the hands around Gavin's throat. She bit the fat fingers, spitting out blood.

"Bitch!" The attacker grimaced, sweat glazing his pale skin. "It won't do you any good. Lindberg is mine."

Gavin went limp.

Bang! A gun went off near April's ear, deafening her. The attacker's mouth opened on a scream she couldn't hear, and he clutched his elbow. Blood leaked through his fingers.

April didn't care. "Gavin!" He didn't respond. Was he unconscious or dead?

Hands pried her away. "He needs medical attention," the black policeman told her. "Let us get him some."

In a daze April followed the cops as they carried Gavin from the cell. She watched anxiously for the slight rise and fall of Gavin's chest. When it came she blinked back more tears—and saw the gate up ahead.

[*Invisible.*] Squeezing in half, thin as glass. She followed Gavin and the two cops through the gate, into yelling confusion.

"Prison fight—"

"Get a doctor—"

"Another wounded—"

" —right now!"

"Had to shoot—"

It suddenly struck April that she'd accomplished half her mission. Gavin was no longer locked up. This could very well be his best chance at escape.

Carefully avoiding the agitated policemen, April crept up to where Gavin lay. His breath sounded no more labored than her own thin gasps, and the cops didn't seem worried about him expiring.

"Where'd the girl go?" one of them thought to ask.

She shook Gavin's arm.

His eyes flew open. [*Lids closed.*] "Shh. We're going to escape in just a minute." Her fingers wrapped around his.

Behind her illusion the real Gavin's eyes were wide with fear. "Who's there?" he croaked.

April squeezed his hand in answer. Her head ached fiercely from the effort of keeping herself invisible and Gavin seemingly unconscious. A trickle of blood started down her left nostril, but she ignored it, taking the crushing weight of mountains on her back for her third illusion. She grunted as the room slowly filled with black smoke.

"What do you mean, 'what girl'? The one who screamed her head off."

[*Black, viscous smoke, curling through the air.*] It didn't smell, but it would have to do. [*Clouds and clouds of smoke.*] Head pounding . . . She pulled Gavin to his feet and let her invisibility run from her hand to him. With her last breath she yelled, "Fire!"

Consternation. The cops stopped arguing.

"Shit!" the blond swore.

The black cop was looking at the space on the floor where Gavin had lain a minute ago, but the gate officer cut him off before he could say anything.

"Begin evacuation procedures!" He pulled the fire alarm that April's pretend smoke wasn't capable of setting off.

April made her feet move, running. Gavin dragged on her arm. He stumbled frequently, gasping and cursing, until April realized she held his wounded left arm. She switched arms.

[*Smoke funneling into the corridor ahead. She and Gavin invisible ghosts.*] Blood in both nostrils now, and pain behind her eyes. Her brain felt as if it were squeezing out through her ears. Move them feet. . . .

They crashed into someone, rounding the corner. Panic gave her extra strength. [*Thick smoke, too black to see. Invisible.*] While the disoriented policewoman looked around, April pulled Gavin after her. He stumbled every third step, finally balking.

"Where are we going?"

Of course. He would see only the illusion, the black smoke, not the clear hallways April navigated. "Trust me."

Farther down the hall, everyone was too concerned about evacuating the building and not losing any prisoners to think much of a trod-upon toe or a flying elbow from two invisible people.

The crush out the doors was a little hairy. Someone kept trying to take up the "empty" space April and Gavin occupied. April lost hold of Gavin's hand, and someone shrieked as he suddenly appeared. Then they pushed through the doors, and April grabbed his hand again. "Run!" She shed the smoke illusion like a snake's skin, clinging only to their invisibility.

Her body was thinner than paper now, and she gasped through her mouth because her nose was full of blood.

They ran five blocks, swerving around pedestrians. April stopped when they reached the gray van Portia had loaned her. "Stop. This is our getaway car."

Gavin doubled over, panting. "Who . . . are . . . you?"

Fumbling with the car keys, April supposed invisible drivers might attract a little notice. She dropped the invisibility.

Sudden nausea made her stagger. Two dimensions ballooned to three.

"April?" Gavin's voice sounded hoarse and grating.

"Surprise." She wiped at her bloody nose. "I found out what my Talent is." She jerked the door open.

Gavin followed her inside, scowling. "Could have been arrested."

April laughed until the pain in her head made her cry. "Now I know you're all right." Ugly bruises ringed his throat, ten large fingerprints, but he was worried about her getting arrested. "You know, you could thank me for saving your life."

A flush built under his skin. "Thanks. In your debt." Pain made him cut off his sentences, but April easily interpreted, "Repay you?" as 'How can I ever repay you?'

"Take me out to dinner when this is all over," she suggested promptly. The moment the words left her mouth she wanted to retract them. When this nightmare ended she was the last person Gavin would want to see—the girl he'd met on the day of Bethany's murder—

"I'd like that," Gavin said clearly.

CHAPTER 6

• 1 •

"You can stay in here," Grandmother Portia said, opening the playroom door. "There are toys around somewhere. Don't touch the dolls. They're Dresden china and very fragile. And stay here. No snooping!"

"I wouldn't snoop—" Kristy started indignantly.

"Don't pout," Grandmother Portia said. "It's extremely unbecoming." She left.

Kristy stuck out her tongue at the closed door. "I'm not pouting, am I, Bobby?"

[*Thpth!*] Bobby stuck out his tongue, too.

Kristy usually talked to Bobby in her head instead of out loud, but right now she was so mad she wanted to shout. She didn't want to be here, in Grandmother Portia's house.

[*Don't wanna be here.*] Bobby repeated, too little to understand he wasn't really there at all. He was in the back of Penny and Jeff's station wagon, driving to Ontario.

"How come adults only listen when they want to?" she asked him, kicking at the rug. They'd let her stay with April to send messages, but they hadn't listened when she'd told them she'd rather stay in Dracula's dungeon than here—well, maybe not the dungeon 'cause dungeons were filled with gross rats—but almost anywhere else in the world from Tuktoyaktuk to China would have been better than *here*.

[*Moo cows.*] Bobby pointed out the car window.

Kristy didn't know why Grandmother Portia had let her stay, but she'd bet her Super Nintendo it wasn't out of grandmotherly love.

Portia thought Kristy was a nuisance. She didn't bake cookies or tell stories like Gran Hillock. Kristy couldn't even imagine Portia wearing an apron. She'd probably burn the cookies.

The image made her giggle, and she sent it to Bobby: [*Portia wearing a frilly pink apron, glaring at a tray of black lumps.*]

Bobby laughed, but she could tell he didn't really understand the joke. She sighed. Sometimes she felt like she'd spent half her life waiting for Bobby to grow up.

Oh, well. At least he could talk now. And he was potty-trained. He used to tell her every time he was wet or hungry or needed to be burped. As if *she* could do something about it hundreds of miles away.

She remembered the day he was born. How the fuzzy black headache she'd had for months had split open like a cocoon, and her mind had been flooded with sensations. White, blinding light. Large hands holding her. Upside-down people. She/he had cried furiously until Penny/Mommy had held her/him and sung the lullaby.

From that day on Kristy had been two people, not one. She was still there, but everything she had Bobby shared. He was always present, like a TV show constantly playing in the background, only instead of just watching and listening to an actor, she felt what he felt, thought what he thought.

Kristy wished all of her was with Bobby watching the moo cows. Anyplace would be better than here. She glared at the row of china dolls on the shelf with their perfect, smooth cheeks and rosebud lips.

Her mother hadn't been allowed to play with the dolls either. Portia had taken the five dolls with her all the way from Germany. She'd left behind everything else, but she'd taken the dolls. Kristy's mother had always smiled when she said that. A funny, sad sort of smile.

Bobby started driving his toy car over the vinyl seat ahead of him. [*Vroom, vroom.*]

Kristy stuck out her lower lip even farther. She didn't want to play with the dolls. Stupid, ugly things. They smiled back at her, blue eyes glassy and vacant. None of them had brown eyes like hers. Or brown hair.

Not like Caroline, the cloth doll her mother had made for her.

Since the time she was two her mother had told her wonderful stories about the new parents she would get when she was five, who would protect her from the old man's evil. She had adjusted easily to living with the Hillocks, calling them Mom and Dad within a few months, but whenever she missed her first parents she hugged Caroline tight.

Thinking about Mom and Dad Hillock brought a lump the size of a peach pit to her throat. They thought she'd burned up in the trailer.

The trailer! Caroline had been in the trailer. Caroline had burned up.

[*Kristy?*] Bobby stopped playing. [*What's the matter?*]

[*Nothing.*] Kristy sniffed, and Bobby wiped his nose. [*Go back to playing with your car.*]

Bobby was uncertain—he knew she was sad, but he picked up his toy car again and drove it over the corduroy ribs of his pants, still young enough to be easily distracted. He was barely more than a baby, really.

Still, if she didn't want him bawling, she'd better think about something other than Caroline. She thought about how angry she was instead. She hated Grandmother Portia, and she hated this house where her mother had been so unhappy.

Grandmother Portia had told her not to leave the room, but Kristy didn't care. She wouldn't snoop. She'd go straight outside.

She started toward the door, then stopped, suddenly remembering the secret passageway her mother had told her about.

[*I'm eating a Revel.*] Bobby informed her.

Kristy chewed her lip, absently tasting chocolate. When Grandmother Portia built the house she'd constructed an underground escape route in case Nigel found them. A trunk concealed the entrance.

Looking around the playroom, Kristy saw a box draped with red velvet below the shelf with the dolls. Ignoring their smug, painted eyes, which seemed to say, You're going to get in trouble, Kristy pulled off the velvet. A large toy box lay underneath.

[*I'm going through a secret tunnel.*] She opened it and pulled out a jack-in-the-box, a beat-up stuffed rabbit, and a regiment of toy soldiers. She felt the bottom of the trunk with her fingers, but couldn't find a handle.

Darn. Kristy sat back on her heels. She'd really wanted to go through a secret tunnel [*like Batman and Robin*] Bobby said. Maybe it was in one of the other rooms.

She put her hand on the doorknob, then snatched it back. The metal was hot! She blew on her fingers and smelled smoke.

[*Fire!*] Bobby yelled, car tires spinning.

The playroom had but one narrow window between a bookcase and a small table. Kristy ran over to it and stood on one of the miniature chairs. She pressed her face against the glass. A one-story drop stared back at her, short grass beneath. If she jumped, she'd break her leg.

Kristy turned away from the window and stopped, caught between the fire and the drop. Her danger instinct struggled to choose between the two.

Smoke leaked around the edges of the door, and Kristy could hear crackling noises like a hundred candy bar wrappers being crumpled. She ran back to the window and stopped again, maddened. She tried to convince herself to jump—a broken bone was better than being burned up—but couldn't make herself do it. You couldn't run very fast with a broken leg. And she had a feeling she might need to run very very fast.

Either way she'd die.

[*Kisty?!!*] A torrent of fear—both images and words—from Bobby overwhelmed her. Her fear sparked his, which magnified hers in an escalating cycle.

Her danger instinct drove her. Door or window. Door or window. Each choice got worse by the second.

[*See-ket tunnel.*] Bobby showed her a fuzzy picture of the velvet-draped trunk.

But the secret tunnel wasn't in the trunk. She threw open all the cupboards, looking for a secret doorway like the one in the C. S. Lewis books, but found only dusty teacups. She swept all the books off the bookcase and onto the floor, but it didn't revolve into the wall.

She was going to burn up like Caroline.

Coughing, the air unpleasantly hot, Kristy stumbled back over to the trunk and scratched the felt bottom with her fingernails. It had to be there. She climbed into the toy box and jumped up and down.

[*Fire and smoke, burning his fingers on a hot stove, falling out of the window . . .*]

[*Not NOW, Bobby.*] Kristy breathed in pants, smoke tickling the back of her throat. Her eyes watered like crazy, and she started to cough. How long before she suffocated?

[*Daddy says cover your nose.*]

Kristy pulled her T-shirt up over her nose. The itch in her throat eased.

[*Crawl around like a baby.*] Bobby's excited thoughts mixed in with Jeff/Daddy's advice.

Smoke rises, Kristy remembered, kneeling.

With a loud, crackling noise the hallway wall burst into orange flame.

Terrified, Kristy pressed against the back of the trunk—and it gave way.

She scrambled through into the dark space between the walls. Smoke overlaid a musty smell. She crawled as fast as she could, feeling a push of heat behind her as the flames attacked the playroom like vengeful demons.

[*Huwwy, Kristy, huwwy!*]

Her right hand slipped off into space. A staircase. Kristy stood up in the dark and let her feet find the way, running down the steps as if it were the last day of school.

A ventilator at the bottom let through stripes of light. Smoke drifted and curled in the air. Was the passageway on fire?

It didn't matter. She couldn't go back so she ran on, banging her arms on the narrow tunnel walls.

She tried to remember where her mother had said the passageway ended. There should be another entrance downstairs—maybe in the living room?—and a tunnel outside.

Or had that only been planned and not dug?

She couldn't remember. She hadn't been much older than Bobby, and—

Whap! She hit a wall, bruising her cheek and one wrist. Bobby cried; she stumbled sideways and followed the tunnel around a corner.

Her cheek hurt, but she kept running with one hand outstretched. The fire was a roaring dragon behind her, belching out foul smoke that hurt her lungs with every breath.

She turned a second corner and saw a window, smack-dab in the middle of the wall. What kind of stupey-doop put a window in a secret tunnel?

Her danger sense prickled, and she slowed even before she heard voices.

"Nigel cursed you until the day he died," a man said.

"Until the day you killed him, you mean," Grandmother Portia cut in, voice as sharp as a sword.

"Yes, of course." The man sounded amused. "Just like I'm going to kill you."

Kristy crouched beside the window and found herself looking into the den with its black-leather sofa and TV cabinet.

Grandmother Portia was standing proudly on the staircase, looking straight at Kristy. Kristy ducked and held her breath, but Portia was talking to someone else.

"Will you kill me because Nigel told you to? Do you still obey him even after his death?"

"I do only what I want." The man moved directly in front of the window, and Kristy saw his broad back and muscular legs.

[*Is he the Bad Guy?*]

Kristy didn't answer Bobby, trembling. She wormed forward on her stomach underneath the edge of the window, praying that he wouldn't turn his head and see her.

"You are unworthy, a coward," the Bad Guy said. "I have Selected you to die."

Kristy eased past. The air was cleaner near the floor, but the smoke was growing. Her danger instinct urged her on, but she hesitated. Grandmother Portia was in trouble. Should she try to help her? If she broke the window, she might distract the Bad Guy, but she'd probably get caught.

"How am I a coward?" Portia demanded.

Kristy tried to picture the den, but couldn't remember a window. Especially one showing a secret tunnel. She'd been dragging her feet following Grandmother Portia, and she was sure there hadn't been a window—

—only a mirror.

A two-way mirror like in cop shows so the person in the secret tunnel could look out, but no one could look in.

"You fled Nigel, that makes you a coward," the Bad Guy said.

"I did not flee him. I could have killed him, but I did not. I hoped that in time he would see the truth of what I was doing."

"So you say."

"A Selector should make his own judgments. Look at me now. Am I running?" The blue curtains on the landing caught fire with a *whoosh*, but Portia didn't even flinch.

"Even a rat will bite when cornered. That isn't courage; it's desperation."

Flames blistered the wallpaper behind her, blackening the cream-and-blue stripes, an evil, spreading stain.

"Trapped? I could have eluded you if I wanted to. I have a number of safe houses outside the city. I could have gone to any one of them, but I came here instead." Portia limped down one stair. "I wanted to meet you. We are not enemies. We share common goals."

The Bad Guy shifted forward, blocking Portia's exit. He held an axe loosely in one hand.

Kristy touched the cool glass, unsure what to do. If she broke it, she might have time to escape down the tunnel while Portia ran, but . . .

But.

There was something going on that Kristy didn't understand. Something that scared her more than a hundred axes. She waited.

"I offer you an alliance," Grandmother Portia said clearly. "You are right to some degree. The Futurists' blood is becoming polluted:

too many are marrying impures. A selective purge is needed, so that the next generation can be raised to greatness. I offer you a place as my right-hand man, my successor."

Kristy dropped flat on her stomach, irrationally afraid that the two-way glass would suddenly turn into a window. An alliance. Wasn't that like being partners?

"How do I know you're telling me the truth?"

"I brought you a gift. The child, Kristy. I locked her in the play-room upstairs." Portia's lip curled. "Although she's probably dead from smoke inhalation by now."

Kristy's heart pounded in slow, hard beats. The tears in her eyes evaporated like spit on an iron.

"You surprise me. Your own granddaughter?"

"Her blood is tainted, and my daughter poisoned her mind against me. Bah, she even looks like her father."

Kristy's chest felt tight. Smoke hazed the air, irritating her throat, but she did not move. She had to find out if the Bad Guy and Grand—no, Portia—became partners.

"You are all tainted. I will sweep aside your 'Futurists' like chaff." The Bad Guy swung the axe like a golf pro, chipping the head off a statuette and sending it flying against the wall.

[Don't like him,] Bobby whimpered. [Let's go, Kisty.]

"And when you finish? Will you kill yourself, too? You are one of us." Flame encased the upper half of the staircase like a living shroud. The banister creaked, tortured wood groaning.

The Bad Guy didn't answer, and Portia smiled triumphantly. "You won't kill yourself. You don't feel inferior; you feel superior. Nigel was wrong. The Talents grow stronger with every generation. If correctly controlled and channeled, the Futurists will become an Aryan superrace. The rulers of the world!"

"No one controls me. I am the Selector, and I have Selected you."

With a tremendous crack! the staircase collapsed under Portia. She pitched forward and landed sickeningly hard on the hardwood floor. She screamed as her clothes and hair caught fire like marsh-mallows dropped in a campfire. Laughing, the Bad Guy walked into the burning hell. He swung the axe—

Kristy looked away. Fear closed her throat, and smoke burned her lungs.

"She and Nigel made quite a pair," the Bad Guy said. "He couldn't believe it when I killed him either."

Then a very bad thing happened: Kristy coughed. The Bad Guy turned toward her hiding place. He had a black mustache and tattoos as if he worked for a circus.

"Fee, fi, fo, fum! I smell the blood of a coward!" He swung the axe at the wall, showering plaster in Kristy's hair.

She lunged to her feet, running into thicker smoke. She tried to hold her breath, tried not to cough, but the faster she ran the more she coughed.

Behind her glass shattered as he broke the two-way mirror.

She hit another wall. Not a corner this time—a dead end.

Axe thudding.

Kristy dropped to her knees and stuffed her fist in her mouth to stifle her coughs. Bobby coughed for her.

Thud. Footsteps in her direction. "You can't run from me. I'll find you." His voice echoed down the hallway, sounding both near and far.

The smoke was burning her eyes, her nose, and her lungs. She had to cough—had to—

Her fingers brushed a latch, and she fumbled to open the door. Escape! Coughs doubled her over as she crawled through. She barely had the strength to close it behind her.

The tunnel had shrunk. There was no longer room to stand up, and the walls were earth, not wood. Damp earth. Dark and narrow as a coffin.

She got dirt on her hands and under her fingernails as she crawled, coughing and coughing . . .

Something wet brushed her face, and she tried to scream, but her throat was so raw she coughed instead. Slowly, trembling, she reached into the darkness and touched several long dangling things. Roots.

Roots couldn't hurt her, but the axe man could. Keep moving.

A terrible coughing spell left her curled in a ball, weak and shaky.

Dizzy. She stopped crawling; it no longer seemed important. Even Bobby's voice was distant now. She sucked in air desperately, breathed in more smoke, and started coughing so hard she couldn't stop.

• 2 •

"Fire!" Bobby yelled.

Jeff stamped on the brakes; the station wagon screeched to a halt. He tore open his seat belt and twisted around, expecting to see smoke roiling out of the exhaust pipe. Instead, all he saw was his crying son.

"Kisty," Bobby sobbed. "I want Kisty," and, "Fire," again.

Penny undid his booster seat belt and helped him into the front seat between them. "What's wrong, honey?" She smoothed his brown hair.

Jeff's initial alarm faded. He couldn't see any fire.

"House on fire," Bobby said.

"What house, baby?"

Bobby looked confused. "Kisty's."

A cold ball of lead dropped into the pit of Jeff's stomach. "Shit. I *knew* we shouldn't have left her." He shifted into reverse, about to do a U-turn, when it hit him that Kristy was 70 km away in Calgary. Too far to rescue.

Penny's expression told him she'd realized the same thing, but her voice was soothing. "We want to help Kristy. Where's the fire?"

"Behind the door." Tears trickled down Bobby's chubby cheeks.

"Is there a window?"

Bobby hiccuped. "Kisty says . . . break my legs."

An upstairs room then. Damn. Jeff was about to suggest tying sheets together when Bobby coughed. "Hurts."

Terror seized Jeff by the throat so tight for a moment he couldn't speak, couldn't breathe. *My God, if Kristy died would Bobby die, too?*

Bobby coughed again, spurring Jeff's mind into gear. "Tell Kristy to cover her nose. There'll be more air near the floor. Tell her to crawl."

Bobby's breathing eased a little.

Penny squeezed Jeff's hand. "She'll be okay. Her danger instinct will save her."

Jeff wasn't comforted. "If her danger instinct was working, she wouldn't be trapped right now."

Both of them looked up when Bobby made a small sound of surprise. "Kisty found the see-ket tunnel."

Trust a psychic to choose a room with a secret tunnel. Jeff smiled until Bobby coughed again. "Why does he keep doing that?"

"The telepathic link between them must be stronger than we thought." Penny sounded strained.

Jeff watched Bobby breathe with single-minded intensity, dreading the next small cough. When it came his hands clenched into fists.

He saw Bobby's tear-filled brown eyes as if in a nightmare, remembering how blue they'd been the day Bobby was born and the fierce love and awe he'd felt when he first held his tiny son.

Fathering hadn't come naturally to Jeff. He'd lacked an example to follow, and the small breakable bundle they'd taken home from the hospital had terrified him. He'd done okay so far, more out of determination and overwhelming love than skill. He would have torn down mountains for Bobby, but he was helpless to save him from a fire 70 km away.

First your house, then your wife, then your son . . .

Coooughh, cough cough cough. Each harsh sound rammed a blade through Jeff's heart. In desperation he turned to Penny. "Isn't there anything you can do? Cut the link between them, or something?"

"I can't, I don't know how. And even if I could, it might kill him." She turned blind eyes to his face. "I always thought telepathy would be like an advanced form of empathy, but I don't know how to deal with this."

Coooughh, cough cough cough. Bobby wheezed like a bad set of bagpipes, tears streaming from his eyes.

Jeff bent anxiously over his son, wishing he could physically put himself between Bobby and the danger.

"For God's sake, will you stop whistling?"

Jeff stared. Had he been whistling? His eyes returned to Bobby's red face. *Please let Bobby live.*

"Run, Kristy, run," Penny whispered. Tears slid down her face.

He covered her hand with his and tried to remember what he knew about CPR.

The coughing went on for what seemed like hours, before suddenly easing. "Pipe," Bobby said. "Air."

Relief made Jeff crush his son and wife to him, kissing the top of Bobby's head. Five minutes later he still couldn't bear to let either of them go, although he became aware once again of traffic on the road and Penny's bulging stomach pressing against his arm. He felt Damaris kick.

His daughter.

For the first time Jeff wondered why Penny had gotten pregnant if she'd only married him to fulfill a prophecy. Penny believed in two-parent families. She would never have conceived a child if she hadn't believed she and Jeff would be married for a long time.

Even if she hadn't loved him when they married, she must feel some affection for him to bear two of his children.

· 3 ·

Ian was dead.

Matt hung up the phone, a fine tremor in his hands. His friend and fishing buddy, Ian, was dead. Matt had phoned Ian, planning to tell him the aliases the Selector had confessed to using and to ask Ian to run them through the computer. Ian's deputy, Norm Kowalski, had answered and told Matt that Ian had been murdered.

The Selector. It had to have been him. He'd broken his promise to Genevieve.

Matt looked over at Genevieve's sleeping body on the bed and wondered how he was going to tell her. She would blame herself.

God knew, he was choking on the bitter taste of guilt himself—it had been his idea to involve Ian.

Genevieve had just wanted to leave town. Matt was the one who'd come up with the clever idea of making a complaint against Crabtree, in order to spike the Selector's guns when the Selector came to accuse them of murder. He would have to remember to emphasize that to Genevieve when she woke up: the Selector would have gone to Ian no matter what they did.

Genevieve hadn't wanted him to phone Ian. Matt almost wondered if she'd had a suspicion the Selector might have broken his word and—

Genevieve's pale face after she'd finished talking to Ian. Matt's conviction that she was hiding something from him. This was what it was. Genevieve had known Ian was dead.

She'd known, and she hadn't told him.

Matt's first reaction was anger. His second one was hurt. He tried to talk himself out of both emotions—she must have been trying to protect him—but anger boiled up in him. Part of it, he knew, was anger over Ian's death, anger he couldn't take out on the Selector because the Selector wasn't there, but a larger part had its roots in the seven months of guessing games Genevieve had put him through when he'd thought she had amnesia.

When she'd finally told him the truth about her past, he'd been determined to put her lies behind them, but now here she was, doing it all over again.

He was angry enough to have woken her up, if the dream she was having hadn't been so important. Matt glanced at his watch. Ten minutes had passed. He had no idea how long that was in dream time. Seconds? Eons? Despite his anger, he became anxious. If the Selector was hunting the other children, Genevieve might encounter the Selector in her dream.

He was on the verge of shaking her awake when Genevieve woke up naturally, three minutes later.

She smiled. "That went better. I dreamed about a twelve-year-old boy. He didn't look like he was in any danger—he was asleep in bed. The name Peter Chambry was written on his binder, and his library books were stamped Thunder Bay Public Library."

"That's good," Matt said. He was glad Peter was alive and okay and relieved that the Selector had not appeared, but mostly he was mad. "Why didn't you tell me the Selector killed Ian?"

She flinched, and her gaze slid away from his, slippery as mercury. "How did you find out?"

"I phoned his house. Kowalski told me. Why didn't you?" Matt wasn't going to let her off the hook this time.

"I was going to, but . . ."

Matt waited.

She looked at him with wounded blue eyes. "He was your best friend, Matt. How could I tell you?"

"We're engaged to be married. I don't know about you, but to me marriage means sharing. Not just kisses and chores, but problems and burdens, too. If you can't tell me, who else is there? You're not alone anymore, Genevieve. Talk to me."

"I lean too much on you as it is."

"Leaning works both ways. I need you, too."

Genevieve said nothing, unconvinced.

She was going to need a demonstration. Matt said the words he'd been avoiding by arguing with Genevieve: "Tell me what happened."

Genevieve bowed her head, then nodded acquiescence. "The Selector went to Ian and demanded to know where we were. Ian wouldn't tell him. So,"—she swallowed—"the Selector shot him in the stomach."

Matt fought the urge to turn his head away. He'd asked for this knowledge. Ian had been his best friend. "Go on."

"Ian still wouldn't tell him. Then the Selector did something to him, something to his mind. He said he made Ian into his hunting dog. Ian said something about 'the claw,' the same thing Crabtree said. Ian said his ears were bleeding, and there was a red film across his eyes."

"So the whole time I was talking to Ian, the whole time the Selector spoke to me through him, Ian was lying there bleeding?" Matt was horrified to hear his voice crack, but the image would not go away: Ian trying to stop the bleeding with one hand while the Selector made him chat into the phone.

"Yes."

Her soft answer destroyed him. "*God.*"

Genevieve's arms came around him, and Matt buried his head in the crook of her neck. "I'm going to kill the bastard." His voice was thick.

"Ian said you would," Genevieve said, rocking him. "That was another reason why I didn't tell you. I was afraid you'd go off half-cocked and do something stupid."

Matt lifted his head. "I promise I won't. But I will get him." He buried his grief under a mountain of determination.

"I'm sorry," she whispered. She touched his face. "Sorry about Ian and about not telling you."

He stroked her hair. "I'm sorry, too. I knew something was bothering you earlier, but I didn't ask you to talk about it."

She bit her lip. "I really blew it, didn't I?"

"Nah. You just need more practice being part of a team," Matt said, making an effort to lighten the conversation. "So what's next? Now that we know you can dream at will?"

"I'll try Eileen next." Genevieve lay back down. She reached for Matt's hand and held it, eyes closed, until she fell asleep again.

Matt kept holding her hand with his left and picked up his pen with his right. He quickly jotted down a few notes on Genevieve's dream about Peter. Too bad the kid had been so young. Too young to be much help. Damn it, there had to be some way to turn the tables on the Selector. He tapped his pen, thinking.

Until Genevieve began to moan.

Matt shook her, but Genevieve just flopped bonelessly in his grasp and didn't wake.

"Genevieve!" Matt framed her face with his hands. He thumbed open one of her eyelids, but her eyes just kept moving in REM sleep. She wasn't seeing him, she was seeing the Selector. "No!" Matt said hoarsely. "You can't have her, you son of a bitch. Genevieve, wake up!"

Her eyes opened, focused on him. "Matt, no! I have to go back. He'll kill her!"

• 4 •

Smoke and flames billowed up like dragon's breath in a blue sky. Only the outline of Portia Carver's two-story riverside house remained. April screeched to a halt at the end of the long driveway, hardly able to breathe. Kristy. Kristy was in there. "She didn't want to stay here. I *made* her stay."

"Danger instinct, keep safe," Gavin rasped, but twin lines of strain bracketed his mouth as he threw open the van door.

April followed, stumbling under a burden of guilt. "Why didn't I let her come with me on the jailbreak? She could have waited in the van."

Gavin grabbed her hand. "Do illusion. Killer may still be here."

April tried to think [invisible], but the stretched-thin feeling didn't come. She couldn't concentrate. Kristy was dead.

"Not dead!" Gavin shook her, and April realized she had spoken aloud.

"She's just a little kid." April couldn't look away from the burning building. "I stopped her from obeying her danger instinct."

"Not dead," Gavin insisted, despite the pain talking caused his bruised throat. "If died in fire, would have screamed. Didn't hear scream, still alive."

April seized the hope with both hands. She blinked back tears and looked around. Even this far away she could feel the heat of the blaze. Portia must have watered the lawn, because the grass was wet, impeding the flames, but nothing could save the proud stand of conifers. They burned like torches, crackling, dry needles exploding.

"Kristy!" she called. "Kristy, where are you?"

Crackling, hissing flames.

Gavin took up the call, "Kristy!"

April walked forward two steps, and someone called her name. "April!"

She recognized Kristy's voice, but couldn't see her anywhere. She spun in circles. "Kristy, where are you? Kristy!"

"Shh." Gavin grabbed her arm, and she heard another weak call. "April?"

"Kristy, where are you?"

". . . here," the disembodied voice whispered.

April looked around frantically, but there was no place *to* look. The nearest trees were on the next property, the nearest building across a paved street. "I can't see you. Where are you?"

"Down . . ." Straining to catch the whisper. "I'm down here."

April looked in the direction of her purple sneakers, but saw only grass.

"Keep talking," Gavin said.

Kristy coughed instead.

In the end April stumbled over the answer: the end of a small pipe hidden in the grass. She knelt down, talking into the tube. "Kristy, are you in there?"

"Yes . . ." More coughing echoed up through the pipe.

Frightened by the sound, April pulled on the rusty metal pipe, but it remained solidly stuck in the ground. "Kristy, is there a handle or door anywhere by you?"

Gavin crouched beside her, listening to the reply.

"Dead end." The words floated up like balloons, followed by another bout of coughing.

Jesus. April tried not to let her fear show in her voice. "Don't worry, Kristy. We'll dig you out."

Gavin was already on his feet. He scooped up a hoe from an untended flower bed and ran back.

The hoe's sharp blade made April shudder—what if it struck Kristy's head?—but there was no choice. "Okay, Kristy, we're going to start digging now. Back up away from the pipe. Some dirt is going to trickle down, but that's okay."

". . . need air."

Sweat fell in icy trickles down April's spine. "Hold on just a little longer, honey. I want you to lie on your back and kick at the ceiling near the pipe. We'll get you out as fast as we can, I promise."

No reply. Had Kristy backed up or passed out because of lack of air? It made no difference, the only thing April could do was help dig. She pushed away the dirt Gavin dug up and clawed grass with her hands.

"How far down do you think she is?"

"At least a foot." Gavin still sounded awful, like Frankenstein's monster talking through a mouthful of gravel.

"Why a foot?"

Gavin pointed to the spot where they were kneeling. "Ground would collapse otherwise."

April still had her mouth open over that horrible image when she felt danger like a blow between the shoulder blades. Instinctively, she looked up and saw a man exit the burning building. Fire consumed his clothes, but other than an occasional swat he paid the flames no heed.

He was a big man, mustached, and his brawny arms looked capable of snapping April in half.

"Dig faster," she whispered, and assumed the mantle of invisibility, smoothing the lumps of sod back into the lawn, erasing herself and Gavin.

She froze when he walked straight toward them. Flames licked at his hair, blistering his face. "Where are you, coward?" Without warning his path changed to random zigzags. His face, which should have been a rictus of pain, showed fury instead. "I'll get you, you little bitch."

He swerved toward them. April held her ground; Gavin worked faster, dirt slopping over into her shoes. Six meters away. Did the man hear the hoe?

Abruptly, he changed direction, shedding little pools of fire. "Where are you? You can't hide from me."

The scarring on his face and back was brutal. Most of his clothes had burned away, exposing a red-and-blue dragon tattoo, wrapped around his back. Blisters and running blood made the dragon writhe, as if devouring him. April bit her lip to keep from crying out. Those had to be third-degree burns. How could he still be walking?

He couldn't.

As fire engines screamed their approach, his zigzags turned into stumbles, and then the stumbles into falls. Three times he fell, three times he got up. April couldn't bear to watch. He was an arsonist intent on killing Kristy, but she couldn't watch, turning her head away. [*Invisible.*]

"Got it." Gavin grunted, pulling out the pipe and leaving behind a wider hole. He immediately attacked that with the hoe, sending dirt crumbling in.

Kristy's air hole vanished.

One last flailing arm movement out of the corner of her eye. The arsonist was dead. April strained to cover him with the grass illusion for the arriving fire engines while scooping dirt.

"Found her shoe!" Gavin dug frantically for Kristy's second ankle, then pulled. Kristy popped up out of the hole like a cork.

For a second she looked dead, and April's illusions blew apart like cobwebs in a fierce gale, then Kristy coughed and fresh tears tracked down her dusty cheeks as she opened her eyes.

She was alive.

• 5 •

Eileen Friestaad did not want to go with her parents to the annual Theroux Institute dinner. She had gone to six previous dinners and had suffered through the last two.

So this year she'd prepared half a dozen impeccable, logical arguments why she should stay home. The dinners bored her. Her nagging to leave early would spoil the dinner for her parents. She had nothing suitable to wear but the too-tight pink dress she'd worn last year. She didn't like the Chicken Cordon Bleu they served every year. Finally—God bless Mme. Meynard—she had a science test Monday, and science was not her best subject.

She presented all her arguments in English, the language of logic and her father's native tongue, not her *maman*'s French.

Not once did she hint at her real reason for not wanting to go. An emotional reason. Her parents disliked emotional thinking, which clouded their scientific judgment.

Andre Theroux would be there.

Eileen hated, loathed, and despised Andre Theroux. Grandson of her parents' employers, Andre *always* came to the dinners, and he'd made the last two a living hell for her.

The dinners bored Andre, so he'd turned to tormenting Eileen for entertainment. She was the perfect age: too old to tattle to her parents when he laughed at her and called her a skinny boy in a dress and too young to tell him to "F—— off." She'd tried to avoid him, but he'd caught her arm and pinched her fiercely. "If you go, I'll get your parents fired." She didn't really think he could, but last year when she'd told him she didn't believe him he'd instantly come up with something even worse—a lie so terrible Eileen hadn't been able to breathe for a moment when he first said it—he'd threatened to tell her father they'd had sex.

This year, at thirteen, Eileen had finally developed something that might kindly be called a bosom, and she would *not* go to the Theroux dinner and have Andre belittle her chest and try to sneak feels. It was not to be tolerated. It could not be borne. She would not go to the dinner.

Her arguments amused her dad, and he agreed. "It's fine with me."

Maman had studied her thoughtfully, sensing that Eileen wasn't telling the complete truth, but she miscalculated the cause. "You're right, you do need a new dress. You should have told me earlier. We could have bought you something pretty to impress Andre."

Maman thought she had a crush on Andre. Whenever there were adults around Andre made a big show of holding hands with Eileen and smiling at her. He was a good-looking boy, and no one but Eileen seemed to notice that his eyes were beady and mean and that he was grinding her wristbones together.

Frightened that her mother would make her go out and buy a new dress, Eileen launched into another rendition of I-can't-possibly-go-to-the-dinner.

Finally, *Maman* became impatient and shrugged her shoulders. "*Bien.* Andre will be disappointed, but he will no doubt find some other girl to talk to."

Eileen let the comment pass without a word.

But now, watching her parents prepare to leave for cocktails, Eileen had a sinking feeling she'd dug her own grave.

She did not want to stay home by herself.

The feeling had grown all day, in ridiculous, illogical leaps and bounds, while she'd watched her *maman* transform herself from a scientist into a woman, black hair down and red lipstick on.

She was on the verge of begging not to be left alone when her *maman* said, "Well, *chérie,* last chance to change your mind and see Andre. Do you want to come?"

Beady eyes looking down her dress . . .

"No," Eileen said on a rush of sanity. "May I invite Janine over to study with me?"

"Janine is a chatterbox," *Maman* said, deftly hooking rhinestone earrings into her earlobes. "You will talk about boys instead of studying." She smiled at Eileen. "I am glad you are taking your science studies more seriously. Study hard." She pressed her cheek against Eileen's, so Eileen smelled Obsession, but *Maman*'s lipstick went unsmeared.

Eileen heard the coffin lid banging down. She did not understand herself. Why was she so frightened? She'd stayed home alone before, once even for an entire weekend.

But all the scientific logic in the world could not slow the waves of panic crashing through her, breaking over her head. When her dad kissed her good night she couldn't speak because fear had closed her throat.

Her dad frowned. "Are you feeling okay, Eileen? You look a little pale."

Oui! Eileen's mind screamed. *I'm sick! I'm dying! Don't leave me alone!*

Maman put a hand on Eileen's forehead. "You do feel a little hot. Do you want one of us to stay home with you?"

Eileen's impulse to play sick died. The Theroux dinner was

238 • N. M. LUIKEN

important to her parents. *Maman* had been nominated for an award. She was being stupid and childish. "I'll be okay." Her mouth tasted like ashes.

Her dad hesitated a second longer. "You have the number of the hotel. Call us if you feel worse."

Eileen nodded, and they left. The second the door closed behind them she clicked shut the dead bolts. She stood by the door feeling abandoned for a moment before obsessively checking every window in the house.

When she'd finished, restless and edgy, she sat by the phone. She memorized the hotel's number and practiced punching it with the receiver down. That look too long, so she punched 911 a few times, too.

After a long half hour spent with her back against the wall watching the living room and hallway, she got out her science textbook. After another fifteen minutes of nerve-wracking suspense she even opened it.

Reading and memorizing helped. Kingdoms and phyla filled her head instead of ghosts and burglars.

She jumped a foot when the doorbell rang.

Eileen shrank back against the couch. Maybe if she ignored the doorbell, the visitor would decide no one was home and go away.

Ding, dong.

Go away.

Ding, dong. Ding, dong.

But if it was a burglar he might break in, thinking the house was empty.

Ding, dong.

Uncertainly, Eileen got to her feet. She crossed over to the kitchen and pulled a carving knife out of the wooden block. The weapon gave her the courage to tiptoe down the hall.

The front door had a peephole. She would look through it, and, if she didn't recognize the caller, she'd tell them to go away. She would be perfectly safe. The door had a dead bolt.

Ding, dong. Ding, dongdingdongdingdong.

Eileen crossed the porch linoleum and put one eye to the peephole.

Even through the wavery fisheye lens the man on the other side was striking. He had blond hair—not the dirty blond that her dad's hair lightened to in summer, but yellow shiny blond blond—and his eyes were the startling green of emeralds, his face sculpted . . . In Janine's words: "a total babe."

At the moment, however, Eileen was far more interested in the fact that he wore a police uniform.

He shifted impatiently and stabbed the doorbell again. *Ding, dong.*

"'Allo?" Eileen said shakily. Had something happened to her parents? A car accident?

"Miss?" His voice enfolded her like warm velvet. "Is someone there? It's the police." He held a silver shield up to the peephole. Montreal Police Department, it said.

"Please, open the door." The man's voice was low-pitched, but anxious. Concerned for her. "You're in danger. Your neighbor reported an intruder entering your house."

An intruder! She had been right to be afraid: there was a burglar in the house. Abruptly, she felt danger breathing down the back of her neck, coming closer. Without another thought, she flipped the dead bolts.

The lock clicked, and the blond man shoved hard against the door, sending her sprawling backward.

Eileen landed hard against the porch steps, and her glasses went flying. She got in one small swipe with the carving knife before he pinned her to the stairs, one hand around her throat.

"You shouldn't have cut me," he said—in English! *Mon Dieu,* he had spoken English the whole time! The pressure on her windpipe increased, and black spots danced before her eyes. Her body strained under his, but could not throw him off. She couldn't breathe; she was dying.

He saw it and smiled, a gift of glory.

Not a babe, an archangel, she thought, and the black wings of a hundred velvet butterflies shrouded her vision.

• 6 •

She cut me! The bitch dared cut me!

The pain was nothing, the cut little more than a scratch, but the insult of being marked by a girl made a red mist of fury swim in front of the Selector's eyes. He was conscious only of the girl's smooth throat under his hands, her bulging eyes. Her body had gone limp before he realized her audacity in attacking him had shown courage.

Breathing heavily, he pulled himself out of the red mists and released her trachea. Impatiently, he began to search her for another sign of inferiority. He was confident he would find one; he had yet to find someone who matched his own superiority. The Selector calculated there were only a handful of Superiors in a million, so it wasn't really surprising he had not found one yet—he had yet to rack up his first thousand kills. Still, he always checked his victims before making a Final Selection.

He started with her body, taking inventory. He ran his hands up over her budding breasts and smoothed down each arm, making sure the bones ran straight and true, counting her fingers. He did the same to her legs, then pushed at her stomach, feeling for nonexistent rolls of fat. Her skin was pale and silky-smooth, untouched by the sun.

Technically, a tan was not a sign of impurity, but it usually angered the Selector so much to see a white woman deliberately turning herself black, that he bent the rule and killed anyhow.

He forced her mouth open, looking for braces or buckteeth and finding neither. Not even a filling.

She moaned, starting to come round, so he pinched her nose closed and held his hand over her mouth until she stopped thrashing. To make sure she stayed under, he banged her head hard against the step.

Her hair was shit brown instead of gold, but her eyes redeemed her: when he thumbed them open he saw that they were a deep, almost navy, blue.

Like Mary's.

Her body was tall and gangly, unfeminine, her breasts just bumps, but however much he wanted to he could not Select her on those grounds: she was still maturing.

That left mental capacity. She had not sounded retarded when she answered the door, merely cautious. Only his Shine had caused her to open it.

A hot surge of frustration choked him. He didn't want Eileen to be Superior. He wanted to kill, to feel her neck snap beneath his hands, to carve her flesh . . .

He had to avert his head for a moment, reining in his bloodlust. He was trying to convince himself she hadn't shown courage at all, had cut him by accident, when he chanced to see a pair of glasses lying on the linoleum floor. One earpiece was bent. He picked them up and began to smile. They were girl's glasses, with pink frames and grossly thick lenses that warped his vision worse than a fun-house mirror.

She was deformed, after all.

He broke the other earpiece off and dropped them back on the floor.

Before the invention of glasses, such poor vision would already have cost her her life. If humans weren't to become myopic as a race, people like her had to be stopped from passing their defective genes onto the next generation.

Lovingly, he wrapped his hands back around her throat.

He'd just started to squeeze when a stir of air lifted the hairs on the back of his neck. His muscles coiled, prepared to spin and lunge, then suddenly relaxed as he recognized the sensation.

"Mary."

Mary was there, and yet not there. Flesh without substance. A ghost.

Her dream image flickered as if made on old film with too few frames per second, and her sneakers made no sound as she drifted through the open doorway.

Her outfit of jeans and a blue button-down shirt disappointed him;

she usually wore a nightgown. He was a Selector, not a common rapist, but there was something deliciously vulnerable about Mary in her nightwear. More surface area to work with.

If he touched her, he would feel warm skin, but at the first prick of his knife she would melt away like snow in the rain.

Hooking was also dissatisfying. He'd forged a bond of sorts between them that pulled her to him during his nighttime killings, but aside from that connection she was a lock that wouldn't open. Whenever he tried to embed his hook, he netted only a scattering of random thoughts before her danger instinct woke her.

Because Mary couldn't be killed or hooked, she was in the unique position of being the only person since Nigel died with whom he had actually conversed.

"I didn't expect to see you again quite so soon, Mary. You're just in time; I was about to start the evening's entertainment." He indicated Eileen's limp body.

Mary wasn't as courteous. "What have you done to her, you bastard? Is she dead?"

"Not—quite—yet."

He'd only intended a simple choking, but Mary's presence changed his mind. Charged him up. He always performed better with an audience.

The cut on his arm gave him an idea. He picked up a drop of ruby blood with one blunt finger. "See this, Mary? She cut me. I think I'll cut her back. That's fair, isn't it?" He picked up the girl's knife. He had one of his own, but the irony of using the blade she'd defended herself with appealed to him. He drew a delicate line down her cheek, from the corner of her eye to the line of her jaw. Red blood welled.

"No!" Mary grabbed his wrist.

It was the first time she'd ever touched him; the Selector felt a shock of pleasure down to his toes. Mary tried to hold him, but she lacked the strength. Inexorably, he moved his hand, repeating the cut on Eileen's right cheek. If the girl had woken it would have seemed as if Mary was helping him. As if they were partners.

Mary dropped her hand with a cry. She turned transparent and for an instant she vanished entirely, [*Matt, no! I have to go back. He'll kill her!*]

The poet man must have listened because she reappeared.

The poet man. Remembered rage overwhelmed the Selector's pleasure in Mary's company. "You slept with him. I smelled it on the sheets."

"Yes." Mary didn't deny it.

"You shouldn't have done that." Mary belonged to him. "I was just going to kill him, but now I'll cut his heart out. I've always wondered: do poet men have red blood or is it pink?"

Mary's face lost color, but she remained defiant. "You haven't been very successful in catching me so far."

What she said was true. To punish her, the Selector traced the two bracketing lines he had cut in Eileen's face. "Not quite symmetrical, but close. Where do you think I should mark her next? Her ears? She already has two holes in them, she probably won't even mind. Maybe her eyes. Her throat?" He held the knife over each area in turn.

"You're sick." Mary was trembling. "You call yourself the Selector, but you're just a sick son of a bitch—"

The Selector frowned. He didn't approve of women swearing.

"—sick in the head, twisted—"

She was making him angry. His hand itched to slap her. "Shut up."

Incredibly, she didn't listen. "—sicko psycho who belongs in a mental hospital wearing diapers and a straitjacket—"

Enraged, he started to reach out, to slam her against the wall—

No. She would wake from her dream if he did that. He tipped back Eileen's slim white neck. "One more word, and I'll slit her throat."

Silence, like turning off a tap. The Selector savored it, confident once more in his power and control. He was the Selector, he—

"Why should I be quiet? You'll kill her anyway."

"Maybe, maybe not. Maybe I'll let you save her, Mary." He turned on all his persuasive charm, Shine so pure and blinding he could have sold a snowmobile to a Sahara tribesman. "Would you like to

244 • N. M. LUIKEN

do that? Save her? If you really want to you can. I'll trade you, just like last time."

"I don't believe you." Flatly. "You killed Ian, you broke your word."

"You asked for the wrong thing. I let him go, as I promised. You forgot to say what condition I had to leave him in. You can save Eileen. If you want."

"What would I trade? My location?" Still suspicious, but like a fish nibbling at a tasty-looking worm.

"No. The price is higher this time. Your sister's life for yours." He held his breath. Mary's death would be worth a thousand Eileens.

She hesitated. She was just sentimental enough to do it.

Come on little fishie, swallow the bait.

"No." An expulsion of air, a gasp, pulling back from the brink. "No."

"A shame." Disappointed, he straddled Eileen's hips and raised the knife high above his head in a two-handed grip. In this position he could shatter her breastbone with one blow—

"Wait!"

Mary's voice stayed his hand. He looked up.

She was milk-pale. "Isn't there . . . something else you want from me?" She took a step forward. Swallowed. "Crabtree said you had a room ready for me."

"You'll surrender yourself to me?" The Selector was unable to keep his eagerness out of his voice. She would belong to him.

"Yes," Mary said. "But only here. In my dream."

Surrender was surrender. If Mary was too stupid to realize that, the Selector wouldn't tell her. "It's a deal. Eileen can live."

"You'll leave her alone? Not harm her in any way? Neither you, nor your minions?" Mary asked anxiously.

"Yes." It went against his principles not to kill someone he'd Selected, but the chance to have Mary was too tempting to resist. "Take my hand."

Shaking, Mary did so. He could feel the tension in her hand, her need to flee, but for once she didn't turn to smoke and vanish. He tipped up her chin.

Her eyes closed, and the Selector realized she expected him to kiss her — that that was the surrender she thought he meant.

The Selector wanted nothing so paltry as that. "Look into my eyes."

Helpless blue eyes stared up at him.

"*Surrender.*" He cast his hook, snagging her soul.

CHAPTER 9

• 1 •

On the day of Al's funeral, Peter got up at 6 A.M. His parents had already decided that he wouldn't attend the funeral — or rather his mother had decided, and his father had sighed and given in. (I won't risk a repeat of the scene that woman made at the ravine.)

If they'd asked, Peter would have told them he didn't want to go to the funeral. He didn't want to see Al's dead body, dressed up in a suit that Al would have hated. He didn't need to "say good-bye" as the woman doctor had urged. Saying good-bye wouldn't make him feel better. Revenge would.

Dressed in dark colors, he crept downstairs. He did not hurry or tiptoe. He and Al had once spent an entire rainy afternoon finding out which floorboards creaked and plotting a silent course through the house.

The thick blue carpet his mother loved was easy to walk softly on; the woods were a challenge. A person really needed moccasins to feel dead twigs underfoot before they snapped. Al had had a pair —

Peter carefully stopped thinking about Al. Remembering made his anger burn white-hot. So hot it frightened him a little, as if it might get away from him. Better to freeze it.

He slipped outside in stocking feet. The ground felt cold and slightly frosty. His mother would complain about his filthy socks, but he didn't care. He needed silence and stealth to catch a murderer.

As dawn touched the horizon, shining pink and gold through the lattice of tree trunks, Peter took an axe and some rope from the shed and walked into the forest. He threaded through the trees with ease.

His mother had forbidden him to go there, but Peter knew the woods had not killed Al. The murderer had.

Peter didn't know who the murderer was, but he knew the murderer would return.

He relived again the tickle of warning that had kept him from crossing the log first. From the seek-and-capture games he had played with Al he knew the tickle only came when he was in danger.

If he had crossed the log first, he would have been the one to die.

Anyone who watched would have known Peter and Al usually met and parted at the ravine. Peter crossed the log and went home for supper; Al went the other way. Except last Friday they'd gone together to fetch a book. So Al, wearing Peter's jacket, had crossed first and died in his place.

Oh, yes, the murderer would be back.

Peter clenched his fist on the sickle scar on his palm. He and Al had sworn to be blood brothers, and his blood brother's death must be avenged.

For an hour Peter climbed trees and knotted rope. Drawing on Al's grandfather's tales and his illustrated hunting and trapping library book, he constructed a trap. When he finished, he stole back into the house.

He had enough time to undress, bury his dirty socks in the hamper, and climb into bed before his mother came in to wake him. Patiently, Peter dressed all over again and ate a silent breakfast with his parents. He read Justice League comic books all morning.

At three o'clock his mother left for the funeral, hugging him goodbye. He squeezed back—just a little. She looked so worried, and she thought all he was going to do was read comic books.

Fifteen minutes later, after his father had settled down in front of the TV to watch sports, Peter slipped out a window and vanished into the silent woods. His trap was missing one vital ingredient.

Bait.

• 2 •

The world twisted around Genevieve as she fell down, down into the Selector's blue eyes.

She woke up in her bedroom, the bedroom she'd lived in for over half her life in Aunt Dorothy's house. She recognized the ballerina wallpaper she'd picked out when she was fourteen and the single bed with its white bedspread. Disorientation flooded her. Was she dreaming? But the room looked as if she'd never left it. There was her stereo in the corner and the careless jumble of her earrings on the dresser. If she looked in the closet, her clothes would still be hanging there.

Her room must have looked like this the day the Selector came for her and murdered Aunt Dorothy.

The sensation of falling came back to her and the deal she'd made with the Selector to save Eileen's life. He'd asked for her surrender, and she'd given it, thinking he had rape in mind.

Instead he'd imprisoned her. Genevieve tried the door, but wasn't surprised to find it not just locked but unopenable, grown into the wall. The window was the same, the scene outside it a static picture of the front yard and street. Wherever she was, it wasn't real.

She was inside the Selector's mind, neatly tucked away in the room he'd made ready for her, his to visit whenever he wanted. Forever.

Genevieve fought down the horror rising inside her. She wasn't going to be imprisoned here forever. She would find a way out.

How?

Genevieve tried the obvious. She went to the door and pounded on it. "Hello? Is anyone there?"

No reply.

Next she tried running at the door with her shoulder and smashing her chair through the window, but only rebounded painfully both times. All she learned was that she could still experience pain — which was hardly reassuring, considering whose prisoner she was.

She went over every inch of her prison cell, probing for a weak spot, but found none. Exhausted, she lay back on her girl's bed. She had no way of knowing how much time had passed, or if time passed here at all.

Back in the real world Matt would be frantic.

Matt. Genevieve closed her eyes and fixed his face in front of her like a beacon. Maybe she could key into him somehow, wake up—

Someone screamed.

Genevieve's heart jumped into her throat. The first scream was still ringing in her ears when the second started and quickly rose to a bloodcurdling shriek.

A lull of perhaps two or three seconds, and then the screams started again.

The sound seemed to be coming from the other side of the wall. She pressed her palms against the fake wallpaper, feeling helpless and afraid as scream after scream rang out. Was the Selector torturing some poor woman? Holding red-hot pokers to her flesh?

Would he come for her next?

Scream after scream after scream after scream pierced the air until Genevieve thought she would shatter into a million pieces like finely tuned crystal—

The walls of her prison cracked like an egg. They fell in tissue-thin peels on the ground, revealing another reality.

The screams stopped.

Trembling, Genevieve walked toward the hole in the wall. She stepped through the portal—

—and into a castle. White marble floors, veined with pink. Rippling blue-and-green tapestries that stretched up and up as if they might touch heaven itself.

The castle was empty save for a young blond woman in the center of the ballroom dancing with herself. She swayed and dipped to unheard music, smiling dreamily up at an invisible partner. Her long blond hair shone gold under her wedding veil, and pearls glittered on her exquisite white dress.

Genevieve recognized her. It was the girl she had dreamed about, the dead girl in the grass.

Did that mean Genevieve was dead, too?

No. She'd been dreaming when the Selector took her, far from her physical body.

"AaaaaiiiieeeeeeeeeeeeeeeeEEEEEE!"

The blond girl fell to the floor and writhed in agony, although, as far as Genevieve could see, nothing touched her. Dying and then being brought here must have driven her mad.

"Ron? Ron, don't. Please, don't. No!" Another shriek as the invisible Ron refused to listen.

Blood appeared, streaking the blonde's face and throat, staining her wedding gown.

Genevieve hurried forward to take the blonde's hand. "It's all right. Whatever you're seeing isn't real."

The blonde stared right through Genevieve, but the contact seemed to soothe her. She started crying. "Gavin, help me! I know you can hear me: you love me. Please, Gavin, you've got to help me!" She wept beautiful tears. "I'll love you forever, if you'll just get me out of here!"

Genevieve's heart twisted in sympathy. "I'll help you," she said, but the woman did not hear her. She kept pleading for Gavin even when Genevieve waved her arms in front of her face.

Ten minutes later the crying eased, and the blond girl slept.

Genevieve hesitated, but she couldn't stay here forever. "If I find a way out, I'll come back for you, I promise."

• 3 •

Penny stroked Bobby's hair, needing the reassurance of touch to believe that he really was all right, unharmed by his brush with death.

He was eating another Revel and making a mess of it, but Penny didn't care. He was alive. He was safe.

In fact, Bobby had recovered better than his parents had.

Jeff was sitting on the other side of her in the backseat, his worry and relief so sharp the emotions snapped like brightly colored flags around his head.

They both needed a distraction. Penny asked him the first question off the top of her head. "Why do you always whistle when you're tense?"

She expected him to evade the question, but Jeff answered slowly, "It's a signal my old man taught me when I was twelve. I'd play lookout while he broke into a car. 'Jingle Bells' meant danger, someone was coming."

Penny couldn't help herself; her mouth fell open. "Your father took you along as a lookout when you were twelve?"

Jeff looked cynical and amused. "Well, I think he was my father." "You think?"

"I never asked. But he looked some like me, and he'd sometimes teach me stuff. Ma's other boyfriends never bothered with me and Todd. He promised me a bike once, but of course he was back in the slammer by Christmas."

Of course. Penny's heart squeezed for the disappointment Jeff must have felt. His father must have been a rat. Might still be a rat. Penny had no idea if he was alive or dead. Yet another item to add to the growing list of things she did not know about Jeff.

It shamed Penny how little she did know about her husband. They'd been married four years, but she'd never heard the story about his brother Todd going to jail before today. Hadn't even known he had a brother.

Her empathy had made her complacent.

Oh, she'd known Jeff didn't have close family ties and that he'd been poor, but she'd always presumed he came from a single-parent welfare family. He'd never mentioned his father or brother.

He hadn't said much about his mother either. Jeff had told her she was dead, but now Penny wondered if that had been a lie, if Jeff had just not wanted them to meet.

She'd sensed some turmoil whenever Jeff spoke of his mother, but she'd passed it off as grief and never probed deeper. She'd just gone happily along, skimming the surface.

Complacent *and* selfish.

She had a lot to make up for.

She didn't know how, but she'd hurt Jeff. Badly.

Jeff showed a hard front, but for those he allowed in, he had a heart like a marshmallow. In a day's time he'd started thinking of Kristy as family.

He still felt hostile toward Gavin, but that was her own fault for using Gavin to make Jeff jealous five years ago.

She'd been so impatient back then. She'd pursued Jeff shamelessly, first striking up a conversation with him at the party, then asking for his phone number. When he hadn't phoned her, she'd phoned him, drawing him into a discussion on movies they liked. When he mentioned wanting to see an action flick; she'd said, "Me too! Let's go together. Cheap Tuesday sound okay?"

She'd badgered him into their second date the same way. Confident of his attraction she'd ignored his hesitation, passing it off as shyness instead of finding the cause and fixing it then.

Now the whole thing had blown up in her face.

"Kisty says Pursha's dead." Bobby licked melted chocolate off his fingers.

Pursha? Did he mean Portia? "Ask Kristy what happened."

Bobby tried to explain, but he obviously didn't understand himself, mangling words and tangling sentences. "Burned up like Caroline. Bad Guy watched. Curtains 'n stairs on fire. Cow-herd. Hit wall. Jack and the Beanstalk . . ."

Beanstalk? Penny and Jeff exchanged puzzled glances.

"Bad Guy. Kisty run, run, run. Coughed."

When Bobby finished Jeff shook his head. "I don't get it. If Portia had the danger instinct, why didn't she leave?"

Penny remembered Portia's erect bearing at the Council meeting. "Pride."

"She wanted the Bad Guy to be a Futurist," Bobby said clearly.

Jeff stared at Bobby as if he'd never seen his son before. "That wasn't him, was it? That was Kristy talking."

Penny leapt to her son's defense. "Don't look at him like that! Bobby is not a freak." *I am not a freak.*

"Of course, he isn't." Hurt filled Jeff's eyes. "I may be a lousy father, but I would never think of Bobby as a freak."

Penny was immediately ashamed of her mistake. Jeff's concern was valid. The depth of Bobby's link to Kristy worried her, too — what would happen when they hit puberty? She had just started to apologize when the second half of his words sank in. "What do you mean, 'lousy'? You're a terrific father." She couldn't count the number of hours he'd spent reading to Bobby, playing with him, building Lego mansions while his son slobbered on the pieces.

"If I'm so terrific, why has Bobby almost died twice in twenty-four hours?"

"That wasn't your fault." [*Rank disbelief.*] Penny tried again. "Do you know why Bobby's favorite cartoon character is Batman, instead of Superman or Wonder Woman?" She didn't wait for his answer. "It's because Batman doesn't rely on powers that he inherited from his alien or Amazonian parents; he uses his brain and his gadgets to defeat the villains — just like his father. Only you're better than Batman because he buys his gadgets while you make yours."

Jeff dismissed her words. "Bobby just likes toys."

Penny opened her mouth, then shut it again. Telling him he was a wonderful father wouldn't convince him. Jeff's psyche was proving to have some unexpected curves, and she needed to learn more before she could offer any instant cures.

After kissing Bobby's forehead one last time, Penny and Jeff resumed their seats in the front of the station wagon and Jeff started driving again. It was a long drive to Ontario and Peter. Penny decided she might as well make use of the time. "Tell me about your brother."

"What's to tell? He was a criminal, now he's dead."

Jeff's flippancy didn't fool Penny; he was as tense as a guitar string. She kept her voice mild. "Well, for starters, was he older than you?"

"Two years." Jeff's clipped tone didn't encourage further questions. He switched lanes to pass a truck.

"Did he look like you?"

Jeff whipped in front of the truck, a little too close for comfort.

"No. Todd was only one-quarter Cree; he looked as white as you. Ma called him her 'blond angel.' "

"And was he an angel?"

Jeff stared straight ahead down the highway. "He could be. When it suited him. When he wanted something."

"And when he didn't?"

Silence. Then, as if the words were being dragged out of him, "A blue-eyed demon. If I so much as looked sideways at him, he'd give me matching black eyes. Then two days later he'd be all buddy-buddy. 'Here's fifty bucks, kid. Go buy yourself something.' And, 'By the way, there's a car-alarm job I'd like you to do.' "

A real user. Penny felt a spurt of anger. "Did you do the jobs for him?"

"Until he killed that poor old woman. I even took the rap for him once because I was under eighteen, a young offender, and he was old enough to be tried in an adult court."

"You loved him." Penny made a statement instead of a question, but Jeff answered her anyway, consumed by bitterness.

"Love? Until we were teenagers I worshiped him. He was my older brother. He could do no wrong, and he could be so damned nice sometimes. Slipping me money for ice cream or smokes, running interference for me when Ma got mean drunk and started with the belt. Todd could always calm her down when she was like that, but just looking at me seemed to make her angry. I always figured she must have really loved his father."

A belt? Penny seriously doubted the woman he'd described was capable of love.

"What happened after Todd was arrested?"

"About what you'd expect. Ma kicked me out. I lived on the streets for a while. I'd probably still be there, but the store I stopped to buy cigarettes in had a broken-down coffee machine. I offered to fix it for the manager and ended up with a job pumping gas. He's the one who told me I should get a student loan and apply at SAIT as a mature student."

"And then you met me," Penny finished softly.

"So now you know," Jeff said roughly. "You're married to a thief. Someone who ratted on his own brother."

Penny felt him bracing himself for a blow, and it suddenly hit her that he expected her to reject him. To be ashamed and repulsed. Nothing could be farther from the truth, and she told him so, voice shaking with emotion. "You make me so proud, Jeff. I always knew you were special, but I didn't know why. You had to be so strong to resist. So many others would have succumbed to the lure of easy money."

[*Astonishment and anger.*] "Haven't you been listening? I'm a thief. My brother was a murderer. I don't deserve you and Bobby."

"You *were* a juvenile delinquent. A troubled youth who merely followed the example of his older brother and father. You're a good, decent man, and any woman would be proud to have you as a husband."

Jeff didn't say anything, didn't look at her, but he couldn't hide his emotions. They surprised her. Instead of sweet relief or heavy doubt, they burned like a beacon inside of him.

[A *flare of hope.*]

• 4 •

Nine hours. Genevieve had been unconscious for nine hours.

Matt was beyond frantic and well into despair. Since she'd slipped away from him, he'd tried everything he could think of to wake her. He'd talked to her and held her hand, kissed her, shook her, yelled at her, even forced himself to slap her twice. He'd yelled, "Fire!" and hoisted her to her feet and tried to make her walk. He'd thrown ice-cold water on her face. Throughout it all she'd remained as limp as a cooked noodle.

Comatose.

No, Matt told himself. *Whatever had happened to Genevieve it was nothing so simple as a coma.*

For that reason he hadn't taken her to a hospital. Yet. He would be forced to soon. Genevieve's body would die without food and water. He couldn't let that happen, but at the same time Matt was convinced that the medical profession would be unable to do anything more than keep her body alive. Genevieve's problem was psychic, not physiological.

The Selector had done something to her. If Matt got his hands on the man he'd—Matt didn't know what he'd do. Try to kill him or beg for Genevieve's life. Either way he'd probably end up dead.

He lay beside Genevieve now, holding her hand, unable to sleep himself for fear he would miss the smallest movement on her part. "Please, wake up. Please, Genevieve . . ."

No response.

Two hours later, when dawn had arrived and Matt had resigned himself to taking her in to the hospital, she woke.

Her eyes blinked, muzzy and unfocused, and her hand moved—it actually moved!

"Genevieve? Are you there? Wake up!"

Her brows puckered. "Water."

Of course, she was dehydrated. Matt sprang to his feet and ran a glass for her in the bathroom. He handed it to her, and she drank it all down. Relief made him babble. "Are you okay? What happened? You've been out for eleven hours."

She put the glass down, still blinking. "Hungry."

Beginning to be worried by her lack of response, Matt quickly gave her a chocolate bar, the only food in the hotel room. He hadn't dared leave her long enough to go to a store and had gotten it and a package of chips from a vending machine. He watched anxiously as she ate, biting back his questions. Hopefully, the sugar in the bar would wake her up and give her more energy.

She fell asleep with a bite still to go.

"No!" Matt shook her. "Don't you dare! Don't you dare do this to me! Genevieve!"

She slept on, oblivious.

• 5 •

An enormous briar patch surrounded the castle, the hedges tall and black and too high to see over.

The only way out was the briar patch, so Genevieve gritted her teeth and waded right in. After a few minutes her face and hands bore scratches and her hair had gotten snagged on bushes twice, but she kept going, fighting her way through the increasingly tangled undergrowth.

She'd just caught a tantalizing glimpse of blue when an imperious voice called out: "Come here, boy."

She turned to look behind her and was astonished and dismayed to discover that she had made almost no progress at all. She still stood on the very edge of the briar patch; she had a clear view of the old man walking toward her across the emerald lawn.

He wore a military uniform and walked stiffly with the aid of a cane. His gray, slicked-back hair had receded to a point, but he had no bald spot.

"Hello," Genevieve said warily, afraid he would start screaming like the blond woman.

The old man stopped right in front of her, gray eyes snapping. "What are you doing here, boy? I told you to clean the pig barns. Do you want a beating?" He raised his cane.

Genevieve crossed her arms. "I'm not a boy."

He didn't hear her. "Answer me, boy! Do you want a beating?"

"No." He was crazy, too, Genevieve decided.

"No, *sir*," the old man pounced. "You didn't call me sir. I'm going to have to cane you." He grinned, exposing yellow, rotting teeth.

Genevieve tried to back away, but the brambles pricked her, and he caught her ear, twisting it fiercely. "Hey! What are you doing?"

He raised his cane—ebony wood carved with a dragon's head—and she ducked free. She raised her hands in front of her face, prepared to defend herself, but instead of chasing her, the old man was flailing about with his cane, beating the briars and grass as if they were she.

He panted, his blows coming less and less frequently. "Take that," pant "and that," pant.

His craziness raised the hairs on the back of her neck, but curiosity kept her from moving more than a few feet away. Who was he? What was going on?

Finally, he stopped, wiping his flushed face with a handkerchief. "I hope you've learned your lesson, boy. We'll make a Selector out of you yet."

Make a Selector? Had this man made the Selector who he was?

As she stared at him a strange thing happened. He froze in place, as if becoming flat two-dimensional cardboard. Then a thirtyish man stepped out of the cardboard, leaving the static image behind. His hair was blond instead of gray, but he had the same pale, pale eyes.

He looked back over his shoulder, an expression of terror on his face, and then started to run. He charged straight at Genevieve, passed *through* her—

A ghost. He was the ghost of the old man's younger self.

—and kept on running, high black boots slopping mud. He'd barely covered five meters when a deafening explosion knocked him off his feet, picking him up and literally throwing him in the air.

Acrid smoke filled the air, burning Genevieve's nostrils.

A WWII tank straight out of old movies lumbered over the hill and swiveled its turret toward the man's prone body like an elephant's trunk sniffing peanuts. The turret steadied, about to fire, when a second, bigger tank hit it broadside. The turret turned toward it instead. Shells whistled through the air, and more tanks chewed up the muddy ground, joining the battle. The noise was continuous and awful as tanks were hit and men bailed out only to die under sniper fire and artillery fire.

At first the ghost man didn't move, stunned to find himself alive. Then he slowly pulled himself up on his elbows and crawled painfully through the mud up a low hill toward the dubious shelter of some scrubby bushes. One leg dragged at an awkward angle behind him.

Someone ran out of the bushes and slung him over his shoulder in a fireman's lift. "I've got you, *Oberleutnant*." He spoke in German, but Genevieve understood him perfectly.

They were Nazis.

Seconds later, under the cover of more gunfire and smoke, the second man carried the *Oberleutnant* farther back into the hills, taking advantage of the bushes wherever possible.

Finally, the gunfire faded into the distance, and the younger man laid down his burden. There were tears on his face. "I told you there was going to be an ambush. Why didn't you listen? Why? We're being slaughtered like pigs." He started to examine the *Oberleutnant*.

The *Oberleutnant's* face was caked with mud and blood, and he moved one leg stiffly, but seemed in no danger of dying. "You shouldn't have brought me here. An *Oberleutnant* must stay with his troops."

"It was retreat or die," the younger man said impatiently. He felt his superior's leg through the baggy black pants. "I think it's broken. I'll have to carry you to Kasserine. If the stinking Americans haven't captured it again."

"We're not going to Kasserine," the *Oberleutnant* gasped. He was in obvious pain. "You must take me back."

"If we go back, we'll die."

The *Oberleutnant* raised himself up on one elbow and drew his revolver; he was pale and sweating but furious. He spoke through clenched teeth. "Are you disobeying a direct order, Grenadier Koehntopp?"

The soldier recognized the trap. "*Nein, nein, Oberleutnant*. I'm just trying to tell you it is futile. We will throw our lives away for nothing."

"How do you know that?" The pale eyes skewered.

The grenadier licked his lips. "The same way I knew about the ambush. There is a special talent that runs in my family. We can sense danger coming. If we go back, I will die."

"Many have died for the glory of Germany. Do you think you are better than they?"

"*Nein*." The grenadier started to sweat. "I'm willing to fight for my country. Just not at Kasserine. Not today."

"But your country needs you to fight today." The *Oberleutnant* smiled thinly. "I order you to fight." He waved the gun.

The grenadier looked aghast. "You would knowingly send me to my death? *I just saved your life.*"

The *Oberleutnant's* face became very cold. "You deserted your post, Grenadier Koehntopp. You are a coward and a disgrace to the Fatherland. Blood like yours pollutes the Aryan superrace. You are a traitor and should be shot as one."

Genevieve remembered the expression on the *Oberleutnant's* face in front of the tanks. He'd been running away when the tank blasted him. He was just as much of a coward as the other man. Genevieve personally thought a person would have to be insane *not* to be afraid of a tank, but apparently the *Oberleutnant* disagreed. He raised his gun.

Disbelief froze Grenadier Koehntopp in place. "You can't do this."

The *Oberleutnant* just smiled, taking aim.

The grenadier offered desperate words like currency to buy his life. "If you have no pity for me, consider my sister. I am all she has. She—" He sprang forward, trying for the gun.

A shot rang out, and the grenadier collapsed into the mud, a small, neat hole between his eyes.

The *Oberleutnant* studied him dispassionately. "A sister, you say?" He continued their conversation as if nothing had happened. "I wonder, is your sister also all that you are? Does she possess the same gifts and flaws, the ability to smell danger on the wind?"

The dead man did not reply. He stared sightlessly at the gray sky.

"Perhaps I shall look her up after the war."

Genevieve pitied Private Koehntopp's sister. Skin crawling, she hurried away from the strange vision.

• 6 •

"Is she sleeping?"

Gavin turned back toward the front seat and nodded. His throat muscles still felt too abused to talk.

Kristy had cried herself to sleep in the back of the van. She hadn't said much, but Gavin had the feeling she'd seen Portia die. Sleep was probably the best thing for her right now. April had been worried about smoke damage to her lungs, but Kristy was breathing easily now, so they had decided to just leave it.

"Poor kid." April sighed.

Gavin adjusted his seat belt and heard a crackling noise. He suddenly remembered the printout and pulled it out of his pocket. The police had only searched him for weapons before locking him up in the holding cell.

"What's that?" April glanced away from the road.

"Suspects." Gavin smoothed the paper down over his knee.

"You did get them! How many?"

"Thirty-four." Raspingly, Gavin told her how he had arrived at the short list.

"Thirty-four is still a lot. We need to narrow it down some more."

Gavin was ahead of her. "Talent," he said.

April caught on at once. "The Voice Will Halvorsen heard. It wasn't one of the Talents you told me about."

He nodded and scanned the pages, searching the Talent field. Ghosting, Seeress, Psychic Agony, Luck, Illusion, another Luck . . . He went through the list twice. "Nothing."

"Maybe the killer was hiding his Talent. Or it went unclassified because it isn't a known category," April suggested. "Does anybody have no Talent?"

Gavin counted them up. "Six. Jennifer Bauer, Paul Brickell, Tracy Weren, Jason Schneider, Greg Nomanski, and Carol Gorman." He checked the date of birth. "All first-year students. Eighteen-year-olds."

There had been young killers before, but Gavin didn't believe that was the case this time. The sniper at the bottom of the stairs had been too well thought out, too cool. The bastard had had *practice* killing, or he wouldn't have caught as many Futurists as he had.

April agreed. "Who's left if you take out the first-years?"

"Sixteen." Still too many.

"Do you know any of them?"

262 • N. M. LUIKEN

"Couple by sight. Only really know Ron Revarc." *More's the pity.*
"It's him." April sounded so certain he stared.

Something hard and ugly rose within him. He wanted it to be Ron, wanted it so badly he distrusted the feeling. He was biased. "Why?" *Why do you think so?*

"Because he knows you. Remember this morning on the highway? Just before he shot himself Will Halvorsen said, 'Lindberg, I'll kill you yet.' *Lindberg*, not Penny or Bobby or Demon. *Lindberg.*

"But Will Halvorsen didn't know you from Adam. *It had to have been the Voice speaking.* Whoever the Voice is, he wants you dead more than he wants the rest of us dead. The only person on that list with a motive is Ron Revarc."

Gavin wanted to be convinced, but he shook his head, playing devil's advocate. "Already thought of him, first thing. No motive. If he was the one phoning Bethany, he didn't need to kill her. Already had her. Kill me, not Bethany. Loved her. Just too possessive."

A gleam came to April's eyes. She liked to argue just as much as he did.

"Let's run through a little scenario," she said. "The killer, the Voice, comes to Calgary for the express purpose of gaining access to the Futurists web. So he joins the Kithkin Klub and starts murdering out-of-touch Futurists like David Calder.

"In the meantime he makes friends with the Kithkinners. Not all the information he needs is in databases."

Gavin held up a hand. "No psychic would befriend murderer."

"Ah, but you're forgetting something, Ron has the—"

"—Shine," Gavin finished. "You're right. I didn't like, but Bethany said jealous."

April paused then continued. "To fit in more, he starts dating Bethany—maybe even falls in love with her.

"So Ron loves Bethany. And then what happens? His possessiveness or Bethany's danger instinct drives her into your arms. How does Ron feel? Well, he hates your guts, and he's very angry with Bethany. Angry enough to kill her."

It was a good argument, but it had a fatal flaw.

"Might be angry, but wouldn't have killed Bethany like that.

Couldn't have . . . cut her up." He had to swallow around his raw throat. "Mutilated her."

Still April didn't give up. She sank the clincher.

"I have another reason for suspecting him. Ever done anagrams?"

Gavin had. He swore suddenly as it hit him.

If you switched around a few letters Revarc spelled Carver.

• 7 •

When Genevieve woke again five hours later, Matt was prepared. He waved a bottle of water in front of her face. "Thirsty?"

"Hmmm." Genevieve sleepily grabbed for it.

Matt held it up out of reach. "Well, you can't have it." He watched her closely to see if that registered. Were her eyes just the tiniest bit more aware? "Genevieve, do you want the water?"

"Thirsty," she slurred, reaching again.

"You can have some, and some food, too—smell that? It's fried chicken—but only if you get up and come with me. Did you hear me, Genevieve?" He had to repeat himself a couple more times, but she eventually stirred, following him outside to the pickup. He coaxed her up into the driver's seat, started the engine for her, and, holding his breath, pushed her foot down on the gas pedal so that they lurched into motion.

Her eyes snapped wide-open, all the way awake. "Matt!" She automatically hit the brake.

"No!" Matt grabbed her chin. "You have to drive. It's the only way you'll stay awake. Go out onto the highway."

She shot him an odd look, but obediently drove out of the parking lot. "How did you wake me? I thought I was lost forever," Genevieve croaked. "Can I have some water? I'm so thirsty."

"I'll let you have some water as soon as you're up to speed," Matt promised. Giving her water and food had been his mistake last time. Thank God he hadn't taken her to the hospital. If they'd put her on an I.V., she would never have woken at all.

"Turn left, and head for Thunder Bay," Matt told her.

"Toward Peter?" Genevieve asked.

"Yes." He'd done some thinking while Genevieve was out and decided that the only thing to do was see if one of her family, another psychic, could help her. According to Genevieve's dream Peter was only twelve, but even if he couldn't help her himself, he might know someone who could. At any rate, it was the best plan Matt had been able to come up with.

When the pickup was going 60 mph he judged it was safe to give her some water. She drank greedily while he explained. "Your danger instinct woke you because you were getting too dehydrated. It should keep you awake as long as you're driving, but as soon as we stop, you'll be out again until your body needs to refuel."

• 8 •

Peter lay pressed to the ground, still as death.

He was waiting, playing possum, eyes closed, legs sprawled out awkwardly, as if he had fallen from the tree house above.

He breathed shallowly and kept his body utterly relaxed. When he and Al had played hunting games, seeing who could get closest to a deer or squirrel, Al had been better at it. Peter had always twitched at the wrong moment or moved too fast. But today he was possessed of an infinite patience that allowed him to lie perfectly unmoving as if dead.

Like Al.

Waiting.

One of his intruder alerts had gone off ten minutes ago. A string tied to a bell.

The alert could just mean his dad or Larry was out walking, but Peter didn't believe it. His heart knocked against his ribs, reacting to the fear he would not allow his face to show.

Patience.

Waiting.

Eyes closed.

Damp earth beneath his cheek.

A twig snapped, loud in the silence. The murderer was coming closer.

Peter wanted to open his eyes, and his knuckles itched something fierce. *Relax. Play possum. Lure the murderer closer. See? I'm already dead, no need to be cautious.*

Look at the tree house. See the broken rung? See the ketchup that looks like blood on my shirt? Come closer and get a REALLY good look, you murderer. Flames of anger licked inside his chest.

Crunching leaves. Peter had arranged some deadfall so there was only one easy approach to the tree house, one obvious path, one point where the path narrowed to a foot, perfect for setting snares. The murderer was very close now. *One more step . . .*

He didn't take it.

"Well, this one looks like the right boy. Had a little accident, did we, Peter? Are you really dead this time? You look real dead."

Limp muscles. Patience. One more step.

The murderer threw a stone, and a rock stung Peter's thigh.

For a fraction of a second Peter tensed, then went still. Dead. Waiting.

"It's not much fun cutting up dead meat. But you know what, Peter? I don't think you're all the way dead. I think you're faking."

It was hard to keep his face expressionless, hard to keep from sucking in a loud breath, while death stood only a few feet away.

Two more stones from out of nowhere, but Peter was prepared even when one cut his face.

Blood trickled down his cheek. The murderer would know he lived.

"Live like a coward, die like one," the murderer said scathingly and took a step forward—*one step*—

Peter yanked on the rope in his fist, releasing the slipknot and triggering his trap.

The bowed-over poplar tree he'd tied down this morning whipped upright and jerked tight the noose—

Peter scrambled upright.

—and the murderer swung high above him, caught in his snare, dangling by his feet. "Son of a bitch!"

Peter grinned in triumph. *Got you, you bastard. Got—*

A shot rang out.

The murderer had had the presence of mind to hang on to his gun, but the rope twisted wildly, spinning, and he missed by a mile, wounding a tree several feet away.

Peter ducked behind the two grown-together spruce trees that cradled his tree house. Coolly, he picked up his bow and nocked an arrow, letting fly before he even got a chance to look at his foe.

He and Al had practiced with their bows all last summer. Peter could hit a twelve-inch target nine times out of ten. The murderer was much bigger.

His first shaft stuck in the blond man's thigh. He was wearing white jeans and a red shirt. Peter's scorn increased. Not earth colors, like the brown he wore, but *red*, a target color.

Swearing viciously, the murderer fired again. A bullet ripped a hole through the plywood walls of the tree house above Peter.

"Drop the gun or I'll shoot," Peter told him.

"I'll kill you!" The murderer twisted on the rope. His next shot tattered some leaves.

Carefully, Peter placed a second arrow in his side. It sank deep, quivering. The murderer reflexively tried to pull the arrow out, and he dropped the pistol.

"Hands away from the gun, or I'll shoot you in the chest," Peter said, voice toneless. All his triumph was internal, banked fire.

The murderer appeared to be thinking about it.

Peter pulled back his bowstring. "I'm not bluffing."

Furious, the murderer placed his hands on his thighs. When he spun away Peter nudged the gun out of reach with a stick. Then he sat down cross-legged to watch.

He sat in silence as the killer cursed him and his parents in language strong enough to blister paint. He sat when the killer changed tactics and tried to persuade him it had all been a joke, a movie plot. He sat and watched as the murderer's blood drained downward, flushing his face, and true blood stained his legs and side.

He felt no pity. This man had killed Al, his blood brother, his friend.

When the killer finally gave up trying to persuade Peter to let him go, Peter began to speak. "You made a mistake when you killed my blood brother, Al."

"Sure did." He smirked. "It was real smart of you to get him to switch jackets. I would have killed you instead otherwise."

Guilt struck Peter's heart, slicing in so clean and deep and fatal he died inside and didn't feel it.

Avid green eyes watched for his reaction.

Casually, Peter threw a large stone at the killer's stomach, causing an *oof!* of pain to escape him. "I didn't give you permission to speak." His rage leapt higher. *Murderer!*

"I don't need your permiss—"

Peter winged two more quick stones, bruising his face and arm.

He shut up, and sullen silence reigned.

"Al was an Apache Indian," Peter continued as if he'd never been interrupted. That was a lie. Al had had Ojibwa, Huron, and French blood. "Do you know what Apaches did to their prisoners?" He stared into the murderer's green eyes and told him. He and Al had read Westerns and taken turns grossing one another out with the torture practices.

The murderer maintained a look of boredom throughout Peter's description of sun-baked carcasses staked out on anthills, but he started to sweat, and that was almost as good. The salt would get into his arrow wounds and sting.

At six o'clock Peter got up. His dad would respect his closed bedroom door, but his mother would check on him the instant she got home.

"Are you going to leave me like this all night?" The man sounded more curious than frightened.

Peter whirled and pelted the stone in his hand. His accuracy was good; the stone left a bruise on the man's chin. Al would have cheered. . . . "No." He collected some rope and a wide roll of tape from the tree house. "Put out your hands."

"And why would I want to do that?" One eyebrow raised.

"Because if you don't, I'll knock you unconscious."

The murderer actually laughed, and Peter came close to killing him on the spot. "Fair enough." He stuck out his hands. "I'm beginning to think I made a mistake about you, Peter."

Head bent to conceal his fury, Peter quickly noosed the murderer's hands together, then came close enough to tie them.

"You're no coward. Perhaps I shouldn't have Selected you."

Peter slipped the noose off, put it around the man's neck, and fastened the rope to a tree well out of reach. If the murderer tried to swing up and free his feet, he'd choke.

"Oh, very clever. You're a boy after my own heart."

Peter taped his lying, mocking mouth shut.

After studying his prisoner with satisfaction, Peter briskly searched him for weapons. He found a knife on the ground several yards away in some bushes where it must have fallen when the trap had sprung, but nothing else.

As a final touch Peter dumped a jar of spiders and other bugs on the murderer's chest. "*This* is how I'm going to leave you."

Agitated, the black swarm crawled in all directions, some seeking protection in the crevices of his clothes, more crawling up his chest, some falling on his neck and nose.

The murderer twisted once, but gave up when the noose tightened around his throat. He raised his eyebrows as if to say, Is that the best you can do?

Peter's anger burned brighter than a hundred candles, but he refrained from throwing the stone in his fist. *Just wait until tonight. Tonight, when your arms and legs ache from hanging so long, and all your blood has pooled in your head, and you're hurt and thirsty, and the noose is choking your neck. See how you feel then.*

part three

Wisdom

CHAPTER 10

• 1 •

Gavin dreamed he was dancing with Bethany. She wore a strapless red dress, and diamonds sparkled at her throat and ears. Straight, shiny blond hair fell past her shoulder. Brilliant blue eyes entranced, and red lips smiled.

The evening was enchanted. An orchestra played a waltz, and they glided to the music, spinning in flawless circles.

When the song ended, Gavin looked deep into Bethany's sapphire eyes and said the words he had never dared to say in real life. "Bethany, I lo—"

A hand fell on his shoulder. "This is my dance," Ron said rudely.

"You don't mind, do you, Gavin?" Bethany draped her arms around Ron's neck, not even glancing at Gavin.

Gavin grabbed her wrist. "Wait. There's something I have to tell you. I love—"

Bethany flicked away his hand as if it were a bug. "I'll catch you later." She smiled radiantly up at Ron and melted against him like plastic on a hot stove. "Let's dance."

Ron swept her away while Gavin watched helplessly. "She's bewitched. He has the Shine, and she can't see past it."

"Yes, I know," a voice beside him said. Gavin turned and saw April's sad blue eyes. "Even if I told him, he wouldn't believe me."

She had her pronouns mixed up—she made no sense—but Gavin was terribly afraid he *did* know what she meant. Deep down he knew . . .

A scream pierced the air.

Bethany's scream.

Gavin started running before the first echo bounced off the ceiling, but the air thickened to mud, slowing him, and he had to push his way through the crowd, knocking people sprawling, fighting to get close to the center, to the screaming.

No one else seemed to hear. The orchestra kept playing, and the dancers kept dancing, twirling around him. Faster, faster . . . He dodged them. *Bethany!*

Into the center at last. Bethany lay in a scarlet heap, blood the color of her dress flowing from a dozen knife wounds. Her mouth hung open and slack.

Bethany screamed no more.

Gavin screamed for her, on his knees, holding her limp hand. Ron had disappeared. The music swelled to a crashing crescendo, and the dancers whirled by, skirts flashing. Green and pink and blue. Yellow and black. Orange. Every color but red. Only Bethany wore scarlet.

SOMEONE SHOOK HIS injured shoulder, and Gavin came awake with a gasp. "Ouch. What is it?"

"We're there." April pointed to the varnished sign by #15 Silverwood Estates which read, NEAL AND EVELYN CHAMBRY.

Ahead of them Penny and Jeff's station wagon turned down the narrow, heavily wooded driveway. April followed, parking behind them.

After thirty-some hours of continuous driving, Gavin eagerly got out of the van. Thanks to Bobby and Kristy's coordination, they'd met up with Penny and Jeff three hours ago, but hadn't stopped for more than coffee. His shoulder ached.

Everyone stood outside, looking as hollow-eyed and stiff as Gavin felt. He peered up at the two-story house and the evergreens standing guard around it. The whole trip Gavin had thought of nothing but getting here. Now they'd arrived. What would they say to Peter? To Peter's parents?

What if they were too late?

"Penny, Gavin, why don't you knock on the door?" April suggested. "You're Peter's brother and sister. The rest of us will wait here."

"Good idea." Penny patted her stomach. "The Chambrys won't toss me out on my ear no matter how bad my story is." Her joke fell flat.

Gavin escorted Penny to the front door. He noticed two cars and a pickup by the garage. Guests? He pressed the doorbell.

A thirtysomething brunette answered the door. She was wearing a tasteful black dress with a single strand of pearls. Funeral clothes. Gavin's pulse leapt as he took in the expression of strain on her face. *Don't let anything be wrong with Peter.*

Penny smiled. "Mrs. Chambry?" A jerky nod from the woman. "I'm Penny Lacrosse, and this is my brother Gavin. I'm sorry to drop in on you so late, but I just couldn't wait." Penny projected nervousness and hope. "Do you have a son named Peter?"

An even jerkier nod.

Penny blushed. "Please excuse the question, but . . . is Peter adopted?"

Evelyn Chambry seemed incapable of speech. She nodded.

"May I — may we — speak to him?" Penny's eyes shone with tears. "I'm his sister. This is his brother. We've come a long way to see him."

A long moment passed before Mrs. Chambry replied. Gavin held his breath. *Please don't say he's dead.*

She didn't. She smiled, a queer, twisted smile. "His sister and brother? Please come in." She stepped back from the door. "Peter's in the living room. He has . . . guests."

Four people occupied the living room. A pale young woman with curly dark hair sat on a low green couch holding hands with a thirtyish man wearing gold-frame glasses.

A man of about forty-five with graying hair sat in the opposite chair. Gavin felt sure he was Mr. Chambry.

The blond, adolescent boy at his feet must therefore be Peter.

Evelyn Chambry spoke, a funny giggle caught in her throat: "Peter, darling, this is your lucky night. Your brother and sister have come to see you."

Her words fell into the room with the impact of a bomb.

Neal Chambry tightened his hold on Peter's shoulder and looked anguished.

The young woman opened blue eyes wide with surprise. Her mouth formed an O.

The man holding her hand looked curiously at Penny and Gavin.

Of them all Peter's reaction was the strangest. His expression did not change one iota upon learning he had a brother and sister.

The dark-haired woman spoke first. "I'm Mary dreams. Who are you?"

Then everyone spoke at once, words jumbling together.

"I'm 'Sister looks'—"

" 'Brother screams'—"

Mary and Penny hugged with instant warmth.

"—so good to see you safe."

"Who's with you, Mary? Is he Firstborn?"

"—any others found?"

"—fiancé, Matt Rutledge."

"Kristy's in the car. And my husband and—"

"I don't care who they claim to be, get them out of my house!" Evelyn Chambry screamed.

"—Selector tried to kill Eileen . . ." Mary's voice dwindled.

Evelyn Chambry's face was pale with strain. Her husband put his arm around her shoulders, but she would not be placated. Finally, he looked up.

"You stories are all very interesting, but it's Peter's bedtime. I'll talk to you all tomorrow." He herded them toward the door.

Penny refused to be pushed. She knelt and took Peter's hands. "Hello, Peter. I'm your sister, Penny."

"Get out of here! Get away from my son! Get out! Get out!"

Gavin took a half step forward, fearing the crazed woman might hit Penny, but Neal Chambry grabbed his wife's outstretched arm.

Penny ignored them, speaking to Peter. "You're in danger, and I want to help you." Something kindled in Peter's eyes, then vanished.

The four of them filed out and exchanged hasty introductions by the vehicles.

Gavin raised his voice over the general exclamations, pointing at the faces at the window. "I think the Chambrys want us out of their driveway. Let's meet down the road."

Explanations followed, fast and furious. The sun went down while they took turns talking. Penny and Gavin went first, overlapping and interrupting one another, and then it was Mary/Genevieve's turn. Gavin listened intently. The Futurist killer—Ron Revarc?—called himself the Selector. Genevieve spoke to him in dreams. She had seen their parents die. In exchange for not killing Eileen the Selector had imprisoned Genevieve in her dreams, which was why she looked so pale and shaky. Only the need for food and water was keeping her awake.

When Genevieve described a vision of World War II that she had seen while imprisoned in the Selector's mind, Penny interrupted. "That must have been Nigel Carver and Portia's brother."

"That makes sense," Genevieve said. She hesitated and looked at Gavin. "I saw someone else in the Selector's mind. Another prisoner. She—"

Just then April gasped.

Gavin turned to his head to see what was wrong, and Peter materialized out of the shadows wearing jeans and a pajama top. He ignored everyone but Penny. "Are you really my sister?"

"Yes, I am, and so are Genevieve and Kristy. Gavin is your brother."

Peter didn't look at them. "I used to have a brother. The murderer killed him."

Gavin spoke without thinking. "He killed Bethany."

"He killed my parents," Kristy said.

"Aunt Dorothy."

"He as good as killed Will Halvorsen."

"David Calder."

"Ian."

"Travis in Calgary," Gavin remembered.

Peter's gaze touched them all. Apparently satisfied with what he saw, he smiled. Unpleasantly. "I have something to show you." Without another word he walked into the woods.

Gavin shrugged and followed, April and Jeff right behind him.

He tried to keep close on Peter's heels, but had difficulty. Peter kept slipping away on him in the dark, threading his way through the dripping dark trees as if it were broad daylight. After Peter had to wait for him a third time, Gavin felt like an idiot, a grass green city boy. He remembered running into the woods after being shot and becoming hopelessly lost. Only his danger instinct had led him to April and safety.

Up ahead, Peter suddenly stopped. "We're here. Watch out for traps."

Gavin passed the message on, but wondered: *Traps? What kind of traps?*

When the others had gathered around Peter removed a flashlight from his pocket and switched it on. A beam of light fell on a pair of eyes in an upside-down face. It traveled up, revealing a blond man suspended by his feet.

Gavin took a step forward, teeth bared. "Ron."

• 2 •

Peter Chambry was dead meat. Any sympathy Ron Revarc might once have felt for him had vanished. After hanging upside down for five hours, he wanted to kill the boy himself.

Five hours of excruciating pain. The arrow wounds in his leg and side burned and stung. His bound hands and legs felt numb, and the noose around his neck choked him with every breath.

Bug bites covered him. He *itched*, and he couldn't scratch. He'd almost strangled himself trying to rub a bite on his nose. To make things worse it had rained a couple of hours ago; his clothes felt clammy and cold, and they clung to him like a death shroud.

Peter Chambry was going to die. Slowly.

The Selector would kill him.

Ron was sure of that despite the Selector's admiration for the boy's daring: *Maybe I made a mistake.* In twenty years the Selector had yet to find anyone who matched his precious high standards. Sooner or later he would find some minuscule fault. The boy was as good as dead.

Normally, Ron felt a distant pity for the people his hands and the Selector's mind killed, but pain had extinguished all sparks of human compassion. Pity was useless anyway.

Whom had it ever saved? Not Nigel, not Bethany, and certainly not himself. He was a puppet, to be taken over and controlled by the Selector on a whim. His life was pockmarked with periods of lost time after which he often woke up in strange cities, wearing clothes reeking of blood.

Ron was helpless to stop him.

Everyone was helpless against the Selector.

Ron vividly remembered Nigel Carver's murder and the utter contempt with which the Selector had treated the law. He'd deliberately left Ron's fingerprints on the murder weapon and allowed him to be arrested. His lawyer had wanted him to plead guilty, but the Selector hadn't allowed that.

When he got off his lawyer had been astonished. *I know you did it, Carver, the judge knows you did it, and the press knows you did it. I don't know how you fooled the jury, but you're one lucky s.o.b.*

But it hadn't been luck at all, only his own Shine, and the Selector's hooking of everyone who disagreed. *Voilà*, one not-guilty verdict.

If the Selector could do that, what chance did Ron have? None. And so Ron had long ago stopped even trying. Why give the Selector the pleasure of blasting him to his knees?

Now Ron did exactly as the Selector said. He jumped when the Selector said jump, brought down prey like a trained attack dog, always leaving the final kill to his master.

Only once had he beaten the Selector—

Shut up!

Ron's mind shied away from the dangerous thought, slipping into another well-worn groove. If he had to hunt and kill someone, why couldn't it be someone who deserved to die? Someone like Gavin Lindberg? Ron wouldn't feel any pity for him. As it grew late, and the blood throbbed in his veins, Ron entertained himself with fantasies of the Selector taking Gavin apart piece by piece. Peter's talk of tortures had given him a few ideas.

He did not fear Peter. It did not occur to him to be afraid.

The Selector had left soon after Peter did, but first he'd pulled strings and triggered hidden hooks to send men to rescue Ron and kill Peter. They would arrive before dawn.

Ron wondered what time it was. Nine o'clock? Ten? Twelve? The sun had set, and a cool wind blew.

He twisted on the rope, like a slab of beef on a hook. Dead meat just like Peter would be.

Noises in the forest—wet leaves squelching underfoot, branches rubbing together. Archfiend Peter returning, no doubt. Automatically, he tried to turn toward the sounds, and the noose choked him. Ron visualized throttling Peter. Killing the boy would leave him stranded, but Ron felt confident the Selector wouldn't let him die.

His Shine made him too useful.

More footsteps. Either Peter had gotten louder or he'd brought the police. Ron grinned beneath the tape. If the police came, he would put the kid in prison.

He was preparing a number of lies and outraged accusations when a flashlight beam stabbed him in the eyes.

Asshole! He scrunched his eyes half-closed.

The beam climbed higher, and Ron counted feet. There must be nine people standing around now.

Standing around. A couple of gasps, but no rush to free him. A sinking feeling had just started in his chest when someone said, "Ron."

Gavin Lindberg.

If Ron hadn't been tied up, he would have betrayed himself and gone for Lindberg's throat.

Lindberg, whom Bethany had called out to in death.

Voices chattered excitedly over him, but he heard nothing until someone cut him down over Peter's loud protests. They kept his hands and feet bound. Unanimous agreement. A small debate over whether the tape should come off. The pregnant woman won, ripping it off.

The tape took several hairs with it. Ron bit back a swearword. He spoke in a pitiful rasp. "Water."

"I'll get some," the man with glasses said.

"Help." Ron lay on the muddy ground and tried to sound weak. It was easy to do. The world looked strange right side up. "Arrows." Both shafts still protruded from him and made him grit his teeth against a scream every time he brushed something.

"There's a first-aid kit in the station wagon," the pregnant woman called after the departing man.

"Who . . . are . . . you?" Ron asked.

"You know who we are," Lindberg said contemptuously. "And we know who you are. You call yourself the Selector and run around killing people. You killed Bethany!"

His last sight of Bethany, slashed and bleeding . . . Blue eyes dazed and uncomprehending at first, "What are you doing, Ron?" Then later, screaming under the Selector's knife . . .

"It wasn't me; the Selector killed her. I tried to save her." Agitated, Ron moved his leg, and the arrow brushed against a stone. Pain cut off his breath. Sanity returned. He had to be careful; the Selector was always listening. He spoke at random, words spewing out from him. "You don't understand. The Selector has triggers set in my mind; when I tried to warn Bethany he took over. He controls me with pain. This arrow wound is nothing—the Selector laughs at pain."

"You are the Selector!" Lindberg sounded furious. "Do you know how many have died since you joined the Kithkin Klub?"

Ron didn't.

"Over fifty," Lindberg shouted. He seemed just as upset over their deaths as over Bethany's.

He probably would have kept on ranting if the thin dark-haired woman hadn't grabbed his arm. "He's not the Selector. I've seen the Selector in my dreams, and he has black hair. This man is just one of his minions."

Lindberg didn't want to stop. "You're sure?"

She nodded. "Black as a raven's wing."

Progress at last. Ron started to smile at the woman—he had the Shine, after all—

The Selector pushed him to the back of his mind.

"Mary, Mary." The Selector spoke through Ron's lips, shook Ron's head. "Always so tenderhearted. That's going to get you killed one of these days."

• 3 •

It was him. It was Ron's voice speaking, Ron's face in front of her, and yet it was the Selector, too. In some subtle, indefinable way Genevieve could see his cold eyes peering out at her from Ron's sockets, his smile in the twist of Ron's lips. She could smell the Selector on him like a whiff of sulfur, and the hair prickled on the back of her neck. She wanted to arch her back and hiss like a cat.

He has two arrows sticking out of him, and he's tied up. He can't hurt you. Except with words. The Selector's barbs slipped under her skin and festered.

"Why aren't you in your room where you belong, Mary?" The Selector ignored the others: they might have been alone on a silent moon. "How did you escape? You're more resourceful than my associate here is. Not that he sets a particularly high standard."

Ron's bound hands yanked at the arrow in his thigh. Blood welled, thick and red, but the Selector showed no pain.

"Leave him alone." Genevieve stepped forward, but stopped short of touching him, alerted by a sudden gleam in his eyes. *That's what he wants. Your touch.* Nausea turned her stomach.

The Selector looked disappointed. He yanked at the arrow again, and it came out, minus the arrowhead.

His hands moved to the second arrow, but Gavin grabbed his arm, and April pinned his shoulder when the Selector tried to roll onto the second arrow.

The Selector laughed. "Gavin Lindberg helping Ron Carver. That's funny. He hates you."

"I used to hate him," Gavin said, holding tight to the Selector's shoulder. "Now I think I'll just hate you instead."

"Why is he talking about himself in third person?" Jeff asked nervously.

"Ron isn't talking, the Selector is. The Selector is hooked into his brain somehow . . ." Genevieve trailed off. "Hooked." Something in the word alarmed her.

"Clever Mary," the Selector mocked. "You're right, he is the first-born, Ronald Carver. 'Firstborn hooked.' His mother gave him over to Nigel's keeping."

Hooked, not hooks. A simple change of tense spelled catastrophe. Ron must have once been the little boy she'd dreamed about, Bad boy Ronnie for crying. The lullaby, *"Who listens seeks to free the one who cried."* To free Ron? Was that what the lullaby meant?

The Selector smiled blindingly with Ron's Shine. "Cat got your tongue, Mary? That's okay, we'll have plenty of time to talk later, after I kill your mortal body."

A tremor passed over his face, and the smirk became a howl of pain. Ron pushed against the hands holding him down, cursing them all to hell.

Matt jogged up, out of breath, carrying a first-aid kit and some bottled water. His eyes flashed to Genevieve, asking a question. She gave a small nod, swaying on her feet. She was fine, just a little light-headed. She was so thirsty. . . .

Matt knelt by his patient. "What idiot pulled out the arrow?" he asked, opening the first-aid kit.

"He did it himself," April said defensively.

"The Selector did it," Gavin corrected. He explained while Matt bandaged the wounds. "So there you have it. We've found Firstborn, but he's no more good to us than a Trojan horse. We're screwed."

Ron laughed. "You're more than screwed, you're dead meat. Every last one of you. Except for her." He indicated Genevieve. "She's even worse off. He'll snag her soul."

"What do you mean?" Penny asked. "Will he hook her, too?"

Ron shook his head. "Snagging is different than hooking. When someone's hooked the Selector controls their body, but they're still in it, like me. Someone who has been snagged's body is empty, and the Selector collected the soul. I don't understand how you're still awake and alive," Ron said to Genevieve.

"He snagged me while I was dreaming and something went wrong," Genevieve explained.

A shift behind Ron's eyes . . . "You're not dreaming now. Look at me, Mary."

Genevieve cringed away from the Selector.

Matt stepped forward and slapped Ron.

The strange expression on Ron's face was wiped away like chalk from a blackboard. "Sorry, a trigger in my mind pulls the Selector in whenever I hear Mary's voice."

Genevieve clamped her jaw shut, quite willing never to speak again if that was the price of the Selector's silence.

Matt was more practical. "Then we'll just have to put you out of earshot, won't we? And for future reference, her name is Genevieve."

"Wait," Penny said when Matt and Gavin moved to tie Ron up. "Ron is part of this, too. He hates the Selector just as much as we do, don't you Ron?"

"Probably more." Ron's lips twisted.

"And I can tell empathetically when the Selector has taken over from Ron. He's the Firstborn," she added softly.

"No," Ron said. "Genevieve's guy has the right idea. Move me out of earshot. No matter how much I may want to help you, I can't, and everything I know, the Selector knows."

Penny gave a short nod, and Matt and Gavin finished trussing Ron up. Then the rest of the group moved fifty yards away.

Even when he was out of sight Genevieve's fidgety feeling didn't leave her. It was time to go. "Now that we've found Peter, I think we should hit the road. The Selector knows where we are."

"You're right." Gavin looked grim. "We've been here over half an hour. The Selector will have sent for reinforcements by now."

"If not earlier." Matt turned to Peter. "What time did you capture Ron?"

"Four-thirty."

Gavin winced. "That's five hours ago. He could be here any minute. Back to the cars."

"No." Peter stepped in front of Genevieve. "I'm not going anywhere, and neither is my prisoner."

"*Your* prisoner?" In the glow of the flashlight she saw Gavin's eyebrows go up.

Genevieve spoke over him. "You have to go. The Selector is coming."

"So?" Peter sneered. "He'll just save me the trouble of coming after him."

"Look, kid, if we have to, we'll tie you up and carry you like Ron here," Gavin threatened.

Peter stood up to him, gray eyes colder than a naked steel blade. "Do you want to kill the Selector?"

Gavin flushed with anger. "Of course I do!"

"Then why run away?" Peter said with simple, stunning logic. "He's coming here. We're never going to get a better chance. There are seven of us, and we have the high ground."

Genevieve saw the possibility and recoiled from it. "We can't. The Selector will bring an army."

"It's too dangerous—"

"We need time to plan—" Penny and April spoke together, words overlapping.

Peter lifted his chin. "Go ahead then. Run like cowards, but Ron stays here."

"Nobody's a coward." Matt's strong, calm voice cut in. "But Peter has a valid point. We should at least consider staying and fighting it out. Right now you're all running on instinct, reacting to the very real danger your psychic powers tell you is coming. But you need to ask yourself if running is the answer or if winning is worth the risk."

Peter put the choice more brutally. "Decide. Are you in or are you out?"

• 4 •

Tension twisted the air like a screw.

A chill bumped down Penny's spine. *This is it*, she thought. This was the moment they had been brought together for, reeled in by the lullaby.

"All in favor of staying to face the Selector," Matt said calmly.

Peter's hand punched the air, a fist of defiance against the night sky. Matt's hand followed. Then Genevieve's, slow and reluctant. April waited until Gavin raised his before lifting hers. Penny was the last to put her hand up, and she did so with a certain amount of dread.

An explosion of fear and anger from Jeff reduced everyone else's emotions to static on a radio. "You're out of your frigging minds! If you want to get yourself killed, I won't stop you, but by God you're not going to kill my children." He snatched up Bobby. "Penny, you're going with me. You're pregnant!"

Damaris moved inside her, and Penny knew she, too, would do anything to keep her daughter safe, but Jeff was going about it the wrong way. "Where will we go? Where can we go that he won't find us?"

Frustration set Jeff's jaw, but he didn't have an answer.

"If we don't stop the Selector, Bobby and Damaris won't have lives to live."

"Bullshit. Give me a day in any major city, and I'll dig up some fake I.D. cards. We'll start another life."

"And the house? The mortgage?" Penny knew how much the security of a house meant to her husband.

"Screw the house. The bank can take it," Jeff said with a ruthlessness that would have shocked her two days ago. "You and Bobby and the baby are what's important. Let's go."

Penny didn't budge. "And when the Selector finds us again? You heard Genevieve; he's good at finding people. What if next time my instinct isn't good enough, and he snatches Bobby from school?"

The muscles in Jeff's throat worked.

"What about all the other parents and children he'll kill if we don't stop him?"

Jeff's brows lowered. "I'm sorry for them, but my responsibility is to you and Bobby."

"Then protect us," she said gently. "I know I'm vulnerable. I promise not to be in the thick of the fighting, but there are other things I can contribute. This may be our only chance to defeat him. Please, Jeff. For the sake of me and Bobby and all those other children out there."

She held his stare for a long moment before his defenses broke. [*Helpless, hopeless love . . .*] "Nowhere near the fighting," he said, but it was surrender, and everyone knew it.

Penny desperately wanted to know why he felt so hopeless, but now was not the time. She slowly turned her attention to Peter, who was snapping out directives like a general.

"The first item on the agenda is weapons. Ron brought a gun, and I have two bows and some arrows. Does anyone else know how to use them?"

A round of negatives.

"The gun goes with Penny," Jeff said, voice hard. "She needs to protect the kids."

"But—"

Jeff didn't let Peter finish. "Don't worry, I can provide all the firepower we need."

"How?" Gavin asked. "Does Penny have a collapsible Uzi in the trunk somewhere?"

"There would be if I'd thought of it while we were in Calgary," Jeff said without humor. "It would take me a day or two to make the right connections in a strange city, so I did the next best thing. Before we met up with you and April again we stopped and bought some stuff. Just let me get it out of the station wagon."

"While he's doing that we ought to lock Ron up somewhere," Matt said. The group split as April, Gavin, Peter, and Genevieve went with him to fetch Ron.

Penny followed her husband to their station wagon, curious. She was sure whatever Jeff had in mind would be brilliant. "You wouldn't tell me what that was all for."

"You'll see." Jeff set Bobby down and opened the tailgate.

"Up, up," Bobby said crankily, arms outstretched.

Grunting a little, Penny lifted him onto her hip. She eyed his scrunched-up expression critically. "Maybe it's time you and Kristy went to bed."

Kristy protested loudly, but Penny won in the end. She put the two of them down with sleeping bags on the station-wagon seats before returning to the group.

• 5 •

Cold fear hatched in Ron's stomach like some hideous reptile. Matt, Lindberg, April, and Homicidal Peter each had an arm or leg and were carrying him through the forest. Genevieve followed, conscientiously trying not to talk.

They had a plan. He could see it in their body posture. They were going to take on the Selector. The thought scared him badly.

On the one hand he hated the Selector. Bethany's killer.

On the other hand, the Selector's destruction would probably mean his own.

Either way he lost, but Ron would lay odds on the Selector winning. That being the case it was just a matter of time before the Selector found out Ron hadn't used his Shine to include himself in their plans. Or worse yet, the Selector would find out about B —

For the love of God don't think about her!

He tried to think of something unrelated — rhubarb and zucchini — something other than his fear of betraying —

Barbed-wire fences. Indian tortures Peter had told him. Yes, good idea, think about what the Selector will do to you when he finds out you hooked Bethany.

You thought about her. Now he'll know for sure!

Ron tried to calm down. The Selector didn't know Ron's every thought or he would have noticed when Ron hooked Bethany in the first place.

Usually when the Selector took over he imprisoned Ron somewhere in his mind, but when he killed Bethany he had only shoved Ron off to the side, so Ron could still hear and see. Watch his own hands kill the woman he loved. It had been punishment, but while the Selector was crazed with bloodlust Ron had reached in and used the Selector's silver thread to snag her soul. It had been surprisingly easy.

If the Selector ever found out what Ron had done, both he and Bethany would die.

Don't think about it.

Ron's gaze swept around the people holding him, searching for a distraction. Lindberg's face was tight with pain—he'd probably strained his bullet wound. *Good.* April and Matt were watching their feet, concentrating on walking backward without falling. Genevieve, the only one who wasn't helping carry him, was clutching at trees for support, shaky and close to the end of her rope. And Peter . . .

Ron hastily averted his gaze, uneasy. Peter's expression was too unemotional, too intense. Too much like—

The Selector arrived. For a moment he and Ron shared Ron's body as the Selector did a quick-and-dirty scan of Ron's memories.

Ron bit his lips, knowing better than to cry out in pain.

"Looks like you've been a bad boy," the Selector said. "Disobeying my orders. You can't be trusted. I'll deal with you later when this is all over." A flick of his fingers, and Ron found himself banished to a tiny, cramped prison cell.

CHAPTER 11

• 1 •

The Selector looked up at his captors and hid a grin. They had tied his hands and feet, but hadn't hindered his greatest power: his mind.

Fools!

The Selector conveniently ignored the fact these particular fools had all evaded him at least once. That had been luck and the danger instinct, nothing more.

The damn danger instinct caused the whole problem. He couldn't simply hook, control, and kill the Futurists because at the slightest hint of danger they resisted. Their brains had security systems.

Without it he could kill them all here and now.

In Penny's case a very touchy security system, but Penny wasn't close enough right now to pick up on his presence, so he had a little time to work.

The security systems forced him to concentrate on the nonpsychics: Jeff or the poet man. Jeff was a risk. Jeff was married to Penny, and she was ultrasensitive to his emotions.

The poet man presented less of a risk. Of the group, Penny was the least close to him.

The Selector bared his teeth. Who was he kidding? He would hook the poet man no matter what the risks because Mary loved the poet man.

In the three years he'd chased her, the Selector had worn blithe, happy Mary Dunstan down to a pale, shivering shadow of herself. Wary. Unhappy. On the edge of falling apart. The poet man was the glue that was keeping her together. His betrayal would sever the rope over the abyss that Mary walked.

Savoring the thought, the Selector turned to the poet man and mentally cast his hook. His first pass snagged nothing more than a memory fragment.

[*Walking through the autumn woods with Genevieve. A falling red leaf caught in her curly hair. He reached up to brush it out and kissed her upturned lips. . . .*]

But his second throw dredged up something more useful. Fear, a welter of it, and guilt mixed in. The Selector smiled. Both fear and guilt could be used to manipulate people.

He hooked there, anchoring it firmly. Then he climbed the silver line out of his own body into the poet man's.

The Selector had followed this procedure so many times hooking came as naturally to him as walking. The barbed hook and the silver line had little to do with what really happened between his brain and Matt's, but the visualization worked. That was good enough for the Selector. He had no use for technical understanding.

He poked around carefully, resisting the urge to use claws on the vulnerable tissues. Stupid as they were, the psychics were sure to catch on if Matt fell to the ground screaming in agony.

Careful proddings produced the original fear memory.

[*Dust and the smell of horses. With sugar cubes seven-year-old Matt persuaded his dad's nervous horse to be saddled. He used the fence to get on, swinging his leg over the horse's back. So high up! Much higher than his pony Red, the largest horse his mother would let him ride. Matt grasped the reins. A flash of fear and anticipation. He kicked the horse in the ribs. A startled neigh, and the horse took off—bone-jolting, reckless-paced. Matt clung, but couldn't stay on. So far down. . . . Mom had been right. . . . Falling . . .*]

The Selector leached everything he needed from the memory before following the paths of associations from fear to fear. Mapping minds was also routine. Easy.

But the poet man's brain twisted unexpectedly, and he lost the particular memory string he had been pursuing in a sudden knot of association. Similar knots lay to his right, curving around a large blockage. All association strings had to find a way around the blockage, resulting in a tangled weaving of strings. It would only take one leaped synapse to create a traffic snarl.

Tempting . . . but he had no time for puzzles. The Selector gave up on the fear memory string. He would have to settle for direct control of Matt rather than subverting from within as he preferred. He set to work planting a trigger instead.

Some of the Selector's more elaborate triggers took hours to set up, but he had to make do with a fairly simple one with the poet man. One that would trigger if Matt threatened him or one of his minions, sending tremors back along his silver line and summoning the Selector.

He didn't know just yet when he would take control of Matt, but he felt sure an opportunity would present itself.

Task complete, the Selector slid back down his silver line just as the group locked him inside a van.

He was alone, but looking through the window he could see the two children lying on blankets in the back of a nearby station wagon. Kristy met his gaze, uneasy, and the Selector smiled at her, using Ron's Shine.

She smiled tentatively back and settled down to sleep.

Foolish girl.

• 2 •

Jeff had arranged his supplies in a semicircle around him: a box of empty bottles, a gas can, three packages of shoelaces, a pair of scissors, some rags, and a jar of matches formed his assembly line.

Matt understood first, laughing, as Jeff filled each bottle with gas, inserted a shoelace, and stuffed a rag into the neck to prevent spillage. "My God. Molotov cocktails. Firebombs."

When Jeff finished twelve of them stood in a row. "If I'd known there would be so many of us, I'd have brought more."

"I think we have a couple of empties in the pickup," Genevieve said.

Matt went with her. "Not to mention a tire iron." ·

When they finished raiding the vehicles their hoard had increased to fifteen Molotov cocktails, two bows and seven arrows, Ron's gun, and two tire irons.

As the pièce de résistance Penny provided a spray can of oven cleaner. "I knew there was a reason I packed this."

Everyone smiled, cheered by the sight of the weapons. Penny allowed them a moment of admiration before bringing them back down to earth. "All right, everyone. It's time to start planning."

"Finally," Peter muttered.

"All of us have different talents and skills. If we're going to win, we need to take advantage of them. For instance, my empathy warns me when the Selector is present in someone he's hooked."

"I can make traps." Peter didn't smile, his emotions all buttoned down.

"I can make illusions," April said.

"I can hear you scream when you die." Gavin broke their rhythm, fists clenched. "Which is to say, I can do fuck-all."

A heartbeat of silence.

"I'm good at plots and puzzles," Matt said quietly.

Genevieve gave a ghost of a smile. "I'm afraid my Talent isn't much more useful than yours, Gavin. I'm on the verge of fainting as it is."

Penny had been thinking about that. "Actually, there is something important only you can do. You can see inside the Selector's mind. You said you saw Nigel Carver in there. You may be able to learn something valuable from one of the other prisoners, the souls he's snagged. Something that will help us."

Genevieve looked startled, then determined. "I can do it, but you should be aware that while I dream, I'm vulnerable. The Selector can pull information from my mind. If he does, he'll know the entire plan."

"Then you'd better leave before you hear the rest of the plan,"

Peter said with a kind of diamond hardness that alarmed Penny.

"All right. I'll go lie down in the pickup." Genevieve sounded calm, but Penny experienced her dread, shudder for shudder. Although the dreams could not physically hurt Genevieve, they obviously exacted a high emotional toll.

Penny had felt tainted just by standing next to Ron when the Selector possessed him, and the Selector hadn't even seemed aware of her presence. What would if feel like to have all that black hatred focused on you?

Matt squeezed Genevieve's shoulder. "You don't have to do this."

She shook her head. "It's only a matter of time until I fall unconscious anyhow. I'll try to only eat and drink enough to sleep for a few hours."

"No, eat as much as you can," Matt said. "You'll need it. The approaching danger should wake you. If it doesn't, I'll put you behind the wheel again." Matt kissed her. "Be careful."

Penny sensed his deep concern, but he was practical enough to stay with them after Genevieve left where he would best be able to help.

Gavin cleared his throat, breaking the silence. "You know, the more I think about it, the less I think we'll actually face an entire army of the Selector's minions. I think the Selector can only control a limited number of people at once."

"Sounds good," Penny said. "Go on."

"I can't see him juggling any more than ten or twelve."

"Juggling?" April asked.

"Yes. Look, the Selector's hooking is a type of mind control, right? Will Halvorsen talked about a voice in his head. Think about it. If the Selector's talking to one person, he can't control someone else's mind at the same time."

Everyone's interest sharpened.

"I don't know about *can't*," Matt said thoughtfully. "We're dealing with something so fantastic we shouldn't rule anything out—but it sounds reasonable to me."

"Most of the time when we've come up against the Selector's

minions it's been a single person," Gavin continued. "Ron twice, the man who attacked Genevieve—"

"Crabtree," Matt supplied.

"—the gunman in Calgary. One man, who could be easily controlled by the Selector."

"Will Halvorsen had a partner," April pointed out.

"I know," Gavin said impatiently, "but let's suppose that, although the Selector can only occupy one person's mind at a time, he can leave three or four others' minds so messed up they'll keep obeying him for short periods of time."

"The demons," Jeff said, unwillingly drawn into the conversation.

Penny instantly understood what he meant. "You mean the reason Will Halvorsen thought we were demons was because the Selector planted some kind of hypnotic suggestion in his mind to make him keep chasing us while the Selector controlled someone else? Only at the end he left it too long, and Will realized what he was doing? And that's why he shot himself?"

"Exactly," Gavin said. "Jumping from mind to mind like that, the Selector can't possibly handle more than twelve or so at once."

"*Can't* again," Matt said mildly.

"I think you're right, Gavin." Penny tapped one finger against her cheek. She leaned back into the curve of Jeff's shoulder. "Except for one small thing. Will Halvorsen was a moral man, whose conscience wouldn't stand for him killing anyone, even supposed demons. The people we face tonight may not be as strong. They may need only the merest excuse to kill. If they're all like that, he may be able to manage as many as twenty or thirty."

April's sigh broke the silence. "Super."

Everyone laughed, a small laugh, but a laugh all the same. For the first time they clicked together as a team.

• 3 •

Bobby dreamed of playing trucks with Kristy.

Kristy dreamed of playing trucks with Bobby.

Kristy got bored and went to play on her favorite piece of play-ground equipment, the swings. She pumped her legs hard, gathering enough momentum to swing really high.

With her legs stretched out in front of her she felt like she could clear the power pole if she let go and parachuted. Legs tucked under her, head forward. Push. Then the downswing, with her head thrown back, looking at the world upside down, her brown braids just clear-ing the ground. And up, reaching toward the sky.

The feeling was glorious, like flying. At the top of her swing she glanced over at Bobby in the sandbox. He liked swinging, too, but he was too little to pump himself. She had to give him underducks and pushes all the time —

Someone grabbed hold of the back of her swing and jerked it out from under her.

She tipped off and dropped three feet onto packed sand. The wooden seat clipped the back of her head, chains rattling and twist-ing, as the swing continued forward, riderless. Kristy saw stars and almost got beaned a second time.

Laughter overhead mingled with Bobby's frightened cries. [*Head hurts. Make it stop.*]

She looked up and saw a dark-haired man standing over her. Without even having to think, she knew he was the Selector, and she dug ruts in the sand with her heels trying to push herself away.

He laughed again, the sound as nasty as cough syrup. "Don't worry, little girl. You're not the one I'm after." He turned away, leaving her bruised in the dirt. Turned toward the sandbox, toward Bobby.

[*Run!*]

Bobby got to his feet uncertainly. He looked from Kristy to the Selector.

[*Run! Head for the slide.*]

Bobby ran on short, stubby legs toward the tall blue slide. The Selector followed, not even bothering to run. He would catch Bobby easily if she didn't stop him.

Kristy pulled herself up and swayed dizzily. Her head hurt, and she could feel warm blood in her hair. She tried to run and soon found she'd wrenched her knee.

Bobby had reached the bottom of the slide, but climbing was a new skill for him, and he was terribly slow.

[*Faster, hurry!*] She tried to impart to him her knowledge of how his legs should move. Only one foot on each step, not first one and then the other. For once it worked, and he ran up the last couple steps, out of reach of the Selector's long arms.

[*Stay at the top. Don't slide down until he's halfway up the stairs,*] Kristy thought as she tore past the sandbox.

Bobby crouched at the top, ready to take the twisty ride down to the bottom. He was used to shorter, baby slides, and she could feel his fear beating at her.

"Slide down, and I'll catch you." The Selector stood at the bottom arms held wide [*just like Daddy.*]

[*No!*] Kristy blanked the image out, horrified.

Bobby hesitated, and the Selector put both hands on the slide handrails. He planted one foot on the steep surface and started to pull himself up.

Kristy came up on the Selector like a silent bullet. She threw all her weight on his legs.

His runners slipped on the slick surface, and he fell, knees banging on the metal. Breathless, Kristy kicked him. She was aiming for his shoulder, but he turned at the wrong moment, and she caught him under the chin in the throat.

His head snapped back, and he gagged. When he came up there was murder in his eyes, and it wasn't Bobby he was after anymore.

He lunged at her, and she took off like it was Track and Field Day. She sprinted past three red teeter-totters, slamming down the seats on her side so they were in motion and the Selector couldn't take a shortcut through them. Then on past a smaller set of swings with safety harnesses and into the sandpit surrounding the wooden fortress.

Chains clinked behind her as the Selector brushed through the swings.

He nearly caught her going up the ramp, but she slipped free into the wide plastic tunnel. She ducked her head and kept on running, but the Selector had to crouch and lost time.

Across the swaying rope bridge, up another ladder, then monkey down the wall of hanging tires.

[*Watch out!*]

The Selector jumped off the eight-foot platform and landed hard in front of her. While he scrambled up off his hands and knees, she turned and dived through one of the tires.

He caught her ankle and dragged her back. Rubber scraped her stomach and arms as she kicked and squirmed.

But he was too strong. He had her out in seconds. "Look at me." He grabbed her chin and forced her to meet his gaze.

His blue eyes trapped her, and she couldn't look away. She stopped fighting, body going limp . . .

[*KISTY!*]

Kristy woke up. Bobby had climbed over the station wagon's seat and was leaning over her, tears splashing her face. She sat up, and his chubby arms went around her neck. [*I thought you were dead. I thought you were dead!*]

• 4 •

The Selector frowned, more disturbed than he cared to admit by the Telepaths' shared dreams.

He'd expected Kristy to run away after he dumped her off the swing, but she had surprised him, coming to Bobby's rescue when she shouldn't even have been there.

If he hooked his victims with silver thread, did iron chains bind them together? The tie made Bobby stronger, but Kristy weaker. Did hooking one mean hooking both?

It didn't matter. The Telepaths held only minor interest for him. They were weak children.

He wished he'd had an opportunity to try to hook Peter instead of them. Peter was neither weak nor a child, despite his age. Peter reminded him of himself.

With the right training he could become a Selector.

• 5 •

Genevieve had feared that she would find herself back in the bedroom the Selector had furnished for her when she dreamed again, but instead she found herself where she had last stood before waking. On the edge of the briar patch.

Ahead lay a garden, to her right a concrete bunker. Genevieve frowned at the bunker. She remembered the garden from before, but she was almost positive the square concrete building had not been there. Curious, she turned toward it.

The bunker was the size of a desk, four-feet-by-three-feet-by-two-feet, lacking both doors and windows.

Her bedroom hadn't had a door.

Obeying a hunch, Genevieve laid her hands on the concrete wall and imagined it cracking and peeling the way her prison had.

The concrete crumbled beneath her fingers like cheap posterboard. Genevieve waved away a cloud of dust and saw the crouched figure of a man who'd been trapped inside raise his head in astonishment.

Ron. "What are you doing here?" Genevieve asked.

"What do you think? The Selector put me here," Ron said shortly. He straightened and brushed the dust from his blond hair.

"He has control of your body right now?"

"Yes." Ron gave her another, Are you stupid? look.

Genevieve ignored it. "Were you still tied up?"

"Yes."

"Good." Genevieve relaxed.

For a moment she thought she saw pity in Ron's gaze, and then he gestured to the remains of his former prison. "Thanks for letting me out. How'd you do that?"

Genevieve opened her mouth, then hesitated. How had she done it? "I think it's because this world isn't real. Most of the time it conforms to what the Selector wants, but if you concentrate hard enough you can . . . bend it."

"So all these years I could have freed myself and didn't," Ron said bitterly.

Genevieve was appalled. "How often does he lock you up?" The bunker had been too short to sit in without hunching and not long enough to lie down in.

"The bunker is special punishment," Ron told her. "He only puts me there when I've displeased him—which happens about twice a week. Otherwise, I'm only in trapped in his mind."

"Then you're familiar with the landscape? The other prisoners?" Genevieve felt relieved; she could use a guide.

"Sure," Ron said. "What did you want to know?"

"What's in the garden?" Genevieve asked eagerly.

"What garden?" Ron asked.

"That one." Genevieve pointed, exasperated.

Ron looked in the direction of her finger and took a step back. "Where did that come from? I don't remember that."

"What was there before?" Genevieve asked.

Ron shrugged, looking uneasy. "There wasn't anything there."

So much for her guide. Genevieve sighed. "In that case we should make it our first stop."

Ron opened his mouth, almost said something, then changed his mind. Still tense, he let her enter the garden first before following.

The garden was blanketed in a glorious profusion of flowers. Tiger lilies, marigolds, poppies, and roses formed a riot of colors, growing wild without benefit of rows amongst the tall, waving grass.

Their overpowering sweet scent hung in the hot, summer air. The farther Genevieve and Ron went the taller the grass grew, until it topped both their heads. In the lead, Genevieve pushed her way through it blindly. Like swimming in a grass ocean.

Also like water, the path they made closed up again behind them.

"Maybe we should go back," Ron said after an indeterminate amount of time had passed.

Genevieve was on the verge of agreeing when she glimpsed something red. "Wait. I think I found something." She parted the grass in front of her face and saw a sleeping boy lying on a bed of grass.

A sleeping, blond boy dressed in a red T-shirt and jeans.

A sleeping, blond boy with black-and-blue bruises on his face and arms.

Ronnie.

With a low cry, Genevieve started forward. She wanted to help Ronnie, to tell him he wasn't a bad boy.

She never got the chance. The grass thickened and turned into briars between her and her goal, growing ferociously, twining amongst itself. Thorns pricked her hands and wrists when she tried to part them.

And then the visions came, too many to count, assaulting her.

Ronnie cringing while the *Oberleutnant* that Penny had said was Nigel Carver caned him.

Ronnie climbing halfway up a rope before slipping and falling. Nigel standing over him, yelling, "Coward! You'll never make a Selector!"

Ronnie crying, rocking himself back and forth. "Bad boy Ronnie for crying. The Selector never cries. . . ."

Ronnie splitting in half. The dark-haired Ronnie kicking Nigel in the shin, while the blond Ronnie watched. Nigel's red, enraged face as he struck the dark-haired Ronnie. The dark-haired Ronnie laughing despite a cut lip. "You can't hurt me anymore, old man. I'm the Selector."

Nigel forcing a knife into Ronnie's hand and holding out a calico kitten. "Kill it." The sudden appearance of the dark-haired Ronnie, who cut its head off while the blond Ronnie wept.

Genevieve turned away, sickened, but she couldn't stop her mind from working and making connections.

The dark-haired Ronnie had green eyes, the blond Ronnie had blue eyes, but otherwise they were identical. Unwillingly, Genevieve looked at the grown-up Ron she had freed from the bunker. If you changed his hair and eye color, he was the spitting image of the Selector.

Ron, Ronald, Ruoon Naiee. Ronnie, not run Mary. Her father hadn't been talking to her at all.

"I don't understand," Ron said, but he looked afraid of the blond boy. "Who is he?"

"He's you." Genevieve explained as gently as she could. Ron and the Selector were the same person, two parts of a multiple personality that had split as a child as a defense against the horrible things Nigel Carver had forced the boy to do.

When she had finished, Ron stared at sleeping Bad boy Ronnie for crying for a long time. "He doesn't look much older than six. Do you think he's been asleep all this time?"

"Probably." At first Ronnie would only have summoned the Selector when Nigel forced him to do terrible things, but as the number of things he was asked to do increased it must have seemed easier to just sleep away the time in a peaceful garden.

"My first memory is of going into grade one. . . . I would have been six years old." Ron looked haunted.

Genevieve pulled him away. "Come on. You have to help me wake up. I have to tell the others what we've found out." That the Selector was their brother and that they had already captured him.

Ron stared at her, uncomprehending, while she first pinched, then slapped herself. "It's not working," Genevieve cried in despair.

She was trapped inside the Selector's mind until her danger instinct woke her.

• 6 •

April gave Gavin ten minutes head start, then slipped into the woods after him. After the planning session, he'd escaped from Penny's Last Supper spread of tuna fish sandwiches and tinned fruit cocktail, saying he had to answer nature's call, but April was sure it was more than that.

She walked carefully, using a flashlight to light her way, while her eyes searched for a second flashlight up ahead. She finally found him sitting on a rock, grimly trying to rotate his sore shoulder with only partial success.

"How ya doin'?"

Gavin snorted. "Oh, I'm in tip-top shape. How are you feeling?"

"Scared." April ignored the dampness and sat down beside him.

Gavin hesitated. "Please don't call me a male chauvinist pig, but you don't have to do this, you know. You can leave."

Men were so clueless. April shook her head. "No, I can't."

"Sure you can. I'm staying because of Bethany, but you can go. The Selector seems to be most interested in those of us related to Ron. He might not even notice you were gone."

"It's too late to back out. I'm needed here now." *Crucial*, Peter had said. Her stomach rolled over and played dead every time she remembered how much of their plan depended on her. She'd only found out she was an Illusionist yesterday, and, while the last hour's practice had gone smoothly, she was still going to feel awfully naked standing up to machine guns with only the thin veil of illusion.

Gavin studied her determined face for a moment, then sighed. "Well, it was worth a try. If I hadn't shown up on your doorstep, bleeding—"

"Kristy and I would have burned to death in the trailer," April finished. "It was my decision to leave. *Mine*, not yours. You bear no responsibility."

"Well, damn it, I feel responsible!" Gavin flared. "Bethany's dead because I didn't stop her, and I don't want the same thing to happen to you."

April softened. "Thanks. As it so happens I don't want you to die either, so we'll both just have to be careful, all right?" She watched his expression closely. He wanted very badly to avenge Bethany, and she was afraid he would count his own life well spent if he took the Selector down with him.

"All right." Gavin grinned crookedly, holding out his hand. "Friends?"

"Of course," April said, even though she wanted to be so much more—and she might be running out of time.

No prizes for the chickenhearted.

She took a deep breath. "Give me a kiss for luck?"

Gavin looked startled, then grim. "We need all the luck we can get."

He bent his head and brushed his lips against hers. He started to pull back, then stopped. His eyes searched hers for a moment, then his head dipped for another taste. April opened her mouth and curled her fingers into his shoulders. His hand gripped the back of her head, deepening the kiss.

When Gavin drew back, he looked a little stunned, but he wasn't looking at her like a friend or a pal or a sister anymore.

He mumbled something about needing a glass of water and backed away into the trees.

April grinned. He was going in the wrong direction.

• 7 •

"Since we're both trapped here for the time being, I think we should try to do some damage," Genevieve said.

Ron was more than willing. "How?"

"I think we should free the prisoners."

Ron looked at her, surprised, and instantly ill at ease. "What good would that do?"

"I've been thinking," she said. "The Selector had a reason for locking up every prisoner here. Every prisoner is someone important to him, someone he hates and fears. We'll start by freeing Bethany."

"Actually I locked up Bethany, not the Selector," Ron said. "She's fine." He smiled at Genevieve, an automatic reflex, trying to influence her with his Shine. "I built her a castle."

"She didn't look fine to me," Genevieve said grimly. "When was the last time you saw her?"

"The day I took her here. Why?" Ron asked, uneasy.

"Why did you take her here?"

"To save her, of course." A little irritation bled through his Shine.

"To save her for what? She may live in a castle, but she spends her time reliving her death over and over. I think she'd rather be dead."

Ron's temper shot up. "Now wait just a bloody minute—"

Genevieve winced and held up her hand. "No, I'm sorry. I shouldn't have said that. You're not keeping her in prison, the Selector is."

"Because he hates and fears her? Tell me another one. The Selector despises all women, and Bethany isn't a threat."

"You're wrong. Bethany is very much a threat to him. You love her."

"Yes," Ron said angrily. "What does that have to do with—"

"Ron Carver was in love with a beautiful young woman. Ron Carver *who is part of the multiple personality that is Ronald Carver* was in love. That's very dangerous to the Selector, who thrives only on hate. He must have been desperate to kill her."

"Then why did he let me save her?"

Genevieve didn't answer directly. "Bethany calls two names. Yours and Gavin's."

"Gavin used to date Bethany." Ron clenched his hands into fists.

"You dislike him." Genevieve made a statement.

Ron bared his teeth. "I hate him. When Bethany started dating him I discovered I was the jealous type."

"You were angry?"

"Oh, yes," Ron said softly, eyes focused off in the distance, remembering Gavin's hand on Bethany's waist, remembering the urge to chop his fingers off for touching her. "Very angry. And very jealous."

"Angry at Gavin?" Genevieve let a heartbeat pass. "Or angry at Bethany?"

Ron's gaze jerked back to hers. "What do you mean by that? I love Bethany."

Genevieve did not flinch. "You loved her, but part of you felt angry at her for betraying you with Gavin. Part of you wanted to punish her. So you locked her up here."

Ron started to protest, but he couldn't find the words. *She's right.* The realization hit him with the force of a blow. His excuses cracked like fragile pottery, spilling onto the ground. He dropped his head into his hands. "You're right, I have been punishing Bethany." Genevieve slipped a comforting arm around his shoulders, but he kept talking, trying to purge himself of the guilt. "And do you know what I've been punishing her for? For following her danger instinct. Gavin was just someone safe. She died because of me, and I punished her."

"Then set her free."

Ron seized on the idea. "Yes, of course. Where is her castle from here? I have to see her."

"That way, I think." Genevieve pointed through the tall grass, and Ron strode eagerly forward.

But ten paces past Bad boy Ronnie for crying, sunshine turned to night. The wildly waving grass become short-cropped lawn, and a cold moon shone down on someone's backyard. A screen door flapped in the wind.

Genevieve caught up with him. "Who else is imprisoned here?"

Ron avoided looking at the darkened house. "There's Nigel. I don't think I can ever forgive him, but I pity him more than I hate him. He's pathetic."

Genevieve nodded in understanding. "Nigel Carver was a monster. Who else?"

"You, but you're already free," Ron evaded.

"There's someone else, though, isn't there?" Genevieve asked. "I recognize that door. I've passed through it in my dreams a hundred times. Gone down that flight of steps."

"Yes." Ron clipped off the word. "There's someone else, but she deserves what she gets."

"You mean, you won't give up your hate for her."

Ron didn't back down. "No, I won't. I can't forgive her for what she did."

"Even if it means the Selector wins?" Genevieve asked softly.

"Even for that, I don't think I could," he said with painful honesty.

"I still think we should see her," Genevieve said. "She is, after all, our mother."

• 8 •

Penny stumbled through the darkened woods, searching for Peter. He'd left the companionship of the camp twenty minutes ago, and she was worried about him. He acted so tight and cold on the outside and felt so much hurt and anger within. He was like a tightly corked champagne bottle — and just as likely to explode under pressure, with possibly devastating consequences.

She would have walked right past him if not for a faint prickle from her empathy. She stopped and looked around, squinting, finally locating him five feet off the ground in a tree house. He was stripping twigs off branches.

"Hello, Peter." His face was closed. Penny wondered how he'd look if he smiled.

"Hello." Peter did not stop stripping twigs.

"Peter, have I told you I'm an Empath?"

He nodded.

"Do you know what empathy means?"

"It's like sympathy." A statement, no curiosity.

"A little bit. Sympathy is feeling sorry for someone." She paused. A drop of water fell from a leaf onto her nose. "I don't feel sorry for you Peter, but I can feel your emotions. I know how hurt and angry you are over Al's death." [*Burning rage and icy distance.*] "In ice he hides . . ."

Peter said nothing. His face stayed blank, but his hands stilled.

"Al's death was terrible and senseless." Penny picked her words with care. "I know you want to punish his murderer — and he should be punished, but not tortured to death the way you want him to be."

"He deserves it."

"Yes," Penny agreed, thinking of Bethany and Will Halvorsen. "But there's something more important than revenge. *You* are more important, Peter, and if you carry out your plan, you'll damage yourself. Torture is wrong. It's evil, and evil corrupts the soul."

"He started it. He killed Al."

"Killing the Selector won't bring Al back," Penny said forcefully.

She got his attention. A crack appeared in his fortress. "The living are more important than the dead. Al wouldn't want you to ruin your life to avenge his death."

She shouldn't have mentioned Al. Peter clamped down again, fire encased in ice. "You're wrong. Al was my blood brother. I have to avenge him. He would have done the same for me." Peter climbed down from the tree and started walking back to camp. His ruler-straight back said clearer than words that their conversation had ended.

Penny followed. She hurt for him, for his grief and loyalty to his dead friend. Most of all she hurt for the real Peter, who might never know daylight and happiness again.

He was only twelve years old.

He shouldn't be doing this, playing a soldier in their war against the Selector. Earlier, during their planning, Gavin had tried to exclude Peter from the fighting, on the grounds that he was too young. Peter had blasted him with frigid gray eyes, and demanded, "Can you steal within five feet of a deer? Can you dive and roll out of a target area just before the arrow hits? Can you?"

Gavin couldn't, of course, and Peter had coldly suggested that *he* go with Penny and the kids because of his wound.

Needless to say, neither of them was going with her. And it was time to leave now.

She could feel the danger almost upon them.

At the camp, she headed straight for the kids. "Come on, Kristy, Bobby. It's time to go."

Jeff met her eyes over their heads, naked fear in his gaze. "Be careful." He pressed Ron's gun into her hand.

Tears made Penny's eyes bright. "That's my line. I'm going into hiding. You'll be the one in danger." She blinked. "I love you."

He hesitated, and she caught a lingering flash of uncertainty before he swept her into a hard hug. "I love you, too." He kissed her forehead, then stooped to pick up Bobby. "You be good for your mom, okay?"

What if she never saw him again? Penny felt as if she was being torn in half. There was so much she wanted to say to him, but the time for good-byes had passed. With every heartbeat, she could feel the danger pressing closer.

She slid open the van door and herded Bobby and Kristy ahead of her. Ron was already inside, seemingly asleep, but just in case the Selector could hear they proceeded with Act Two.

Matt came rushing up, carrying Genevieve. "I still can't wake her. I don't dare wait any longer. If the Selector finds her like this, she's a sitting duck. I'm sorry, I'm going to have to leave with Penny."

"Leave if you like, coward," Peter spit. "We're staying."

"I would if I could," Matt said. He followed Penny into the van, hoisting Genevieve into the driver's seat.

Matt fired up the engine for Genevieve, working the pedals from behind, while Penny was still strapping Bobby in. They drove off into the darkness.

The night swallowed them whole.

CHAPTER 12

• 1 •

Genevieve woke up behind the wheel.

Her fingers tightened spasmodically, her heart rate jumping from the shock of sudden transition as the Selector's mental landscape was replaced by the dim interior of a van and the glistening black highway rolling under the wheels.

"You okay?" Matt asked. He half crouched beside her, ready to take over if she fell asleep again.

Genevieve nodded, even though she was less than fine. She pressed her foot down on the accelerator, desperate to keep her danger instinct engaged and stay awake. The van sped up to 60 mph.

"Don't fasten your seat belt," Matt warned. "You didn't wake up until I unhooked it."

In the rearview mirror she noted the van's other occupants. Penny sat between Kristy and Bobby in the next row. Bobby was upset because "Kristy" wouldn't play with him, and Penny was trying to distract him with a game of pattycake.

In the third row was Ron. Or rather the Selector. He seemed to be sleeping, but Genevieve didn't believe it. She felt chilled.

"Here's the plan," Matt whispered, for her ears alone. "Gavin thinks the Selector can only inhabit one mind at a time. We want you to speak to Ron and trigger the Selector's presence, distract him so the others have a chance to move against the minions he's sending."

It was a good idea, but when they made the plan they hadn't known what Genevieve knew now. "I found out something important while I was dreaming," she said urgently. "Ron and the Selector—"

She didn't get a chance to finish.

Matt made a strangled sound, and the black flowing river of the night was torn to tatters. Her danger instinct, which had only been humming before, shrieked into life, too late.

Matt's body fell across hers, his hands fisting at his sides in the throes of a grand-mal seizure. His weight tore her arms from the steering wheel, and the van rushed across the yellow line.

In the backseat someone screamed, but Genevieve paid no attention. She pulled one arm free of Matt's waist and grabbed for the wheel. One-handed, she overcorrected, and the van veered too far to the right.

She got her second arm free barely in time to keep them from hitting the ditch. Matt's body continued to lie rigidly across her lap, tonic, his legs kicked straight out, and his jaw muscles knotted and bulging like a movie Frankenstein's monster.

One of his arms dangled by her legs, getting in the way when Genevieve hit the brakes.

The sudden deceleration made Matt's body roll forward, slipping toward the floor pedals. Genevieve grabbed a fistful of Matt's shirt with one hand and held on for dear life, desperately trying to brake and steer at the same time.

It was working. The van had slowed to 30 mph and was under control when Matt went into clonic phase.

His arms and legs flailed convulsively. His head banged against the steering wheel, and one elbow slammed into Genevieve's ribs. All the air left her lungs in a choking gasp.

Simultaneously, Matt's leg stamped up and down on the gas pedal. The engine roared, and the van leapt forward like an enraged bull charging a matador's cape.

The orange needle on the speedometer swept up to 45 mph.

Genevieve bent forward, hooking one arm around Matt's thigh, trying to pull his leg away from the gas pedal and steer at the same time. The van crested a small hill, hard to see in the dark.

Matt's other foot caught the edge of the brake, and Genevieve lurched forward. Her head banged into the steering column, her teeth clicking shut hard enough to draw sparks.

Eyes tearing, Genevieve looked up and saw blacktop highway with ghostly white lines screaming down at her.

They were on the wrong side of the road.

"Shit!" She let go of Matt's leg and jerked the wheel to the right, away from the ditch while his arms beat at her legs and stomach. His foot hit the gas again, and Genevieve swerved left, then right again, all over the road and on the shoulders.

The speedometer needle jumped past 65 mph.

A bullet through the night.

Genevieve clung to the wheel as Matt's convulsing body beat at her own, struggling to pay attention to the lane lines. Ghost lines that disappeared into the dark.

If she could just hang on a little longer, last the attack out . . .

She was trying to locate the brake with her foot when Matt's head connected painfully with her funny bone. Her left arm went numb and lost its grip on the wheel for a second.

Lines curving . . .

A corner! *Screeee!* Matt hit the gas just as she veered away from the ditch. Forget the lane lines, she'd be happy to just stay on the road—

Oncoming headlights exploded out of the dark as they swung around the corner.

Genevieve whipped the steering wheel to the right, and they hydroplaned, slewing sideways, but the other vehicle swerved in the same direction. Desperately, she steered left, left, cranking the wheel, but it was too late, they were too close, still skidding and she had no control, none—

The front of the pickup smashed into the van, and Genevieve flew forward, smacking her head against the windshield. The last thing she saw was the spiderweb of cracks radiating outward like a nova.

• 2 •

Impact.

Metal screeched sickeningly against metal; Penny was thrown forward, then jerked back by her seat belt. One window shattered, spewing safety glass, and the side door slid open on metal tracks.

Even when the van stopped moving a car horn kept blaring a warning. Her nerves jangled with a message of danger. Frantically, Penny put a hand to her stomach, kneading the taut surface. She almost cried in relief when Damaris pushed back as strongly as ever. The distress Damaris was feeling had no physical cause.

Bobby next. He was crying and clutching her skirt; she ran quick hands over his body, but couldn't find any injuries. He was just frightened. "Shh, Bobby, everything's going to be okay." She kissed his forehead and started looking around, assessing the situation. The van had swung crazily across the road, and now lay half-in half-out of the ditch. Ron looked unharmed. Kristy had already undone her seat belt. She was fine.

The same, however, could not be said of the other two passengers.

Matt's body still thrashed, and Genevieve slumped sideways, unconscious.

"Stay here," Penny told her son, as she heaved herself up. She couldn't do anything for Matt, so she ignored him, bending over Genevieve.

A red line marked her scalp, and her nose was bloodied, but she seemed to be breathing. Penny picked up her wrist, feeling for a pulse, and peered outside at the car horn.

The dark pressed in like a living thing. They'd lost one of their headlights so only a single spot of yellow illuminated the other vehicle, a pickup on its side. She hoped the passengers were all right.

Penny winced as Matt's head banged against the steering column. She should move him somewhere where he couldn't hurt—

A light came on in the pickup's cab, and Penny saw that the passengers were not all right after all. A man was hanging out of the windshield. Dead. Spots of blood on his glasses.

The driver had been saved by his airbag. Penny watched as he reached up and opened one of the side doors. He jumped up, hoisted himself out, then lay flat, stretching one arm back inside, fishing for something.

He pulled it out and held it up to the light. A handgun.

Not innocent passersby, injured by Matt's accident: some of the Selector's minions on a mission to kill.

"No!" Bobby yelled. "Kristy stop. It hurts."

His childish fear and confusion scattered all her other concerns like a bowling ball; Penny turned.

Yelling and red-faced, Bobby pulled away from Kristy. Kristy—whose face and emotions were a blank page as she knelt behind Ron and untied his hands.

Untied his hands.

The greatest puppet-master of them all.

The Selector smiled at her. Not Ron. She knew whom she faced. In an instant she knew the black depths of the Selector's soul.

• 3 •

The Selector smiled, gratified at the way Penny gasped and blanched. He felt pleased with what he'd wrought even though events had not gone exactly as he planned.

He'd intended to take over the poet man's body, but when he jiggled the silver cord the poet man had had a seizure instead.

The van's crash had provided a wonderful distraction while he hooked Kristy and made her start untying his hands. He'd clamped her vocal cords to prevent her from crying out, but he'd reckoned without Bobby.

Linked to Kristy's mind, but not hooked with her, the little brat had started crying and attracted Penny's attention.

"Kristy, no!" Penny tried to pull the girl away.

Penny had a strong Talent, but her pregnancy made her weak. The Selector made Kristy headbutt her in the stomach. While Penny stumbled back, clutching her abdomen, he made Kristy resume untying the knots.

One knot undone. The Selector could see them through Kristy's eyes, giving the room an odd double perspective.

[*Untie them or I'll kill Bobby*] he told Kristy. Of course, he had every intention of killing the boy no matter what.

Bobby shrieked and ran out of the open van door.

Penny hesitated a moment, torn between stopping Kristy and going after her three-year-old. She must have seen the killers in the pickup that had crashed into them, because her maternal instinct won. "No, Bobby, come back!" Stark terror showed on her face as she ran out into the night.

• 4 •

When he heard the crying, Eric Szmata giggled.

He was playing the most advanced virtual-reality game on the market, Commando Death Raid. Instead of his own skinny five-foot-five self he was in the body of a big tough son of a bitch with muscles like Schwarzenegger back in his early movies before he wimped out doing comedies, and he had a gun like a cannon, an Uzi automatic. He'd asked for a rocket launcher, but the VR Commando captain had said no.

That had pissed him off—after all, in VR a rocket launcher was only graphics—until he'd realized the programmers were probably saving the rocket launcher for the next level of the game.

Commando Death Raid had only one life per turn, and Eric was determined to go as long as possible without dying. Virtual-reality games cost a lot of dough, and it might be months before he had a chance to play again, especially an ultrasophisticated game like this one that was almost too real in places—flying to the mission drop really had seemed to take hours—so Eric wasn't going to do anything that might make [GAME OVER] flash across his screen.

The car crash had been really wild: a kaleidoscope of colors as the vehicle set off the land mine and rolled over, the sound of glass smashing, and the choke-tight hold of his seat belt. The graphics of his dead companion were absolutely over the top. The body lay slumped over the Land Rover's hood, neck torn open by the jagged metal frame of the jeep, glasses dangling from one ear. Somehow they'd gotten the smell and texture of blood as well as the color.

Eric figured his fellow soldier's death had to be part of the game plan to force him to continue solo, one man against an entire Viet Cong village.

He'd escaped into the jungle before whoever set the land mine could find him, firing a burst at a movement in the dense foliage. He still couldn't get over the reality of VR—the gun had actually seemed to kick in his hands.

The lighting was a little too dark, though; if Eric had written this module, he would have included night-vision goggles. He couldn't see where the crying was coming from, where his wounded prey lay.

It could be a trap, of course, but Eric grinned, unafraid, because he had a flak jacket, technology the little gooks lacked.

He aimed his Uzi at the jungle ferns where the crying originated, finger on the trigger—

Someone burst from the trees behind him. In surprise, his gun jerked upward, squeezing off a burst—too high, damn it—and he spun around, expecting to hear another gun open up and the Commando theme music to play, flashing [GAME OVER] and taking him back to being a skinny, pimpled computer nerd.

But it didn't happen; the figure just kept on running. He almost shot her in reflex, but the moon came out from behind a cloud and revealed his quarry was a woman.

Killing an unarmed civilian would probably mean a penalty, but if he let her get away she might warn her village. He gave chase, ignoring the too-real branches scratching his hands as he jumped logs and ducked vines.

Something primitive about the nighttime silent pursuit heated his blood. In real life Eric was reluctant to venture out after dark for fear of getting mugged, but here in the jungle his Uzi made him the biggest predator of all. He laughed, and adrenaline flooded his pumped-up system. He'd always been a good runner, but in this body he was a superb running machine, gaining on the woman with every step. Any second now, he'd be close enough to catch her sleeve, drag her down . . .

He wondered if raping would end the game and how big a cock his VR body had.

The woman crashed through the jungle, gasping for breath.

Eric's fingers touched her coat, then slipped off.

She swerved left, leaving him clutching thin air. He stumbled at the sudden change in direction, and his foot slipped in loose shale, almost going over the edge.

In the dark he hadn't seen the ravine. Had it even been there two seconds before? Damn cheating computer.

He'd beat it anyhow. The woman was tiring, gasping liking a wounded cow. He put on an extra burst of speed and tackled her.

They fell together on the wet ground, among the soggy dead leaves and branches. Eric groped her breasts in a frenzy of lust. He forgot all about the possible [GAME OVER]; he was pulling down his zipper when she spoke right in his ear.

"Please, I'm pregnant."

The English confused him; he'd expected her to speak Vietnamese. In the dark he couldn't tell her race, but a hand on her tummy verified she had a bun in the oven.

Eric reared back, outraged. What kind of shitty combat game was this? He was supposed to be a commando fighting the Viet Cong, hucking grenades and blowing up villages.

He had no intention of rescuing some pregnant woman, and fucking her would be no fun, with the kid squirming in between.

He started to climb off her and triggered the hook in his mind.

THE SELECTOR SHOVED Eric Szmata's personality aside as if walking through a beaded curtain.

His irritation faded when he got a look at the woman pinned beneath his minion's body. Penny Lacrosse.

So. He would have expected her to be still hiding safely in the woods. A quick rewind of Eric's memories enlightened him. She had broken from cover to lead him away from Bobby. Her maternal instinct had overruled her danger instinct.

The kind of maternal instinct his own mother had lacked.

The Selector shook the thought off, angry. He never thought of his mother except to gloat over her death.

"You don't really want to do this. Please let me go," Penny said, her voice low and intense, designed to soothe a nervous teenage boy.

The Selector laughed when he realized she was afraid the boy would rape her. "Don't worry, Penny. I'd rather swim in a cesspool."

The boy's desire for Penny disgusted him. Desiring any woman implied a weakness, and she was pregnant, a mosquito-infested swamp crawling with larvae, a breeding ground for the cowardly and impure.

Underneath him, Penny stilled. "You," she breathed.

"Yes, me." A grin stretched his face.

The baby kicked in between them.

With one hand the Selector anchored her wrists above her head. "You know what? I think the kid wants out. Maybe I'll help him." With his other hand he yanked up her cotton skirt, exposing the obscene white bulge of her belly. She looked ripe, ready to burst.

He reached into his belt and pulled out the machete he made all his minions carry. He would carve her open like a jack-o'-lantern, and the kid would pop right out, all wet and slimy—

Penny kneed him in the crotch, and pain knifed through him. Before he could clamp down on the offending nerves she wrenched her arms free and threw herself backward into the ravine. She fell down the cliff, showering rocks and dirt.

The Selector scrambled to the edge of the gully and shone his flashlight down. What he saw made him gnash his teeth in frustration.

Penny still lived, trapped at the bottom of a gully. The Selector could get down to her, but the sides of the ravine were too steep for his minion to climb back out, and tonight the Selector needed every minion he had.

Damn, he would have to shoot her. Bullets just didn't satisfy him like knives did. They weren't as . . . intimate.

He studied her for a moment, drinking in the scrapes and disfiguring bruises. She blinked in the flashlight beam, her breathing fast and shallow.

He picked up the .38 Eric had thought was an Uzi and aimed it carefully. First shot in the belly, second in the face — She moaned suddenly and clutched her stomach, face contorted with pain.

The Selector lowered his gun, and a slow smile played across his minion's lips.

The fall had brought on her labor. Eve's punishment. During the long hours ahead while she screamed in agony, she would wish he had killed her right away. And if by chance she didn't die from childbirth, he could still kill her later.

Decision made, the Selector instructed Eric to find Bobby, Eric's perceived "wounded man," and reached out with his mind to talk to his troops.

• 5 •

When Genevieve disappeared, Ron started to walk past the screen door. His mother could rot; Bethany was more important.

He took four paces then stopped, hands clenched.

What if Genevieve was right? What if freeing the prisoner could defeat the Selector?

Reluctantly, Ron turned back. Put his hand on the screen door. Pushed it open.

He paused on the threshold, disturbed. The house looked ordinary from the outside, but there was no main level, only a flight of stairs leading down.

"Shit," Ron said and started down the steps.

The basement held a fireplace, sofa, and a clutter of clocks. Only all these clocks had stopped, frozen, at nine o'clock, the time of Terisa Richmond's death.

His mother sat on the couch.

"Hello, Ron." Terisa smiled sadly. "My precious child. Is it finally happening as I foresaw? Is it time to leave my prison yet?"

Ron said nothing.

"Of course you don't know," Terisa answered herself. "You can't see the future."

The other prisoners Ron had met were locked into their own fantasies, unaware that they were even in prison. "If you want to leave, why don't you just walk out the door?" he asked.

"Guilt binds me."

His anger at her returned. "Guilt for letting Nigel have your kid?"

Terisa did not take offense. "No. Guilt for not killing my child. I foresaw my own death. I knew the Selector would kill me when I abandoned him. Watch."

Ghost images sprang up in front of Terisa. They solidified as she faded.

A young woman and her husband faced a fiftyish Nigel on a staircase. The young man had a gun, but couldn't use it. Nigel dangled a screaming toddler upside down over the railing.

"Put him down, or I'll shoot."

"Drop the gun, or I'll dash its brains out," Nigel countered. He rattled the child like a toy, and the boy's screaming whoops filled the air.

Terisa made a quick motion of distress, and her husband's knuckles whitened on the gun. "If you do, I'll kill you. We'll both lose. Give him to us."

Another razor-edged smile. "If I hand him over, you'll kill me. I'll keep the child, thank you."

"If it's a hostage you want, take me," Terisa said. "He's just a baby; he's of no use to you!"

Nigel shook his head. "I think not. You're too old to learn new tricks. I made a mistake letting your mother raise you. I'll be more careful with my grandson. He won't turn into a coward; I'll mold him into one of my Selectors, the evolutionists of the new human race."

Terisa moaned, eyes black with anguish.

An alarm went off outside.

The man looked torn between his wife and son. "Terisa," he said urgently.

"Make your choice," Nigel said. "Your child dead or your child raised by me."

The little boy in question screamed endlessly.

Terisa's green eyes locked with Nigel's dirty ice. Her face was deathly pale. "If you raise him in hate, he'll kill you when he grows up."

Nigel snorted. "Do you think I'd believe your lies?"

"No lies, only truth, Father."

The blood of rage suffused his pinched face. "Don't call me that, you hell-spawn!"

"But I am your daughter. The daughter of Portia Koehntopp and Nigel Carver. Neither of a superrace nor a cowardly one. I see the future. And I tell you again: he will kill you. He will also kill me. That is the choice you offer me: either let you kill my firstborn child or be killed by him twenty-three years from now."

For the first time Nigel looked unsure.

Vehemently, she swore, "I will *never* kill my son."

Nigel smiled in triumph.

"Terisa!" Her husband was frantic. Someone banged on the door, breaking it down.

"Bye-bye baby." She blew a kiss to her screeching child, then fled down the stairs.

The ghost images dissolved into acid, and Terisa faced Ron once again, clothed in guilt.

"I was too weak to let Nigel kill him. Because of me seventy-three people are dead."

"You didn't abandon Ronnie. You chose his life over yours," Ron said.

"I chose his life over mine, my husband's, my children to come, and countless others. I had no right to make such a choice," Terisa said harshly. "I had no right to give birth to more children and give them up for adoption just to save my firstborn."

"No," Ron said. "You don't deserve this punishment. You didn't know about the others the Selector would kill. You only knew about yourself and Nigel."

He stepped forward, hands outstretched. "I should have known the Old Man lied about you abandoning me, the same way he lied about everything else."

"You were only three years old. You couldn't be expected to know."

"Neither could you." Ron took her hands. "I'm sorry for punishing you so long. Please come out of your prison, Mother."

She smiled, radiant in her tears, and vanished.

• 6 •

Even after the Selector left the terrible compulsion to untie him remained with Kristy.

Somewhere inside, her danger instinct shrilled, telling her to stop, that if she untied Ron, the Selector would kill her, kill Bobby, kill everyone—but she couldn't stop.

The little voice wasn't as compelling as the echoes of his last command and the memory of pain he'd inflicted when she tried not to hit Penny [*Mommy*] in the stomach.

With a great, wrenching effort she managed to make her fingers work on the knots holding Ron's feet instead of his hands, but they would not stop altogether. They kept working like busy elves on Christmas Eve, working even though Genevieve was unconscious and Matt kept banging his head on the steering wheel.

Even though Bobby had run outside into danger.

Independently, her fingers untied another knot. They bled, making the knots slippery, but her fingers did not hurt. The pain was separate, too.

Kristy had been divided into a bunch of different boxes. Untying knots in one. Her danger instinct in another. Screaming terror. Bobby. Pain in her fingers.

The bonds around his feet slipped loose.

Over her danger instinct's protests, she started on the knots hold-ing the Selector's hands together.

[*Kisty?*]

At first Bobby was distant, too, locked in his separate box, but he soon got out. [*Kisty!*]

Her hands stilled.

[*KISTY!*] His thoughts came to her in a jumble, like a toy box spilled out.

[*Mommy's gone/Yelling/Shaking/Bad Guy found me/Upside-down/ Screaming/Nose full of snot.*]

The onslaught of images and thoughts scalded Kristy like ripping off a bandage. Bobby pulled her one way, the Selector another. There was no contest: the chains won; the silver thread snapped.

Kristy scrambled over to the van door. Genevieve moaned as she passed.

Away from the van's single eye, it was very dark outside, but Kristy didn't hesitate. Bobby's frantic cries dragged her through the ditch and into the woods like iron to a magnet.

[*Grip on his/her ankles. Upside-down, swinging in circles. Like the airplane game Daddy sometimes played with him only Daddy held his hands not his feet, and he didn't swing him near trees.*]

Kristy felt the pine needles scratching Bobby's face, heard his screaming, and was dizzied by the arc the Bad Guy swung her through, yelling, not making sense. "Where's your village, you little gook? Tell me now or I'll forget about Game Over and dash your brains out."

Only something in the words troubled him, because he hesitated. "Dash its brains out." He shook Bobby. "Dash its brains out." He sounded like a stuck record. "Dash its brains out."

Kristy leapt on his back, biting and clawing.

Startled, the man dropped Bobby. He swore, reached behind, grabbed a handful of her hair and yanked. Kristy clung tighter, kick-ing.

He backed up into a tree, slamming her against it.

[*Kisty?*] Bobby stopped screaming, but didn't run away. His chubby, dirt-smeared face held uncertainty. [*Kisty?*]

[*RUN!*] Slam against the tree. Breath knocked out of her. She barely held on, felt her arms lose their strength, tried to keep her pain from reaching Bobby. Slam. Pain exploded in her head and back. Dazed, she slid to the ground.

"Vicious little bitch," the man panted. His ear bled where she'd bit him. He pressed a gun to her temple. "Tell me where the village is or I'll kill you."

Kristy spat out a mouthful of wet leaves, in too much pain to be properly frightened. "I don't have a village, dummy. Thunder Bay is east of here."

"What?" He shone a flashlight in her face. "What is this? First pregnant women, now little kids. Some Death Raid. I don't care how many points you're worth, I am *not* a baby-sitter." Disgusted, he walked away, crashing through the bushes.

Kristy stared after him. He was nuts. Her body ached, bruised and stiff. Bobby crept up to her, and she put an arm around his shoulders. [*****] His thoughts had degenerated into baby talk.

CHAPTER 13

• 1 •

The Selector's minions had arrived.

Even before the three pairs of headlights turned off the road, April knew it was them by the way her stomach tightened. She fought down the urge to flee and gripped the tree branches where she was sitting eight feet off the ground. Peter had dictated that the perch would give her a better "field of vision" for the battle to follow. The battle in which she, April Rae Jongkind, formed the first line of defense all by herself.

The responsibility terrified April.

As the vehicles stopped, lured in by the sight of Jeff and Penny's station wagon and Matt and Genevieve's pickup, April drew an illusion of part of the tree over herself like a blanket. [*Brown bark, twisted branches, green leaves.*] Experimentation had shown that the tree illusion was easier to maintain than pressed-flat invisibility.

Doors opened and eight armed men got out.

April had hoped that the Selector's minions would come in trickles of twos and threes, but Peter had been positive from the beginning that the Selector would throw all his forces at them at once. Chalk up another one for Peter. At least April *hoped* eight men were all the Selector had sent.

As they walked in front of the headlights April strained her eyes, searching for a man who matched Genevieve's description of the Selector: twentyish, muscular, black hair, extremely good-looking. If they could take the Selector out, the others might crumble.

She didn't find him. Four of the men were too old—three bearded biker-types and one businessman in an expensive suit. Two were too young, skinny teenagers with pierced noses. The two remaining minions were about the right age and had dark hair, but April wouldn't have called either of them handsome. Or all that muscular.

If the Selector didn't show up in person, the whole point of the trap they had laid was wasted.

Unfortunately, April was pretty sure the eight men below wouldn't be agreeable to calling off the fight.

She took a deep breath and sent out an illusion.

[*Peter, in jeans and a white shirt instead of the black he was actually wearing, darting out from behind the cover of some trees and running down the forest path.*]

"Get him!" one of the bikers whooped, and the shudder of machine guns broke the night's silence.

If Peter had been real, he would have been shot into doll rags, but April made the illusion Peter keep running [*zigzagging*] and three of the minions took off after him while the others fanned out in the trees at April's feet.

If the Selector had been directly controlling the biker minion in the lead, the whole balance of the battle could have shifted then. Warned by his danger instinct, the Selector would never have fallen into Peter's trap. But Genevieve must have been doing her job of distracting the Selector because the biker's foot came down in just the right place on the path.

Snap! The tree Peter had bowed over whipped upright, snatching the bearded biker up by his feet.

Now. Concentrating fiercely, April threw up two more illusions in addition to the running boy and her own tree disguise, as Peter had made her practice earlier.

[*A blanket of invisibility over the bearded, upside-down biker.*] And: [*An exact duplicate of the upside-down biker swinging wildly back and forth six feet to the left of where he actually was.*]

She couldn't do anything about the real biker's yells for help other than hope his companions wouldn't notice the noises were coming from a point six feet away from where they saw the biker mouthing curses. Keeping the four separate illusions complete in her mind was hard enough, akin to juggling flaming torches.

One brand up in the air—

[*Peter running deeper into the forest, limping now as if he'd finally been hit.*]

One of the minions, the skinny punk, kept following illusion Peter into the trees, still firing wildly, but the other stopped to cut down his fellow biker.

Throw the second brand while the first still fell—

[*The bearded upside-down biker, invisible.*]

Toss the third brand from the right hand to the left—

[*The duplicate biker, spinning as he swung, shooting his automatic up at the rope that held him. Face red with fury and the rush of blood.*]

Catch the first falling torch in her right hand—

[*Peter, running.*]

No, wait! She'd forgotten one—the tree illusion hiding herself. In a moment of panic, April almost dropped all the illusions, burning her fingers. She grabbed wildly at the two most important, Peter and the illusion biker.

The invisible biker winked back into existence just as the second biker fell neatly into the trap in front of the illusion biker.

Snap. Swing. To April, Peter's trap was poetry in motion. That had been way too close.

The second biker dropped his gun in surprise. He started yelling for help, but still didn't warn the others about illusions. The Selector's obsession with Genevieve was costing him. Two of his men were out of the action now, helpless but alive.

Matt had pointed out that the Selector's minions were not to blame for the things the Selector made them do and should not be killed out of hand. "All of them have families, girlfriends. We want to kill the Selector not them."

Which was easy to say, but not so easy to do when the hapless minions carried automatic weapons. And so the traps. It was Peter's job to disarm the trapped minions and tie their hands so they couldn't free themselves.

April had her own job.

[*Peter running, growing smaller, an occasional flash of white among the trees.*]

She concentrated until the punk and the false Peter both passed out of her sight and range. The punk was Gavin and Jeff's problem now. April tried not to think about the hail of bullets the punk was firing and how vulnerable the men were.

She turned her attention back to the upside-down minions to see if Peter needed any help, but it didn't look like it. The first biker, the one who was armed, now had an arrow sprouting from his leg. She smiled. No doubt Peter was warning the biker to drop his weapon or take another arrow —

April's smile died. The armed biker, furiously trying to kill Peter, shot his fellow minion hanging next to him instead. The second biker went limp, arms hanging down, dead.

Damn it. April looked away. The five other minions were her responsibility, not the trapped ones. Peter could aim his arrows at nonfatal spots, but Gavin and Jeff with their Molotov cocktails had no choice but to kill or be killed.

April was determined to spare them as many burning deaths as she could.

The five remaining minions, wary of more traps, had ignored their companions' calls for help. They had spread out, searching the forest and spraying bullets at the slightest rustle of leaves.

For her next target, April picked the minion nearest her and farthest from the others. She studied his appearance as well as she could in the gloom, then crafted a double. [*A solidly built man with a thick chest and legs. Bushy red sideburns. Large hands. Camouflage pants and hat.*] Only she added a few extras to her doppelganger version. [*Vampire-pale face, bulging eyes. Gory wound in his chest, blood-soaked clothes. The shambling gait of a zombie . . .*]

Sideburns stopped and stared when his double appeared ghostlike in front of him. The double came closer [*drool running down its chin*], and he fired at it.

The bullets went through the illusion, of course, but instead of breaking the spell the ineffectiveness of the bullets convinced Sideburns it was a real ghost he was seeing, a vision and warning from the future. He gave a strangled cry, dropped his weapon, and fled back to the vehicles. He scrambled into a jeep, gunned the motor, and screeched off.

April was congratulating herself on a bloodless victory when a burst of flame and a man's scream told her that the first Molotov cocktail had been thrown. Her stomach lurched.

The four remaining minions also heard. They abandoned their search of the bushes and ran toward Jeff and Gavin's hiding place.

She panicked and threw up another of the prepared defenses she'd gone over with Peter: [A *blaze of headlights suddenly switched on, showing a ring of cop cars and twenty policemen pointing guns at the minions.*]

She forgot Peter's instructions not to use this particular illusion unless he or Jeff or Gavin was close enough to provide voices for her illusion cops.

It started to work — one of the minions dropped his gun and sank to his knees, hands on his head — but another one started shooting. "You won't take me alive! I know you're aliens!"

April tried to adjust, to keep the illusion viable: [*Cops ducking behind car doors, one man wounded in the arm, another in the leg, being dragged to safety*] but it was no good. Her illusion cops couldn't fire back; their guns made no noise.

Even the minion who'd surrendered cautiously looked up when the return fire failed to materialize.

And then the Selector finally made an appearance himself, speaking through the minion in the expensive Italian suit. "They're not real, it's an illusion! Forward!"

One of Peter's arrows took the alien paranoid in the throat, but his death wasn't enough to turn the tide. The minions charged April's illusion, going through it like smoke. She dropped it. Shit. She'd blown it. Jeff and Gavin —

There was trouble coming her way.

Danger instinct shrieking, April abruptly focussed on the Italian suit, who was coming toward her. "Where there are illusions there's also an Illusionist," he said.

[*Bark, branches, leaves.*] April brought her own illusion up like a shield, but it was too late: he'd seen her in her tree.

"Well, well, what have we here?" The Italian suit had dark eyes and hair and a thin mustache. He was handsome in an elegant, dangerous way, but not muscular. He carried a neat little handgun instead of a semiautomatic, but April found him more threatening than twenty bikers and suspected she might have even if the Selector hadn't been possessing him. As he walked toward the tree where she was hiding, she fumbled for her only weapon. Her fingers closed around the cold metal of a tire iron.

[A *fanged beast, leaping at his throat.*]

But the Selector just chuckled and let the white wolf with the spotted coat of a leopard pass through him. He stood under her tree and raised his gun. Even though he could no longer see her, he couldn't miss her at that range.

April dropped her illusions and jumped out of the tree on top of him, swinging the tire iron like a golf club.

She took him by surprise. He had no time to duck. No time to protect himself.

Only one chance.

But the Selector only needed one. He met April's angry eyes and threw a silver hook like a harpoon.

• 2 •

Move! Gavin's danger instinct warned him.

His second Molotov cocktail had missed a punk with chains and a bleach job. The punk laid down fire, quartering the bushes where Gavin was hunkered down. Gavin rolled to his side, but refused to crawl away on his belly even while bullets battered his former resting place.

Peter's remark about running like a coward bothered him. Did his instinct to avoid danger make him—involuntarily—a coward?

If he had been a little braver, would Bethany be alive?

Run! his instinct screamed.

Gavin ignored the compulsion. He was tired of running; all he'd done since Bethany's death was run, both from the Selector's minions and his own memories. He'd almost welcomed the peril of demon-hunters, because they meant he didn't have time to remember.

You stupid asshole, didn't you hear me? You're in danger. D-A-N-G-E-R. Move!

Gavin didn't move. He crouched down among the thornbushes and made himself remember, made himself face his own guilt. As if from a film unwinding, he saw Bethany's face. Not the terrible sight of her bloody body, but the last time he'd seen her alive. Her last words: "No, I'll go get the strawberries by myself. I won't be long." The kiss she'd blown him, the minxish smile that had told him clearer than words that she wasn't just doing the caterer a favor, she was going to meet another man.

His instinct threw a tantrum. *We're going to die!*

He'd guessed that she planned to meet Ron, but he'd still let her go, knowing Ron could become dangerous. Knowing she was letting herself in for some heartache, but unable to make her mistakes for her.

Heartache.

He'd thought her ex-boyfriend would break her heart a second time. He hadn't known Ron would take her life, hadn't even suspected the existence of the Selector.

Gavin probed the feeling carefully, like touching a sore tooth. He'd sensed that Ron's jealousy could make him dangerous, but had he thought *Bethany* was in danger?

No. The answer came freely, easily. He'd thought Ron would smother Bethany's spirit with possessiveness, maybe punch out any man that she flirted with, but hurt her? No. Bethany captivated all men; Ron hadn't been any different.

The guilt smothering his heart fell away.

Gavin felt oddly light. He could let go of Bethany now; he would no longer be haunted by her screams. He would obtain justice for her, and then he would move on.

Justice . . .

A flick of his lighter, and he touched the fuse of another Molotov cocktail. Counted to ten and hurled the firebomb at a silhouette. The bottle smashed against a tree, splashing gasoline onto the punk's hair and clothes. Fire ignited in its wake. *I hope you felt that one, Selector,* he thought hazily, as the man screamed and beat at the flames with his bare hands. *I hope you enjoyed it, because I intend to kill more of you today.* His hand closed around another cocktail.

[*GAAVIIINNNN!*]

The scream blossomed in his mind like a monstrous black orchid, deadly and shattering in its beauty.

It blocked out all thought, closing Gavin's mind to the knowledge that more minions were hiding in the dark, attracted by their blazing comrade. It propelled him forward as if out of a slingshot, turned the red bursts of agony in his shoulder to pinpricks, deafened him to the bullets whining around him, tugging at his clothes.

He had only one thought, born of the two previous times he'd heard the death scream of someone he'd loved and failed to save: *Not again. Never again.*

His toes dug into the muddy earth as he ate up the ground between him and the place where they'd left the pickup and the station wagon.

Dear God, not April, too.

• 3 •

The Selector held the knife he made all his minions carry at the Illusionist's throat, trying to decide where to cut her first. Her throat? Her breasts? Her belly, as he had planned to do to Penny? She wasn't conscious to feel it, but the job still required some artistry—

Footsteps.

The Selector looked up and saw Lindberg charging toward him. Unhurriedly, he got to his feet, still holding the knife. He was amused to note that Lindberg held no weapon.

Triumph tasted golden on his tongue. Lindberg had once taken something that belonged to him. The Selector had later judged it inferior, but that did not erase the offense.

Lindberg didn't understand his peril. He flung himself at the Selector, without thought or grace. He knocked the knife spinning and closed his hands around the minion's throat in a storm of rage.

Grinning, the Selector brought his fist up under Lindberg's guard and punched his weak shoulder. To his surprise, Lindberg cried out, but didn't let go.

The Selector did it again, same result.

The Selector couldn't account for it until he realized this particular minion was a hit man by profession and not terribly muscular. In addition, the blow the girl had landed with the tire iron had done more damage than he had thought. Blood wet one entire side of his face, and he staggered sideways, dizzy. That was a bad sign. Pain was easy to shunt aside, but balancing the fluids in the inner ear required a delicate touch, and the Selector lacked the concentration to spare in the heat of battle.

He stumbled and fell, dragging Lindberg down with him.

Lindberg kept on top, kneeling heavily on the minion's chest. His hands fastened around the Selector's throat again, choking him, lost to rage.

The Selector's vision blackened around the edges like paper catching fire. Twist as he might, he could not dislodge Lindberg or grapple him to the floor. He was actually losing until Lindberg chanced to see the Illusionist's limp body.

Lindberg let out a hoarse cry, and his attention wavered.

The Selector heaved, flipping Lindberg onto the bottom, but his hit-man body was too weak; Lindberg rolled him back over within seconds. Cords stood out on Lindberg's arms, and a pulse beat at his temple. "What have you done to April?"

The Selector saw no reason to lie. "I snagged her soul."

"Give it back!" Lindberg banged the minion's head against a rock embedded in the damp earth and dug his knee into his stomach.

The Selector felt no pain, no concern for his minion. He shook his head, enjoying himself. "If you want her, you have to come and get her."

Lindberg hesitated, and the Selector thought he whispered, "Never again."

"Take me there," he said. Wrath fired his eyes.

"Certainly." The Selector's voice rang with malice. " 'Step into my parlor, said the spider to the fly.' "

A brief moment later he pushed Lindberg's limp body off his wounded minion. He started hunting for his knife, but his vision doubled annoyingly. It took all his concentration to keep the minion from passing out.

When he finally found the knife, he gently pressed the point of the blade into Lindberg's throat and watched the slow trickle of blood, savoring that last instant before he made the kill.

He adjusted his grip for a quick, ripping slash—

—AND HIS DANGER instinct yanked him back to the van.

His fortunes had changed somewhat.

The poet man lay on the floor, still thrashing but irritatingly alive. The little girl had broken his thread and slipped off. His feet were free, but his hands were still tied.

Finally, of far more immediate concern, was the gun Mary pointed at him with shaking hands.

• 4 •

Jeff threw his last Molotov cocktail, missed, and scrunched down behind a log as bullets thudded into the trees around him. He felt dim surprise when none of them hit him.

But then the whole attack had gone amazingly well. Only four of the Selector's minions had made it as far as Gavin and Jeff's position, so April's illusions must have worked. There was only one minion left now, and everything would have been fine if Gavin hadn't taken it into his head to run away. Jeff had been forced to show himself in order to keep the man from killing Gavin, and now the gunman had Jeff pinned down.

Another bullet whapped into the log.

Think, damn it. Penny keeps saying you're as good as Batman. Prove it. Invent something.

He blanked. He had no weapons. If he raised his head an inch, he'd get it shot off.

In desperation his hand closed over a rock. A small rock. He tried to force himself to stand up and throw it. David had done it, right?

But Goliath hadn't had a machine gun. Splinters struck Jeff's cheek from another bullet.

If he stayed here, it was only a matter of time before the gunman figured out he wasn't armed and came close enough to finish him off.

On the count of three.

One.

Two.

He couldn't do it.

He burrowed deeper into the damp earth. Maybe if he stayed very still, the soldier would walk right by—the way Todd had that time in the city, swinging his baseball bat, banging on garbage cans, calling—

"Come out, you coward!"

For a second time doubled, and he heard Todd calling. Even though Jeff knew his half brother had died in a prison fight, he'd never really believed it. It was Todd, looking for his brother who had ratted on him. . . .

"Coward!"

Jeff couldn't bear it, couldn't bear waiting for Todd to walk up and put a bullet in his head while he cowered in the dirt. Screaming, he leapt up and hurled his stone—

—just in time to see Peter put an arrow in the blond soldier. He toppled over, clutching his chest.

Not Todd. Just a soldier.

Jeff kept repeating the assurance while Peter efficiently disarmed the dying man. "Nice distraction."

Jeff tried to swallow. Couldn't. Not Todd.

"That's the last of them," Peter continued. "The attack is over, but April and Gavin are both unconscious. I can't see any wounds on them. The Selector must have snagged their souls."

Jeff's worry changed directions. "At least everyone in the van's safe."

The dying soldier laughed, blood bubbling on his lips. "Not so . . . Selector said to tell you . . . Matt's flopping around . . . like a fish . . . Guess . . . where . . . your wife . . . is."

Your wife. The words echoed terribly, starting a slow avalanche in Jeff's mind. Penny was supposed to be safe. "What have you done to her?"

"Penny . . . is in . . . gully . . . having baby."

Boulders came crashing down on his head. It was too soon, he thought stupidly. She was only eight months pregnant, there was still a month to go. But thinking it didn't change facts. Penny was in premature labor, giving birth out in the wind and cold, alone, without a doctor to dole out painkillers or intervene if there were complications. Far from the oxygen tents and incubators that preemies often needed.

And Bobby. If Penny was in a gully, where was Bobby?

First your house, then your wife, then your child . . .

Jeff's lips skinned back in a snarl of defiance. "Not a chance in hell, Ma."

• 5 •

"Mother."

At first Penny thought the voice was a hallucination, so she kept her eyes closed, moaning as a contraction ripped through her body. Pain. That was reality.

She was caught in her worst nightmare. The steep walls of the gully and her pregnancy trapped her more effectively than chains. The fall had ruptured the amniotic sac and thrown Penny pell-mell into the second, active, phase of labor. It had taken a goodly portion of her strength just to wriggle out of her panties and spread her jacket underneath her hips. Climbing was out of the question: she couldn't risk another fall.

As far as her empathy could ascertain Damaris hadn't been hurt from her slide into the gully, but she was premature. She shouldn't be born for another month yet.

No one knew where Penny was, so she held out little hope of rescue. She was going to give birth to Damaris right here in the dirt and cold.

No wonder the Selector had laughed. Penny pictured her daughter, blue-faced and covered in blood, struggling for breath, squirming on the wet rocks beside her dead mother.

Penny didn't kid herself that she wasn't in mortal danger. If Damaris happened to be a foot breech birth as Bobby had been, or Penny had a uterine rupture, she would die.

Blood gushing out as her Caesarean scar split open . . .

Penny's doctor had assured her that uterine rupture was rare and that the "once a Caesarean, always a Caesarean" rule no longer held—that women had had successful vaginal births after three or four Caesareans—but she could not eradicate the image from her mind.

Bloody, painful, brutal death.

And if she died, who would protect Damaris and Bobby?

Bobby's distress had eased ten minutes ago, but Penny could not tell if it was because he was safe or unconscious. Or dead.

Jeff was too far away to pick up, and she worried about him, too. If the Selector had sprung one trap, why not two?

Her labor was playing merry hell with her empathy. In between contractions she felt sensitive to every blade of grass—every stick and stone poking into her back seemed part of a complex organism, alive—but during her minute-long contractions she could pick up only her own pain and fear, reamplified and echoing. An army could have marched by, and she wouldn't have noticed.

"Mother, look at me."

Mother, not Mommy as Bobby always called her, and the voice wasn't right either. Pain temporarily over, breathing in gasps, Penny opened her eyes.

She saw a little girl sitting on a rock several feet away. She had dark, shiny hair tied back with a yellow ribbon.

That wasn't the problem. A dozen little girls could sit on rocks, and Penny wouldn't care. But this little girl *shimmered*.

At odd moments Penny could see through her to the black rocks beyond. That was another problem. It was dark out, but Penny could see the girl quite clearly, right down to the daisies embroidered on her yellow overalls.

"Mother, are you listening to me?" She sounded impatient.

There was that, too: the girl kept calling her Mother. Definitely a hallucination. Her daughter wasn't born — yet. Penny put a protective hand on her stomach.

The little girl looked grave. "You must stop having contractions. I'm not supposed to be born yet."

Penny fought back tears. "It's not . . . that easy."

"I know," the little girl said sadly. "That's why I'm here to help you."

To help. If she was going to hallucinate somebody to help her, why hadn't she hallucinated a doctor? Or Jeff? He was almost as good as a doctor, smart and resourceful. She needed him desperately, even if only to hold her hand and keep Damaris warm.

But she didn't have Jeff or a doctor. She only had a hallucination. "Who are you?"

"I'm Damaris." The girl stopped shimmering and became almost solid.

Of course. Who else do you hallucinate about during labor, but the child you're going to lose?

Penny felt tears start from a different kind of pain. Her daughter was dying. Damaris, whom she had sung to and loved for eight months already. Misty-eyed, she drank in the vision of what her daughter would have looked like, talked like.

"Mother, pay attention. You listened to me last time," Damaris grumbled.

"What last time?"

"When I told you to marry Daddy. I was very tiny then, but I whispered, and you heard me."

Penny felt a sudden chill that had nothing to do with the damp seeping into her clothes. "I fell in love with Jeff at first sight."

"That's what the love-at-first-sight Talent is: a baby Seeress sees the future and tells her mother to marry."

"Unborn babies? For everyone?"

"Yes." Damaris nodded, shiny hair bouncing. "Aunt April, too."

Baby seeresses . . . "Funny, it was a Seeress who told me to marry Jeff."

"Grandma." Damaris smiled, showing her dimples.

Grandma? For a moment Penny was confused, thinking of her adoptive grandmother and Portia, but then she realized Damaris wasn't talking about Penny's grandmother, but Damaris's grand-mother. Terisa. She'd met her mother and never known it.

The Seeress had had green eyes like Penny's own.

Looking back, it was obvious Terisa had attended the Kithkin function solely to talk to Penny. She'd lain in wait for Penny in the washroom. Penny had been with her friend Carrie, and Terisa had told Carrie a little about her future, about a stray cat she would find, but Terisa's attention had all been focused on Penny. She had been warning her daughter. And when Penny had looked around a few minutes later to see if the Seeress would tell some of her friends' fortunes, the Seeress had already left.

Pain overtook her. Jesus God, it hurt. Something had to be wrong; she wasn't meant to give birth this way; Damaris must be a breech. She would just strain and strain to no end, until something gave. She wondering if she would feel her skin tearing, or just a warm, wet gush . . .

Ride the pain. Don't think about it. Don't scream because the Selector might hear you.

She grunted, biting her lip. She wasn't riding the pain: it was riding her, spurs digging in, bit slicing her mouth.

When the contraction finally ended, she felt light-headed; her thoughts spun. Something in what Damaris had just said bothered her.

Her mother had been a Seeress. Unborn Seresses telling their mothers to marry . . . Portia falling hopelessly in love with Nigel

Carver, a monster. The whisper of an unborn child . . . The same baby who'd later cost Portia her husband and caused her to flee for her life.

No wonder Portia had hated her own daughter.

Dear God, she'd been so lucky to fall in love with Jeff instead.

CHAPTER 14

• 1 •

"Well, Mary," the Selector smiled intimately. "Alone at last."

Genevieve bit her lip. *He's tied up, and you have a gun. He can't hurt you.*

But she was afraid that he could.

When she'd regained consciousness she'd been horrified to discover Matt still having a seizure God knows how many minutes later. She'd moved him onto the floor and put a jacket under his head to prevent him from hurting himself too badly, then picked up the gun Penny had left behind when she went wherever she and the children were now.

Her gaze had fallen on the Selector/Ron and she'd known instinctively that he was responsible for Matt's unnatural seizure. The Selector had woken up as soon as she pointed the gun at him.

"Stop his seizure, or I'll kill you," Genevieve told the Selector. She was very serious.

The Selector smiled, Ron's Shine radiating from him like the heat of a small sun. "Go ahead, kill me. Kill me and April and Lindberg. I snagged their souls."

April *and* Gavin? Genevieve weakened for a moment, then rallied. "I have only your word for that. Release Matt, or I'll kill you."

He kept smiling in the face of her threat. "What about poor old Ron? If you kill me, you kill him, too."

Genevieve felt sorry for Ron and Bad boy Ronnie for crying, but they were bound up in the Selector. She had no choice. "Ron hates you, too. He'll understand."

"Kill April, Lindberg, and Ron? Little Miss Mary Wouldn't-Harm-a-Fly?" He shook his head. "I doubt it."

Matt's arm hit her in the shin.

She couldn't lose Matt. She loved him. God, why had she waited so long to tell him? She'd shortened their time together to a few measly days.

Face dead white, she repeated, "I'll kill you." This man had already cost her Aunt Dorothy, her parents, the pretty life she'd had planned. He would take Matt over her dead body.

The Selector raised an eyebrow. "Why, Mary, I think you really mean it. No qualms about blowing away three of your siblings?"

Genevieve didn't let herself flinch. "For all I know, killing you is the only way to return April and Gavin to their bodies." She glanced to her side. Matt's lips were blue. "Let him breathe!"

The Selector smiled. "No."

She shot off his kneecap.

The Selector screamed as the bullet shattered his kneecap and ricocheted into his flesh. Genevieve ignored him. She knelt by Matt, her eyes stinging with tears as his seizure halted and his chest began to rise and fall.

The Selector stopped screaming; it was too undignified. He swore instead. "You bitch. You're going to regret that." His eyes promised murder, his face contorted in pain.

Genevieve no longer felt frightened. "If you give Matt another seizure, I'll shoot your other knee." He was tied up, and she had a gun. He couldn't hurt her.

"And when Lindberg and the others fail to come back, will you kill me?"

"Yes." She would never be safe as long as he lived.

The Selector bared his teeth. Blood poured down his leg in a red tide, drenching his white jeans. "You do that, Mary. And the instant the bullet enters my brain I'll hop a silver cord into someone else's body. Guess whose." He smiled maliciously.

Genevieve froze. She had a gun; he couldn't hurt her.

It was a lie.

• 2 •

"April," a voice said.

April unglued her eyelids. She looked up and saw Bethany standing over her.

"Shit!" She scrambled backward, falling onto the marble floor. She stared at her cousin in disbelief and horror. "Bethany," she said through a mouth as dry as cotton. "You're dead."

Bethany's beautiful face puckered. "I am not! You take that back. You're just saying that because you're jealous."

Well, that was true enough. April got to her feet. "I'm sorry." Why upset her? Bethany was dead, and since April was here, talking to her, she must be dead, too.

April studied the fairy-tale palace that set off Bethany's beauty and instantly felt grubby. Funny, she hadn't pictured death like this at all.

"So how have you been?" Bethany asked. "I've been dying to hear some gossip. What's new at home?"

"I don't know." April picked her way through a minefield. "I left the day after you did." She risked a question. "Why did you leave?"

Instead of being disturbed, Bethany looked up through her lashes and smiled coyly. "An old friend called and invited me out."

"An old friend?" April's stomach began to sink.

"Weeell, not really an old *friend*. More of an old flame." Bethany gave a tinkling laugh.

April had always envied Bethany's laugh, but now the sound made her shiver.

"I might as well tell you," Bethany said. No doubt she had been *dying* to tell someone. "It was my old boyfriend, Ron. He begged me to meet him in the clearing west of town. He brought a big picnic basket and a bottle of wine. Isn't that romantic? Then he brought me here. Only he hasn't been back to visit me."

"You agreed to meet Ron?" April kept her voice neutral with difficulty. "I thought you were dating Gavin."

"Oh, that was nothing serious."

April clenched her fists. Gavin loved Bethany, and she'd betrayed him without a second thought. "You've been gone a while. Don't you think Gavin might be worried about you?"

"Yes." Bethany had the grace to look slightly ashamed. "After Ron didn't come back, I called out for Gavin, but he hasn't come either. So here I've been!"

Why, she's scared. She's terrified. And Bethany once more became her beautiful, slightly thoughtless, but never cruel, cousin.

"You know, April," Bethany's voice wobbled, "sometimes I have the most terrible dreams."

"It's okay, Bethany. You're not alone anymore." She held her cousin's cold hands.

"Thank you," Bethany said humbly. Then she put her smile back on. Did she think she always had to smile to be liked? "So how have you been? Any boyfriend yet?"

"No," April said, conscious of the terrible irony.

"What have you been doing? Tell me everything."

"Actually," April said, feeling weirder by the minute, "I've been having an adventure. I was baby-sitting Kristy Hillock Friday night—" God, was it only two days ago? "—when I heard a knock on the door."

"Who was it?" Bethany's eyes danced. "Prince Charming?"

"No," April said. Too quickly. "It was this boy—Garett—I knew him from parties," she improvised. "And he had been shot. There were armed men chasing him, so after I bandaged him up I helped him escape."

"Wow," Bethany breathed. "How did you know he wouldn't hurt you?"

April hesitated, stuck. *Because I love him, and I knew he couldn't have killed you.* "I just knew he wouldn't. My danger instinct would have warned me if he was dangerous."

"Oh, April!" Bethany squeezed her arm. "So you are a psychic. Welcome to the Klub."

"Thanks." Sudden tears sprang into her eyes. Since she'd fallen in love with Gavin, she'd forgotten how nice Bethany could be. "He—Garett—is a Kithkinner, too."

"That's great. That's how I met Ron. And Gavin," Bethany added as an afterthought.

"Yes." April swallowed. "So Ga—Garett and I drove to the nearest web house. He wanted me to drop him off, but I insisted on at least going up to the house with him."

"Why April, so forward."

April blushed, and Bethany crowed with delight. "You're in love with him, aren't you? Admit it."

Red-faced, April nodded. She'd never been able to keep a secret from Bethany. "I fell like a rock."

"Love-at-first-sight," Bethany said knowingly.

Curiosity overcame April. "Did it happen to you? Have you ever been in love?"

"Oh, yes." Bethany turned serious. "It wasn't love-at-first-sight, but I fell in love with Ron Revarc last November."

"What happened?"

"I'm not sure." Bethany twisted her hands. "Everything was great for a while. Only . . . only sometimes Ron would act like a different person. It scared me. We started having fights, and we broke up."

"Then you started dating Gavin."

The tension left Bethany's face. "Yes. Gavin's such a sweetheart. And he's so dependable. I knew he'd never let me down."

Like Ron did.

"For a while I thought I could love him," Bethany confided. "But then he started to irritate me, and when Ron called I knew I still loved him." Tears sparkled on her eyelashes. Bethany even cried beautifully.

"Then—then—" She went into full flood. "I wish I'd never met Ron Revarc. I hate him," she said without conviction. "I hate him. I want to go home."

Feeling inadequate, April patted her on the back and told stupid, meaningless lies. "It'll be all right. Gavin will come get you."

She couldn't help wishing Gavin would come rescue her, too.

As if she'd conjured him up, she heard his voice. "April? April, where are you?"

Her neck hairs prickled, and she couldn't speak.

"There you are." Sounding relieved, Gavin walked through the palace wall.

April blinked. Gavin didn't go away, but she did see the door he'd used. "Hi, Gavin," she said weakly. What could she say, good to see you, sorry you're dead?

Bethany raised her tear-stained face. "Gavin? Is that you?"

April watched, heart aching, as his face went from shock to incredulous joy.

"Bethany?" His voice cracked.

"Gavin." Bethany threw herself into his arms. "I knew you would come. I called and called, and you heard me."

That's not fair, you told me you loved Ron. April stared off into the distance while Gavin hugged Bethany tight, pressing his face into her hair, eyes closed. "You're alive!" he said over and over.

April pretended she couldn't hear the emotion in his voice, pretended she was alone in her room at home. She sat on her bed and tried not to cry.

Eventually, they remembered her.

"April," Gavin said, "I was so worried about you." Her bedroom wall crumbled, and she returned to Bethany's fairy-tale castle and Bethany's fairy-tale Prince Charming, with his earnest expression.

That was worse, April decided in some remote part of her mind. He was fond of her, but he loved Bethany. "I'm fine."

"You gave me an awful scare. I thought the Selector had killed you."

"He did."

Gavin's face showed pity. "Is that what you thought? You're not dead, April. The Selector separated your body from your soul. You're in a coma." He touched her cheek, and April flinched back. Gavin withdrew his hand, looking hurt.

Bethany interrupted before she could apologize. "You two know one another?"

April shook her head frantically, but Gavin didn't see her, smiling warmly. "We met a few days ago. April saved my skin. I'd been shot, and she bandaged me up."

"Did she?" Bethany's voice was a little too high. She'd just realized who "Garett" was. April felt sick.

"Are you okay?" Gavin asked, concerned. "You look a little pale."

"I'm fine," April lied. "I just don't like it here. If you know a way out, Gavin, why don't we leave?"

"Of course," Gavin said, and they exited into a hallway. After following it for five minutes, April realized Gavin didn't know where they were, but she, too, said nothing. The habit of protecting Bethany was too strong.

• 3 •

A flash of white.

Jeff stumbled to a stop, playing the flashlight beam over the bottom of the gully, trying to relocate the white spot. His breath came in hard pants as if he'd been running for hours.

He'd been in constant motion since the Selector told him Penny was in labor.

First the dash to the station wagon, then the wild drive down the highway until he sighted the van in the ditch and slammed to a stop half a mile away in case the Selector had minions about. He had ignored the van and taken off into the woods where Peter had told him the ravine was. He was afraid for Bobby, but Penny needed him, and he couldn't be in two places at once.

He found the ravine by nearly falling into it. Only one arm hooked around a tree branch saved him from sliding over the edge.

He chose a direction at random and started running alongside the muddy ravine, searching for Penny with the flashlight.

He forced himself to a half-skipping jog, torn between his need to hurry and his fear of missing Penny in the dark. He dared not call out to her for fear the Selector's minions would hear him and hunt him down. His eyes scanned restlessly, picking out clumps of grass and craggy stone. Tree branches like upthrust fingers, broken stickmen blurring by . . .

A flash of white.

There.

The pale beam of the flashlight snagged on a white limb, an arm. He followed it up to Penny's face.

A red line scratched down one cheek, and a livid bruise sat just under one eye. She looked white and dead, lifeless, until he saw her hands tear at the grass.

She was having a contraction.

"Penny!"

Her eyes stayed closed.

Jeff played the flashlight over the lip of gully, searching desperately for a way down. "Hang on, baby, I'm coming." The yellow beam made the gully appear curiously harsh, black and white, its shadows sharp enough to cut.

The walls were too steep. Jeff almost scrambled down anyway, crazed in his need to get to her, but common sense pulled him up short. A hell of a lot of good he'd do Penny trapped in the gully with her.

"Penny!"

Her eyes opened. "Jeff!"

Her voice was the sweetest music he'd ever heard.

"Jeff?"

His mind kicked back into gear. "How far apart are your contractions? Has your water broken? Is there time to drive to the hospital? Did you hurt yourself during the fall?" All the information he'd read up on for Bobby's birth and not needed came flooding back.

Penny stared at him, bemused. "My waters broke when I fell. The contractions are quite strong and coming fast—no more than a minute or so apart. My ankle hurts; I think it's sprained. Damaris is all right—she's just a month early. She needs hospital care."

"She'll have it," Jeff promised fervently. "I'll have you and Damaris at the hospital in two shakes. What about Bobby?" Jeff asked as he tore off his T-shirt and draped it over a branch as a marker.

"I think he's okay—I can't feel any distress coming from him," Penny said. "Stay away from the van. The Selector hooked Kristy, he'll have taken Matt and Genevieve captive—" She grunted as another contraction hit.

She didn't have much time.

Jeff ran back into the woods. His breath felt hot in his chest, but he ignored it, coldly going over his list of supplies. He had rope, his toolbox, some camping equipment, and Bobby's toys.

The rope was the most immediately useful; Penny's secret cache had contained a hundred feet of strong, nylon rope, the kind used by rock climbers. But he couldn't haul Penny up in a rope harness; if Damaris was born in that position, she would fall headfirst onto the rocks below.

He needed an elevator, but he didn't have one. Minimum requirements were a platform for Penny to lie back on, a pulley, and two or three men to pull her up.

He had rope, what else? He crashed blindly through the brush, probably missing the station wagon by a mile, but trying not to worry about it. As long as he kept going in the right general direction he would cut across the road again.

Clothing, cans of food. Had Penny packed her sewing kit? A butane curling iron. Gasoline. Matches. A blanket.

If Gavin and April woke, Peter would send them to help, but Jeff couldn't count on them. Peter wasn't strong enough. Matt and Genevieve were out of the picture. Jeff would have to save Penny all by himself. If he could rig up a winch he might be able to pull her up.

The highway appeared in front of him. Jeff swooped down into the ditch, stepping in ankle-deep water, then rising out—

"Don't move, sucker." The barrel of a gun screwed into his head, just behind his ear.

"That's right," the voice said, when Jeff stopped cold, one foot still in the water. "Now then you and I are going to go on a little trip together to your village. There's some Missing In Action vets I'm going to rescue before I torch the—"

Jeff didn't wait for him to finish. He ducked under the gun barrel and spun in the same movement, driving his flashlight into the soldier's throat.

The move was stupid, even suicidal, but it was also unexpected. The boy—and it was just a boy, a teenager in jeans and a black nylon jacket—fell backward, gagging. His grip loosened on the gun, and Jeff ripped it away. He shone his flashlight in the boy's eyes and dug the muzzle of the gun into his left breast pocket, which was stitched with the name Eric.

"I'd kill you now, but it's either you or a winch, and I don't have one. Get up."

"A wench?" The boy looked angry and surprised, but not afraid. He got to his feet, leering. "If you want a woman there's one stuck in a gully back there."

In two seconds Jeff had Eric flat on his back, with the gun to his forehead. He was distantly amazed at how fast old habits came back. Old habits and old violence. "One more word about my wife, and I'll cut your tongue out."

Eric blatantly ignored the warning. "How come you speak English? Are you a communist spy?"

Jeff didn't reply. Time was ticking down. "Go." He grabbed Eric by the scruff of his neck and shoved him up onto the highway. He glimpsed the station wagon to the right. "That way. Run."

Eric surged forward, trying to leave his captor behind, but Jeff kept close, gun pressed into the small of Eric's back while his feet ate up the tarmac. "Faster."

At the station wagon, Eric turned suddenly and sprang for his throat. Jeff pivoted sideways and let Eric fall bruisingly to the pavement. He put his foot on the back of Eric's neck. "Try that again, and you'll be dead." Every instinct screamed that he was wasting time, dooming Penny, dooming Damaris, but cold logic told him he needed Eric to save them, and he needed Eric afraid and cooperative, not cocky and aggressive.

"Go ahead and shoot me. When the game's over I'll just start another one."

"Game?" Rage built inside Jeff's chest, swelling his rib cage like a balloon. *The van sideways in the ditch. Penny laboring in the gully, Bobby God knew where.* "You think this is a game?"

Eric's eyes spit black hatred. "You're nothing but a computer graphic, a construct, a bunch of zeroes and ones. Some colored pixels in a virtual-reality program."

"And yourself?"

"I'm the commando who's going to burn your village." He showed his teeth in a snarl.

Jeff understood then. It was like Will and the demons, only worse, because Eric *wanted* to believe, wanted to be a big strong killing machine.

"This is not a game."

Eric smirked contemptuously, and Jeff slid into the role Eric had created for him. "This is war, and you're my prisoner."

He knew instantly that he'd made an error. Eric's face came alive with almost holy ecstasy. Being a prisoner gave him the opportunity to be a hero. Eric wasn't dangerous because he was invincible: he was dangerous because he thought he was.

Penny in a gully, having contractions.

Jeff had to reach Eric, and quickly. "Put your hands on the car."

"Gonna frisk me?" Eric grinned as he leaned against the car.

"Spread your fingers."

Eric spread them.

Jeff slammed his knee into the kid's back, pressed the gun between Eric's middle and index fingers, and shot out the webbing of skin.

Eric squealed. He stared at the blood on his left hand. "Hey, that hurt."

"You bet it did. Your pain centers are wired into the game. I can shoot off half your body parts before the game will allow you to die. You got that?" Jeff jammed his knee harder into Eric's back. "Or do you want me to shoot off something else?"

Eric shook his head, wary. He would wait for a better opportunity before he attacked Jeff again.

Penny had taught Jeff there were decent people in the world, but he also knew there were Cornys and Todds and Erics who enjoyed hurting others. The trick was not to give them a chance. Not one. Ever.

He tossed Eric his car keys. "Open the tailgate."

Sullenly, Eric did so. Jeff was happy to notice that he was right-handed.

"See the white first-aid kit?" Jeff pointed it out with the flashlight in his left hand while holding the gun in his right. *He* was ambidextrous. "There's rope inside, take it out. Then the toolbox beside it. Open it."

Eric flipped the latches.

"Take out the screwdriver."

Eric stirred slowly through the box.

Penny in labor . . .

"Throw something at me, and I'll nail you."

Eric held up the green screwdriver, innocent as a lamb.

"Set it down." The kid was too damn slow, and he couldn't be trusted. "Lie down on the pavement, over there." He pointed to the white line on the middle of the highway.

Eric sauntered over.

Jeff fired a shot over his head, and the kid dropped to his knees, then glared. Jeff pinned him with the flashlight, but it was too dark. He would need the flashlight to see what he was doing; he couldn't watch the kid, too.

Eric smiled, enjoying his dilemma.

"Close your eyes. Facedown." He sent another bullet flashing off the pavement, and Eric put his head down.

Jeff slung a heavy box under one arm and walked over to the kid. "Hold still."

Eric tensed.

Jeff set the box down on Eric's back, stamping on the kid's fingers when he tried to trip Jeff. The box was full of cans and cutlery; Eric couldn't get up without making a lot of noise.

"What if a car comes?" For the first time Eric seemed to notice he was staked out on the white line.

"Hope they have good brakes, because if you move, I'll shoot you."

Penny groaning in agony . . .

Adrenaline stormed his system, making him feel as if he could rip the station wagon apart with his bare hands, but he forced himself to pick up the screwdriver instead. A fine tremor passed over his hands. Penny's and his daughter's lives depended on his speed and ingenuity.

You're no good for nothing.

The screwdriver slipped, and he gashed his arm. Eric's head came up, a wolf scenting blood. Jeff pointed the gun at him, and Eric turned his head back into the wet pavement. Jeff's heart raced, his palms sweaty. *Calm down, damn it. Penny needs you. If you fail her now, you really are good for nothing.* Ignoring the slippery spill of blood, he turned back to the car. Back up a step. Was the tailgate the best choice for a platform? What would work best? One of the doors? The spare tire?

Yes. The tire.

Jeff shifted three boxes aside, then lifted out the spare tire. Eric watched Jeff openly. "What are you doing?"

"Shut up." Jeff concentrated on the tools in front of him. He had a rope and a seat for Penny and manpower. Miraculously, he had a small pulley. Had Penny put it there, warned by her instinct? But two pulleys were needed to halve the work of lifting a heavy object. The second would have to wait until he reached the ravine and saw a likely tree. Was he forgetting anything?

Yes.

He needed to attach the rope to the tire.

He picked up the coil of rope and starting threading it through the slots in the hub.

Some half-comprehended instinct made him look up. Eric was on his hands and knees, box balanced between his shoulder blades.

"Go ahead," Jeff told him softly. "I'm waiting."

Eric lay back down, unfazed. "How come a commie knows how to whistle 'Jingle Bells'?"

Bastard. Keeping a wary eye on his prisoner, Jeff bent back over the tire. He pulled on the line between the second and third slots, creating so much slack he had in effect four ropes, which he then knotted together into a tent shape. He cut the rope with a pair of wire cutters and hooked the pulley onto it.

"Okay, kid, you can get up now." Jeff watched Eric's hands and feet, anticipating a move.

"Now what?"

Jeff gestured him over to the station wagon. "Put the blanket on the tire."

Eric did so, draping the coils of the rope overtop.

"Lift it."

Awkwardly, Eric picked it up. "It's heavy."

Jeff threw a roll of duct tape and the wire cutters on top of the blanket, then carefully placed the gun on the tire so that he could blow a hole through Eric's abdomen if he did anything stupid. Jeff kept one finger curled around the trigger guard, while his other arm took some of the tire's weight. "Now move."

Jeff shoved the spare into Eric, forcing him to walk backward or fall down. He hurried him back through the ditch and into the woods, running in spots, never going slower than a fast walk, keeping a constant pressure on the tire and Eric off-balance. Fear for Penny goaded him like a cattle prod. They were too slow, too slow. . . .

"Stop," Eric panted. His eyes were wide, the whites showing in the dark. "The ravine—I'll fall in."

"So?" Old rage flamed anew. "You let my wife fall, didn't you? Pushed her in?" He shoved hard with the wheel, one hand on the gun.

"No!" Eric dropped to one knee, but didn't lose his grip. "I stopped chasing her when I realized she was pregnant, then . . . then . . ."

The Selector, Jeff realized. He'd forgotten who Eric was, who he could become at any moment. Eric was a straining hawk; the Selector would be a leaping tiger.

Jeff's hand tightened on the gun, but just then he saw the blue of his shirt fluttering on a tree branch a few feet away. Penny.

"Hold on." Jeff barely gave Eric time to react before letting go of his end. "Now put it down." Eric dropped it. "Lie down, hands over your head."

Shakily, Eric got down on his stomach. He looked tired, but Jeff knew better than to give him an opportunity. He held the gun against

Eric's skull and knelt on his back. No chances, ever. He shone the flashlight over the lip of the ravine. "Penny? I'm back. Are you okay?"

The flashlight revealed her drawn face, her bloody, bitten lips. "Hurry," she gasped, moaning from a contraction.

Jeff jumped back to his feet. "Up," he told Eric. "Start looking for a tree with branches strong enough to use as a pulley." He pushed Eric ahead of him.

"She in labor?" Eric asked, sharp eyes searching for a weakness.

"Premature labor, thanks to you." Jeff's bitter eyes held Eric's. "If she or my daughter dies, I'll kill you."

For a second Eric looked unsure, then his confidence returned, and Jeff knew he was thinking this was all a game. "For God's sake, I'm Mètis, do I look Russian to you? Does this look like a jungle?" He slashed at a pine tree.

Eric mumbled something about poor graphics and computer programmers with weird senses of humor.

Jeff gave up. Five meters farther on he found what he was looking for: a huge beech tree with thick branches stretching nearly all the way across the ravine.

Holding the gun on Eric every step of the way, Jeff made him carry the tire over to the tree.

Understanding and anticipation dawned on Eric's face. Both men's strength would be needed to pull up Penny on the tire. Jeff would have to trust him at some point, either leaving him at the top alone or down at the bottom with his wife.

Jeff smiled ferally. *Not a chance, boy.* He made Eric lie down again and swiftly knotted one end of the rope to a thick branch. He then threaded it through the pulley attached to the tire and slung it back up over a second tree branch at a spot between two smaller limbs to center the rope and prevent it from sliding off the end of the branch.

He studied it a moment, despair rising. It was no good. The friction would make it too hard to pull. He glared at Eric, who was waiting patiently now that he knew his chance was coming—and got an idea.

"Take off your jacket."

It was made of slippery nylon and unlined. Jeff used the duct tape to fashion it into a crude wheel, keeping the rope from touching the rough bark of the tree. He pulled on the rope and the nylon circle turned easily. With Penny's weight on the bottom there would be some friction, but it was better than nothing.

Eric held the flashlight as Jeff dropped the extra rope over the side of the gully. One-handed, Jeff took up the slack until the ropes tented over the tire. He passed the rope behind his back, holding it with his right hand and lifted the spare tire half a foot off the ground. "Swing it out over the gully," he told Eric.

Eric pushed it out.

"Now get on it."

Eric stalled. "I don't like heights."

"You'll like a bullet in the leg a lot less."

Reluctantly, Eric crawled out onto the swing, slowly shifting his weight. Jeff compensated by pulling harder on the rope. The weight was too heavy for Jeff to lift, but he could lower Eric swiftly instead of dropping him.

The instant Eric's head dipped past the level of the cliff Jeff swung himself over the edge, dropping several feet in the space of a second. The move was accomplished so swiftly Eric didn't have time to attack. Jeff pulled once he was level with Eric, swinging beside the tire, knees and ankles locked on the rope, so his hand was free to use the gun. "Don't even think it," Jeff warned. "If I let go, you fall."

He tucked the gun in his waistband and let several feet of rope slip through his fingers, jerkily lowering both himself and the swinging, bumping tire in fits and starts.

"Bastard," Eric gritted out, fingers clutching the pyramid of ropes.

Jeff laughed. He let another foot slide. Two feet. Three.

Eight feet from the bottom, Eric jumped off.

Jeff had been expecting the move and simply let go of the rope. He, Eric, and the tire crashed down simultaneously. Eric's foot twisted in one of the ropes allowing Jeff enough time to jam the gun under his chin. "I know every thought you think before you think it. Get up."

Eric got up, limping slightly.

"Trying out for *Richard III*, are we?"

Eric glared, but started walking normally.

"Jeff?" Penny called in the distance.

"Coming!" Jeff grabbed the flashlight and prodded Eric into a run.

"Who's with you?" Penny asked as they approached within a couple of meters. "He hates you."

"I know," Jeff said impatiently. "Down." In what was becoming a routine move, Eric lay down on his stomach while Jeff applied murderous pressure with his knee.

Jeff forgot about him and held his wife's hand. "How long between contractions?" Did they still have time to reach the hospital? First babies were supposed to take hours to be born. Damaris was their second, but since Bobby had been Caesarean, he wasn't sure that counted. . . .

"Don't know. No watch. Not long." Penny panted.

How long was not long? Two minutes, less?

Didn't matter. They had to try. "Can you walk? Between contractions?"

She looked doubtful. "I don't know if that's a very good idea."

They didn't have much choice. "It's only fifteen meters. Eric, don't move." He handed Penny the flashlight and helped her to her feet.

"What about him?" Penny trembled, tears shining in her eyes as she put pressure on her injured ankle.

"Crawl, Eric." Jeff supported Penny with one arm while keeping Eric under his gun.

Penny waddled, legs spread, gamely walking until another contraction hit halfway there. "Stop!" Jeff told Eric.

Penny crushed his hand. "Did I ever tell you" — teeth gritted, face intense — "that I hate pain?"

Jeff felt helpless, and because Penny was an empath he inflicted the feeling on her.

"Shh . . . it's — okay. I used to think" — grunt — "pain was the worst, but — it's being — alone — that's hell. Just your — being here — helps."

"How touching," Eric sneered.

Jeff kicked him. He didn't think he was helping a hell of a lot. It hurt him to stand by and do nothing while Penny was in pain.

When the contraction finally eased he couldn't even let her rest, half-cajoling, half-dragging her to where the tire and blanket rested at the bottom of the ravine.

"Your carriage, madam." Eyes on Eric, he spread the blanket over the tire by feel and lifted the ropes so she could crawl under them.

The thing looked flimsy as hell, but Penny didn't express one word of doubt, awkwardly seating herself, legs spread wide. Her back arched with a new contraction. "Help me, Jeff."

"I will." He brushed back the sweaty hair on her forehead. "You just concentrate on Damaris, let me handle everything else."

"I love—you," Penny said, closing her eyes.

For the first time in forever, he believed her. Tears stung his eyes. "I love you, too." He didn't have time to say more, turning to Eric. "Get up."

Now came the dangerous part; this was what he needed Eric for. Just as he had no choice but to trust the rope would hold and the tree branch not break, he had no choice but to use Eric; he wasn't strong enough to pull Penny up by himself.

He passed the rope behind his back and wrapped it twice around his right hand before transferring his gun to that hand. He made Eric stand in front of him and kept the gun trained on him at hip level. "Grab the rope and walk backward."

Even with two men pulling, it took a moment for the tire seat to leave the ground. It swayed, spinning, and Penny cried out.

"Slow and easy," Jeff rasped. The rope burned his hands and bit into his waist, but he hauled harder on the rope. He had to work quickly before Eric got brave enough to try something. His shoulders strained, pulling, pulling. They walked backward, raising the tire one blistering inch at a time . . .

Eric waited until Penny was three-quarters of the way up the gully wall, at her most vulnerable if she fell, before halting. "That's far enough, commie. Give me the gun or I'll let go of the rope."

Jeff had been expecting this. "If you let go, I'll shoot you."

"Will you?" Eric grinned. "I don't think you will. You'll be too busy trying to hold on to the rope. If you cooperate now, I might even help you."

Jeff's heart was beating hard enough to knock a hole in his chest. "What do you want?" He followed the script Eric expected him to.

"Tell me where your village is."

There is no goddamned village! Jeff wanted to shout, but he played along instead. Eric wouldn't believe him if he betrayed his "village" too easily, so he stalled. "What village?"

Eric let go.

• 4 •

He was crippled, his kneecap shattered beyond hope of repair.

The Selector had shunted away the pain, suppressed the troublesome nerve endings, and stimulated other areas of his brain to produce chemical endorphins. He felt no discomfort, but the thought kept creeping in: *He was crippled. No longer perfect.*

Of course, he was different from other cripples. He wasn't restricted to one body. So while the loss of his knee was upsetting, there was no need to Select himself for death because of it.

No need at all.

With effort he concentrated on the woman holding the gun.

Mary looked shaken, but just in case she hadn't understood his threat, he spelled it out for her. "If you kill my body, I will take over the poet man. You'll never be able to trust him again."

The idea held strong appeal. How much fun it would be to pretend to be Mary's poet man. To raise her hopes that he was the man she loved. Maybe even to marry her. To bide his time until she trusted him totally, and then—

—the knife.

That would be very sweet.

The Selector drank in the thought of the betrayal she would feel. It almost made him wish she would kill him.

But Mary looked stricken. The gun no longer pointed at him, but at the floor. Pitiful little tears formed in her eyes.

Victory. He gloated. He had waited years for this moment. Years. "Untie me, or I'll give your poet man another seizure."

"If I untie you, you'll kill both of us."

Stalemate. The Selector gnashed his teeth. Not now. Not when he was so close.

In desperation he considered triggering the poet man's epilepsy. If he couldn't kill Mary, he could at least hurt her. She cared more for the poet man than for herself. The Selector stopped short. *She cared more for the poet man than for herself.* A smile shaped his lips.

"I'll make a deal with you. Kill yourself, and I won't kill the poet man." A twitch of his silver thread, and the poet man's body went rigid.

Mary gasped, her horrified eyes on her weakling lover.

"Do it, Mary. Shoot yourself, and I'll let him breathe again." He would snag her soul as she died. Mary was his talisman. Once he possessed her, everything would come to him.

Everything . . .

"He's dying," the Selector said brutally when Mary hesitated. "You can save him. Put the gun to your head."

Slowly, slowly, she raised the gun barrel to her temple.

"Now pull the trigger." The Selector tasted triumph. She was going to do it. He could count on Mary.

His enemy and his confidante.

Her finger tightened on the trigger—then stopped. "How do I know you won't kill him once I'm dead?"

"I give you my word." The Selector meant it. Something about that fact disturbed him. He was the Selector, and the poet man wasn't worthy of life. But the world was crawling with inferiors

(cripples)

and there was only one Mary.

She didn't question his word. "Thank you." She closed her eyes, then opened them. "May I ask you something first?"

The Selector was feeling generous. "Certainly." He would promise her other lives if she wanted.

But she surprised him. "Will you tell me why? Why do you want to kill me? What did I ever do to make you hate me so much?"

"I Selected you to die because you're inferior. You're a coward."

"But you tried to kill me before I ran. You tried to kill me in my dream. Why?"

He should have said, Because you're a stupid bitch, or, Because I enjoy your terror. But he had waited years for this victory. None of the others mattered as much as Mary.

Mary was special.

And so he told the truth. "Because when I met you I realized I wasn't an only child." Although his parents had abandoned him, they'd loved and protected their other children.

"Yes," Mary said softly, "I understand now why you hate me. I would probably have hated me, too, in your place."

The Selector didn't want her understanding. It made him uneasy and impatient. "Hurry up, your friend is dying." He watched Matt bang his head on the floor with pleasure.

"It won't work, you know." Mary's words brought his gaze back to her face. She was pale, but composed. "Even if you snag my soul and lock me up in a room somewhere for all eternity, I will never belong to you."

Her words shouldn't have mattered, should have been just empty defiance, but they slipped past his guard like arrow shafts and lodged in his flesh.

They made him furious. She would belong to him, *would*, would smile at him the way she smiled at the poet man, would listen to his plans and praise him and not flinch from his touch, or he would make her sorry, make her bleed and cry, snap her bones like brittle sticks, one by one, until she admitted it; he needed her to admit she belonged to him.

He needed her.

The truth struck him with the force of a hurricane, straining his personality.

He was the Selector, a perfect specimen, superior in every way—

He was crippled, lame, fit only to be taken out and shot like a horse.

No. Injured racehorses were sometimes kept alive to breed, because their genes were still superior. He was still superior—but Superiors didn't need anyone, especially inferiors—

His danger instinct kicked in. The Selector grabbed wildly for his hate, and felt the first cold tickle of fear. His hate was gone. All of it. For his mother. For Nigel Carver. For Bethany. He felt only a growing coldness. Emptiness.

He heard his mother's voice: "Be whole again, Ronald."

Terrible forces pulled and tore at him.

He made one last desperate effort to save his disintegrating personality.

• 5 •

When the Seeress disappeared, the ground rocked under Ron's feet as if from an earthquake. Clods of yellowish-gray matter tumbled from the ceiling.

"What the hell was that?" Ron asked the empty air. Had it been good or bad?

He decided to assume it had been good. Freeing his mother had literally shaken up the Selector.

Time to free Bethany.

On his way to her castle he had to pass through the garden. He stopped, staring in amazement. The briars had all been uprooted, and the grass squashed flat. Bad boy Ronnie for crying was gone, and when he got to the castle so was Bethany.

• 6 •

Gavin was lost, but he stubbornly refused to admit it. If there was a way in, there had to be a way out.

All he had to do was find it. He glanced at Bethany, still dazed by her presence. A miracle had brought her back to him. He couldn't fail her again. Or April—

The floor bucked underneath him.

Gavin fell to his knees, and Bethany screamed. He shielded her body from the falling debris, squinting fiercely through the rising cloud of dust. Where was April? He glimpsed an orange blur that might have been her shirt before his eyes started to water and he had to close them. The hallway shuddered and wheezed like an asthmatic.

When the earthquake finally stopped, Gavin rolled off Bethany and helped her sit up. Tears made tracks down her dirty cheeks, but, seeing no blood, he turned to April. "Are you all right?"

"I'm okay." She winced as she stood up. "A little bruised, but okay." She surveyed the torn-up floorboards and fallen paintings. Squares of dirt showed where the paintings had once hung instead of walls or blue sky.

Where the hell were they? Uneasy, he took hold of Bethany's arm and started her moving again. "It shouldn't be too much farther," he lied.

The passageway curved and branched randomly, more like a worm tunnel than a straight hallway. Things also shifted disturbingly.

There—hadn't that wall been covered with rose-sprigged wallpaper just moments before? Now it was stark white. And where that bare bulb dangled, hadn't there been a light fixture?

He and April exchanged glances like secrets; neither said a word to Bethany. They kept walking.

White faded to dingy beige and then a yellowish clay that gave off a dim luminescence and a moist heat that seemed almost organic. When a cave-in blocked off the tunnel Gavin was only too glad of the excuse to turn back.

"I think we took a wrong turn. We'll have to go back."

"Good." Bethany shuddered and pressed close to his side. "I don't like it here."

Typically, April didn't listen to him. "I see light." She pointed to the upper corner of the tunnel. "I think we can get through." She gouged the yellow clay with her bare hands. "Come on, if this wasn't a way out, we would have taken a different tunnel."

Reluctantly, Gavin started digging.

Bethany hung back and watched. He had to bite his lip to keep from snapping, "We aren't your slaves." He didn't understand his irritation. Bethany had been saved by a miracle, and he was quibbling over a little digging?

The clay felt warm and humid, and it clung unpleasantly to his fingers, but it crumbled like sponge cake. In no time at all he and April had cleared a two-foot hole.

April squirmed through, and Gavin followed. Bethany made icking sounds as Gavin helped her through. He felt obliged to soothe her even though he felt uncomfortable himself. Thank God, April didn't complain.

It seemed odd to remember he had once liked Bethany's clinging. It had made him feel protective and needed. Now it annoyed him.

It was just the situation, he told himself. Bethany was the same enchanting girl he'd fallen in love with, but April was more competent, someone he could rely on in a crunch. He waited impatiently as Bethany picked clay out of her hair.

"Look." April had stopped a few feet ahead. Coming up behind her, Gavin also halted.

The tunnel ended in a huge hexagonal chamber. Each side held one or more doors opening to it, and light poured out from a dozen flashing silver cords that rose up and up from the center of the room.

"What are they?" April asked, wandering closer to the hum of electricity.

"I don't know . . ." Gavin started to say.

"They're his hooks," a voice behind him said. "The Selector's hooks."

Gavin turned and saw Ron Revarc standing there. His gaze snapped to Bethany to gauge her reaction.

She paled and gripped his hand harder. Gavin's insides loosened a little. The Selector had killed her using Ron's body.

But Bethany wasn't dead, so the Selector couldn't have killed her. But what of the bloody body he'd found in the meadow? She'd felt dead.

She must have been in a coma. Like April. He shoved down the knowledge that Bethany's body had been bloody and lifeless while

April's had breathed. Her breathing had given him hope.

And she was alive. Gavin studied April with relief while she asked Ron about the silver cords. What on earth had she been thinking, attacking the Selector? When they got out of here he would have a little talk with her.

"This is the center of his power." Ron sounded excited. "If we cut his hooks, the Selector will be handicapped."

"So how do we cut them?" April asked. The silver cords crackled and swayed, giving off sparks. Gavin frowned when he saw how close to them April was standing.

"The world we're in is malleable. All we have to do is shape it to our thoughts. Now what disrupts electricity? Damn, I never paid much attention in class—"

"Insulators. Ceramics, rubber, and glass are the most common," April said crisply, then blushed when Ron looked admiring. "I always liked physics."

It was that damn Shine, Gavin fumed.

"Let's do it." Triumphantly, Ron held aloft a large pair of glass scissors.

"That one's pulsing." April pointed. "I think the Selector might be using it. Cut it last, so he won't realize what we're doing."

"Good idea," Ron said.

Gavin hung back with Bethany while April and Ron cut the Selector's hooks. The silver cords burned out in a flash of light as the glass scissors sheared through them.

"Don't!" April cried, when Ron approached a cord that was thicker than the others were. It looked like it had been double-threaded. "That's not a hook, it's a snag."

Ron nodded, wiping away sweat from his brow. He left the double-threaded cord and another that they found a few minutes later, but cut a shadowy snag that he and April decided must be Genevieve's. Ron was just about to cut the pulsing cord that the Selector was using when it burned out in a painful flash of light.

Gavin threw up a hand to shield his eyes, bringing it down warily a moment later. He half expected the Selector to suddenly show up, pissed, but he didn't. Gavin cleared his throat. "So how do we get out of here? Just hop a rope?" He took a step closer to the double-threaded silver cords.

April looked worried. "There are only two snags, and four of us. Two of us can't go."

A second's appalled silence, then Gavin knew what he had to do. "I'll stay. You girls go."

Bethany burst into tears and sobbed into Gavin's shoulder.

"No, I'll stay," April said. "You and Bethany deserve some happiness."

She was in her stubborn mood; Gavin could tell from the set of her chin. But this time she wouldn't win. "No way." He disentangled Bethany's arms so he could argue better. "I got you into this. You're going, and I'm staying."

"That's very noble of you, but I'm staying," April said.

"Not if I have to tie you up and—"

"You have to go, you idiot! One of the bodies is male—"

"Whose cords are they?" Bethany asked, face pale.

"One of them is Gavin's, and the other one is yours," April said. "I'm staying; you're going."

But the other cord was April's. Gavin knew it. He'd held Bethany in his arms and had known no life or breath would ever touch her again.

"No." A bear trap closed around his heart. Bethany was his dream, but he couldn't find happiness with her at April's expense. "I can't let you do it. It's too big a sacrifice."

"What are you saying?" Bethany asked sharply. "April says it's mine, so let's go."

"I want to do it!" April ignored Bethany, focusing only on him, eyes fierce as hawks. "I want you and Bethany to be happy together."

"Bethany's—" *dead.*

"Shut up!" April spoke quickly, "It'll be okay. My Talent is illusion—with a little practice she'll look just like she does now. She might not have her Shine, but she'll be alive. She'll be Bethany, and you'll marry her and have kids."

Bethany had the Shine. The revelation should have shocked him, but somehow it didn't. Funny, how he'd known Ron's Talent immediately, but had never asked Bethany's.

Had part of him always known?

"You can't seriously mean to leave me here!" Bethany's nails dug into his shoulder.

He shrugged her hand off, concentrating on April. "I can't let you do it. It's wrong. You're going, and that's it."

April was shaking her head. "You don't understand—"

"I'll marry you," Bethany said.

"—I love you, you idiot! I don't care where I am so long as you're happy."

"What did you say?" Gavin was talking to April, but Bethany assumed he was speaking to her.

"I said I'll marry you." She looked beautifully determined, a martyr. "We'll have kids together just like you wanted." Her voice broke. "I'll do anything, Gavin, only please don't leave me here alone!"

Looking into her tearful eyes, Gavin's heart softened just like always. But this time he saw more than her beauty, he saw the fear behind her eyes. "Of course, we won't leave you here alone. But you don't have to marry me for that, and you can't take April's body. We'll think of something else."

Even if he had to lay her spirit to rest along with her body, he would do it. It would be sheer cruelty to leave her in solitude forever.

Bethany had always been afraid of being alone.

"Think what you're doing," April hissed. "Are you—"

"You won't be alone. I'll be here with you," Ron said.

Bethany turned toward him, blond hair swinging. "Do you mean it? You'll stay with me?"

"Forever," Ron swore.

Gavin felt like he was watching a sappy old movie as Ron opened his arms and Bethany ran into them. Ron swept her up in an embrace. Together they radiated sunshine.

A tiny part of him was still jealous, but what he mostly felt was relief at the solution to the problem. Somehow, in the last few days, he'd fallen out of love with Bethany. And that was a relief, too.

Gavin took one more look at the Shining pair who were still joined at the lips, then slung an arm over April's shoulder. "You know, I think they deserve one another."

She smiled shyly up at him. "I think you're right."

Together they approached the tall silver cords. "How does it work?"

"How would I know?" April asked. "Hopefully, if the owner of the cord touches it, they'll be drawn back into their own body and not electrocuted."

"I guess we'll find out." Gavin grabbed the nearest cord.

CHAPTER 15

• 1 •

The pain in his knee took Ronnie by surprise. He screamed.

It hurt, it hurt! He almost retreated to the half-sleep that had cocooned him for so long, but he pushed the pain back instead. He'd learned how to block out pain while living with Grandfather Carver.

Like locking a door. Ronnie knew a lot about locking things up. Pain in one compartment, fear in another, until he'd locked himself up and refused to come out.

He'd been a cow-herd, just like Grandfather said. Grandfather was mean. But now, Ronnie knew Mommy hadn't wanted to leave him with Grandfather. She'd loved him. The knowledge had given him the courage to open his prison door.

The pain faded. Ronnie risked a quick look down, then moaned, wishing he hadn't. His knee bled buckets.

He hated blood. The horrible bright redness of it, the smell and the sticky warmth.

Queasy, he looked away—and saw the woman.

She had curly dark hair and blue eyes. *Mary*, his mind whispered. She looked scared, her eyes huge.

He was scared, too. "Hi." His smile wobbled, and he tried not to cry. Grandfather always hit him when he cried, and for some reason it was worse to cry in front of girls.

Mary crouched down on the floor. "I'm sorry. Your scream startled me, and I dropped the gun."

The gun? Ronnie didn't like guns. They were loud, and they made things bleed. Like his knee. Had she hurt his knee?

Mary picked up the gun.

Tears welled in Ronnie's eyes. "Don't hurt me."

He didn't really expect her to listen. Grandfather never had. But Mary was a girl. "Please." Tears rolled down his cheeks.

Mary hesitated, lowering the gun. "Please?"

Was she stopping, or only pretending like Grandfather did sometimes? She didn't look mean. "Please don't kill me, Mary."

She flinched. The gun came back up. "Nice try, but no one calls me Mary but you."

She was going to hurt him. On the verge of retreating into himself, Ronnie noticed something strange: she'd pointed the gun at herself, not him. Curiosity stopped his tears. "What are you doing?"

"Killing myself so you don't kill Matt, remember?" She pressed the gun against her forehead.

"Who?" Ronnie asked, bewildered.

"Matt!" Mary said sharply. She pointed to the man lying on the floor. "You said you would kill him."

Ronnie shrank back. "I don't like killing things. Please don't make me."

Silence. Mary didn't say anything for so long Ronnie began to fidget. Having a body wasn't as nice as he'd remembered. He'd forgotten about the blood and pain. Maybe he should go back. . . .

But Mommy had told him to come here. Ronnie decided to wait a bit longer.

Finally, Mary asked, "Who are you?"

"Ronnie."

"How old are you, Ronnie?" Mary watched him closely.

"Six."

Mary put the gun down. "Ronnie, do you know who the Selector is?"

Scared, Ronnie nodded. He'd created the Selector to do the things Grandfather made him do, but the Selector hadn't wanted to leave afterward, so Ronnie had left instead. The Selector wasn't very nice.

"Do you know where he is?" Mary asked.

"He left."

"Where did he go?"

"He went down one of the cords. But someone cut the cord so he can't ever come back." Ronnie didn't know how he knew that—the answer tickled at his mind—but he knew it was true.

"God, no." Staring at the man on the floor, Mary began to cry.

• 2 •

Penny's full weight jerked Jeff off his feet; he slid two feet over the rocks before Eric grabbed hold again. Above them Penny cried out as she plummeted several feet.

"All right, all right, I'll tell you!" Jeff's mouth felt bone-dry as he struggled to remember the pat lie he'd made up. "Follow the gully for a mile until you come to—" To a village. Eric was looking for a village, and if he found anything, a house, a town, a school, he would walk in with his gun, and when he didn't find any MIA soldiers to rescue he would torch the place. Kill everyone inside.

For the sake of me and Bobby and all those other children out there. Penny had pleaded.

"Come to a what?" Eric urged.

No, Jeff thought. *Don't ask me to do this. Don't ask me to save the world. What has the world ever done for me? I just want my wife and my children.*

"To a what?" Eric demanded. He took one hand off the rope, increasing the murderous pull.

"To a fork." His tongue felt thick, halting. "Take the left one. At the end you'll find what you're looking for."

Eric smiled fiercely, and Jeff shot him in the kidneys.

Eric collapsed against him for a moment, clutching his arms. "Is it . . . Game Over?"

"You bastard." Jeff wept. "You would have dropped her anyway."

Screaming, Eric fell sideways in slow motion, letting go of the rope.

Penny's life hung from Jeff's good-for-nothing hands. His feet were braced on the rocky bottom, his whole body angled backwards, but nothing could have prepared him for the terrible extra weight.

He didn't drop her, didn't break her spine on the rocks, but it took all Jeff's strength to hold her there; he had none to spare to pull her to the top.

He hauled on the rope anyway until he felt like he would bust a gut. His arm muscles trembled with strain, and the skin on his palms tore, making the rope even more slippery. His shirt was still waving from a tree up top, and the rope laid raw a strip of bruised flesh at his waist.

He couldn't do it.

He called up to Penny. "Baby, I need your help. Find the rope going down and pull on it. Do you understand? Pull on the rope."

Silence, then, "I can't reach it."

Jeff closed his eyes. Part of him knew that he should give up and lower Penny back to the ground while he still had the strength—he might be able to save her, if not Damaris—but he couldn't make himself do it.

And eternity stretched by, his back and arms in agony, tendons stretching their utmost, ligaments threatening to detach from their bones, until Penny said, "I think someone's coming."

It was another of the Selector's minions. Jeff felt a black despair so total it was like plunging down a well. The Selector was coming, and he could not do a thing—

The weight from above was removed so suddenly Jeff staggered and fell. It took him a moment to react to Gavin's voice. "Jeff, are you all right?"

Gavin.

Penny was safe.

Jeff's muscles went limp and spongy. He sat on the cold, hard ground next to Eric's whimpering body and wondered why he wanted to weep.

"Hurry, Jeff, I don't think Penny has much time." April's words were meaningless chatter, but Penny's moan brought Jeff to his feet.

He clawed his way back up the bank, slipping and sliding, holding to the rope as Gavin and April pulled from above. When he finally hauled himself over the edge the first faces he saw were Kristy's and Bobby's.

Bobby was hovering anxiously over Penny. "Don't cry, Mommy." He gave her a wet kiss.

Jeff pulled him back, voice hoarse. "Mommy has to rest now. Kristy, take Bobby back to the car." He, Gavin, and April bent to pick up the tire, carrying Penny on it like a stretcher.

"This is one hell of a contraption," Gavin said. "Where'd you find it?"

"Jeff made it," Penny said between pains.

Jeff didn't say anything. His palms were bleeding again, and his arms ached, but he was determined not to stumble, not to drop his precious burden—

He was aware only of Penny groaning and writhing on the blanket, pushing. Her time was very close.

Someone drove the station wagon while Jeff crouched on the floor in the backseat, holding Penny's hand and stroking her forehead. "Hang on, Penny. We're going to make it." He spoke nonsense. Only Damaris could decide if they were going to make it or not.

Worse than useless to try to comfort an Empath. Penny patted *his* hand. "Of course we'll make it." She tried to tease him, "The Seeress said you would save my life, and you have."

A day ago he would have bristled angrily—Is that why you married me? Well, don't think I'll give you a divorce just because my usefulness is over!—but tonight Jeff heard the pride in her tone. He managed a weak grin. "Batman without the cape."

"Yes." Her eyes closed again on another contraction.

Screaming sirens and flashing lights announced three cop cars. After a moment of shouting out the window, they acquired a police escort.

Jeff barely noticed, watching Penny. There was scarcely any space between contractions now, and no time to think.

The doctor delivered Damaris within minutes of their arrival at the hospital. Jeff barely got a chance to look at her tiny, perfect wizened face before a nurse whisked her away into an incubator. Her lungs seemed fine, but the doctor wanted to observe her for a while.

Penny looked exhausted, but when Jeff gently told her to go to sleep she held on to his wrists with impressive strength. "Not just yet, buster. We have some things to straighten out."

Jeff stayed still, expecting some question about how he'd found her or who Eric was, but Penny stared him straight in the eye instead.

"No more evading the issue. Why have you been so mad at me these last few days?"

Jeff shifted uncomfortably. The issue was better left buried, but he was too grateful for her and Damaris's health to lie. "I panicked a little when I found out the real reason why you married me."

Her forehead puckered into a frown. "The real reason? What do you mean?"

"It doesn't matter." He kissed her knuckles.

Her brow became even more furrowed. "I think you'd better start from the beginning. Why do you think I married you?"

It didn't matter, Jeff reminded himself, but the words still hurt his throat, like chewing glass. "You married me because the Seeress told you to."

Penny collapsed back on the pillows in amazement. "Because someone told me to? Jeff, my dentist's been telling me to floss my teeth for years, and I still don't do that. No one could have made me marry you if I hadn't wanted to—if I hadn't loved you.

"It might have been Genetic Instinct that made me fall in love with you, but it isn't why I've stayed in love with you. It's the patience you show Bobby, the hours you spend building me gadgets, the way you won't let me lift the smallest thing when I'm pregnant."

But those are little things, Jeff wanted to say, but emotion kept him mute. The strings binding his heart loosened just a little.

"I even love the way you whistle. That proves it's true love"—she touched his cheek—"because you can't carry a tune in a washtub."

• 3 •

Matt's head felt like someone had run a truck over it, and his mouth tasted vile. He croaked Genevieve's name.

No reply. He pried one eyelid open. "Genevieve?" He thought he saw her. "What happened?"

If she told him, he didn't hear. His head spun. Disoriented. "Where . . . am I?" He seemed to be lying on his back, staring up at a blue ceiling.

Van. He remembered a van. There was something else he should remember. Something important. Dangerous. He looked around for Genevieve. He had to make sure she was okay.

She was there. The buzzing in his ears faded enough for him to hear her crying.

Other faces hovered over him, but he couldn't remember who they belonged to.

"—be kinder just to do it—" someone said.

There was something he should remember . . .

He stared at Genevieve. Why was she crying? Feebly, he tried to touch her cheek.

She recoiled, and for the first time Matt noticed the gun in her hand. He tried to consider that important fact, but it kept slipping away. It didn't make sense. Genevieve wouldn't point a gun at him. Genevieve loved him.

"Love you," Matt managed to say. His tongue felt thick.

Genevieve's face contorted with pain. "I can't do it." She put down the gun, weeping.

"That's cruel," another voice said. Female. Angry.

Matt didn't listen, focusing on Genevieve. She mustn't have heard him the first time. "I love you."

"I love you, too, Matt." Her voice didn't sound right. Too husky.

"Don't—cry." He tried to touch her face again.

She cupped his hand against her wet cheek. "Oh, Matt."

"Careful," the man said. "He could attack you."

"I don't care." Genevieve's tears trickled over his fingers.

The world faded away.

When Matt woke a second time he felt more clearheaded. He remembered the Selector; he recognized Gavin and April, but he still didn't understand why someone had tied him up.

For the moment it didn't matter. "Where's Genevieve?" He needed to see her.

Gavin pointed the gun at him. "She's outside."

"I'll get her." April got up.

"She's alive then?"

Gavin nodded.

"Thank God." Matt closed his eyes in relief. "What happened?"

"What do you remember?" Gavin evaded. His eyes never left Matt's face. The close scrutiny made Matt nervous.

"I remember driving away in the van. Nothing after that. I presume I had another seizure?"

"Yes." Gavin hesitated, then shut up, alarming Matt. What had happened? He didn't see Ron anywhere. Had he escaped?

A second later the door slid open, and Genevieve and April climbed inside. "Matt?" She hung back, almost fearful. "Are you okay?"

"My muscles are a bit stiff," Matt said. A feeling of unreality settled over him. Why was everyone staring at him?

"He says he doesn't remember what happened after his attack."

Matt did not miss the lack of trust in Gavin's words.

"Of course he doesn't remember," Genevieve said fiercely. "He was unconscious."

Matt had spent months coaxing things out of Genevieve. "Tell me what's wrong."

Genevieve turned away, unable to speak. April told him in a calm, neutral voice. "The Selector caused your seizure. He hooked you. He told Genevieve that if she killed him, he would take over your body."

Cold understanding seeped into Matt. She could never trust him again. He could never trust himself.

There would be no June wedding, no happily ever after.

He memorized her face, the curly dark hair and the blue eyes full of sorrow instead of secrets, then turned to Gavin, voice rough, "For God's sake, whatever you do, don't untie me."

• 4 •

"I know it's Matt. Let me untie him." Genevieve was annoyed to find she was crying. She felt furiously angry with Gavin. "Think about it, you idiot. Would the Selector have told us *not* to untie him?"

"Maybe, if he were being clever." Gavin didn't budge from his position in front of the van door.

"I'm telling you, it's Matt." She made another move to go around him, and he caught her arm. He winced when she jerked free, but refused to let her by.

"Look," he said, so patient and reasonable, Genevieve wanted to claw his compassionate brown eyes out, "it wouldn't make any difference if it were Matt. If the Selector's inside his head, he can turn into the Selector at any moment. We can't untie him. There are kids around. Jeff would string me up if I untied Matt while Bobby was within a hundred-mile radius."

"All right," Genevieve said calmly, but it was a brittle, false calm. "A hundred-mile radius it is. I'll give you all a head start before I untie him."

Gavin was appalled and showed it. "But the Selector will kill you."

"If the Selector's in Matt at all."

Compassion turned to pity. Genevieve waved him off before he could start. "No. I shouldn't have said that. We have to presume the Selector did do as he threatened, that he is inside Matt somewhere— but Matt's in there, too! I can't just abandon him."

"You're talking as if you just found out he leaves the toilet seat up. Having a homicidal maniac inside your brain is a little more serious than a character flaw. He could kill you!"

Genevieve turned bitter, intense eyes on him. "At this point, do you really think I care?"

That silenced him.

"I was going to kill myself earlier today. I had the gun pressed against my temple when Ronnie suddenly showed up. Any life I have after this is a gift from God, and I damn well am not going to waste it!"

Gavin was staring.

Genevieve swallowed back the tears and rage inside her. "I've wasted too much time with Matt already because of the Selector. Because I wouldn't allow myself to be human enough to have problems. However much time the Selector gives us together before he springs his trap is worth it to me."

Gavin was still looking at her as if she were crazy. Any second now he was going to call in reinforcements, and they would forcibly separate her from Matt.

She made herself calm down. "Look, there's something you don't know. The Selector made a mistake when he hooked Matt; whenever he uses his hook Matt has a seizure. The seizure will give me enough warning to tie him up."

"And how will you know when the Selector leaves again? He'll just pretend to be Matt and wait for you to untie him. That's what he's probably doing now."

But Genevieve had already thought of that. "I asked Matt to write me a poem. 'Green eyes full of secrets/ Memories locked away/ I searched for the key but/ You knew them all the time/ Blue eyes full of sorrow/ I try to shut Pandora's box,' " she quoted. "Trust me, it's really Matt. The Selector can't write poetry worth beans."

"Even if you're right and it is Matt in there now, it won't work. The next time the Selector takes over, he'll never let Matt out."

"Yes, he will."

Gavin looked surprised at her surety. Genevieve was a little surprised herself, but she knew she was right. "He'll make a deal with me. For some reason I'm important to him."

"Yeah, he wants to kill you real bad."

"No, he wants to *possess* me. He's killed people for the pleasure of five minutes of my company."

She struggled to convince him. "The Selector is a supremacist, the Naziest Nazi of them all, right? He despises weakness of any kind, was ready to kill Eileen because she wears glasses. And yet he's confined himself to the body of someone he thinks is a wimp, a poet man with pink blood, an epileptic.

"The only thing Matt has that the Selector wants is me. If I offer him equal time, he'll take it."

"Jesus," Gavin breathed. "Think what you're saying. Equal time with a monster?"

"I'll try for a seventy-thirty split, but to keep Matt I'll settle for fifty-fifty." Genevieve pushed past him, back to the van. "Now, if you'll excuse me, I'd like to spend some time with my fiancé."

• 5 •

"So then Mom told Nigel that I would grow up and kill both him and her if he raised me," Ronnie explained in a soft voice. He flushed under the attention of so many eyes.

It was seven in the morning and everyone but Penny and Jeff were gathered around a small campfire, sharing their stories. April had covered them all in illusion when the police arrived to investigate the gunfire. After she skillfully directed them to the now-confused man hanging in the trees and another wounded man trapped in a gully, they'd all sneaked away to a campsite Peter knew of a few miles down the road.

Gavin was having trouble adjusting to the notion of the Selector and Ron as multiple personalities. The little boy's voice coming out of Ron Revarc's twenty-nine-year-old body kept throwing him. "But Nigel wouldn't listen. So she made her choice and left," Ronnie said sadly.

"How terrible." April shook her head. "And all this time you thought your mother had abandoned you to that monster."

"Nigel treated you terribly," Genevieve said. "I don't blame you for creating the Selector to deal with the abuse."

Nods of agreement, except from Peter. "I don't care. I'm still glad I killed him."

Shock.

"What do you mean, you killed him?" Gavin leaned forward. "He escaped down one of the silver cords."

"Down a silver cord into the body of one of the dying soldiers," Peter corrected. "He tried to hook me, but I burned him up."

"You threw a Molotov cocktail at him?"

Peter didn't answer directly. "You never asked me what my Talent was."

Gavin stared curiously. He had a Talent, so did Penny and Genevieve and April—even Bobby and Kristy did. What was Peter's?

Slowly, Peter rubbed his fingers together. A small flame appeared. *Peter burns.*

Genevieve stood. "I have to tell Matt."

"Wait." Gavin grabbed her wrist. "It would be cruel to give him false hope. We have to be absolutely sure. Tell us exactly what happened, Peter."

"I waited until Jeff had left, and then . . ."

• 6 •

Peter took out the knife in his belt and fingered the bone handle. It was Al's knife, the only thing he had left of his friend, picked up unthinkingly when he'd found it at the bottom of the ravine.

He wished he could use Al's knife to kill his murderer, but the Selector wasn't the kind of enemy who could be dispatched by such simple means.

Other methods would be necessary.

Peter had been left behind to guard April and Gavin from any more minions that might show up. He sat beside their bodies and studied his quarry.

The man April had hit with the tire iron was dying, but not yet dead.

Peter squatted on his heels by the man and pricked his neck with Al's knife, just hard enough to get his attention. "Hey, you. I need to talk to you." Another prick, in the little hollow just below the ear.

The man's eyes flickered, and he groaned.

"I need to talk to your master."

"Master? Huh?" The man's eyes started to slide shut.

Peter made a careful nick in the rim of his ear. The minion's brown eyes opened again, confused and dull. "I have no quarrel with you at the moment, but if you don't fetch your master, I will cut both your ears off."

The man chuckled weakly, the sound a rattling wheeze. "What do I care?" Peter had to bend low to catch the words. "I'm dying."

Peter shrugged. "As you wish." He began to saw through the man's left ear. Dark blood welled.

The man decided he did care, after all. "Stop! What do you want?"

"I wish to speak with your master, the Selector. You may not know him by that name, but he is the Voice in your head, the one that orders you around."

The man puzzled over that for a moment. "You mean the Mafia don that ordered the hit?"

"Yes."

"I don't have his telephone number."

"That's okay. Just close your eyes and call him." The hit man looked as if he might protest, so Peter pricked his neck again. The brown eyes closed.

Peter sat perfectly still, practicing patience. His face was calm, but inside his anger raged, furnace-hot behind a wall of ice.

His muscles were strung tighter than barbed wire, but when the hit man said he'd gotten a busy signal, all he said was, "Keep trying."

He passed the time talking to Al's spirit. *I will avenge your death today, blood brother. Your killer shall die by my hand. I will be strong.* He imagined himself as an iceman, coldly capable. When the Selector arrived he would be ready.

But when the Selector came, he came in a heartbeat.

The brown eyes opened, and Peter saw that they were clear, no longer cloudy. They touched Peter with approval.

"I was right about you, Peter. You've done very well; I count two men dead by your hand. I'd killed a dozen when I was your age, but you've made a promising start."

Peter ignored his words. "Are you the one who calls himself the Selector?"

"I Select who lives and who dies. I am an evolutionary judge. I weigh each person's life in my hands, and if they fall short, I end their genetic line. I've been a Selector for twenty years and in that time I've only found one other person who is worthy of life. Superior. Do you know who that person is?" The Selector's eyes were hypnotic.

Doggedly, Peter asked the next question in his revenge script. "Did you kill Al Ghostkeeper?"

"You, Peter. You and I alone are worthy of life. We are brothers."

"Did you kill Al Ghostkeeper?"

"Would you like to be a Selector, Peter? I know you like to kill. You hate the inferiors, don't you? The ones who thought you killed Al? The ones too stupid to listen?"

Peter felt a flicker of anger as he remembered how nobody had believed him when he'd said someone else had shot Al. His parents had taken him to a psychiatrist as if he'd turned into a monster.

He's trying to trick you. He's the one who killed Al.

"DID YOU KILL AL GHOSTKEEPER?"

The Selector looked impatient. "I was hunting you. That was before you proved your worth."

Peter realized he was shaking. Liquid shifted and melted behind his block of ice. "Did you kill Al Ghostkeeper?"

The Selector frowned, annoyed that he kept harping on the same subject. "He was unworthy."

The air began to get thick and hot. "He was my friend."

"He had mongrel blood. Aryans do not mix with inferiors. They don't need them, only kill them, eliminate them—"

"You killed my blood brother." Peter fed his rage into the air, heating it. *Al's broken body at the bottom of the ravine, neck snapped, head at an unnatural angle. Dead. Never to smile or laugh or be beaten at archery again.*

Beads of sweat condensed on the hit man's face. His swarthy skin turned pink, then red. Like boiling a lobster.

"Are you doing that?" The Selector sounded curious. "It is a very good Talent. The two of us in conjunction will be unstoppable."

Crank up the heat. Blisters formed on the dying man's cheeks and forehead.

"Ah, Peter," the Selector smiled, and his lower lip split open, bleeding. "You and I think alike. This is just what I would do."

"I am not like you." Peter's control shattered. [*Ice melting. Polar blue turned to incandescent flame . . .*]

"You are. Superior, perfect, not crippled . . . I can begin again, train you." The Selector sounded feverish, desperate. "Your first lesson is that I am your master. You will obey me in all things and call me 'sir.' "

"No," Peter said softly. [*Blue flame burning, a gas jet ready to erupt.*]

"Yes," the Selector said, with equal determination. "Look into my eyes."

"I wouldn't do that if I were you." Peter met the Selector's gaze squarely.

The Selector didn't listen, launching a hook at Peter's mind with the speed of a javelin.

[*FIRE*]

His mind touched flame, and he recoiled, screaming, as the delicate cord he'd attached to his hook caught fire.

"Burn." Peter loosed the molten anger he had been hiding behind a wall of ice.

The Selector screamed, but his cord had burned up; he had nowhere to retreat. He screamed as he burned.

And for the first time since Al's death Peter felt tears touch his cheeks.

"THEN I CAME back here," Peter said.

"The pulsing cord burned out in a flash of light," April said. "If the Selector was down the cord at the time—"

"He had to have been to have used the hook," Gavin interrupted.

"He's dead." Peter's voice was very final.

Genevieve left at a run.

"Sit," April said, when Gavin started to follow. She smiled. "Leave them alone. Matt and Genevieve have a wedding to plan."

• 7 •

It was over. All April wanted to do was go home, but she couldn't as long as Gavin was wanted for murder.

She persuaded Gavin to drive with her into a hospital in Thunder Bay. They dropped Ronnie off to get his knee and arrow wounds treated and stopped to see Penny and Jeff's baby. While Gavin peered at Damaris through the nursery glass, April located a pay phone. It took all of her change to place a call home.

Four rings, then the answering machine clicked on. "April, if that's you, don't hang up." Dean's voice.

"We caught Bethany's murderer. It was a cop. Jerry and I tackled him just before he opened fire at Bethany's funeral."

Opened fire. April blanched.

"We clobbered him," Jerry said, voice full of satisfaction.

"Yeah," Allan added.

"Thanks for the warning, sis," Dean said. "I might have ignored my danger instinct otherwise, thinking I just felt the normal reluctance to go to a funeral."

"You can come back now, April." Her mother's voice. "You won't be arrested."

"Please come home," her father said. "We love you."

Beep!

April cleared her throat of its lump. "It's me, April. I'm so glad you're safe. Dean, Jerry, thanks for clearing Gavin's name. I'm on my way home. The danger is over." The tape would cut her off soon. "Don't be surprised if I bring a guest."

She remembered something Gavin had said when they woke back in the woods. He'd asked if she was all right, then started to lecture her. "Jesus, April, what were you thinking, getting that close to the Selector?"

April had calmly pointed out that she had been using an illusion. "The Selector didn't see me until the last second." She hadn't really minded his lecture, but she'd teased him back. "So what was your excuse for getting caught?"

To her surprise Gavin had flushed. "I, uh, ran straight at him when I heard you scream." He squeezed her hand. "I couldn't bear to lose you, too."

Gavin had heard her scream—her *mental* scream.

People with the Talent Psychic Agony only heard those they loved.